LUCKY THE HARD WAY

LUCKY O'TOOLE VEGAS ADVENTURE

BOOK SEVEN

A NOVEL BY

DEBORAH COONTS

Book published by Austin Brown, CheapEbookFormatting.com

Cover Design by Andrew Brown, ClickTwiceDesign.com

ISBN-13: 978-1-944831-82-0

PRAISE FOR DEBORAH COONTS' NOVELS

"Deliciously raunchy, with humorous takes on sexual proclivities, Vegas glitz and love, though Agatha Christie is probably spinning in her grave."

—*Kirkus Reviews*

"Complete with designer duds, porn conventions, partner-swapping parties, and clever repartee, this is chick-lit gone wild and sexy, lightly wrapped in mystery and tied up with a brilliantly flashing neon bow. As the first in a series, *Wanna Get Lucky?* hits the proverbial jackpot."

—*Booklist*

"*Wanna Get Lucky?* is a winner on every level. Deborah Coonts has crafted a first-class murder mystery coupled with a touching and unexpected love story. Against a flawlessly-rendered Las Vegas backdrop, Lucky's story is funny, fast-paced, exuberant and brilliantly realized."

—Susan Wiggs, *New York Times* bestselling author

"Get ready to win big--with a novel that will keep you glued to the pages all the way to the end. *Wanna Get Lucky?* is as entertaining as the city in which it's set."

—Brenda Novak, *New York Times* bestselling author of *Trust me, Stop Me, and Watch Me*

Wanna Get Lucky goes down faster than an ice-cold Bombay martini—very dry, of course, and with a twist.

—*Douglas Preston, New York times bestselling author of Impact.*

Wanna Get Lucky? Is an amazing debut novel, a mile-a-minute read, with fantastic characters, dry wit, and the gritty neon feel of Las Vegas. Bravo to Deborah Coonts—I see a great future ahead.

—*Heather Graham, New York Times bestselling author of Night of the Wolves.*

NOVELS IN THE LUCKY SERIES

WANNA GET LUCKY?
(Book 1)

LUCKY STIFF
(Book 2)

SO DAMN LUCKY
(Book 3)

LUCKY BASTARD
(Book 4)

LUCKY CATCH
(Book 5)

LUCKY BREAK
(Book 6)

LUCKY THE HARD WAY
(Book 7)

LUCKY NOVELLAS

LUCKY IN LOVE

LUCKY BANG

LUCKY NOW AND THEN
(PARTS 1 AND 2)

LUCKY FLASH

CHAPTER ONE

*T*OO many questions, no easy answers, and no one to shoot—
not exactly a great Christmas.

Okay, I didn't *really* want to perforate someone. Not on
Christmas. To be honest, I'm not exactly a point-and-shoot
kind of gal anyway. Probably a good thing, since the woman
standing in front of me was campaigning hard for a spot in the
crosshairs. This is where that concealed-carry permit, had I
had one, could've gotten us both into trouble.

But there was a difference between imagining shooting
someone and wanting to see that person dead.   One a
euphemism, one a finality—so don't take me too seriously. I'm
known for talking a talk I could never walk—a shortcoming I've
learned to carry with shame.

Miss Minnie, the aforementioned woman standing in front
of me, was the proprietress of Miss Minnie's Magic Massage
and one of the most difficult people I know, which was saying a
lot. Dealing with difficult people all day, every day was at the
core of my job description, but when I was off the clock? Well,
that just seemed wrong.

In a questionable neighborhood on the opposite side of
Interstate 15, Miss Minnie's was light-years away from my
hood, the glamour and glitz of the Las Vegas Strip. A long,
narrow retail space, it was a perfect layout with closed rooms
on either side of a narrow hallway, a laminated counter up

1

front, chipped and stained, and a threadbare couch pushed up against the wall as an afterthought. Muted music thumped from the rooms. I blocked out the other, more human, sounds.

As with most things in Vegas, Miss Minnie's hid reality behind the thick whitewash of a fantasy. I was raised in a whorehouse; I could smell them a mile away. The cloying scent of sex masked by ammonia and room deodorizers—a noxious combination to churn even the most ironclad stomach.

Minnie's girls worked as independent contractors—another clue. Alone with a client behind closed doors, each girl could negotiate her own deal—business dealings repeated multiple times in parking lots of the strip clubs and in hotel rooms all over town. Most of Minnie's girls chose the profession, or so my mother told me, and she was somewhat of an expert. They weren't the ones I worried about when the noise of life quieted and daylight thinned. But they were not why I was here. Not tonight.

Tonight I needed help.

The Miss Minnies of the world were parasites capitalizing on human frailty. Of course, I ran a casino, so who was I to judge? Before I slipped out onto that slippery slope and outlawed gambling, drinking, and other excesses, thereby turning Nevada into Utah, I reined myself in and tabled that bit of unnerving parallelism.

Using my ten-inch and fifty-pound advantage, I stared down Miss Minnie, willing her to break.

One of the junkyard dogs of the human race, with a bite worse than her bark, she met me glare for glare.

A walking fashion faux pas, tonight Miss Minnie channeled her Geisha-Gone-Wild look—with my apologies to geishas everywhere. She looked like a silk-encased human hotdog. The sheath of delicate fabric captured her Himalayan breasts several inches shy of respectability, then tapered to a tight opening at her ankles. The seams held, defying every law of physics. With her stride silk-limited to about six inches and teetering on platform shoes, Miss Minnie had no choice but to hold her ground, which she did with tilted chin and fists planted on either hip. A white face, the powder cracking and flaking, and a jet-black wig appropriately styled and lacquered completed the look. And the flashing pink of the faded sign in the window added a comical color, but this visit was anything but funny. Her red bow-tie mouth knotted tight and her dark eyes throwing daggers, she met me stare for stare as anger rolled off her in waves.

Wasn't anger outlawed on Christmas?

"Minnie, you know why I'm here. I need your help." I cringed as I said it—the last person on the planet I wanted to owe was Minnie, a high-ranking priestess in the cult of Paybacks Are Hell.

My name is Lucky O'Toole and as the Vice President of Customer Relations for the Babylon, Vegas's most over-the-top strip casino/resort, I was slumming, but for a good cause—at least that's what I kept telling myself, but I wasn't an easy sell. As Christmas night wound toward an end, I wasn't at all pleased to have been lured out of my bit of the jungle, especially with a warm bed and a hot French chef waiting for me.

"You bring man who killed my Sam, and I help you." Minnie's staccato delivery perforated my veneer of civility, thin as it was.

As I worked to hold onto my notoriously absent patience and regain my thick shield of self-delusion, I stared at Minnie. And I wondered how she stayed in business. One look at Minnie and any self-respecting male should turn and run. There was a warning in that thought somewhere, but I chose to ignore it.

"Irv Gittings shot Sam," I said, telling her what she already knew. "You know I'd gladly risk twenty-to-life to shoot Mr. Gittings myself, but I have a minor problem—I need to find him first. That's where you come in."

"Me?" Miss Minnie's voice rose on a wave of forced incredulity. "What I know?"

Despite knowing her well, Minnie didn't scare me...much. I seemed to have the same effect on her. Familiarity breeding contempt and all of that. "Minnie, Irv Gittings hopped a private jet with your husband."

"He not my husband anymore." A faraway look lit her eyes for a moment, a look I couldn't exactly read, other than I saw a hint of homicidal...and terrible hurt.

The Madam and the Diplomat—a B movie if there ever was one. I doubted it played well in halls of power in Beijing. "Your daughter, Kim, was along for the ride, too. Don't you want me to find her?"

Miss Minnie flicked a glance my way. I'd say it was inscrutable, but that would be cliché and bordering on non-PC, wouldn't it? Not that I didn't normally blow right through those boundaries.

"Kim? Girl? Bah." From her tone and puckered mouth I actually thought she might spit. Thankfully, I was wrong. "Girls no good for nothing but trouble."

I couldn't argue, other than with her double negative. Kimberly Cho, Miss Minnie's daughter—a recent revelation that still had me a bit on my heels—had run me in circles in my own town, played me for a chump, and then had hot-footed with her father and Irv Gittings, a wart on the ass of humanity.

"Last I heard they were headed to Macau." I threw that out there, a hook perhaps to catch Minnie's complicity.

Her pupils pinpointed. "Then why you need me? You already know where they go."

"Macau is a maze. Tiny winding streets, thousands of miniscule apartments—a spot of an island with six hundred thousand people on it." Taking a deep breath and counting to ten, I worked to not wring the life out of Miss Minnie. Truth of it was, I needed a lead and she was the best hope I had—yep, a new low. Life was trying to teach me something—either that or Santa had a huge bitch streak. "Three needles in a very large haystack. You can tell me exactly where to start digging."

Minnie burbled like a teakettle ready to boil. I braced myself.

"You killed Sam!" she shrieked, as she launched herself at me with a growl, trying to rake me with pointed talons.

Actually, she didn't launch herself so much as lean like a small tree felled in the forest. I stepped to the side and watched as she face-planted on the carpet that probably hadn't been visited by a cleaner since it left the factory.

And I'd thought this was going so well.

A landed carp, she wiggled and thrashed, trying to throw her bound body over. Curiously detached, I watched and marveled at the incongruity of my life. *This* was my Christmas.

A life intervention! That's what I needed. And I'd thought I had a pretty good handle on my life. But that was before Teddie came back. Then everything had gone on tilt, and I hadn't found my footing since.

Miss Minnie flopped a few more times then quit. The floor was as far as she would get without help.

Bending, I grabbed her, pinning her arms at her sides, and lifted her up. A tiny human, she was as light as she looked, which was a good thing. While I could throw my weight around, I wasn't as strong as my size might lead one to believe—intimidation rather than force was my game.

I held her while she fought, making sure to keep out of the reach of her teeth. One wooden-soled shoe connected with my shin, evaporating my thin veneer of restraint. I carried her to a small couch in the corner of the vestibule and tossed her down, her geisha finery immobilizing her better than I could have. One breast escaped and fell like an under-inflated water balloon. That was a bit more of Minnie than I needed.

She didn't appear concerned. Instead, she struggled to lean forward, scooching to the edge of the couch to get her weight over her feet. Each time she almost got there, I pushed her back.

Finally, she tired of the game. "You kill Sam." Her voice had lost its fight. Now she sounded like a mother who had lost her son, which she was.

I didn't feel bad about the shooting Sam part, but my heart constricted for the mother-losing-a-son part. No matter how bad the child, a mother was always a mother—or so my own mother, Mona, told me—but Mona couldn't always be trusted.

In a logic kind of mood, I gave it a shot, knowing full well reason never trumped emotion. But, hope springs eternal and all of that. "Irv Gittings shot Sam. And Sam had it coming." Considering Sam had killed Holt Box, effectively ending a county and western comeback story, and then had framed Teddie for the murder, I wasn't feeling at all charitable toward the former Sam Cho. He also then attempted to kill both my father and me, thereby solidifying his name close to the top of my shit list. Irv Gittings had earned a permanent place in the top spot, but that was a long story.

This time, Miss Minnie spat, narrowly missing my left foot. "You know nothing. Sam a good boy."

"Sure, all the good boys I know try to kill people." No logic in that. And it dawned on me that I really didn't have the time to soften-up Miss Minnie—if that was even possible. Or maybe I didn't want to take the time. Whatever. Time to play my ace. "I have Frank." Frank was Sam's brother, Miss Minnie's second son, and the Dr. Jekyll to Sam's Mr. Hyde.

"You bring Frank?"

A glimmer of interest, which fanned the flames of my hope. "Maybe," I told her, not feeling at all remorseful about the lie.

Her narrowed-eyed look told me she didn't trust me. I knew how she felt—I didn't trust me either.

Frank was a guest of the Silver State at the High Desert State Prison outside of Indian Springs, forty-six miles north of Las Vegas, so him being the good son was relative. My cohort, Detective Romeo, a detective-in-training (my characterization, not his) for the Metropolitan Police Department, was working on remanding Frank to my care, but his mother didn't need to know that. Frank would be my bargaining chip in Macau. His mother didn't need to know that either.

My plan was to bring Kimberly Cho back, find a way to rid the world of Mr. Gittings without taking the fall for it, and do the same to Mr. Cho if it turned out he was behind the recent assassination attempt on my father.

What can I say? I'm an over achiever.

And then there was Teddie to think about.

Teddie.

But, before I went all vigilante, I needed some information. "You need to tell me what game your ex-husband and your daughter are playing."

"Why you think I know?"

I gave her the what-do-you-take-me-for look.

She didn't buy it. "What make you think anybody tell Minnie anything? I just a small-business owner."

That was like calling a Great White just another shark.

Logic clearly wasn't the winning gambit. "Stupidity, I guess." Keeping an eye on Miss Minnie, I glanced around the entrance area to the massage parlor. Faded carpet, unraveling in places, with a dark track from the door to the counter then continuing around the desk and down the long hallway toward the back, large windows fogged with dirt, a pink neon sign blinking from high in the corner, the sizzle of aging bulbs audible above the low thumping music from the back, the place reeked of sexual desperation. I still didn't understand the whole prostitution thing. Never would. But I'd learned enough about human peccadillos to read Minnie like a book.

"To be honest, Minnie, I don't even know why I'm here. Really stupid of me to think you might know something, that you might be able to help me find your daughter and stop her father." I gave her the benefit of my full attention. "I mean, really, who would tell you anything? You're right. I'm sorry I bothered you." I moved toward the door, but I didn't turn my back on her—a rabid dog, she was waiting for the chance to bite me in the ass.

"You bring my son home?" She managed to stand, weaving a bit before finding her balance. "You give me back Frank?"

One hand on the door, I paused. "It depends. What do you have to trade?"

She eyed me, a butcher weighing meat on the hoof. I countered with my best I'm-out-of-here attitude. At a momentary impasse, I called her bluff. Showing her my back, I pushed the door open.

"Wait."

I wiped the gloat off my face before I turned.

The large glass storefront to my right exploded.

Instinctively, I flinched away, my arms covering my head,

my face tucked to the side. Ducking down, I waited for the next shot. It didn't come. Outside, tires squealed. I looked up in time to see brake lights flash as a car turned, fishtailed onto the road and then disappeared into the darkness.

The hallway doors opened disgorging girls and guys in various stages of undress, excitedly chattering.

"Get back." Still in a crouch, I motioned them to stop. "Go back to what you were doing. Excitement's over." My unfortunate choice of words actually amused me—sex one paid for couldn't be exciting, at least not by my standards.

They hovered barely inside the hallway, but at least they didn't step out into the open.

"Minnie, you okay?"

Standing, I brushed my slacks down as I kept my eyes looking out the window for more shooters. The fact that I was more pissed than scared probably should bother me, but frankly, being shot at had gotten to be a bit old-hat.

Miss Minnie didn't answer.

One of the girls stepped around the corner. With a hand to her mouth, she screamed. I swiveled to look.

Slumped on the couch, Miss Minnie's eyes were wide, her mouth slack. She pressed a hand to her chest. Blood seeped through her fingers.

"Shit!" I grabbed a towel from the front desk. Kneeling beside her, I gently moved her hands. Pressing the towel to the neat little hole, I then put her hands on the cloth. Her eyes followed me.

"Hold this, okay?"

I felt her hands press down—not much, but enough.

"You shoot me?" Her ragged voice held the hint of respect.

What a world she lived in. "Don't be silly. I need you. When I don't need you anymore, then I'll shoot you." I hit the emergency button on my iPhone. When the 911 dispatcher answered, I barked instructions. Finished, I left the call open but put the phone down, turning back to Miss Minnie.

"You real funny girl," she gasped.

"And I'm the best hope you have to get your kids back.

And I don't know what game your ex is playing, but I'd hazard a guess it isn't for your benefit."

Even through the haze of pain, she looked like she was mulling that over.

"Besides, my father would kill me if I shot you now."

That got a hint of a reaction. She and the Big Boss went way back to old Vegas when the Mob ran the town. Hard times bred unusual friendships. "Your father a good man."

The look on her face told me she didn't think he'd passed on that bit of DNA to his daughter. "I know." I put my hand on top of hers and added pressure.

She covered mine with her other hand. "You remember that."

That struck me as odd, but now was not the time to go into it. "Of course. Who did this?"

"It not matter. Minnie old. Tired." She worked to pull in a deep breath. "In Macau, you find Sinjin. He help you."

"Sinjin? He have a last name?"

She pursed her lips like that was a stupid question.

I wasn't going to argue. "How do I find him?"

Her voice grew weaker. "Maybe he find you. Sinjin know everything."

I could feel her blood, warm and thick, leaking through the towel. "Okay. I'll find Sinjin. Be quiet now." Sirens sounded in the distance, quickly growing louder. "Stay with me. Just a minute or two more."

Sinjin knows everything. I wanted to ask her what she meant, but I couldn't. She would expend her last bit of energy trying to tell me and then she *would* die. Not a fair trade. Still...

I only considered it for a nanosecond, a victory, considering the task ahead. I'm not normally quite so virtuous.

Did Sinjin have all the answers? Is that what she meant when she said he knew everything? God, I hoped so. But I also knew better. Life never was that easy, at least, not mine.

As the ambulance skidded to a stop in front, its strobing lights painting the walls red, her eyelids fluttered, then closed.

"Minnie!"

She didn't answer. A thready pulse beat under the two fingers I pressed to the hollow of her neck, and I breathed a sigh.

An EMT brushed me aside with a muttered thank-you, his hands replacing mine as his co-worker took Miss Minnie's vitals. "What happened?"

"Drive-by shooting. One gunshot."

His eyes flicked to mine. They were blue. Recognition flared. We'd met before. That time it had been a bomb. "Lucky."

The way he said my name, well, it sounded a bit ironic. I knew what he meant. When my mother named me Lucky, she'd unknowingly invited the Fates to prove her wrong.

Apparently they'd accepted her invitation.

"Hey." I couldn't remember his name, if I'd ever known it. I felt sure I had, but my brain had reached capacity years ago, and, so far, I hadn't found anything worth forgetting so I could remember him. He was cute, but cute only got you a second look, not a permanent place in the gray matter.

He turned back to his work. "When are you going out to dinner with me?" He was pressing; blood was oozing. Miss Minnie still hadn't opened her eyes.

"Seriously? A woman is dying, and you're thinking about a dinner date?" I looked at him, bug-eyed. Men were scary. Mona had told me that, how many times? She'd phrased it a bit more delicately—something along the lines of men were different—but this was the first time I understood she had been underselling her theory.

"She's not dying," he said.

"I'm engaged."

"You're not married."

"She's crashing," the other EMT said, his voice calm, his demeanor not so much. The banter fell away.

Giving them room to work, I crossed my arms and stepped out of the way. A few of the girls eased closer, angling for a look. My glare sent them scurrying back to their rooms.

Who would want to kill Minnie? The list was probably long, but standing there, with her blood on my hands, killing became all too real in its horror and I couldn't think of anyone who would want to do that...including me.

Even when it came to Irv Gittings.

I talked a big game, sure. But all in all, I'd rather someone else be responsible for the rope, the hood, and pulling the lever to drop the trap door.

I worried a button on my sweater that already hung by a thread. It popped off in my hand, and I hurled it through the broken window.

At a loss as to who to call, what to do, I lapsed into my normal state—pissed off.

If I could only get my hands around Irv Gittings' neck. I wouldn't kill him—that I'd leave to the pros. But I wasn't above making him wish he was dead.

Someone had shot Minnie! The thought that had angered me before now took my breath. While I didn't like her, I respected her, which was more important. A woman hacking and slashing her way through a man's world—and teaching them how the game was played—she was a force. A lot like my mother. Of course, I would never tell Mona I respected her— she'd punish me forever.

The night air sent shivers through me. Or maybe it was the breath of Death, cold and close. As I pulled my sweater tight around me, I noticed frayed threads. A closer look. The threads bracketed a tear.

I looked at the window, remembering where I'd stood. Then a glance at Minnie.

The bullet had grazed my shoulder.

That close.

I guess I had been a good girl after all, or at least had enough karma points to trade for a little more time.

But Minnie? Why Minnie? She ran a semi-respectable business, which was far above the norm in Vegas. As far as I knew—and as a well-connected, native Vegas casino brat, that was a lot—Minnie kept her nose clean, steered clear of trouble and paid off the right folks.

So why would someone want her dead?

CHAPTER TWO

CHRISTMAS.

Okay, technically it now was the day after Christmas, but I hadn't had a Christmas yet, and I was enough of a kid to hold that against the Fates.

I'd asked Santa for a sexy Frenchman in his skivvies—my kind of package.

But, instead of getting what I asked for, I'd gotten an attempted murder in a whorehouse masquerading as a massage parlor and a night talking to the cops.

Clearly, when it had come to the naughty-or-nice thing, I'd fallen on the wrong side of that line. I planned on holding that against the Fates as well.

But I was alive, so there was that.

Yes, I had lost my Christmas cheer, which wasn't unusual. Cheery was not an adjective anyone would include in my epitaph. Living down to expectations, it's what I do.

The Metropolitan Police Department, Metro to those of us who held it in low esteem—and deservedly so—had kept us for hours. Thankfully, Detective Romeo had ridden to my rescue and busted me out early. Miss Minnie was still hanging on, but when I'd checked an hour or so ago, the doctor had said it would be touch and go once she came out of surgery.

Nothing to do but go home.

Home. A lantern in the storm.

The streets of Summerlin were quiet, everyone sleeping off

Christmas. One neighbor already had put his tree to the curb, decorations and all. I didn't even want to think about what had precipitated that. I'd had enough sad for the night.

My borrowed red Ferrari easily recognizable, the guard waved me through the gate.

The garage light clicked on as the door rose. I still couldn't reconcile my life with a house in the suburbs, a fiancé, a future stepchild, and a garage door clicker with the me I used to be. Funny that. Life choices. The suburbs or the Strip? Jean-Charles or Teddie? And why did choosing one always mean losing the other?

Tiptoeing through the mudroom into the kitchen, I tried to be quiet as I set down my keys and purse. The lingering aromas of dinner—something Italian maybe—curled around me. Toys littered the floor. A game of Operation had been shoved to the side of the large country table. Four place settings. Mine still had a knife and fork atop a clean napkin folded, waiting.

I felt the guilty prick of unmet expectations.

The strains of *Moonlight Sonata* led me to the bar off the kitchen. Jean-Charles had waited up for me.

He stood in front of the fire, attired as I'd asked for, his hands clasped behind his back, worry pinching the skin between his eyebrows into a slight frown. His eyes closed, he swayed to the music, lost in it. A few inches taller than my six feet, my fiancé...yes, my fiancé...had waited and worried, making me feel lucky indeed. The Fates be damned.

To be honest, I still couldn't get used to the idea of getting married. And to such a man! Tall enough, as I said, trim in all the right places, with full lips, chiseled features, wavy brown hair he wore just a trifle long, and a smile that lit his robin's egg-blue eyes, he was a feast for sure. And he could cook! An added benefit, since I'd never been known to pass up a meal. But it was the way he looked at me, the way he listened, and the way he made me feel that had won my heart.

My heart.

The one I'd taken back from Teddie.

Sensing me standing there, he opened his eyes. His smile

warmed me to the core, banishing my murderous evening. Holding his arms wide, he welcomed me into an embrace.

Tucking my face into the crook of his neck, I let him hold me. And I knew I could get through anything if this...if he...was waiting for me at the end of it all.

"You are okay?" he whispered, his breath warm against my cheek.

I tried not to think about Miss Minnie, the look in her eyes—imploring, scared. Even though I'd washed off her blood, I could still feel the warmth, the vitality...her essence...as it leaked out of her. I could feel her fear, her fight. I shivered.

"What's the matter?" Jean-Charles sensed my discomfort.

I pulled him over to the couch then curled under his arm, tucking my feet up under me after I'd shucked my shoes.

And I told him.

The song started over twice before I had finished. Jean-Charles hadn't said a word—he'd simply held me tight and let me talk. When I'd finished, he kissed my forehead. "You are going to Macau."

It wasn't a question—he knew I had no choice. Well, I guess we all have a choice, but letting Irv Gittings get away was not one of them. But we both knew that wasn't exactly why I was going.

Teddie.

I'm not sure I could find the words to describe all that Teddie had been and continued to be to me. Best friends, my first love, my biggest disappointment, and now, back to best friends, even though it still rankled that he looked better in my clothes than I did. Teddie had been Vegas's foremost female impersonator. I'd even let him wear my vintage Chanel and my Manolos, even though he stretched them out. If that's not love, I don't know what is...was. The break in my heart still hurt when I thought of him.

Unfortunately, our relationship had been a bit one-sided. Teddie had fallen more in love with himself than with me. In the race of love, a distant second wasn't what I was hoping for, wasn't what I needed.

Teddie left.

I'd let him go.

Then he came back—a ruse created by my parents, but I couldn't exactly prove it. That's where things had gone from bad to abysmal.

Teddie had fled house arrest for a murder he didn't commit. Somewhere in that pea-sized brain of his, he thought it would be a good idea to go off half-cocked to Macau to bring Irv Gittings to justice and, according to Mona, me back to his bed.

So not happening.

But, regardless, somehow it was my fault, in a roundabout sort of way—I hadn't handled Teddie's return very well. My friends and family argued with my assessment. But, my fault or not, I felt responsible. And the only way to live with it was to make it go away.

And somehow, some way, I needed to put my feelings for Teddie to bed. Okay, a bad analogy, but I needed to get him out of my head and my heart. Time to move on. But I couldn't let him die for me.

A martyred love—just what I needed. Of course, it wasn't all about me, but right now I was feeling a bit put-upon.

A fly the spider had singled out for dinner.

So, yes, for a myriad of reasons, I had to go to Macau.

Teddie was ill equipped to deal with Irv Gittings and the Chos, and the God-knew-who-elses of the Chinese underworld. Unlike Teddie, I had a lifetime of dealing with lowlifes. So, the job fell to me.

There was that irony again.

While Jean-Charles wasn't pleased, to put a nice spin on it, he *was* trying to be supportive.

"And Cielo?" he asked, still holding me, still loving me, but a slight mock in his voice, as if choosing Teddie over a hotel was an incomprehensible choice. To be honest, I agreed with him.

Cielo. My very own hotel. The Grand Opening loomed—

New Year's Eve.

My birthday.

And I had to go to Macau. I couldn't even begin to process how stupid an idea that was, so I didn't.

Maybe, just maybe, the police would do their job and I wouldn't have to go.

Right. And maybe Irv Gittings would turn himself in, the Chinese would stop trying to game the system, and Teddie would be alive.

Teddie. Are first loves ever forgotten?

I pulled Jean-Charles's other arm around me. "Everything is in place. I'll have my phone. And maybe you will help me stay on top of things?"

"Of course. However it is not ideal."

"But it is inevitable."

He kissed my forehead. "I do love that about you, always riding to the rescue."

Tilting at windmills that had developed a habit of shooting back—that's my gig. I lifted my face to his for a long, sweet kiss.

"Macau will be dangerous," Jean-Charles said after I released him, his accent making the whole thing sound somehow wonderfully delicious and exciting.

"No more than here." In the last couple of days, I'd been shot at more times than I could count. Frankly, it was getting old. Maybe a change of scenery would change my luck. Yeah, even I didn't believe that.

"I cannot argue with that." He toyed with the large diamond on my left ring finger. "You owe it to me to come back."

"I know." Desperate to change the subject before we ruined Christmas, I placed my hand on his stomach, skin to skin. I gasped at the sizzle, the electric connection that arced through me. It happened each time we touched, but still surprised me.

Jean-Charles pulled in a deep breath through his nose. He felt it, too.

I let my hand wander. "I haven't had my Christmas yet."

He chuckled, a low rumble in his chest. "And what did you ask for?"

"A handsome Frenchman wearing very little."

"Then you must've been a good girl." He pulled my shirt free and worked a hand under it. Cupping my breast, his thumb teased the nipple to a peak through the thin fabric of my bra.

"I am always good," I said in my most suggestive voice. Somehow I didn't laugh. "But I'm feeling naughty." I worked my hand down to test just how...engaged my Frenchman was—an embarrassing lack of control, even for me. Could I plead unfulfilled homicidal tendencies, all that unused adrenaline? That and the fact that I was head over heels, all contributed to my taking what I needed.

My Frenchman had already risen to the occasion.

He stood, then pulled me to my feet. Wrapping my arms around his neck, I captured his mouth as I pressed myself against him.

His tongue tangled with mine. He groaned when I deepened the kiss. "The bedroom?" he managed.

"The kids?" I figured he had that well in hand, but it never hurt to ask.

Jean-Charles had a five-year-old son, Christophe. A head full of blonde curls, a smile to match his father's, and eyes a deeper blue, the boy, taking a lead from his father, had wormed his way into my heart before I'd known what was happening. Jean-Charles' niece, Chantal, a culinary student intent on following her uncle into the business, was also bunking at her uncle's place. Two kids, two of us—we were horribly outnumbered.

"They are asleep." Jean Charles sounded less than certain.

"Here?"

"Yes." He broke away for a moment and closed the double doors as I shucked my shoes. "Kids," he added, tossing the word like water onto a fire. Nothing like children to kill the sexual mojo.

"Always plotting," I said, completing his thought in the same way he completed me.

Sex with kids in the house was a bit different than my usual pick-a-partner-and-a-piece-of-furniture-and-have-at-it. I'd learned this lesson the hard way. Jean-Charles and I had about herniated ourselves in the bathroom, doors locked, the theme song to Thomas the Tank Engine at a decibel level suitable for torture. Mind-blowing sex, but that song now conjured physical reactions I didn't think the creators intended.

The bar, with its windows and louvered doors, presented a new challenge.

As I shucked my clothes, I lowered the blinds and secured the doors. Ever the Frenchman, Jean-Charles lingered over the perfect wine. If he thought we were easing into this over a perfectly chilled Sancerre, he had another thing coming.

"For later," he said with a smile, as if he could read my thoughts.

He probably could, which should have terrified me—my brain is hallowed ground, sacred in its weird rituals—but I guess he truly was the One, because I no longer cared if he saw behind the curtain.

As I stepped out of my slacks in the middle of the room, Jean-Charles paused, his eyes alight. Then he thrust the bottle into a bucket of ice and moved around the bar.

He stopped me as I hooked a finger through the fine lace that Mona assured me passed for functional underwear. To me, the stuff gave me a perpetual wedgie, but the effect it had on my Frenchman made me willing to suffer through.

"My turn," he whispered, his breath warm against my cheek. Deliberately slowing the pace, he reached behind me and undid my bra with a simple flick that always left me in awe. I'd been fastening and unfastening bras far longer than he had, but perhaps not as often as he did, and I couldn't do it with such skill. I'd love to know his trick, but even I knew some things are best left to lie.

I let him slow it down—history had taught me that slow was definitely better...especially with Jean-Charles—he delighted in each nuance. I was good with that—as long as he stroked all the right buttons.

As it turned out, all that slow and sensuous was way out of reach for both of us. Fear prodding us, love entangling us, we tore at each other with an intense need for connection in the face of a long goodbye.

Goodbye sex is like makeup sex, but with desperation replacing the languid surety of a bit more time.

THE tingle of sex still sizzling through me like a shorted wire brought me slowly to consciousness. Enjoying the memory, savoring the heat from my Frenchman wrapped around me on the couch, I lingered in the half-awake state...until I realized the sizzle, which was really a vibration, came from my phone.

Irritation dampened the afterglow, and life came back into focus.

Reality, such a downer...at least parts of it.

Worn out, a bit defeated, deflated at the thought of heading across the Pacific to face God knew what, and totally unwilling to disturb Jean-Charles, I let the call roll to voice mail. For a moment, peace reigned...then the damned thing vibrated a new.

"Perhaps it is important?" Jean-Charles's voice was husky with sleep. Awake, he decided to nibble on my shoulder, which made it damned hard to not call his bluff.

"Everyone who calls me thinks it's important. I rarely agree." I wormed my arm around, my hands searching for the vibration. "Stop that," I said, pleasure and a giggle infusing each word, which sort of defeated the purpose.

He switched to my ear, making me shudder deliciously.

"That's not what I meant." Despite my best intentions to be dour, I giggled. "What time is it?" I asked, trying to get a foothold in the day.

Jean-Charles found the phone under his left thigh, which rested on my right one. I didn't want to think about how it got there, or if I had inadvertently butt-dialed someone in the past few hours, giving a whole new meaning to the term phone sex. Used to humiliation, I didn't worry about it too much—except for the host of media-types on speed-dial. Reading about my tryst in Norm Clarke's column, or his replacement's—I still couldn't believe he'd retired—in the R-J tomorrow...later today...would not add to my Christmas cheer, even lacking as it was.

"Still early," Jean-Charles said between nibbles.

"So helpful." I glanced at the caller ID. The Big Boss, Albert Rothstein to the masses, Father to me, was the god of the Babylon properties. And as such, mentioning his name usually prompted a genuflection or some other sign of supplication—not from me, of course. I knew his secrets, one of which was that he was human, and, right now, more human than I could handle. Still, he was one of the few people who centered my world.

As I swiped my finger across the face of the phone, all vestiges of warmth, sleep, happiness, and hopes for a normal life evaporated. "Is everything okay?" I was proud I hadn't shouted.

"Ah, Lucky," he sighed. "I heard what happened at Minnie's. When you didn't call..."

With a sinking heart, I realized I'd added to his worries. He'd already been shot; he didn't need another load from me. "I'm so sorry, Father. I only got home a couple of hours ago. Calling you in the middle of the night didn't seem like a good idea." Of course, I hadn't thought of calling him, which added a huge line item to my guilt list.

This whole family thing was pretty new, and it still surprised me that there were people who worried about me. Until recently, Mona and the Big Boss had kept his paternity secret. It was complicated, but I understood—apparently even in Vegas and even thirty years ago, it was a felony to have sex with a minor. Mona had lied about her age, but that didn't change the facts—she was pregnant with me. So, instead of ruining the Big Boss's career, they'd lied. But now they'd come clean, and my family had doubled in size. And my father was a worrier.

My mother, not so much. Mona had always been there for me, but she slept until noon and wouldn't even consider worrying until fully caffeinated and the police had issued a nationwide APB. Awakening her usually resulted in an evisceration. To shift from fiercely independent to interconnected at my age was asking a lot. "How did you hear about Minnie?" I asked my father.

"I know people." That line was a joke between us, considering the Big Boss had come up through the ranks of the Mobbed-up Vegas. But now it didn't sound so funny. "We need to talk." His voice held the nobody-fucks-with-my-family tone.

Jean-Charles started to move off of me.

"No." I pulled him back down.

"No?" My father didn't sound pleased—he wasn't used to having that tone ignored.

"I wasn't talking to you."

"Oh." Now he sounded confused and perhaps chagrined, as the light must've dawned. Used to having me at his beck and call, the Big Boss was still transitioning to the concept of my having a life, a real life, outside of the Babylon. Of course, we both knew that was a clever bit of fiction, but we'd been keeping up the farce.

Jean-Charles caught my lips in a sensuous kiss. I focused all my attention, savoring, making a memory.

"Lucky?" The demanding voice of my father in my ear.

Slowly, reluctantly, I relinquished Jean-Charles's lips. "I'm here," I answered my father as I shifted into good-daughter mode. "Are you okay? Mother? The twins who have yet to be named?" Yes, despite my advanced age of thirty...ish, my parents had just given birth to twins. Of course, my mother had been fifteen when she had me, but still. She'd been a hooker after all—you'd think she would've learned something. My thoughts took a hard left. My father *had* been awfully happy lately.... Still squeamish about my parents' sex life, I shuddered, then wrestled my thinking back on track.

Good at procreation, bad at protection, Mona still couldn't settle on names. I wondered what that was about.

"We're all fine. But," he hesitated, which made my heart skip a beat.

I waited, then felt compelled by worry to jump into the silence. "You know I hate buts."

My father was more the bull-in-the-china-shop than a beat-around-the-bush type. Still, he hesitated as my blood pressure spiked. "We need to talk. There are some things you need to know."

Ah, the payoff for all that worry—there really was something to worry about. The Big Boss wasn't good at hiding things either. "Okay. When?"

"On your way to the airport. They are readying the Gulfstream."

"Now?" I clutched my Frenchman to me.

"It's important."

Two simple words, yet they lodged like bullets in my brain. "Did you send someone to pack for me, too?" Being railroaded was a sure way to piss me off. My father knew that. He did it anyway. I didn't like what that implied.

"Lucky." Now a tone of exaggerated patience that wheezed into imploring. So not like the Big Boss. He never implored anyone other than the Virgin Mary, which was sort of funny, all things considered. Rothstein wasn't a Catholic name, but we each are entitled to our own beliefs and superstitions.

"Where exactly am I going?"

I must've still sounded pissed.

When he answered with a "Lucky, please," he sounded tired. No, more than that—defeated.

Oh, this was so not good.

CHAPTER THREE

DAYLIGHT was still a pale harbinger of the brightness to come, brushing the eastern sky with color. Like a string of pearls, the lights from the long queue of arriving planes draped against the pinks and oranges. The tourists came from everywhere, all looking for something. A constantly changing kaleidoscope of cultures, genders, races, sexual orientations, we had them all and we made magic.

Vegas.

In contrast to the streets barely beginning to fill, the Babylon was already firing at full bore. When I pushed through the heavy glass door, noise and energy buffeted me. Normally I would've found joy in that, but not today. Well, okay, I lied. I always found joy in that, even today as I staggered under the weight of the proverbial other shoe.

I'd lingered in Jean-Charles's arms, then taken a moment to go upstairs and kiss Christophe. I hadn't meant to awaken him. He'd looped his arms around my neck, holding me tight, as if somehow he'd known I was going far away.

"You must be back for your birthday," he'd whispered in his lilting French accent. "I have a very good present, but Papa made me promise not to tell." He smelled of baby soap and mischief.

"I will." New Year's Eve. Six days to travel halfway around the planet to save the world as I knew it.

Piece of cake.

"Promise?" he whispered.

There was that word. I took a deep breath. Squeezing my eyes shut, I took the leap. "I promise."

"Want to know what I got you?" Still clutching me tight, he held me with those big blue eyes.

I brushed a curl back from his forehead. Holding a little person was so visceral, bringing peace and contentment—like a puppy, but way better. My reaction had been unexpected. "No. I love surprises," I lied. The top three things I hated were meanness, untruthfulness, and surprises...and cockroaches, but, well, they weren't really important now.

He smiled as sleep tugged at his lids. "No, you don't like surprises." Christophe sounded as if that was a crime against nature. He was probably right. "Papa told me."

"He was accurate, but not clear. Bad surprises I don't like. But presents from boys I love. I like those kinds of surprises."

With the hint of a smile teasing his lips, his eyelids had closed and he'd drifted off.

And I'd left—no lingering, no long goodbyes.

Almost running for the door, I'd taken a passionate kiss from Jean-Charles, then jumped in the car and left all that happiness in my rearview as fast as possible. A moment longer in that house, in Jean-Charles's arms, and I wouldn't have been able to break myself away.

I had no choice, not really. Not if I was to live with myself.

And if I didn't keep my promise to that little boy, I couldn't live with myself either. So I had to go, and in doing so, I risked never coming back and breaking a little boy's heart.

He'd already lost his mother.

How did normal people shoulder all of these emotional burdens?

Whether I stayed or went or never returned had never mattered much before. Now it meant the world.

Hamstrung by my choices, immobilized by emotional responsibility, I paused for a moment in the doorway to the Babylon, absorbing the energy, the happiness. Behind me, the valet eased the Ferrari from the curb, its five hundred horses at a low growl. Irv Gittings had blown up my Porsche and darn near with me in it. The death of a vintage 911—another in the long list of insults and indignities I'd suffered at the hands of that man. My mechanic had wept when I'd told him. Of course, my temperamental car and I had put three of his daughters through college, but I think he really loved that car.

All I had left of it was the emblem from the center of the steering wheel. A sacrilege and a loss I was still processing. Gittings had torched my apartment, too. And if I hadn't been up in Teddie's place right above mine when the bomb went off....

Everything I used to be had vanished in a few moments of white-hot heat.

All the magazines touted the magic of personal reinvention. Personally, I thought they were full of it. I liked the me I used to be. But I would never be that me again.

The guys at our in-house Ferrari dealership had let me drive one of their loaner cars while I tried to make an impossible choice: Italian or German? I had yet to commit, which didn't surprise anyone who knew me well.

When I dropped my suitcase at his feet, the bellman nodded and smiled.

"Give me an hour, maybe not even that long."

"I'll keep it right here, Ms. O'Toole."

A twenty made his smile even wider. "Could you also please have Paolo waiting? I need to go to the airport." As I said it, the trip became real. Most people would jump at a trip to Macau. Sometimes being me wasn't all I'd hoped it to be. I wondered if everybody felt the same way at one time or another. I suspected they did, but that didn't make me feel any better.

Turning back to the lobby, I stopped and drank it in. The huge room of white Italian marble inlaid with bright mosaics topped by a soaring ceiling covered with Chihuly glass— hummingbirds and butterflies arcing in flight always settled me. The beating heart of the Babylon—a first impression if you will, and as such, hugely important and a priority of mine. My staff would gladly attest to that, generally with an exaggerated eye roll.

The nighttime playlist filtered through the speakers: Sinatra, Dean Martin, Sammy Davis, other crooners...an *homage* to the Rat Pack era which birthed the modern Vegas. That was my favorite era in Vegas. I had lived it vicariously through Mona's and the Big Boss's stories, which probably obscured the truth under rosy-tinted half-truths. History is always better in the remembering.

To the left, reception desks marched down the wall under bright tents of cloth. At this time of the morning, the lines were short or non-existent. Only two cocktail servers worked the lines, offering flutes of free Champagne. Give it an hour or two and the lines would swell, requiring an army of beverage servers wielding full trays.

To my right, across the lobby from reception, floor-to-ceiling Lucite windows separated the lobby from an indoor ski slope, replete with rope tow and man-made snow. The grooming crew readied the hill for another day of skiing in the Mojave—an affront to Mother Nature that attracted young and old.

Occasional shouts emanated from the far recesses in front of me. The casino lay just beyond the lobby and was separated by our own version of the Euphrates, a meandering stream bounded by reeds and grasses and populated by far too many ill-tempered waterfowl that had apparently studied the rabbit's method of procreation. The vet on staff earned her keep.

Bridges arced over the stream, providing access to the casino and the opportunity for great photo ops.

To my immediate left, before reception, the opening to The Bazaar beckoned. A trail of high-end shops with wares worthy of the most extravagant sultan. The Bazaar also held our wedding chapel, The Temple of Love—frankly, I thought we could've done better with the name. Something like the Hitch-n-Git, or The Ball and Chain, or maybe even The Life Sentence, appealed to me, but the Big Boss hadn't seen it my way. Never having taken the plunge, I didn't argue. Also in The Bazaar was Samson's, a ziggurat of beauty and pampering with scantily clad young men, each a personification of the namesake, ready and willing to do a woman's bidding—my kind of place. I'd been rescued from peroxide in that place. Another new-me thing... Teddie had helped with that.

Teddie.

We'd been best friends. That was the part I missed the most.

The Babylon even had its own version of the Hanging Gardens, one of the Seven Wonders of the Ancient World. Ours were the only tropical climate in the middle of a desert; at least that's how the marketing department described it. And I was willing to buy into the web they wove. Thankfully, the web worked and the Babylon captured more than its share of the forty-five million visitors drinking, partying, and gambling throughout our fair city.

All of these parts together were my home, my Shangri-La, brought to life by the people who gave it heart. If I left for very long, I had no doubt I would cease to exist.

Leave it to me to have a symbiotic relationship with a place. Okay, not only a place, but *Vegas.* A smarter woman would've picked San Francisco or Paris or Rome even, despite the Italian's penchant for ignoring the necessities of life like fiber optic cable, high-speed Internet access, and some semblance of a workweek.

Briefly, I considered swinging by my office on the mezzanine, then even more quickly abandoned the idea. Miss P, my right hand-man, was on her honeymoon with the Beautiful Jeremy Whitlock, Vegas's preeminent private investigator. Brandy, Miss P's assistant, was in charge—and she had Detective Romeo to fall back on, which didn't exactly give me warm fuzzies, but, well, birth by fire and all of that. I just hoped no one burned down the Babylon while I was gone. Yes, I have an exaggerated sense of self-importance—one of my many coping mechanisms along with sarcasm, self-delusion, and a penchant for bad clichés.

But, as Customer Relations people, our job was to keep the cops away and the hotel off the nightly news or the front page of the local rag, the *Review-Journal.* Brandy was young, but she was good. And Jerry, our Head of Security, had her back.

Even more telling, and slightly alarming, especially to me and my huge need to be needed, nobody had called me. I'm a pleaser. As part of my Lucky O'Toole Self-Improvement Plan I was working on that, but the work was tedious and slow, and I lost interest fairly regularly.

I checked my phone. Yep, no missed phone calls. That was sort of odd, but I tried not to let it worry me.

Maybe just this once, Santa would lighten my load for a bit.

Yeah, right.

THE BIG BOSS'S apartment sat atop the west tower of the hotel—a commanding view from the fifty-second floor. My keycard gave me access to the private floor and started the elevator on its ride to the top. Leaning against the back wall, I stared at my reflection in the polished metal of the doors. Sad to say, I looked as tired as I felt, although just a hint of very satisfying sex softened the sharpness of worry that widened my eyes and etched lines that bracketed my mouth. My hair, back to a soft brown from its original bottle-blonde, just touched my shoulders. A fringe of bangs brushed my eyes. My hips were a little wider than the Standard American Emaciated Look so popular with the younger crowd, my tummy a little softer, but, as Mona said, I should be thankful for my height, which helped camouflage most of my imperfections. All in all, I guess I looked like an older version of the me I used to be.

Whether I was wiser was still a topic for debate.

As the elevator whooshed to an easy stop, I pushed myself off the wall and straightened my sweater. My clothes were all new—my collection of vintage couture collected over a lifetime had vanished in a cloud of thick smoke when Gittings bombed my apartment.

Effectively, he'd wiped out the physical talismans to who I

was, and, in doing so, inflicted the worst kind of pain.

He was good at that.

At the time I got out with the clothes on my back and my bird, Newton, a foul-mouthed Macaw, who had, despite my best intentions, chosen me as his human. To be honest, I would've chosen a few other things before the bird, but the bird was what I got. I still wasn't sure what message the Universe was sending me through that little bit of serendipity.

Now wearing non-vintage felt odd, as if I wore someone else's skin. I was me, and yet I wasn't, which was unnerving but liberating.

I ran my fingers through my hair, which seemed determined to hang limp and lifeless. This Pavlovian need to arrange myself well for presentation to my boss was an ingrained habit from years ago. I was fifteen, an eager employee, and for all I knew, the Big Boss was simply that, my boss. I should be mad at my parents for denying me the stability of family, but I didn't have it in me. And I wasn't sure ours would ever have been considered stable, or even functional.

Family: folks who you forgive when you would shoot anyone else for the same transgressions.

The Babylon had saved me, molded me, until I was as much a part of it as the stucco and stone.

As I stepped into my father's, and now my mother's, main living area, I started running my mouth. Even though my father was just home from the hospital, offense was still the best defense.

"You do know I have a hotel of my own opening in five days. You do know that, right?" I raised my voice to carry through the room. "I've got no business running halfway around the world chasing one idiot, two fools, and a girl who would be wise to steer clear of me."

The light in the large room came from the low glow of dimmed spots trained on the various works of lesser masters that dotted the upholstered leather walls and the kaleidoscope of neon flashing through the wall of windows at the far end that painted the walls with its dizzying display. That view of the Strip mesmerized, drawing everyone who entered the room like moths to a flame. I was no exception.

Mona had rearranged the furniture, couches and chairs made from hides of various former animals and exotic woods. Personally, I didn't like the whole skins of dead animals thing, but I still wore leather shoes and ate meat, so making a distinction seemed a bit hypocritical.

My father hadn't answered, but I knew where to find him—the couch in front of that window, looking at Vegas preening, even as the dawn muted its vibrancy. On my way, I stopped at the bar to add a splash of Chambord to a flute of Champagne that waited for me.

A Kir Royale cured most of the world's ills—well, Champagne in general was a universal panacea. Most days I drank too much, to the point of worrying about it. I used to be a Wild Turkey 101 gal, but I'd switched to bubbles and felt virtuous in that bit of self-delusion.

Quite simply, life was better with bubbles. Unlike Hemingway, I didn't drink to make people more interesting. I drank to make them less terrifying. Or perhaps to cast a rose-colored hue on the starkness of a sometimes-harsh reality.

Not good—a line item in the syllabus of my self-improvement plan. Hadn't gotten that far.

I plopped down next to my father, who acknowledged me with a pat on my knee. "Where're your keepers?" I asked, surprised to see not one nubile young thing in attendance. Of course, Mona had a chilling effect on the amount of pulchritude orbiting my father, so the lack of youngsters in attendance was not surprising. However, finding him alone was. "They made me promise you would keep nurses around the clock for a few days. That's how we sprung you from the hospital. The surgeon—I forget his name—he was apoplectic. Made me swear on all my future children."

"Pretty safe bet," my father groused, ignoring my irritation.

"You don't need me to procreate to leave your legacy. You're doing just fine adding to the family line as it is. You sent the nurses away, didn't you?"

"I have your mother."

"To take care of you? I'm not even going to dignify that bit of ridiculousness with an argument. But you also have the nannies, which seems appropriate."

He gave me a huff, which served as a slight chuckle. Pale, thinner than normal, his face showing his struggle, my father shifted as if rearranging the pain. He gave me a wan version of his victory grin. To the casual observer, he looked like himself. His chin still stuck out, as if begging to be hit. As usual, his salt-and-pepper hair was cut short and styled—a power cut, he called it. Whatever it was, it suited him. His face was clean-shaven—a nick on his chin dotted with dried blood, his cheekbones sharp enough to have been carved of granite. Today they accentuated the hollowness of his cheeks. His shoulders broad, his arms thick, he cut an imposing figure despite his short stature—even today, just barely back from the brink. Today, as every other, his shirt was starched, his slacks were creased, his feet bare inside a polished pair of Ferragamo loafers. His open collar was the only nod to the earliness of the hour and the fragility of his health. The tape of his bandage barely visible in the V of his collar was a stark reminder of how close Death had lingered.

Still, he wouldn't look at me.

"Any news on Minnie?" I asked.

"Holding her own. Millimeters they said."

Millimeters. That's what the doctors had said about him. "A fine line between life and death."

He shot me a quick glance but wouldn't meet my eyes. "Please don't tell me that as you get older you're going to turn into one of those pundits always spewing profundities they've overheard or read somewhere?"

"What do you mean 'turn into'?" I tried for indignation. I thought I achieved it. "I'm there and I own it."

Always good for a laugh, this time I only scored a tight smile from the Big Boss. Whatever I'd been summoned to hear, it was weighing heavily on him.

He tried for a positive spin. "It's actually good timing that you are going to Macau now."

"Good timing?" My voice rose on a wave of anger. "I'm

opening a hotel in less than a week."

"Yes, of course." He let the silence stretch uncomfortably between us. He knew I could rarely resist jumping into the abyss.

I fought a losing battle with myself. Which seemed an impossibility—if I won, how could I lose? But the losing me didn't disappoint my father. "Okay, what makes you think the timing is good?"

"The priceless watch exhibit opens tomorrow."

I knew that, but it had fallen way down on my priority list. An exhibit of amazing timepieces, each of them valued at over five million each, with the top one, an extremely rare Patek Phillipe, worth at least four times that. The Chinese, caught up in Western commercialism, loved collectibles, the rarer the better. Showing one's success in a somewhat understated way was a favorite pastime the Chinese elevated to great sport. And timepieces were perfect—only those in the know would be impressed.

"It'll be good that a representative of the hotel is there."

I angled my body so I could look at him squarely from the side. "I don't think I'll have much time to glad-hand."

He pinched the bridge of his nose. "Yes, of course."

What part of all of this was he pretending didn't exist? And why?

"Sometimes it's best to let things go," he said, apropos of nothing. Finally, he turned and looked at me. "Let Cho go."

"No." I put my hand on his arm. "Cho's got you in a headlock. You can't keep that kind of secret from me—I can read you like a book." Okay, not that well, but I had a pretty good bead on him. "I need to know exactly what he has on you. I'm a Rothstein. And..." I raised an eyebrow, urging him to finish the unofficial family motto.

"No one fucks with my family." He still didn't look convinced. "You could get killed."

"Any time, anywhere." I decided to lighten the tone while he mulled over the options he thought he had. In reality, he only had one—to tell me—but pushing would only be met with stonewalling.

My mother's breast pump sat on the side table. Diapers, thankfully clean, were stuffed in the crevices of the couch. I leaned to the side, raising one cheek, then reached under and pulled out a plastic rattle, which I put next to the pump. "I love what mother's done to the place."

That got the crack of a smile from my father—still avoiding my gaze as he sipped amber liquid from a cut crystal Steuben tumbler.

"Is that the Fifteen or the Twenty-Five?"

He hand jerked, rattling the lone ice-cube. "The Twenty-Five."

Oh, so not good. He only broke out the expensive stuff when faced with matters of life and death.

I braced for what was coming, whatever it was, and for a moment I was a little girl wishing I was anywhere else but here.

Before he had a chance to tell me what exactly threatened life as I knew it, my mother shuffled from the hallway leading from the private areas.

"Oh, Lucky. I'm so glad you're here." Her tone didn't match her words. Glad didn't exactly ring true.

I didn't take it personally. With Mona, it rarely was. "Merry Christmas, Mother." I rose and gave her a hug, then returned to my spot next to my father. I didn't let her greeting get me all excited. When it came to me, my mother was an emotional porcupine. Best not to let my guard down.

Her perfect face and flawless skin crumpled into a frown. "Christmas?" She pretended to be confused—a ruse men found absolutely fascinating, much to my consternation. "Is it really Christmas?"

A new sparkler on a gold chain flashed at her neckline—she knew full well it was Christmas.

She pushed at her disheveled hair as if embarrassed by her un-pulled-together state. In fact, by Mona's standards, she had let herself go. Still whippet thin and maintained to within pinching an inch of perfection, she looked like my younger sister. Even messy she inspired envy...and insecurity. Wisps of brown hair curled next to her face as she cocked her head to one side and she gave me the once-over. "Is that a new outfit?"

"Of course."

She looked at me as if she'd forgotten that her firstborn, her only-born until a short time ago, had nearly been immolated. "Have you gained weight?" she asked.

Mona, both a boon and the bane of my existence. At least she was consistent.

Another sip of Champagne helped me absorb the blow. "Mother, have you forgotten? We have a holiday moratorium on insults." She loved me; I knew that. After all, I was always the one she called when she'd gotten her ass in a crack, which happened with alarming regularity. Giving me an opportunity to save her was an expression of love in my mother's convoluted way of thinking. Frankly, I could do with a little less motherly love.

"The truth can't be an insult," Mona said with surety as she waded into quicksand.

I'd discovered that, with my mother, the more confident she sounded, the less sure she really was. Dazzle them with bullshit would be a fitting epitaph.

"From where I'm sitting, it sure sounds like one." I sipped my drink and drank in the Strip. "I believe you're mixing legal theories with reality. Truth is an absolute defense should someone decide to sue you for libel or slander—but truth is not a defense to intentional infliction of emotional distress."

My father raised an eyebrow.

I was shoveling as fast as I could. "My job puts me in contact with far too many lawyers. They breed like rabbits and they all have a beef with me...sorta like Mother."

Mona blinked several times, obviously trying to figure out a counter. "There's a moratorium?" A dodge rather than a counter—so like her. "I wasn't insulting you. I just asked a simple question." She mustered the energy for a moment of indignation, then gave it up.

"I'm not in the mood to parse words with you, Mother." I

didn't need Mona right now. Not with her perfect ass, her perfect ankles, her perfect nose, and her perfect ability to punch every button I had by simply walking into the room. Mothers and daughters—and now she had two more. I took special delight in that. "Go back to sleep. We can cross swords again later today," I offered with the illusion of fair play. Funny how promises could sound exactly like lies. I'd be half a world away by the time she'd regained her strength.

"Oh, Lucky, I'm so tired." She motioned me to move over so she could squeeze in next to me on the couch. It was a tight fit. "See, if you'd just maybe try that cleanse that all my friends swear by." She wasn't giving it up...even in the afterglow of Christmas.

"Mother, water, lemon juice, maple syrup, and cayenne would not ever constitute a meal. An alternative to waterboarding, maybe. But a meal? Never." I felt my father's shoulders start to shake, but he kept his expression impassive, his eyes straight ahead.

Mona looked at me with a clear lack of understanding. "Well, I still can't fathom how you can eat *bread*."

She made it sound like a mortal sin or something. "It's okay. I say three Hail Marys and one Our Father, and all is forgiven." Turning my attention to the light show outside, I retreated from the fray.

She put a dainty hand on my knee and went all sanctimonious. "It's okay. I accept you for who and what you are."

I narrowed my eyes. "If that were true, then you wouldn't keep pointing out how I can improve."

"But then I wouldn't be your mother."

"Truer words were never spoken."

She seemed pleased. She didn't get it.

Mona adjusted her robe, arranging the folds to cover her legs. "I've been meaning to talk to you about something."

A flank attack, and just when I'd been feeling so smug. I braced myself for impact. "Great timing, since you've softened me up by being so nice and all."

She ducked, letting that salvo sail right by. "With you leaving town this week, someone needs to be managing the last-minute preparations at Cielo."

Panic gripped my heart and squeezed. "Oh, no. Oh, no, no, no." I shook my head and gripped my father's knee. "Mother, a lot of someones are doing just that." I tried to shut her down with a cold tone. It never worked, but I had to try.

"Well, I know."

She pouted. I didn't even have to look; I could hear it in her voice. Besides, this was a classic Mona gambit.

"Mother. You are not to do *anything* at Cielo." I turned to face her so she could get the full force of my sentiment. "Nothing. Not. One. Thing."

"Aren't you being a little harsh?" She used her tiny voice now.

Against all I knew to be sacred, I weakened. "Mother, please, I know you're trying to help, but I've got this. Everything is in place. My team is well trained; my staff knows what to do. Besides, Jean-Charles will be at the restaurant. And I'll be in constant contact."

The forlorn look on her face made me feel bad. Being trapped all day with two tiny babies had to be one of Dante's Circles of Hell—I didn't know which one, but probably the closest to the Pit of Despair, if he had one of those. Or was that *The Princess Bride*?

Teddie and I used to have movie nights. He brought the popcorn...

Mother and I were at an impasse when I was saved by a wail. One baby, either Thing One or Thing Two, as I dubbed them, let loose a piercing shriek, followed closely behind by her sibling. If Mona didn't name them soon, the Thing names would stick, which would be karmic justice, all things considered, although the girls would pay the price, which wouldn't be fair. Having Mona as a mother was burden enough.

She cast a weary look at me, then an imploring one at her husband.

"I need to speak with Lucky," the Big Boss said in his kindest voice that rode on an, "I'm sorry." He reached across me and squeezed her hand. "Then I'll come help. We won't be long."

"You two always have something to talk about. Can't I help?"

The babies wailed in stereo.

Mona shot a worried glance in the general direction of the cries. Even I had to admit there was a primal reaction to a baby's cry.

"Perhaps now is not the best time," my father said, kindness and love infusing his voice with warmth.

"Maybe not." Mona rose. She paused, wringing her hands—caught between two worlds. "But you'll let me help sometime?"

Neither my father nor I had an answer to that. She seemed to accept that, which made me sad. Mona would have to find her own spot. I had. My father had. And she had, too, but she'd given that up for him. Would she think the price worth it? Women were expected to do so much, give so much, while men were praised to the moon for changing one diaper.

We both watched Mona shuffle back the way she'd come, disappearing into the hallway tunnel. "I want to tell her she had it coming, but she looks so pathetic I can't even muster one good gloat."

"She's so cute." My father sounded like a lovesick teenager.

"Cute wasn't the adjective I was searching for." I squeezed my father's leg, hard. "You can't let her do anything at Cielo."

He shrugged. "You know your mother."

"I do. That's why you have to promise you'll keep her away."

"I'll do my best."

That meant he might try, but if she was determined, he wasn't going to throw himself in front of the Mona bus. "Coward."

He didn't disagree, evidence of the true depths of his

cuckoldry.

The wails diminished, and, after a few minutes, silence once again reigned. To be honest, looking at my father's face, his hard eyes, his clenched jaw, I figured I might have a better chance of survival with the twins.

Knowing that my father would get to his point, his way, and in his own time, I sipped my dainty drink and hoped life wasn't about to implode.

"I know the timing on this whole thing is bad," he started, his voice lacking its normal force.

"Understatement." Sorry that I hadn't opted for something higher-octane, I took another slug of my Kir but couldn't find the anesthetizing warmth.

"Unavoidable." He shot a glance at me as he threw back the last of his drink, then put the empty glass on the floor by his feet. Then he pulled his wallet from his back pocket, extracting a hundred-dollar bill. By rote, he started working the paper, folding, creasing, unfolding—ingrained steps that would turn the bill into a tiny piece of origami art. "It's worse than you know."

From the first three folds, I knew this one would be a crane. The Chinese symbol for peace and longevity.

I waited, and I knew that moment of terror experienced by jumpers once they'd left the bridge but before they hit the water.

"You read our financials, right?" my father started again, his focus on the small figure taking shape in his hands.

"I help the auditors prepare them." I softened my voice. He'd been through so much, fought so hard, built so much not only for himself but for all of us and our several thousand employees. The years, the battles, had to have taken a toll.

Not to mention Sam Cho's bullet.

He pulled in a deep breath, wincing against the pain. "Right. Then you know in recent years our Macau operation has been more important to our bottom line, to our financial health, than our Vegas properties."

It was no secret the economics of Vegas were changing,

gaming revenues diminishing, and club and entertainment revenues gaining, but falling short of covering the shortfall. "Of course."

"The Chinese Government is cracking down on money laundering in Macau. Most of the diplomats are on the take, but the government won't do anything about that."

I finished the story. "The bribes flow out of China into Macau, are laundered through the casinos, then invested overseas."

"Yes, hard to prove, hard to track, but we have a big problem. The launderers have been working our property pretty hard. If some of the activity comes to light, we could lose our gaming concession. It's hard enough to get the allocation of tables promised—the government has most of us over the barrel."

My brain ticked into corporate mode, strategizing a solution to the problem. "Okay. I can work on that." I'd always worried about doing business, investing as much as we had, in a place where the law was malleable and readily bent to suit the local government's whim. I hated betting on the largess of a bunch of officials, some of whom were corrupt, some not, but impossible to distinguish. So few understood that we'd had to invest hundreds of millions, paying folks off at every step of the construction process, with no guarantee of even getting a gaming concession, much less an allotment of tables that would give the property a chance of paying off the construction loans. High-stakes gambling at its most elemental. Yes, the potential profits were huge, but with the odds stacked against the foreign players.

"There's very little time." My father's fingers worked the delicate folds. "If you don't figure out what is happening in Macau..." He stopped, shaking his head as he focused on his small work of art taking shape.

With a hand on his shoulder, I made him look at me. "How bad is it? I need to know the truth."

He didn't answer until he'd finished the crane. Taking my hand in his, he pressed it into my palm, closing my fingers over it.

"Cho came here to tell me he had me over a barrel. I think he wanted me out of the way, thinking you would be easier to deal with." He smiled at that idea as he touched his chest where the bullet had managed to miss everything vital. "He was so wrong."

I wasn't so sure. My father pretty much had a lock on strong-arming. "Dad?" I leveled my sternest gaze, a parent quizzing a child. "How bad?"

The first time I'd called him Dad—I saw the softening in his eyes as he met my gaze.

Sadness lurked there. "I haven't exactly been honest with you."

The thought clearly pained him, but I don't think as much as it did me. "You lied to me?"

He winced. "Not overtly." He straightened his back then turned and looked me in the eye. "But by omission, yes."

I picked up his glass off the floor and headed to the bar. Fortification was clearly in order. A ruse to give me time to process.

His voice followed me. "I thought I could handle it. I even believed I still had it under control when Cho showed up."

I didn't say anything as I stood in front of the racks of bottles, all expensive, all with the anesthetizing power I was looking for. I chose my poison and refreshed his, adding one fresh cube of ice.

I handed him a fresh drink, then took mine to my normal position in front of the window—a bit of distance in case I felt like doing something I'd regret. The Champagne hadn't had enough octane for this conversation. This time I opted for a tumbler of Wild Turkey. Old habits died hard.

My father had lied to me...about casino business. "Tell me about Cho. He's not really a Chinese diplomat, is he? That's why I wasn't notified of his arrival."

"No. Not a diplomat. Only half Chinese." My father shifted; I watched his reflection in the glass. One of his nervous tics. "He's mostly Macanese. One of the power players."

I didn't like the way my father said that. "Which strings does he pull?"

"He's a junket dealer. Runs a real shady operation called Panda 777. Has his fingers in a bunch of pies, all rotten. If there's a bad angle to play, he's in on it. He's like somebody I knew back in the day."

"Not the time for a swing down memory lane."

"Maybe it is." He took a sip of his drink, his thoughts parading across his face. "He's like one of the wiseguys, throwing his weight around, intimidating everyone, killing those who don't bow to the pressure. He's got some game going on in Macau. In our property. We need to shut him down."

"But not get caught by the government looking like we are one of the players."

"Exactly." My father looked defeated.

I wasn't feeling it. Maybe it was the Wild Turkey. Maybe it was being cut loose from the bonds of fair play—nothing like having nothing to lose to free one up to do what was necessary.

Clearly, my father warred with himself. He glanced toward the hallway down which Mona had disappeared. Lowering his voice, he said, "You need help in Macau."

I thought of Miss Minnie's Sinjin. "I think I have a bead on that."

"There are all kinds of help, Lucky." He leaned forward, resting his forearms on his knees as he stared out the window, the lights of the Strip painting his features. "In Macau, life is not as precious as it is here. It's merely another commodity that, after it is gone, its absence can be repaid."

"Meaning?"

"Some there kill without thought, knowing they can pay the price to the family." He let me absorb that for a moment. "You will need someone you can trust to have your back. Many will see you as a problem to be eliminated."

All the juice I'd felt from the bolt of anger melted out of me. "Well, it won't be the first time."

"Go see Vito Morgenstern."

"Vito? Morgenstern?" I would've laughed if he hadn't looked so pained.

"His mother was Jewish." My father acted like that explained everything. "He crossed some lines. Had to leave Vegas."

"And how do you know him?"

He licked his lips, a nervous habit. "We were partners."

My eyebrows shot upward. First I'd heard of a partner. "Really."

"Don't believe everything he tells you."

Which of course meant it all was true. And it meant I'd be wading in where this Pollyanna didn't want to go. "Sure."

My father did not look happy—he knew that monosyllabic response was my way of saying Hell no. "I know you're angry," he said. "Rightfully so. I've played this hand too far. Vegas was one thing, Macau a whole other ball game half a world away. I'm out of my depth."

"And resorting to my penchant for clichés."

"Apparently you're rubbing off on me."

Not enough, but I didn't say so. My father would always be a bit of a gunslinger. I liked to exact my revenge a bit more precisely—better odds that way. "What's Cho's angle? Laundering? Game on the side?"

"He's running a laundering operation out of the Panda junket room at the hotel. I know it's true—our auditors found it."

"What exactly is he doing?"

"The gamut, I suspect. We're just digging into it now. But so far we've seen evidence of Politically Exposed Persons putting huge sums into play."

"I'm assuming they were never reported to the Macanese authorities."

My father shook his head. That alone was enough to put our gaming concession in jeopardy. "What else?"

My father waved a hand as if swatting at a fly. "Allegations of wiring anomalies. Lots of cash flowing through the casino, but not much of it being put into play. All the stuff the

Macanese government takes a dim view of."

"We're still in business, so I'm assuming they don't know about it."

"Not yet."

"And the auditors sniffing it out prompted a visit from Mr. Cho. You threatened his business, so he threatened yours."

"Pretty much."

My mind whirled. We couldn't ask the authorities for help—Mr. Cho had seen to that. As my thoughts turned to other possibilities, I must've smiled.

"When you smile like that, I don't know whether to be happy or scared as hell."

"Me, either, but I do like a bit of revenge, don't you?" I turned my back to the Strip. "We need to give Mr. Cho a taste of his own game."

"How?"

"Not sure yet." I took a slug of bourbon, which brought tears to my eyes and a welcomed burn all the way to my stomach. It'd been a while. I felt a bit more like me. "But we do have one thing Mr. Cho wants."

"What's that?"

"His son, Frank."

My father pursed his lips. "I've got a few markers I can call in, maybe get him remanded to you. It's a long shot."

"I'm already on it. Romeo is out at Indian Springs as we speak. I used my influence with the FBI."

My father looked impressed.

"It's a new world, Dad."

He seemed to wilt a bit. Nobody liked to have their waning relevance rubbed in their face. "Clever. But, you do understand if the play in Macau goes south, we could lose everything."

CHAPTER FOUR

PAOLO waited for me out front, standing at attention by the rear passenger door of one of the Babylon's limos. As usual, the Babylon's machinery worked flawlessly and I felt insignificant, which was silly considering the anvil the Big Boss had dropped on my head.

I longed for a mundane problem to solve, anything other than the ones I'd been given. And I wanted to go home.

"Airport, Miss Lucky?" Paolo, a small man, his black hair combed straight back, his normal megawatt smile turned to dim, his uniform impeccable, sensed my mood as he opened the door for me. A nod sufficed for the normal pleasantries. I handed him the tiny origami crane. His smile flashed as he pocketed it—he knew it was for his daughter. "Where to this time?"

"Macau," I sighed as I grappled with reality.

The valet stowed my suitcase in the trunk, and Paolo stowed me in the back seat. The television was off—smart man, he remembered how much I hated being bombarded by bad news wherever I went. The fact that most people needed constant noise in their heads confused and alarmed me. Only in the quiet could I process my thoughts, make my plans, control my emotions, fit the pieces of life together.

And, boy, did I need the quiet now. I'd made my father go through it all, each detail, while I made notes. Nothing leapt out at me, but I'd go through it all again on the flight over. Before engaging in battle it was always nice to have a plan. Strategies might change as the war commenced, but a starting point and a goal would help.

My thoughts whirled, my emotions tumbled, I hadn't even begun to make order out of them when I felt the car slow and Paolo turn in through the gate at the private jet service at the airport. Leaving the Babylon, the short drive, the sun peeking above the horizon, none of that had even registered.

The sunlight radiated off the silver skin of the sleek Gulfstream 650, one of two in the Babylon's fleet. A magic carpet, the Big Boss called it. The door was open, a set of stairs extending to the ground. The ground crew worked with quiet precision, fueling, loading, and provisioning the plane for the long flight ahead. The captain walked around the plane, running through his preflight checklist.

Soon the lights would tick off as the sun broke above the horizon. A new day, a new set of problems. Problems I had no idea how to solve.

I had one name: Sinjin. And a back-up, in Mr. Morgenstern...maybe. Taking my cues from my father, I had a feeling that messing with the likes of Vito Morgenstern would exact a price I wasn't willing to pay.

Detective Romeo waited at the bottom of the steps. Frank Cho, in handcuffs and an orange jumpsuit, stood next to him. Both of them looked unhappy.

That made three of us.

"Thanks for getting Frank remanded to me," I said, as I levered myself out of the car. "Although I appreciate it, I didn't expect you to personally deliver him. Don't you have transport services for that sort of thing?"

"At this hour of the morning, they're not exactly standing around waiting to be called. But...you're not going to like this." He paused, eyeing me as if wondering how bad my bite might be.

"I don't like any of this." I watched the pilots stow my suitcase, then paused, one foot on the first step, a hand on the railing. "But what exactly am I not going to like?"

"It's not as simple as we'd hoped." Romeo dug a toe into the tarmac, or tried to. As usual, he looked rumpled and no more than twelve. His raincoat hung off his thin frame. His suit had a sheen to it, the collar slightly frayed on the tip. His shirt, a bright white, looked new, but not his tie, dotted as it was with a few drips of mustard. His light brown hair was a bit longer than his normal Number Two scalping—probably Brandy's influence. Damp, his hair showed evidence of a recent combing, but his cowlick had refused to be tamed, waving like a flag in the slight breeze.

"It never is. What's the catch?"

"I'm going with you." He raised a hand to stop the argument he knew would be forthcoming.

He was wrong. I had no fight left. Besides, the Big Boss's words were echoing in my empty head. I needed backup. And I had a feeling my father had arranged some. Romeo wouldn't have been my first choice, but right now he was my only choice. "Okay." I launched myself up the steps. "You have your passport?"

"Of course." Romeo put Frank in front of him, then prodded him up the stairs. "That's it? Are you sick? What's wrong?"

"I'm assuming the sheriff didn't see fit to hand over a convicted felon to an average citizen, so why argue?" I reached the cabin and turned around to help get Frank inside.

"You are *so* not the average citizen," Romeo muttered, looking like I'd stolen his thunder.

"I'll take that as a compliment."

Shackled and handcuffed, Frank took a bit of maneuvering. His-jet black hair cut short, his face round and soft, his eyes dark but not angry, he gave me a smile. "Thanks again for the art stuff you got me. The warden gave it to me. You keep your word."

"I try." I'd traded art supplies for information. I wondered how that was going to play for Frank on his home turf. He'd given up his own brother and Gittings. I'd been one step too late, but that hadn't been Frank's fault. But squealing on family, that had been his choice.

While perhaps not as luxe as Sheldon Adelson's two personal 747s, the G-650 was about as nice a way to travel across the Pacific as I could handle—anything more would be considered gauche, by my way of thinking. Configured with two bedrooms in the back and a lounge/meeting area up front, the plane had all the comforts of home—a bar, soft couches, satellite connectivity to several flat screens that arose when summoned from clever hiding places. Stocked with all the best elixirs and, if my nose could be trusted, a hot meal or two from the Babylon's kitchens, it was home away from home. My stomach growled—even though used to the normal liquid sustenance, it didn't necessarily like it.

The best part about the plane? I could stand up straight in the center aisle. I tossed my handbag in one of the club seats facing aft. I felt Romeo behind me.

"This is amazing." His gaze trailed over the leather and wood. "The last time I was in here was when that dead guy got stuck in the lav. I don't remember it like this."

"Different plane. We traded that dog in." I shot him what I hoped would be a grin. The dead guy Romeo referred to had been one of the Big Boss's best friends and I was glad this wasn't that plane. "Why don't you put Frank in the last row over there." I motioned to where I wanted him—close enough to keep an eye on but far enough away he wouldn't be in my face.

I stepped to the side to let Romeo and Frank pass.

Frank Cho. I needed to think about him. His brother, Sam, had been bad business. A lousy shot, which was odd for an assassin, but everything about this whole business stunk. By all appearances, Frank was the good son—good being relative, since he was incarcerated and all.

Miss Minnie wanted him back.

I needed to think about that, too.

And Mr. Cho, he wanted him, too.

Yes, another thing to think about.

After checking with the pilots to make sure all our passports and paperwork were in order, I confirmed Hong Kong as our destination—the FBI thought it best to ride in to

Macau under the radar in a commercial hydrofoil, not that I
had much choice—the airport in Macau was less than ideal. I
grabbed two bags of Peanut M&Ms on my way back to my seat.

Romeo dropped into the seat across from mine and we
buckled in.

I tossed him the bag of candy. "Have you booked your
return flight?"

He ran his hands on the smooth leather of the armrest.
"What do you mean? I'm riding back with you, whenever that
is."

"No." My voice was as sharp as an icepick.

Romeo's attention snapped to me. "No?" An angry cloud
passed over the light of his smile, dimming it.

Choosing a different approach, I stepped back from my
demand. "Look, this is my problem. And it's going to get
hairy."

"How?"

"Like the gunmen running around Vegas recently, except
more of them and nobody to help us."

Romeo seemed to weigh that for a moment. "When I
chose to go to the Academy, that's what I signed up for. And
there is no way I'm going to leave my best friend without
backup."

Touched, I didn't know what to say. I didn't want to be
responsible for Romeo. I looked at his eager face, lines
bracketing his eyes and mouth, a world-weary truth in his eyes,
and it dawned on me: I wasn't responsible for him. He'd
grown up on me. And now he was responsible for himself and
his choices.

As hard as it would be, I had to honor that. And I had to
be prepared to live with the consequences. Although I spent a
lot of time and effort trying, nobody could protect him or
herself from loss—not even me.

I could admit that, but that didn't mean I liked it.
Somehow I'd figure out a way to send him home.

Only vaguely aware of the crew buttoning up the doors and
then settling themselves, I tried to stop the whirling in my

mind.

I could lose Romeo.

My family could lose everything.

And I could lose myself.

Determined to get over myself, I pulled in a deep breath, cleared my thoughts, then hit the M&Ms. "Eat up, Grasshopper," I said to Romeo, as I poured the candy into my hand and started eating one color at a time. "One of the perks."

The sound of the engines spooling up shot a jolt of energy through me—or maybe that was the chocolate. My body practically purred. I pressed my nose to the window as I watched our progress toward the active runway and fought the overwhelming desire to stop the plane, make them turn back and let me out.

We could lose everything. I needed to find a way to muzzle that inner idiot that kept whispering that in my ear.

I had no choice. I knew that. Time to get over it and get on with it.

My father, recovering from a near-miss gunshot, wasn't exactly up to strapping on the six-shooters and riding off to take down the bad guys. Mona? I shuddered at the thought. No, it was up to me. Lucky me.

"Make a note," I said to Romeo. "When we get back, I'm changing my name."

He looked at me as if I was kidding.

"I'm serious." I waggled a finger. "Make a note of that in your damn notebook."

Reluctantly, keeping an eye on me, he did as I said. "Your bark is a little bit worse than normal today."

"I'm entitled. Trust me." At the end of the runaway, I leaned back and closed my eyes. The engines whined, then screamed. The plane gathered speed. I felt it lighten on the wheels, then take to the air, and I smiled.

Maybe life held little magic right now, but flying...that would always be a miracle.

*S*OMEWHERE over California, Romeo and I had our first drink. We hadn't even leveled off at cruising altitude when I twisted a top and poured.

Romeo took a sip and his eyes widened, but he didn't choke. "What is this? Smooth but with a hint of lethal."

As his whiskey-drinking mentor, I was proud. "You are learning, Grasshopper. Macallan Twenty-Five."

"The Big Boss's private stash?"

I savored a sip. "He owes me."

"More than he can ever repay," Romeo said, ingratiating himself enormously. "You going to tell me what we're walking into? From the look on your face, I can tell things have changed." The kid wasn't just learning about Scotch.

And clearly I'd lost my poker face. I lifted my chin, indicating Frank in the back. "Slap some headphones on him. This conversation is for you and me only."

Frank didn't look put out, but he made sure Romeo chose some acceptable music for him to listen to. They bickered about it for a few minutes.

I rooted in my Birkin handbag, a gift from the Big Boss years ago. Who knew such an expensive bit of silliness could actually be functional? I pulled out a wooden box and a small sketchbook. "Here," I said, shaking them to get Romeo's attention.

He grabbed them then handed them to Frank, who insisted his handcuffs be shifted to his right hand.

Romeo sagged back into the seat across from me. "Do you have anything in your bag for me, Mary Poppins?"

"A Taser if you don't behave."

He unbuttoned his jacket to expose his sidearm in a shoulder holster. Then he hiked up his pants leg—a small gun, just as lethal, in an ankle holster. He ran his hand across his face and darted a look toward Frank Cho. "Why is it everybody feels so entitled these days?"

"A way to feign power when you don't have any."

He seemed to accept that. "Man, that guy and all his wants and needs just piss me off. It boggles my brain to think that is your job every day, twenty-four seven. How do you do it?"

"Everyone carries a load. Remembering that, and trying to figure out what it might be and lighten it a bit, that's the key."

"Empathy."

Like I said, he was learning. "As a cop, how do you handle the everyday ugliness?"

"It's my job," he said, answering his own question and mine.

I freshened our drinks, then checked with the steward, a tiny Asian woman I didn't know. She had an odd tattoo on the inside of her forearm. "That's interesting. A dragon. What does it stand for?"

She glanced at the tattoo then pulled the sleeve of her sweater, which she had pushed up, down to cover it. "Dragons stand for good luck for those who deserve it."

That left me out. "I like it. Very dramatic. What's for dinner?"

Her smile didn't hit her eyes, obsidian orbs in a flawless face. "Chef Bouclet arranged some special things for you. You will not be disappointed."

"I'm only disappointed that he is not going to enjoy it with us." I stepped out of the galley and returned to face Romeo, handing him his new drink as I plopped into my seat. "Any word on who shot Minnie?"

"Not a peep, which is odd."

"Not really. Given the recent stuff with the Chos, it could've been a hit from outside."

"That doesn't make me feel better." With no concern about mixing colors, Romeo popped a couple of M&Ms into his mouth.

I wanted to correct his candy-eating etiquette, but I didn't, showing a great deal more self-restraint than normal. "Homegrown is easier to handle?"

"At least I know the rules."

"Rules that only apply to you. Bad guys don't give a shit. Which is a nice segue to Macau. Our biggest problem there is we don't know the framework, don't know how far we can push it, don't know the players, don't have anyone to call if we get into a bind." I didn't count Vito Morgenstern in that category. Something about him, something I didn't know, yet I did, scared me. I could see it in my father's eyes. There were things I didn't want to know.

"And we're foreigners—don't underestimate that disadvantage in a place like Macau," I continued, droning on about the obvious—it helped me put things in order in my head. "It's like not being part of the Family when the Mob ran Vegas."

"A Mission Impossible. Thank you, Mr. Phelps." Romeo didn't soften that with a smile. Instead, he looked out the window as he chewed on his lip.

Somehow I'd turned into a grownup and Romeo was stealing my lines. But I resisted one-upping him and let him think. This so wasn't our normal dead body in Vegas.

"Not much to see out there," he remarked to no one.

"Nothing but water between here and Hong Kong."

When he looked at me again, his eyes were saucers. "That creeps me out."

"Of all the things we could be facing, *that* gives you the willies?"

He shrugged.

I reached across and squeezed his arm. "This is way out of our ordinary." I leaned back and drew down my own drink. "*Mission Impossible* is a good analogy. For all the obvious reasons, and for this: you do get an opt-out. When we get there, I'd really like it if you'd go home."

"You said that already. Give it up. Brandy knows the score." He was starting to get his back up, turning all huffy.

I raised a hand, cutting off further argument. "I'm not going to tell you what to do. But think about it. Okay?" I wanted to tell him that I had more responsibility than I could shoulder and he'd add to it, but, as I thought about it, I wasn't so sure that was the case.

He didn't resist. I took that as a positive sign. "I do have one ace up my sleeve. Well, not so much an ace, and maybe not really anything that would help." I punched a button to raise a flat screen, then picked up the satellite phone and started dialing. The number I knew; the extension I had to double-check on my phone.

Romeo eyed me with interest as he sipped on his firewater and watched the screen rise from its slotted hiding place. "An in-flight movie? This bird comes with all the bells and whistles."

"No movies, even though it has a full library. We need to plan then we need to sleep. Do you remember Agent Stokes?"

Romeo's smile disappeared. "The anti-terrorism FBI guy from Central Casting?"

I gave him a look, and Romeo wisely tabled the wiseass. He threw back his drink. He didn't even blink—not one cough or tear. I had nothing left to teach him about drinking. I wasn't sure how to feel about that, but guilty sprang to mind.

He hooked a thumb toward the back. "I'm going to stash Frank further back. What's back there anyway?"

"Bedrooms." I saw a quip forming. "Stifle it. Just find a place to attach him to something solid, okay?" I didn't want to think about Frank Cho wandering free in this pressurized tube that hadn't been de-weaponized. He could take us all out, but he'd go, too. I wasn't willing to bet my future on his will to live.

How did I go from a customer relations gal to a felon-keeper? Clearly, I needed to learn to just say no.

"I'll send one of the crew to watch him until we're done."

While he figured out where to put Frank, I rounded up one of the pilots—there were three for this trip—and sent him to the back. When Romeo returned, he let me see the hint of nervous running under his b.s. He tugged at his tie, loosening it.

My look stopped him from shucking his shoes. "No way. We can't vent those dogs. You unleash those puppies and the pilots will mutiny. Such a bother at forty thousand feet."

For a moment, he thought I was kidding, but I wasn't. There weren't enough of those odor things on the planet to make living in this confined space with the noxious fumes from Romeo's feet even remotely tolerable. "Besides, on long flights your feet swell. Easier to keep your shoes on than try to wedge puffy feet in them on the other end. Been to Macau before?" I asked. A quick shake of his head as he left his feet encased in his shoes, saving the rest of us from being gassed. "Been outside the U.S. before?" Another shake.

Terrific. Looking at his earnest face, I felt like a Boy Scout leader. "I could've used your help at home riding shotgun on Brandy."

He gave me his best shut-it-down look. "I've earned the right to sit at the big-kids' table."

"Indeed. But, for the record, it's not all it's cracked up to be." I worked with the phone and the electronics panel in front of me. The connection sizzled to life and an image popped up on the screen—a bit fuzzy, but there. Considering my considerable lack of technical skills, I was impressed.

Romeo, not so much.

Special Agent Joe Stokes appeared on the screen. Blond, military-style crew cut, square jaw, kind eyes, Stokes was the FBI's point man in Vegas and the agent from Central Casting, according to Romeo. Personally I thought he looked like he should have his own action figure, or at least an invitation from Barbie to ride in her pink Cadillac and maybe, if he was really good, to live in her dream home.

"Lucky. Nice to see you again." Deep timbered and authoritative, his voice held a serious tone.

"Stokes. What can you tell us?" Okay, a bit harsh, but pleasantries were overrated, especially when talking on satellite hookup.

The kindness fled from his eyes. What can I say? I often have that effect on men.

"An agent of ours, working undercover in Macau, will make contact. It's pretty dicey right now, and best not to trust much sensitive information to these unsecure connections. Cho is surrounded by a bunch of guys we've fingered as Triad.

Can't prove it...yet, but your man Cho is in deep."

Of course he was in deep—he was a junket dealer, not the most upstanding citizens, if reputation could be trusted. Triad did the junket dealer's dirty work, collecting debts, breaking kneecaps, cutting off fingers...the usual. "Under Chinese law, gambling debts aren't legally enforceable."

"Hence the need for another kind of enforcement," Romeo said, finishing my thought.

"Sam Cho was smuggled into Vegas by his father, ostensibly to execute the hit on your father." Stokes shifted his gaze to Romeo. "That's how we became involved, Detective. And that's the limit of our authority here."

Meaning he wouldn't ride to our rescue. Feds with no balls—completely worthless.

"And Holt Box?" In all of this I couldn't forget the country western singer who had been killed and Teddie blamed for it— a classic case of wrong man, wrong place, wrong time that set in motion a series of events that still had me chasing the guilty, the innocent, and my own tail.

"We're still working with the authorities in Vegas to exonerate your friend, if that's what you're asking."

That was exactly what I was asking, and we all knew it. I still had Teddie to think about. In all of this craziness, I had to remember that I couldn't let him take the fall for a murder Sam Cho committed.

"The plans for Frank Cho, to trade him for Teddie, that's still the plan, right?"

The agent nodded, but his eyes gave him away. He had another plan for Frank Cho.

And he wasn't going to tell me.

God, we couldn't even trust the good guys.

"What are you going to do?" he asked me.

Poker face, Lucky. "Well, since I'm here, I'll just check on operations. We're building a new support center across the border. Wouldn't hurt to take a look."

"Good then." Stokes seemed to buy it. "We'll be waiting in Macau."

"And your agent will find me?"

"Affirmative. The jetfoil will be waiting—the captain knows where to take you. We've chosen a place that has a bit more privacy than the Ferry Terminal. There will be a car waiting. You can hand him over then."

"And you can take Detective Romeo and myself to the hotel." It wasn't a question. "You screw this up, Stokes, I'll have your head on a spit." I pressed the disconnect button and his image disappeared, flashing to a black screen. Ever the puppet master, Stokes pulled the strings, leaving me to do as he said. Playing well with others was not my strong suit, and I chafed under the hair shirt of my forced compliance.

Fascinated, I watched as the screen disappeared into its slot. "So helpful," I groused, to no one in particular. "And so like the Feds and their need-to-know bullshit." If they wanted my help...and they would...Stokes would have to learn to play nice. I may not know the down and dirty in Macau, but it couldn't be too different than Vegas—and that kind of game I could play. But this time I'd be walking the high wire without a net.

"Did you get the impression Stokes has a different plan for Frank Cho?" Romeo asked.

"Loud and clear." With hours of twiddling my thumbs in front of me, I leaned back and tried to relax. The Scotch was helping, its warmth spreading through my body.

"You don't like him," Romeo said.

Not really a question, I answered anyway. "He's playing us. He wants to make all the rules, give orders, and that's not going to work. I know how this is going to go down—Macau now is just like Vegas when my father was coming up through the ranks. There were cops like Stokes back then who pushed and shoved their way around, looking for Communists and wiseguys under every rock. And leaving the honest men like my father to find ways to protect their own, establish their rank in the pecking order. The trick then, as it will be in Macau, was to cultivate the right friends."

Romeo sat up a little straighter. "I can handle the Mob."

For once I was thankful I was too tired to smile. "Nobody

can handle the Mob. Who wants to? And the Triad is worse."

A chink appeared in Romeo's armor of confidence.

I sipped at my Scotch, wishing for wisdom. "Kid, the trick is to stay out of their way, go around them. Maybe divert their attention away from us to someone else."

"You sound like you're hatching one of your plans." Romeo didn't look happy. "Silly me, I thought we were going to hand over Frank Cho to the authorities, get Irv Gittings and Teddie, then beat feet back home."

"It's not that simple."

"With you it never is. I know that, but I keep hoping one day you'll surprise me." He slumped back, his glass of Scotch cupped in both hands in his lap. "We're not dealing with the police, are we?"

"No, the police have no interest in Frank Cho. But his father does. Which I find interesting."

"So we're dealing with him."

"Best to keep your enemies closest."

"I'm not sure I buy that, at least, not in this situation."

"Yeah, me either." I contemplated a lie—it was sitting right there ready to trot out, to keep Romeo in the dark. But I couldn't. Not anymore. "Miss Minnie gave me a name. Sinjin."

"Sinjin who?" Romeo cast a dim view of Minnie; he had yet to learn the value of high people in low places, although I'd opened his eyes a bit.

"That's all I got."

"So helpful," Romeo groused, sounding just like someone I knew far too well.

"The Big Boss gave me a name, too." Romeo perked up but my scowl shut him down. "Not anyone we ever want to call on—a port of last resort, if you will."

"So we aren't flying completely blind." Romeo connected the dots.

"In this case, our friends might be more dangerous than our enemies. Everybody will expect something in return; remember that. And we may not want or be able to pay it."

"Got it." Romeo pretended to be engrossed in checking his weaponry.

"Ramboing up?"

"Any better suggestions?"

That shut me up...for a moment. "If it makes you feel any better, no one knows we're coming except for the FBI."

"Really?" Romeo sounded like that was a bad plan.

"We need to get our bearings. We'll play it from there."

And I didn't tell him the Babylon hung in the balance.

And I didn't mention Vito Morgenstern.

Come to think of it, I was keeping the kid in the dark. The thought that that wasn't a good idea did fire across my synapses.

"What else don't I know?" Romeo pulled his notebook out of an inside pocket.

"You know as much as I do." The lie rolled off my tongue so easily, which should've bothered me. Sometimes the less one knows, the better. Okay, I was justifying, but sharing family dirty laundry wasn't on my to-do list at the moment.

His eyes widened. "That's all you got?"

"I have a whole network of people who work for me, the eyes and ears of the hotel. Now would you relax? I got this. And the FBI has our backs." That last little tidbit was a total lie, and we both knew it. Agent Stokes would cover his own ass before he pulled ours out of the fire.

Romeo reached for the bottle and refreshed his drink, then offered the bottle to me.

I waved it away. "Drink up, Grasshopper. Then get some sleep. I have a feeling you're going to need it." And I was going to need to be sharp, as sharp as I could muster.

I didn't like dragging him into this—whatever the hell *this* was.

No, I didn't like it at all.

AFTER his third Scotch, Romeo's eyelids got heavy. As he listed to the side, I took the glass out of his hand before he dropped it. Stuffing a pillow under his head, I pressed him down. "Sleep. We've got a long way to go." He didn't argue. Feeling protective, I put a blanket over him.

And then I went to have a little chat with Frank Cho in the back.

His head bent over a drawing, he didn't look up when I took a chair close to his, leaving an empty seat between us. "How're you doing, Frank?"

His hand jumped. He sighed, removed his headphones, then reached for the eraser.

I put my hand over it. "I'll repeat, how are you doing?"

Finally, his eyes met mine—dark, flat, they could've held hatred or happiness. "How would you be doing?"

"This isn't about me." Something flickered across his face, so quick I might have imagined it. "Or is it?"

"Why would you think that?"

"I've got something you want."

He snorted. "What would that be?"

"Legitimacy."

"My father is an esteemed diplomat."

I leaned on my shoulder against the back of the seat so I could keep facing him. "Really?" I put all the sarcasm I could muster into that one word. "He's a junket dealer trolling the back alleys like a mongrel, feeding on leftovers, preying on the weak."

His eyes flicked from mine as he bent his head and concentrated on his drawing.

A woman. Dark, slanted eyes. Long dark hair. I knew her. "Is that Kimberly? Your sister?"

"What?" He looked confused for a fraction of a second, then his expression cleared. "Yeah. My sister."

"You want to see her again?"

He shrugged but wouldn't meet my eyes.

I tugged on his arm until he looked at me. "I can make that happen," I lied. I had no idea how to even find Kimberly Cho, much less present her to her brother, but desperate times, desperate measures and all of that.

He gave me a long, appraising look.

"I've delivered on my promises so far. Remember that." Man, I was so busy promising stuff I had no idea how to make happen that it had become easy—like sinking in quicksand, the more you moved, the faster you sank. "Now, let's talk about your father."

Frank's face closed; his eyes went all flinty.

"He thinks he has my family over a barrel. Maybe he does; I don't know." I waited until I was sure I had Frank's attention. "What I do know is this. I will take him down and you along with him. If I lose the property in Macau, so be it."

"Your company couldn't survive that loss."

"Maybe, maybe not." I bluffed. He was right; I knew it. I prayed he didn't.

"My father, he's analyzed..." Frank trailed off, his face coloring a bit.

I leaned back a little giving him a look. "Has he now?" We were small in comparison to Sheldon Adelson's operation, or MGM, or even Steve Wynn. And there's no denying losing Macau would certainly be a huge loss, maybe one from which the Babylon would not recover.

Irv Gittings would like that. This whole thing had his stink all over it. He'd already tried to frame my father for murder. I guess when that failed he went looking for a stronger ally. With Mr. Cho in his pocket, his odds improved greatly—couldn't fault him that.

"Your father has overplayed his hand." I leaned back into him. "One thing I can promise you and your father, I will destroy all my family has built before I let you have it or let you tarnish our name." I did my best De Niro impersonation. If only I had a baseball bat.

Frank glanced away, telegraphing the truth of what I told him. To be honest, I was making this up as I went. Oh, I had a good idea how things were going down. The trouble was proving it, connecting the dots, and putting the guilty away forever. A minor complication.

"Your father is wanted back in Vegas for ordering the hit on my father. Pretty convenient he got his own son to do it."

I was all puffed up and proud, when Frank stuck a pin in my balloon. "Or pretty damned dumb."

Well, there was that, but I wasn't about to let the truth trifle with my mojo. "Hey, in America stupid criminals have their own television show."

One side of his mouth curled up. "You don't know anything."

"So your mother told me." His eyes flicked to mine. "Aren't you going to ask me how she is?"

"I talked to her yesterday. She called. They record every conversation at the prison, so I'm sure you know that. Probably know what we talked about."

I didn't, but I assumed if it had been important somebody would've told me. "So you know somebody shot her?"

Surprise flattened his smirk. "What?"

I nodded. Then I shot a look toward the forward cabin where Romeo still slumbered. "He didn't tell you?"

"Cops," Frank huffed. His tone said it all.

"Yeah, cops." I tried to match his tone. From the look on his face, I could tell he wasn't exactly buying my buddy-buddy act.

To be honest, while I didn't necessarily disagree with the route the cops had taken—the last thing they needed was Frank Cho demanding to hold vigil at his mother's bedside—I did feel withholding that sort of information was a bit...cruel. Although, it's not like the Chos were a close family—murder, theft, assassination, larceny, bribery, money laundering...oh, yes, and prostitution...the ties that bind. They made my family look like the Huxtables.

But I bet their family dinners were far more interesting.

"She okay?"

Frank's voice brought my attention back. "So far. Any

idea who would want her dead?"

His dark eyes held mine—this time I'd swear they held laughter, like somehow the joke was on me. "You sure they were shooting at her?"

"Well, they hit her, and, if it was a professional hit as I assume it was, those guys usually don't miss." For some reason, Sam Cho sprang to mind. He'd missed... twice.

His shoulders drooped. "I have no idea why anyone would want to shoot Minnie."

He seemed sad; maybe I imagined it. Maybe I knew it wasn't up to me to pound information out of him—that was the FBI's job. Maybe I was too tired to think straight.

But maybe, just maybe, I was right about Frank Cho.

"You're in my world now," he said. Benign words that clearly held a threat.

"You think you hold all the cards." I leaned hard, my elbow on his hand. He flinched as I pressed down. This whole thing reminded me of an overblown Hollywood B movie. "Be careful, Frank. I'm not nearly as stupid as you think I am. And, I promise you, there will come a point...I don't know exactly when, but it'll happen in the next few days... where you'll be begging me for help."

He scoffed, but I could see the fear behind his bravado.

"You ratted out your brother. Pointed a finger at your father. You've been tight with Irv Gittings, and, I assure you, that will come back to haunt you." I pushed myself up, but not before grinding the point of my elbow into his hand. "You know where to find me." I swaggered out with my last erg of courage.

In my absence, the flight attendant had set up for dinner, pulling a table from its slot, securing it between Romeo's seat and mine, then draping a white cloth. She disappeared back into the galley then reappeared with fancy silver and crystal. The dinner would be plated on Babylon china before being served.

All this had been done while Romeo napped.

When I sagged back into my seat, Romeo opened one eye.

"Guess it's time to eat."

"Time to try something new, since we have the drinking part down." Wonderful aromas infused the small space. It smelled like Jean-Charles had outdone himself.

Romeo pushed himself upright, then shook open the cloth napkin and tucked it in his collar. "Learn anything?"

"Planted some seeds, more like." On barren soil or rich, I didn't know.

Make it or break it time.

CHAPTER FIVE

THE BIG BOSS told me that flying was like riding a magic carpet, picking you up in one world and dropping you in another. With my nose pressed to the window, I believed he was right. Below us the lights of Hong Kong and Kowloon brightened the night. Clusters of tall buildings along the water rose like fingers of light toward the stars. Huge tall buildings with choreographed lightshows dancing up the sides of the tallest. Roads and lower buildings outlined the dark hulks of low mountains that pushed up through the city. And in the middle of it all lay Victoria harbor, one of the most magnificent harbors in the world with it sleek boats, jetfoils, rusted tankers, and brand-new gleaming ones, sampans and junks, and the ubiquitous transports of the Star Ferry.

After a repast worthy of my multi-starred chef, I'd slept fitfully.

I tapped Romeo on the shoulder. "Kid, wake up. We're in Neverland."

He awoke with a start, took a fraction of a second to get his bearings, then joined me at the window.

"The airport used to be right here in the thick of the action," I told him, trying to convey some of the magic I felt. "A runway along the water that required a tight turn to final over an apartment building. That first trip I sat over the downwind wing and I remember looking down this long

65

expanse of metal and seeing an old woman hanging her laundry on the lines on top of the building. She was so close I thought I could reach out and touch her." I thought back. The first time I'd come here had been with the Big Boss. I was twenty-one and had just graduated from the Hotel and Restaurant Program at UNLV. "Actually, I thought we were an air burble away from taking her out. We didn't, of course, but the whole near-miss feeling always started a trip to Hong Kong off on the right foot."

"You're pretty strange, you know that?" The kid didn't seem surprised.

"Yep, for a long time. I won't tell your superiors that it's taken you this long to catch on, Detective." Turning back to the sights outside the window, I continued with the travelogue, whether he wanted it or not. "They use the old airport now as a dock for the largest cruise ships."

We both fell quiet as the pilots made a lazy turn around the city as I'd asked them to.

Feeling the tug of the unknown, I waxed poetic, surprising myself. "Travel changes you. You leave and then you come back different, in a good way. Different people, different traditions, they make you think and you realize that maybe we don't have all the answers. Maybe there is room for differing opinions, differing lifestyles, differing ways of putting together a life. It's actually freeing in a way, all the possibilities."

"I've never heard you talk like that. Be that real. You ought to let down that wall more often."

With a hand to my chest, I feigned indignation. "Please, the wizard never lets anyone see behind the curtain."

"Right. You may not know it, but you're pretty much an open book."

He'd just said otherwise, but I didn't argue. "Well, don't tell anybody. And let me have my little fantasy that I'm hiding the real me behind jokes and bullshit."

"Why?"

"Why the bullshit?" He nodded. "If folks don't know what you're thinking, what you believe, they can't judge."

"People always judge. If you don't give them the truth, they make it up. Human nature." He sounded like he knew that from experience.

Didn't we all. I gave him a nudge. "Now look who's being profound."

"But if they don't know the real you, then how can they be your real friend?"

I don't think he expected an answer. If he did, I didn't have one. "I'm not comfortable being all out there."

"Hence the sarcasm."

"No, the sarcasm is a result of my shallowness."

That made him laugh. "Okay, I let you have that point. You know I'm right, even if you won't admit it." Despite all the chatter, his eyes had never left the window. "This is an amazing place."

"You have no idea. Hong Kong was my first time out of the country, just like it is for you. And a more foreign place you couldn't find, at least not easily. Although today it's more international. Macau, on the other hand, is still strictly Asian. Much less Anglicized."

We made another circle around the city as I'd asked. Romeo deserved to feel the awe. First times are so important. First trip to a faraway place. First kisses.

First loves.

Each of those things leaves a mark.

The approach to the new airport wasn't nearly as dramatic. So, as we left the lights behind, I left the window and leaned back, savoring the last moments of feeling comfortable in my element, cocooned in a metal tube where the world couldn't get to me.

The new airport was a large expanse of concrete on an island comprised of reclaimed land. There still was a bit of insecurity to it—one minor earthquake...I guess the Chinese hadn't heard about liquefaction. That was the theory that would give us Las Vegans beachfront property when the Big One took out most of California, sliding it into the ocean.

The Big Boss must've paid a fortune for a landing slot—the

Chinese weren't all that thrilled with the elitism of private air travel, and they made it as difficult as possible.

After taxiing to a far corner of the tarmac, the pilots shut down the engines then lowered the steps, letting in a rush of cool damp air. Humidity—my skin practically sat up and did a dance, a mummy rehydrating. I breathed deep—so healthy compared to the desiccating wind that scoured Las Vegas, mummifying everything and everyone.

Romeo got up and started making plans to disembark.

"Slow down, Grasshopper. We have to wait for Customs. Make sure your paperwork is in order."

The four guys who showed up gave me the willies. Two Customs agents and two cops. They had the right uniforms, the right questions, but they didn't have the right...something. Something hit my bullshit meter, but I couldn't figure out what it was.

Maybe I was just being paranoid. A strange land, an unpleasant business—as my father used to say when talking about a dead body found in the desert. I guess I was entitled to a bit of paranoia, but I hoped my unease wasn't prophetic.

While the Customs guys poked and prodded and worked at looking official, I wondered what time it was in Vegas, what Jean-Charles was doing. And I wished like hell I could wiggle my nose and be back there.

The men checked our paperwork while I checked their credentials, such as they were. They looked legit, but I didn't like the way they sniffed in every corner, the way they looked at us, the looks that passed between the head dog and Frank Cho. They took a particularly long time questioning Romeo about his prisoner, analyzing his paperwork, asking Frank questions.

Then they made a big stink about Romeo's guns. For all of us Great Unwashed guns were illegal in this part of the world. Of course the police could carry them, but it took Romeo some time to establish his bonafides.

I watched and stayed out of it, figuring I would only piss somebody off and make things worse—that was one of my best things.

A voice at my elbow startled me.

"You're just transiting Hong Kong?" the lead dog asked. He had slits for eyes and a mean, thin mouth.

"Yes, delivering Mr. Cho to the FBI in Macau."

"And you?"

"Hotel business."

He gave me a long stare.

Authority triggered a deep-seated guilt response, whether I had anything to be guilty of or not, especially this kind of authority—the kind that wore a gun and an attitude and could throw me in jail and leave me to rot. I crossed my arms across my chest as I attempted a look of authoritative cooperation, whatever that was.

"Any money to declare?" He made it sound like an accusation.

"What?" I patted my pockets.

"Cash. Are you bringing large amounts of cash into the country?"

"No. The point of doing business in Macau is to take money out, not bring it in."

"That's illegal."

"Not for me." I met his flat stare with one of my own.

He flinched first. He and his compatriots finally signed off on the customs forms and let us into the Special Administrative Region of Hong Kong. Our stay would be short—just long enough to get to the dock chosen by the FBI.

Once the officials cleared out, a black Rolls pulled to the foot of the stairway. I half expected Paolo to jump out and open the door for me as he did back home. But instead, it was a young woman, reed thin, a sour look on her face, at least the bottom half. Several sizes too big, her chauffeur's hat rode low, hitting just above her eyes, the brim shading most of her face. Reaching for the door handle, she exposed the inside of her forearm, where the tail of a tattoo curled toward her wrist. It seemed all the young women had tattoos—guess I'd aged-out of that fashion statement.

We all piled in for the short ride to the dock—it wasn't far, still on Lantau Island. A large red arrow of a boat nestled into the pier waiting for us. I'd wanted a helicopter, but the Big Boss muttered something about not getting a landing spot from the local authorities, that they preferred a less flashy arrival. Only from Americans, I thought, as I eyed the parade of helicopters heading south.

An empty, bright red jetfoil wasn't exactly subtle. At least it was one of many similar jetfoils ferrying passengers between Hong Kong and Macau.

The captain and a skeleton crew, no more than three deck hands, welcomed us aboard.

The televisions hanging in the corners remained dark, the huge main cabin surrounded by windows normally held hundreds, but tonight only three. "Like walking into a ghost town," I said under my breath.

Romeo kept close. "Creepy, huh?" he whispered as he helped Frank down the aisle, escorted him to a chair in the middle of a sea of them, then handcuffed him to the armrest of a chair bolted to the deck. Romeo took the term "secure" seriously. Personally, I thought the sharks in the South China Sea were enough of a deterrent, but what did I know?

The young detective returned to stand at my shoulder, joining me to stare into the inky darkness.

I picked up where I left off. "Everything about this has my teeth on edge."

He wiped a hand across his eyes—they were red-rimmed and a bit bloodshot. "You're just tired."

Ah, the complete cluelessness of inexperience. "Maybe so, but keep at the ready. We're strangers here, and we'll never see them coming." I still couldn't shake the feeling I'd missed something, something big.

Once at sea and up to speed, the hydrofoil riding high, I started breathing a bit easier. The FBI would be waiting for us in Macau, a short sixty-minute ride. Sixty minutes. Ready to offload Frank Cho and scurry into the comforting world of our casino, to me sixty minutes sounded like a lifetime.

The emptiness of the jetfoil added to my discomfort. Sometimes one could hide in the crush of people. Here, we were exposed. Unfortunately, the FBI hadn't seen fit to have them open the bar for our journey. Probably just as well.

There was Sinjin to find.

If Minnie had been jerking my chain, I'd shoot her myself when I got home.

And there was Teddie to think about.

I wondered where he was. Was he okay? I hadn't let myself think otherwise—to think it would make it real. I had to believe he was alive and well and waiting for me to show up so we could kick some ass. Maybe he even had some answers. Or maybe he knew who the hell Sinjin was.

Yeah and maybe he'd jump out of a friggin' cake dressed in a hot pink tutu and tell me this was all big joke.

The joke wasn't happening. But the tutu? My mind wandered to my closet...a fashion show...his arms around me....

"Help me." I tossed the words out of the side of my mouth to Romeo.

"What?" Looping an arm around my shoulders, he gave me a quick squeeze.

Curiously, I felt comforted. "I'm going all Throw-back Thursday, trippin' down Memory Lane."

Romeo jammed his hands in his pockets and hunched his shoulders. "Teddie's a nice guy."

Jeez, maybe the kid was right and everyone could read me like six-inch-tall letters on a well-lit billboard. "Not helping."

He shrugged. "Quit worrying about it. Your heart will choose."

"When did you get all grown-up on me?"

"When you weren't looking." He didn't smile.

"A lot of stuff had happened while I wasn't looking. What time is it?" I asked Romeo, as if he would have a clue. We'd wasted time getting off the ground in Vegas, and then a whole lot more jumping through official hoops in Hong Kong.

He pulled out his iPhone and worked some magic. "Dinner time, if you like a stylishly late dinner." Pleased with himself, he glanced up. At my scowl he said, "Just a touch after eight p.m."

"What day?"

"Tomorrow."

"Terrific, we lost a day already." So now five days to accomplish the impossible. I mentally ticked through the schedule: find Teddie, find Sinjin, set up Mr. Cho, leave Irv holding the bag. Still doable. It'd be tight, but marginally within my superpowers. Yes, I laughed at myself, but at some point, my luck would have to turn.

"But we'll gain the time going back."

"Small consolation, but I'll take it." Antsy, I stared out the window into the darkness, wondering about the lights on the shore. The moon had yet to rise and the water was dark, the land only sparsely dotted with lights. Other boats, their lights shining in the distance, helped me feel not quite so alone. For a moment, I marveled at being here—just a half a day ago, a little more, I'd been in Vegas, wrapped in Jean-Charles's arms, secure in my ignorance of the precarious financial situation my family now found itself in.

"Why didn't the FBI meet us here?" Romeo asked, breaking my reverie.

"Everyone thinks Hong Kong and Macau are both parts of China now, but that's not entirely true. The Chinese Government runs each as Special Administrative Regions with their own governments, sets of laws, police, and all of that. So, there are borders between Macau, Hong Kong, and mainland China. My guess is the FBI has established itself in Macau and didn't want to go crossing borders and raising eyebrows."

"Does that seem kosher to you?" Romeo was definitely learning.

"Yes and no. Stokes was holding things close to the vest, riding under the radar. But I'm sure the presence of the FBI doesn't go unnoticed. Someone had to have had eyes on them or he would've met us. Maybe it's best this way—if no one pays much attention to us, then maybe we can sneak in unnoticed." No maybe about it—I was banking on it.

Romeo pulled a pistol from the holster under his left arm and racked the slide—one round chambered. I didn't know whether to feel comforted or alarmed. Guns made me twitchy.

I was more of a hand-to-hand kind of gal. When push came to shove, I wasn't above breaking a nose or two, but I probably would always run like hell when presented with the opportunity. Live to fight another day and all of that.

All this pent-up energy had me ready to explode. Having sat on my ass for the better part of fifteen hours, I could feel it expanding by the minute—Mona would be apoplectic. I needed to walk—for my ass and for my nerves. My staff used to tease me about going on my walkabouts through the hotel—a habit that settled my nervous energy and helped focus thought. Here, a walkabout was problematic. Streamlined, the boat didn't have a walkway around the outside. Okay, I couldn't walk, but I could get some air at the rear. After checking that Frank was secure, I left Romeo in charge and opened the back door, stepping as close to the edge as I dared.

Salt spray riding the wind scoured me as I stepped out of the doorway, then ducked around to the fantail. Mother Nature delivered the wet cold slap that I needed.

The noise of the engines, a dull thrum inside, grew louder with the door open, drowning out anything else. Impossible to hear, impossible to see, impossible to completely avoid the spray and the wind, this still beat sitting inside on go with nowhere to...go.

I hated not being in control. Worse, I hated not even being able to conjure the illusion of control.

My phone vibrated in my pocket. Terrific. I pulled it out and squinted against the spray. A number I didn't recognize. I tucked back inside just a tad, sheltering myself from the elements. It took three tries sliding my finger across the face of the thing before it finally let the call through.

Jamming a finger in my open ear, I pressed the phone to my other. "O'Toole." I raised my voice, but didn't shout.

"Lucky?" The voice was small, scared...familiar.

"Who is this?" I squeezed back up into the far the corner of the main salon—it was the only place I had hope of hearing anything.

Frank Cho gave me a disinterested stare, which told me he was anything but.

"You know who this is." A female voice. "I used to work for you."

Kimberly Cho.

A chill chased through me. Funny, I was expecting the hot prick of anger. "Still do, as far as I know."

She didn't argue the point. "Don't say anything; just listen. I know you don't trust me."

"With good reason." I closed my eyes and pressed the phone to my ear as hard as I dared, as I concentrated on the sounds in the background. A continuous pulsing noise hard to identify. "Where are you?"

"Be careful," she said.

"Of what?"

"People are not who they seem. I can't tell you more, not now, not here, but don't trust anyone."

Noise in the background. Music. Shouting. I thought I'd lost her. "Are you there?" I shouted against the noise, against my fear.

"You're coming; I know. You have..." The line went quiet.

"Yes." I knew she meant I had Frank. Someone must be listening on her end. She seemed to be choosing her words almost as carefully as I was.

"I need your help." Her voice was stronger now.

And I need your father. I wanted to believe her—she'd never given off even a hint of bad. I'd be willing to risk a lot to find out if I was right. I wanted to look into her eyes as she told me her story—then I would know. "Where can we meet?"

"I'll find you."

With that she was gone.

The boat fled through the night, the engines roaring, the wake a swirling and iridescent tail behind us.

Darkness had fallen, but on which day? Romeo said tomorrow. So the twenty-seventh? Crossing the International Date Line always messed me up. While I liked the idea of reliving the day going home, I didn't like losing one coming west. And this time less than most—time was precious enough as it was. Especially with no do-overs, just do-mores, as if I didn't have enough to do already. And now I had to worry about Kim Cho and how she factored into all of this.

The night sky was an inky black, the stars gauzed by the humidity. And the temperature was cooler than I'd expected, or maybe I felt it more with little sleep and even less food. Tugging my sweater tighter around me, I shivered, but welcomed it as the fuzziness of travel left me and my thoughts cleared. This operation would take cunning and subtlety— neither of those were strong suits.

Lost in that imponderable, I staggered when something hit us from the side. I grabbed a handrail with one hand but still was thrown to a knee. The boat slewed to the side, yawing.

Holding tight to the rail, the twist threw me around. My knees absorbed my fall, skin scraping raw on the rough deck surface. Then I pivoted around my arm, my hand a vise on the metal, cold and slick with spray. The torque wrenched my shoulder, but I wouldn't let go. Finally, the boat wallowed. I landed on my butt, my back to the railing. The burn of pain. The heat of anger...and fear.

Someone pulled the engines to idle and the boat settled into the water. The deck leveled.

I waited several heartbeats before I reached up with my free hand and pried my fingers from around the railing. One fingernail was bloody, my knuckles scraped raw. Pushing up, I glanced inside. Romeo lay draped over three chairs. Frank was in the aisle, sitting next to his chair, holding his arm. The jolt probably wrenched it pretty good, handcuffed as he was.

Squinting against the spray, which was much less now, I looked for what we had hit, or what had hit us.

The black hull of another boat angled into us. With the roar of the engines idled, I could hear the thrum of the other boat as it maneuvered to come alongside.

Figures moved like wraiths over the deck.

Excited shouts ripped the eerie quiet. Several shots hissed over our heads.

On hands and knees, I got my feet under me. As I started to turn and run toward the bridge, a shot at my feet stopped me.

"Hands up." Masculine. Sure. With a hint of British.

I did as asked, turning toward the voice.

He kept his face in the shadows. His four other henchmen, all armed with automatic weapons, did not. One had his weapon trained on the bridge where I guessed he was holding the captain.

The others scurried over the side. With automatic weapons held across their chests, they brushed past me into the main salon. One figure, lithe and small—the hint of a dragon tattoo on the forearm.

Her eyes lingered on mine for a moment.

Yep, I'd missed something big.

Who the hell were these people? Cho's men?

Hands in the air, Romeo looked around them at me, a question on his face, easy to interpret. I shook my head. There were too many. Live to fight another day and all of that.

Still, I seethed and looked for any possible opening, a weapon close at hand, but...nothing. Romeo must've let them take his weapons, then he tossed them the keys to Frank Cho's handcuffs.

With one guy in front and the young female with the tattoo trailing, they escorted Frank and Romeo single-file. She was the chauffeur. Hat too big, sloppy uniform, and I'd missed it. Well, not missed it, but the significance had been lost on me. And I'd lost the chance to gain the upper hand.

This was my fault.

They came through the door I had been standing in, elbowing me out of the way.

The man in front stepped near me, motioning Frank over the railing. Frank didn't need to be asked again—he hopped over, landing on the deck of the waiting boat. From below he gave me a look—I couldn't read it. Then the woman behind prodded Romeo with the barrel of his gun. "You, too."

"No!" I shouted. Without thought, I lunged for the man behind Romeo.

The woman stepped near, swinging the butt of her gun. I ducked, but she caught me in the temple. I staggered. I thought I heard her whisper, "It is best." Then she hit me again.

My world went dark.

CHAPTER SIX

SOMEBODY slapped me lightly on the cheek. "Lucky?" A man's voice. One I knew.

He slapped me again, harder this time.

Anticipating his next slap, I reached up and grabbed his hand before he made contact. "Stokes, you hit me again and I'll break your arm." My head hurt like a mother as it was.

"Right."

I felt him move back a little, giving me room. Wherever I was, the floor beneath me was cool and wet. I tried to remember. The plane. The boat. I bolted to a sitting position. "Romeo?" My world spun, but I gritted my teeth and pressed my hand to my temples. "Damn." An involuntary epithet as I forgot and pressed where the butt of the gun had raised a large goose egg. "Where's Romeo?" I reached out, grabbing Agent Stokes by the front of his all-black shirt, and my world steadied a bit. Blinking furiously, I worked for focus. "You have him? You got him back, right?"

"No."

"We've got to follow them, get Romeo back." Leaning on one hand, I tried to lever myself up. My world spun and I sagged back. Panic flooded through me. I couldn't lose Romeo; I just couldn't. The thought squeezed my chest until I fought for breath. "You're going after them, right?"

Stokes still sported a crew cut and the square jaw. The

hard eyes were new. "Your ship was boarded. You were no more than twenty minutes out. They took Romeo and Frank Cho. The captain brought you in." He pointed to my temple. "You've got a nasty bump."

My eyes went slitty. "Curiously, in Vegas they don't grow women as stupid as you think they do. What part of all that did you think would be news to me?"

His skin flushed pink—probably from anger, but it should've been from embarrassment.

"Where did they go?" I asked, trying to ignore the pounding in my head.

"I don't know."

I tried for patience, then gave up. "Damn it, Stokes. What's the IQ the FBI requires now? Single digit? Which *direction* did they go?"

"Back toward China."

"The Fire Swamp," I whispered. We were on our own. And Romeo was God knew where. My vision cleared a bit and I focused on Stokes. And I had to deal with a Rodent of Unusual Size, lucky me.

"What?"

"Movie reference." I extended my hand. "Make yourself useful, if possible. Find that boat and the smug English guy who stayed in the shadows."

"Everyone around here sounds like they're British. You didn't see his face?"

"No, I didn't. But you let them take Romeo," I said, which was only a small part of the truth. *I'd* let them take Romeo. And I couldn't live with that. So intent on my own weak hand in this game where folding wasn't an option, I'd been blind to life upping the ante.

Stokes didn't offer a platitude, which was the only thing that saved him from a broken nose. No, I wasn't above taking my anger out on him—a character flaw I'd live with.

"Why didn't you come get us?" Shaking shivered through me, rattling the last shreds of confidence. How could I have let this happen? "This is your territory; you're running the show.

You wanted to be in charge. Worse, I let you run the show. Fool me once, Stokes." My fists balled at my side—an involuntary fight reflex.

Stokes seemed unaware of how close to serious bodily harm he was. "They were watching us. We didn't want to alert them to your arrival. Frankly, I have no idea how they found out you were coming in tonight. Are you sure you kept it in-house, with only your father in on it?"

That redirected me—a leak, an inside job? I didn't want to admit it, but it was a good explanation, but one among many. "The pilots knew, of course, but they've worked for us for years; we went through that. And don't go putting your screw-up on me." Minnie had known, maybe. If not known, then certainly expected. But she hadn't known when. And since she'd been shot, I doubted she'd had the ability to crow about it. Secrets so hard to keep—I don't know why I'd thought this one would be any different. Maybe because it's Christmas.

Most likely because I'm a fool.

"We're debriefing the pilots, looking for any communications out of the ordinary," Stokes said with the flat affect of a federal intelligence officer, which, in his case, inflated the oxymoron.

Anger brought me back to normal—well, except for my head, which felt like it had a meat cleaver buried three inches deep. "Feds." I shook my head, then instantly regretted it as my brain oozed out my ears. "A great cleanup crew, but as a lead-off hitter, you guys suck. You need to learn how to stay one step ahead, Stokes." I chastised him, but really it was time to clean my own house before I started ridiculing anyone else for their dust bunnies under the couch.

Stokes stood, then extended me a hand. Small consolation, but he looked pretty bummed about the whole thing. Still, I really wanted to rearrange his nose. I had no idea what the penalty was for assaulting a Fed was, but I was perilously close to throwing caution to the wind and learning the hard way. Wouldn't be the first time.

Instead, I scrambled to my feet, ignoring his offer of help. Too little, way too late. The world tilted, and I gritted my teeth against my weakness. That wouldn't do—not now, not when Romeo needed me. "We need to find Romeo and get him back. Now!" Somehow, I found solid footing.

"I've got my agents on it. Let them do their work. They'll figure out who took him and where they're keeping him."

I raked a hand through my hair, but knots and tangles stopped me halfway. "Frank Cho I get, but Romeo? Why did they take him?"

Stokes scrunched his face like that was a question I expected him to answer. "Because he's important to you?"

"Thank you, Dr. Watson."

"Look..." Stokes started.

"No, you look." I met him eye-to-eye. "You didn't protect us. That was your only job, and you didn't do it. You made the arrival plans. I followed them, and now I've lost a dear friend." My voice hitched as I waved my arm in a semicircle. "He's somewhere out there with God knows who." I didn't want to think that Irv Gittings might have him. If he did, he was the type to punish Romeo for my perceived transgressions. Irv was never one to pick on someone his own size...no, he was way beneath that. My anger ran white hot. "This isn't my turf; it's yours, as you don't miss a chance to remind me. Now, go do your fucking job and bring Romeo back in one piece." A poke in the chest emphasized each point.

A tic worked in Stokes's cheek, but he took it like a man.

I had no idea what to do, where to go, how to find Romeo. Powerless, clueless, I had nothing to do with my anger. "We need to report it to the police."

"They've been alerted. There's some question as to whose territorial waters you were in. As you can imagine, piracy is a bit of an issue in the South China Sea."

"Pirates? That's your story?"

"I understand you're upset..."

"You don't understand anything. I'm assuming you haven't found Teddie either?"

He brushed aside my question. "We got it covered, Lucky." He lowered his voice. "There's more going on here, a lot of players, a lot of money. The politics are very delicate."

"Well, while you smooth ruffled feathers, my friend's life hangs in the balance." I figured if he had Teddie, he'd tell me. No reason not to and every reason to want to throw me a bone, if he had one.

So, no Teddie. Which meant they hadn't found him, but it also meant he hadn't washed up on the shore somewhere, so not all bad news.

Stokes glanced around, looking for eavesdroppers. He needn't have worried; his staff had seen to that, clearing a large perimeter around us. "Trust me. We have this."

Hands on my hips, I stared at him and couldn't shake the feeling that he so did not have this. "Take me to the hotel."

Apparently, that much he could do. The Premier of China wouldn't have had a better motorcade through town than I did. As I said, the FBI is great on cleanup.

The damage had been done—and they had Romeo.

And still, I had no one to shoot.

The traffic was heavy, the going slow, even as the scooters darted in and out of the cars hung up in the gridlock. I flinched at each turn, at each corner—I would need some time to get used to driving on the wrong side of the road in the long-standing British tradition.

I'd been to Macau many times, but always on business, with my schedule and movements carefully orchestrated. Now, with time, I paid attention to the city parading by. Although long after dark, the sidewalks were still crowded, Christmas decorations very much evident. For some reason, I never equated the Far East with Christmas, but Macau, especially the Macanese, had embraced the Catholicism of their former occupier, Portugal. While Hong Kong had thrown off most of the vestiges of British rule, Macau still embraced much of what the Portuguese had left behind. The ruins of St. Paul's Cathedral stood high on the hill in the middle of town. At night, with its dramatic lighting, the cathedral reminded me of the ancient ruins on the hills that dotted Athens. Around every corner, colonial buildings still in use added a historical anchor, which contrasted sharply with the overbearing casino properties with their tacky neon come-ons.

For me the whole thing had a bit of déjà vu. The Wynn properties here looked exactly like the two at home and were named to match. These were his earlier properties and right around the corner from our own.

Wynn had a new property opening here soon, the Palace. It would be his third in Macau. I thought he was nuts. But it was out on the Cotai Strip, ditto the Venetian, which looked like the one back home, only larger. The Cotai Strip was the new flashy part of the gaming business here. I didn't much care for it. After the hustle and bustle of the Vegas Strip, the Cotai, with no shops and a super-wide street so folks didn't wander between the hotels, seemed like a ghost town—a far cry from the insanity of the tight and crowded Vegas Strip.

Central Macau was one bridge and light-years away from the new stuff.

In many ways, the city center seemed like home except with tight, narrow streets that wandered, colonial buildings that reminded me of Florida, and signs I couldn't read. People crowded the narrow sidewalks. Apartments draped over the streets, tiny cubicles that looked unappealing and sad from the outside. Rectangular air-conditioning units clung to the exterior walls, one for each unit, like alien growths. And there were no sirens. That commonality to each large city whether they be fire, police or ambulance was missing here leaving me with the odd feeling that help was way more than a simple call away.

Alone in the car with Stokes at the wheel, I asked him, "Do you know a guy named Sinjin?"

"Sinjin?" The lights of the city played over his face so I couldn't be sure, but I thought he had a flash of surprise before he hid it behind his normal pretense of competence. Then he said, "I do, actually," which surprised the hell out of me. "He's a regular lowlife around here. Fancies himself a modern-day Robin Hood, in a way."

"How so?"

"He's a Chinese champion of truth, justice, and the American way, always lathering up the locals with his talk of fighting corruption and graft."

"Does he carry a baseball bat?" This story reminded me of the vigilantes who patrolled Vegas back in the day, taking out the guys who didn't play by the rules. The big question was, whose rules did Sinjin play by? "Any idea how to find him?"

Stokes snorted. "The guy's a ghost." He shot me a sideways glance. "It's my understanding you don't find him; he finds you. And you'd better be prepared when he does."

"Terrific, I'm playing a game, and not only do I not know who the players are, I don't even know the rules." I turned back to watching the city saunter by outside my window.

"Welcome to my world."

If Stokes hoped for sympathy, he wasn't going to get it. Not until he helped me find Romeo.

Finally, we pulled up underneath the grand entrance to our property, the Tigris. We couldn't call it the Babylon, as someone else had already claimed the name. Some thought the name choice unusual—we already had a world-renowned restaurant in the Babylon known by the same name. But there were no worries that we would open an outpost of our restaurant here in Macau. The Chinese didn't pay for fancy American feasts—they thought the food too heavy. A high-end steakhouse from the states had boldly gone where few would dare and had opened in a property not far from ours. Last time I'd been, I could've shot a rifle through there and not been in danger of hitting anyone. I had no idea if it was still open. Fancy food couldn't compete with gambling for the Chinese attention and money. Watching the locals run upstairs with their little pots of dehydrated noodles to heat and rehydrate them then rush back to the tables, actually warmed this casino boss's heart. Time away from the tables was money that didn't hit my bottom line.

Still, the whole food thing was odd, especially to someone who could wax poetic over anything sublimely prepared...as long as I could identify it. That was sort of up for grabs in China as well. The eating guessing game...not one of my favorites. But then again, I hated games. Here, I usually opted for a grab-n-go hamburger and prayed I wasn't eating Fido or

Fifi.

A young lady stepped up to greet me, a pressed uniform, a lovely smile. "Are you here for the Timepiece Exhibition?" She extended a pamphlet toward me.

I took it. "Yes, thank you."

She gave me directions to the room where the watches were to be displayed. "It's an amazing collection. I'm told the value is well over one hundred million U.S."

I knew that—I'd negotiated the insurance piece by piece. "Thank you."

She stepped away to greet another patron, and I stuffed the pamphlet in my Birkin. I waved the porter off and then shooed the FBI away. Standing on the curb, I watched the motorcade of black vehicles, all American, all huge, snake its way into the night.

The last car passed, revealing Agent Stokes standing on the other side. Apparently, the Feds decided I needed a keeper.

I didn't bother showing my irritation—it wouldn't do any good. "Subtle." I nodded after the disappearing motorcade.

He joined me on my curb. "Standard Federal issue. I take what I'm given."

That's why I didn't like him! Finally, an answer to why the man burrowed under my skin like a chigger. "People who never rock the boat never make waves, Stokes."

He looked like he understood...or was being patronizing. Hard to tell with him—another irritation. He picked up my suitcase and pushed open the large glass door.

Even though I knew what awaited us inside, it always startled me.

The lobby looked the same as the Babylon, but it wasn't the same. The vibe was totally different—everyone patient and deferential. Even though I'd had the course, I still was unsure as to the proper etiquette, which kept me a bit off balance. The last thing I wanted to do was insult someone important when I didn't intend to.

The chatter was indecipherable. The music, though, that was very much a bit of home. Although right now, I could swear *La Vie en Rose* was playing.

Different, yet eerily similar—like a funhouse.

While the outside of the Tigris didn't look like the Babylon, and the inside didn't feel, smell, or sound like home, many of the design components were similar from the Chihuly glass ceiling to the mosaic tiles. The indoor ski slope hadn't made the transition, though. And pawnshops replaced the high-end boutiques of The Bazaar back home. Also, no quickie wedding chapel, which personally suited me just fine.

The pawnshops always intrigued me. A cog in the wheel of money laundering sitting there, operating in plain sight—some in the casinos, most of them just outside lining the side streets. The Chinese limited the amount of money a citizen of the People's Republic could take out of the country—and Macau was considered "out of the country," a difficult thing for Westerners to keep straight. So, Chinese nationals, and anyone else who wanted to circumvent their own country's cash-n-carry laws, would stop in at the pawnshop of their choice and buy a very expensive watch on credit. Then, they'd turn around and sell the watch back to the pawn dealer for less than they'd just bought it for. That way the pawn dealer was happy with a percentage and the player had his stake.

And the government looked the other way, knowing they would get their cut of the money put in play. They were making waves about curtailing purchases of luxury goods, but so far the Chinese Government had done only that, make waves. The credit cards issued to the Chinese Nationals were state-issued, so Big Brother not only had one eye in your bedroom, deciding how many children you could have; they also had a hand in your pocket, deciding what sort of purchases the collective wisdom supported.

The whole credit card thing actually was sort of funny. Americans always think they are going to export democracy and free-market economics. What they don't understand is Russia and China, and many of the other countries struggling with offloading the constraints of Communism didn't have the infrastructure to make the Western way of life possible. No banks, no individual property, no credit.

The first attempt at credit in China had also included portable credit-card machines, much like we had back home. The problem was, the merchant would carry the credit-card machine to Macau, find an Internet connection, and start issuing credit to Chinese Nationals, as if they all were still in China, thereby bypassing the legal limitations of the exportation of money.

That always made me feel somewhat comfortable, actually. No matter how different we appeared on the outside, on the inside we all were equally as larcenous and as criminally clever. Human nature shared by all. Diversity my ass. Throw money into the mix and we're all just a pack of hungry dogs.

I was just adjusting to my surroundings when I felt a presence at my shoulder. In China, no one touched anyone else. As a touchy-feely, huggy kind of gal, stifling myself made me twitchy. Inevitably, I would end up with a faux pas or two...or three. I jammed my hands in my pockets and tried to start off at least pretending not to be a bourgeois American.

"Miss O'Toole?" A small woman, brilliant in her flawless skin, silky black hair that cascaded down her back, almond eyes, and perfect features, looked up at me.

So much for riding into town unnoticed. Of course, a six-foot-tall American woman with light hair never really went unnoticed in Asia and never failed to illicit a response, sometimes inappropriate, sometimes irritating, always disconcerting. Some anger, some interest, some touchy-feely in defiance of local convention...a kaleidoscope that kept me on guard and off-kilter. I'd forgotten. The stares as everyone in the lobby turned reminded me. "Yes."

The lady flicked a glance at Agent Stokes, then concentrated on me. "You must come. Please. We need your help."

Without waiting for an answer, she turned and walked toward the casino.

I started after her, Stokes falling in trail. "Don't you need to go find Romeo?"

He didn't answer. I didn't argue.

Standing a head taller than everyone else, I found it easy to follow the woman's progress through the crowd. Darting quick glances over her shoulder to make sure we followed, she hurried toward the far end of the large room, then disappeared through a door.

Two steps behind, I caught the door as she let it swing closed. The minute I stepped inside, I recognized the hostess employee lounge. A gaggle of silent young women looked at us with opaque eyes and unreadable expressions. They parted to let us through.

The sight in front of me brought me up short. The agent behind me grabbed my shoulders to keep from bowling me over.

"Shit." Stokes and I said it in unison, but probably for vastly different reasons.

So much for finding Kimberly Cho.

The surroundings were foreign, but the dead body made me feel right at home.

Miss Cho's body had been carefully arranged in a circle of gold stars embedded in the dark wood floor. "I'll find you," she'd said when she'd phoned out of the blue. I don't think this was exactly what she had in mind.

She'd called me, and now she was dead.

This one was on me, too. I should have known I couldn't sneak into town to catch a killer. While I hadn't brought him, I'd chased him here.

And he'd wasted no time in letting me know how the game would be played.

Careful not to contaminate the murder scene, I pressed two fingers to the hollow of her neck—her skin was still warm. Feeling for a pulse...praying for a pulse. I held my breath, although the lifeless look in her eyes told me all I needed to know.

Kim was dead.

Romeo and Frank Cho were gone.

Not hard to connect the dots.

And that left me flying solo. I didn't count Agent Stokes as an asset. The über, by-the-book Fed, who didn't believe in rocking boats would be a huge hindrance if I couldn't think of a way to ditch him. I tried to ignore the cold seeping through my veins. The killer had killed Kim Cho.

And he had Romeo.

Sitting back on my heels, I stared at the lifeless body, willing it to give up its secrets.

Since I'd last seen Kim in Vegas, she had traded Western make-up for a fresh face, highlighting her youth. And she'd left behind Western fashion, clothed now in a form-fitting silk dress with silk-knotted buttons and a high collar that accentuated the graceful arch of her neck. Dyed a deep vibrant turquoise, the fabric perfectly accented her dark hair and porcelain skin.

I tried to ignore the ivory handle of the knife protruding from her stomach and the seeping dark splotch as I stood rooted to the spot by a desperate need for revenge.

The image of a dragon had been tattooed on the inside of her right forearm. I'd seen it before on the young woman who chauffeured us to the dock from the airport, the same one who'd coldcocked me on the boat, and the flight attendant—it was cropping up enough to take notice. Using my phone, I snapped a couple of photos.

Squinting, focusing, I shifted my attention to the knife. Old, ivory, something about it rang a distant bell. I captured a few quick photos, some panning out to capture the scene, others zooming in to grab the details of the knife. Feeling the pressure of every set of eyes in the room boring holes in my back, I felt the need to hurry, but consciously slowed. These photos could be important. Murder scenes always surprised me with the secrets they held. Some they hid far longer than they should, and photos were often the key to unlocking the truth.

Behind me, the music from the casino filtered in, the volume increasing with each opening of the door, and then muting as it shut, leaving the silence of shock. The women I sensed gathering in the back of the room said nothing, their clothes rustling as they strained to get a better look.

I stood but didn't turn around. "Who's in charge here?" I

used my grown-up voice, even though the child in me cried. Good or bad, Kim didn't deserve her fate.

"I am," a voice called from the crowd.

I knew that voice and that quiet don't-fuck-with-me air. "Cindy Liu!" If it was possible to visibly sigh, then I did. Finally, someone I knew, someone I could rely on, someone I could trust.

A good foot shorter than my six feet, dark hair, flawless skin, almond eyes—green, not the expected brown—she looked like a delicate doll as she stepped out of the crowd to stand in front of me. At the last minute, I stifled my urge to wrap the tiny woman in a bear hug, saving us both an awkward moment.

"Cindy, it's been a while."

"Yes, Miss."

Cindy and I had single-handedly pulled this property together and had opened it on time and in grand fashion. So much in synch, she could anticipate my every wish—I hoped we still had some of that magic. I so desperately needed a point man...and a friend.

"Call Security," I said, as I worked through a mental checklist. "Then the police. Make sure no one." —I used my height to impress my point; after the last two days it was all I had—"and I mean no one..." I waited until I got another crisp nod. "No one gets near the video streams from tonight. All of them."

Sadness lurked under her mask of efficiency as she glanced at the lifeless form of Kimberly Cho, then turned to go. "The police have been alerted."

Ah, that old black magic....

"And..." I started to say, but she cut me off.

"I will clear the room and have Security keep the girls close by."

"The police will want to question everybody," I added, somewhat unnecessarily, or so I thought.

That got a slight smile as she stepped away. "Yes, Miss," she said, but her tone said, "Yeah, right."

She turned back, bridging the distance with a hand on my

arm. "I will help you."

I gently touched the goose egg on my head—a throbbing freight train of pain. "Some ice, maybe?"

She gave me a look that wasn't hard to interpret: *There are things you need to know. You can trust me.*

"Of course. Thank you."

Words fled, and I clamped my lips together and my eyes tight as I fought my emotions too long held in check. *What if Romeo....* I glanced at Kim Cho, then squeezed the thought away.

Logic, Lucky, logic. You gotta hold it together.

I'd trusted Cindy Liu with my hotel, but could I trust her with my life? Same thing, I reasoned after a bit.

My vision swam and I bent over, putting my hands on my knees, which made the throbbing worse but the standing-without-throwing-up easier. Apparently, I'd reached the end of my proverbial rope. Hanging on by my fingertips, I was swinging over the abyss.

All I had to do was let go...

If I lost it, there wouldn't be anyone else to make all this right. Pulling myself to my full height, I took a deep breath, opened my eyes, and worked to get over myself. Where was Miss P when I needed a kick in the keister?

Cindy Liu would have to do.

One look at her stiff spine, the jut of her jaw, and I knew she would be up to the task.

"Thank you, Cindy." My gaze took in all the women clumped around us paying partial attention. I was amazed my voice sounded normal, in control. "Do you have the ability to talk with Security directly?"

She produced an iPhone from a hidden pocket that I would've bet was out of the question in her skin-tight uniform. "Number two," she said as she handed the phone to me, then started herding our audience out the door. I glanced at the throng all angling for a look. All Lilliputian. Terrific—I felt like enough of an outcast without having my Amazonian proportions on display. Life always worked out a way for me to

DEBORAH COONTS

stand out when all I wanted to do was blend in.

A lone tall figure hugged the back wall, her face averted. Something familiar tugged at me. Before I could place the feeling, she blended with the crowd and disappeared.

I hit the button Cindy had indicated, pressed the device to my ear, and closed my eyes. Maybe if I stayed this way reality would disappear and I would've been in time, and Kim Cho would still be alive.

A male voice answered in Cantonese.

"Is this Security?" I said in English. I didn't dare use the Cantonese I knew, most of which I'd learned from a hooker at my mother's whorehouse when I was seven.

"Yes, ma'am." A clipped accent, not entirely British but with hints. "How may I be of assistance?"

He didn't interrupt me as I galloped through all of it.

"On my way."

"No, send a team, the police will be here soon. There's something else I need you to do."

He waited while I explained, then we worked through the logistics of patching. I had to patch Jerry, our head of Security, through from home. Thankfully he was at work, whatever day it was and whatever time. I'd given up trying to keep track.

After I'd told the two men what I wanted, I'd rung off, letting them work their magic. After taking a deep breath, I finally dared open my eyes.

Kim Cho was still there, still dead.

And I was still far from home and in over my head. Two killers against one mediocre corporate muckety-muck and a pansy-ass Fed. Not odds even this Pollyanna would take.

I stared at the phone I still clutched tightly, imagining a connection to Vegas, to home. Where would Jean-Charles be? What time was it? Was it daylight or dark? Yesterday or tomorrow? What did it matter, since I wasn't sure what today was. "Is it possible to feel any further out to sea?" I whispered. Emotion tugged at my already ragged edges. A woman dead. I found myself far from home, far from the man I currently loved, and chasing the one I used to love. The killers had

92

Romeo—now they were the ones with a bargaining chip. "Could you maybe, just once, give me a simple problem to solve?" I muttered, imploring the Powers That Be.

Agent Stokes stood like a statue next to me. He hadn't moved, hadn't said anything. I'd forgotten he was there. Ineffectual is easily overlooked.

From the red splotches on his face, he looked like he wasn't breathing either. "You think that was a good idea?" he said.

Okay, still breathing, but something was bothering him...I mean beyond the obvious. I could only imagine he referred to the job I had given my two Security guys. "No, I think it's a terrible idea. That's why I chose to do it."

The sarcasm didn't faze him. "The local authorities will take a dim view. They like to keep a lid on their investigations."

"And I like to cover my ass. Besides, I don't give a damn what they do. It's my property."

Agent Stokes turned and looked at me—something in his gaze brought me up short. "That's where you're wrong. Private property is a malleable concept to the Chinese. And human life is easily distilled to a dollar figure."

Since I had a Ph.D. from the do-it-first-beg-forgiveness-later school, and Stokes was apparently a dropout, I didn't bother explaining. Besides, he looked green underneath the red. "This your first dead body, Stokes?"

When he turned to look at me, his eyes, now all dewy, flicked from mine. "My first female team member to die on my watch."

Jet-lagged to the max, still reeling from the blow to my head, that little stink bomb staggered me. "Kimberly Cho worked for you?"

The FBI pansy nodded; the muscles of his jaw knotted, making him look like GI Joe without the balls and the finely-honed sense of justice.

I'd finally found somebody to shoot.

I gripped his arm. "Why didn't you tell me?" I asked, even

though I knew the answer.

"Need to know. The more who knew, the more at risk she was."

What if I had known she was an ally? My gaze lingered on her face. How different would it have turned out for her? We'd never know, and Stokes would have to live with it—as the head of the team, the choices had been his.

Yeah, I wanted to shoot him. Right now, he might welcome it.

My phone vibrated at my hip, forestalling my homicidal tendencies. The ID said "Unknown." Knowing caller ID was a long shot in these parts, I answered it. "Lucky O'Toole."

"Oh, Lucky! I hope I didn't awaken you." Mona.

Where was my gun when I needed it?

"Lucky, am I catching you at a bad time?"

With Kim Cho in front of me, Mona wanting to chat, and all eyes burning tiny holes in my flesh, I felt ensnared by indecision and incongruity. There were so many things wrong with this picture, this moment...Mona's question. Since when did she worry about catching me "at a bad time"? This was a bad dream; that had to be it. I turned to Stokes. "Pinch me."

"What?" He looked irritated. Understandable.

Then Mona said, "Lucky, don't be silly; I can't pinch you."

"Hang on, Mother." I lowered the phone then said to Stokes. "Okay, don't pinch me, but punch me in the arm."

That he could do—with relish. And it hurt. I put the phone back to my ear. "Damn, not a bad dream. A nightmare, yes, but no dream."

"Lucky, are you drunk?" Mona's voice held disapproval.

"Just high on life, Mother. What can I do for you?"

Agent Stokes moved away, his phone pressed to his ear as he quietly spoke into it. Miss Liu wove through the crowd, giving instructions in a hushed tone as, with heads bowed, the girls looked at me through their lashes.

I was an island in a sea of curiosity with the added pain of Mona in my ear. "Oh, Lucky, I've done the most wonderful thing, and I want to tell you about it."

The pit of my stomach hit the floor. I looked around the room, hoping for a window I could jump out of. Oh, yeah, a casino. No windows. My luck. Pressing my eyes closed, I squeezed the phone. "What did you do, Mother?" I tried to keep my tone light, hoping for the best.

"You know that block of rooms at the Babylon you were holding back for no reason?" Her voice was breathy with excitement.

Something I didn't share. I had a reason for holding back the rooms. Clearly that possibility had been lost on my mother, like so many other things, such as thoughtfulness and logic. "Hmm." That was all I trusted myself to say.

"I've rented the whole block, and at a premium, too!" She sounded so self-satisfied, so productive.

Okay, okay. I slowed my breathing, worked for calm. This wasn't a disaster. This could actually be okay. Brandy and I could rework the room allotment. There were some rooms at Cielo as well that I'd held back. I found myself letting a bit of her enthusiasm leak into my dour mood, just a little bit, but the panic that had tied my stomach in a knot was loosening. "That's terrific, Mother. Who to?" I cringed against the anticipated blow of her answer—experience had given me a bit of wisdom at least, although not the kind I really needed.

"A group of the nicest young people. A convention called CrackHack." She must've heard my sharp intake as she rushed on, hurrying her words. "I know. I was leery, too. So I made sure they weren't one of these medical marijuana groups or anything." She dropped her voice to a conspiratorial whisper. "At first, I thought maybe they were one of those sexual fetish groups."

If panic hadn't once again constricted every blood vessel and working organ I had, I would've laughed. And I wanted to know just what CrackHack conjured in that addlepated brain of hers. TMI, I know, but I'm a glutton for punishment, although I didn't have the stomach for it right now.

With my free hand, I pinched the bridge of my nose. "Guess you covered most of the bases, which is good—not perfect, but good. There's only one minor problem. Mother, do you know what they do?"

"Something with computers."

"That's like saying NASA does something with air travel. They are a group dedicated to hacking into other people's computers."

"Oh," Mona's voice went all flutter...sorta like my heart.

"They wouldn't do that. They're such nice young people."

"Cancel their reservations, now, Mother. There isn't a hotel on this planet that wants them in-house with access."

"But I can't; they're already here."

I counted to twenty. Didn't help. Didn't think counting to one hundred would either, so I gave it up. "Well, I'm only half a world away; I ought to be able to handle this."

"Lucky, there's nothing to handle."

I couldn't tell whether she sounded contrite or indignant— I didn't care. "Oh, that's where you're wrong, Mother. I have a lot on my plate: two killers, a missing, ex...oh, wait, make that two missing exes." Yes, I had once fallen for Irv Gittings' personal brand of sleaze. Not a proud moment, but a long time ago...when I'd been even more stupid. "A couple of enforcers for the Triad, a murder to solve, and one to plan." I couldn't tell her about Romeo.

"You're going to kill somebody?" Mona's voice dropped to a theatrical whisper. "Who?"

"You." I disconnected before I said anything I didn't actually mean.

CHAPTER SEVEN

AFTER saying three incantations to dispel the lingering aura of my mother and hopefully rob her of her powers, I opened my eyes and reoriented myself.

Still in Macau. Kim Cho was still dead. Miss Liu had cleared out the girls and she now stood deferentially to my side, something that always had bugged me—like women here were taught four paces behind was their place.

Agent Stokes had disappeared.

I pulled Miss Liu around to face me. "Did you make sure no one leaves until the police arrive?"

"Yes, Miss. I left everyone with Security. But the man who was with you...he said he would take care of this and to turn the police away."

"Always a good idea at a murder scene. Where did he go?" I didn't think Stokes had any jurisdiction here, certainly not when it came to a Macanese citizen, and certainly not enough to be circumventing the local authorities.

"He said he'd be right back." That only raised more questions without answering the one I'd asked.

As I was trying to fire up a few more neurons, Agent Stokes returned with a uniformed cop in tow. The cop looked familiar, but then again, as an American, it was hard for me to catalogue the subtle nuances in Asian faces. And I was beyond exhausted, which didn't help.

"This is Primary Guard Uendo with the Public Security Police Force. He and his officers will be processing the crime scene."

Uendo, completely unexceptional in his blandness, nodded, then turned to his work, gesturing to his men who flowed in behind him.

"Where's the coroner?"

"The police do that work here." Stokes watched the men as they set up around the body of Kim Cho, chattering animatedly in the Macanese dialect—a Portuguese, creole, patois, Cantonese mash-up that was as indecipherable as it sounds. "Murder is unusual here, and it's not that big of a deal."

The thought that murder wasn't as unusual in my world took the last breath of wind out of my sails. "Not that big of a deal."

It wasn't a question, but Stokes missed that subtlety and echoed what the Big Boss had already told me. "No, the Chinese have an odd way of looking at it. They figure the person is dead already, so what's there to do? Pay the family some money and be done with it."

"Really," was all I could say. Words seemed inadequate—the one I came up with certainly was.

"Yeah," Stokes continued. "On this whole island, they have like thirty people in jail."

When compared to the ginormous prison population in the States—I couldn't do the math or make the comparison, nor really make any sense out of it. "Money as a cure-all." There was some sort of cosmic depravity in that, but I couldn't quite grasp it, being a Vegas gal where money is king. "Hell of a playground for those with murder on their minds. Certainly not helpful when trying to catch a killer."

Stokes shrugged, but he didn't look happy. "Up to us, I should think."

"Add it to my list." I sounded flip, but was anything but.

*H*AVING arrived after Kim Cho had been killed, and having spent that time in the company of the FBI, I'd been released by the police and had wandered to the casino bar and had taken a seat at the counter. The lights were too bright, the red too red, and the gold too much—apparently, I didn't share the Asian fascination with bright colors.

The city was a maze, I had lost Romeo, and I was no closer to finding Teddie or saving our hotel.

The bar was a much more understated and underutilized affair than its Vegas counterpart. With a bored look, the bartender swiped at a delicate glass with a bar towel.

"Champagne."

I must've looked lost or desperate. "We have stronger."

"Champagne, make it pink," I said in my best Vegas mobster growl, amusing only myself.

The night still young, I was his only patron. The bar top looked like petrified wood inlaid with various semiprecious stones in a swirl pattern. The stools were contemporary and as uncomfortable as they looked, which made me squirm. I couldn't avoid my reflection in the mirror behind the bar, so I used it to look over my shoulder. The bartender put a flute of Champagne in front of me. I didn't touch it.

I'd lost Romeo. I'd lost Teddie. I'd lost Kim Cho. And I was on the verge of losing everything else. One hell of a losing streak. Tired of waiting for luck to turn my way, I thought it time to force Luck's hand.

After I'd dialed a familiar number, I pressed the phone to my ear and waited, imagining the electronic pulse traveling half the world, under oceans, over mountains. With a glare, I sent the bartender scurrying to the far end of the bar, well out of earshot.

Finally, Jerry answered. "Can you talk?" he asked without preamble.

"No. That's why I called."

"Smartass." His voice held a chuckle.

"That's Vice President Smartass, to you."

This time I got the laugh I'd wanted. "How could I forget? My apologies."

"Don't let it happen again." I flipped my serious switch. "We have to assume that no matter where I am, while in Macau, everything I say can be overheard." I glanced to my right and left, then behind me, using the mirror behind the bar. No one seemed particularly interested, other than the normal interest I attracted here anyway. The Chinese were so amusing to watch. Even coupled up or with friends, each of them stared into their mobile devices, completely ignoring their compatriots. I bet dating was a blast. "You got delivery?"

"Transmissions came through fine." Jerry's voice mirrored my serious tone. "The tapes of tonight are clear, but there is a lot of footage to go through."

"I know."

He heard the unasked questions. "I'll be looking for Miss Cho and anyone showing peculiar interest in her, as well as anyone we recognize. That what you want?"

"Absolutely. As soon as you can."

"We're on it."

A man entered the bar to my right. The hotel operations manager by the looks of him—officious, with a nametag and a service pin stuck in his lapel. With a tight smile, he worked the patrons and the employees, greeting each one. "You're a peach, Jer," I said, keeping my eyes on the man. He looked familiar.

"Please remind my wife. But one question. Why me? Why not local? The Security guys there could give you the inside skinny."

"You I know I can trust." With that I severed the connection. Hearing his voice, knowing he was so far away, everything I knew and loved was beyond my reach, the emotions welled and I felt so alone. Too much booze, too little sleep, and the whole world-hanging-in-the-balance thing had me slipping over the edge.

Where was Romeo? What were they doing to him? The imaginings derailed thought and churned my stomach.

And Teddie? I sat on that thought until it quit torturing me.

What I would do for a friend.

Pressing my face in my hands, I worked to pull myself together.

When I felt a hand on my shoulder, for a brief instant, hope surged. *Teddie!* Heat raced through me.

But the voice, too deep to be Teddie's, dashed my hope.

"Lucky? I'm sorry to interrupt, but, as the Operations Manager, I feel I should extend my personal welcome." There was a hint of familiar in the deep tones—the man I thought I had recognized. He extended his hand. "It's been a long time. Ryan Whitmore."

"Ryan Whitmore! Of course." He hadn't opened the hotel—I'd been here for that. The Peninsula had hired that guy away—he was that good. Ryan had been a third-string stand-in, and I was surprised the Big Boss hadn't replaced him. If it'd been my responsibility, he'd have been long gone.

I thought I'd recognized him, but I hadn't been sure. Funny how, in a foreign place, people started looking like someone from home. It happened to me every time, but this time more than others. Perhaps I missed home more.

But with Ryan, I'd been right.

He was someone from home.

Ryan Whitmore.

Years ago, I'd trained him when our careers had momentarily traveled the same path. We both had been pups barely whelped. Now he had grown into a set of broad shoulders tapering to a thin waist then ending in long legs that put him eye-to-eye with me. His green eyes reminded me of a Texas guy I once knew, as did his wavy brown hair and easy manner. He even oozed the same slickness. Although younger than Ryan by a year or two, back in the day I'd been a few rungs higher on the corporate ladder—still was. I'd wanted it more, worked harder. Ryan had relied mainly on his charm. Since I didn't have any, that wasn't an option for me.

Ryan gave me a warm look, which pissed me off—I was still

his boss. Some men never got it.

He hadn't impressed me then, and he sure wasn't getting off on the right foot now. "You should have let me know you were coming."

"It was spur of the moment. I had some non-hotel business to take care of in Hong Kong." That sounded legit, even to me, and I knew it wasn't true.

"Glad you stopped by, in any case." The words tripped easily off his tongue, but the subtext, if I read it right, negated the words. "Bad business, this."

If I'd been in his shoes, I would've felt put out at a sneak visit from a corporate type, but I've always been a bit touchy. In contrast, Ryan had a smooth polish. He was better than I thought.

Bad business? I tried not to flip out. "Truly. Do you lose workers often?"

He shrugged, then deftly changed the subject. "I've been watching you—from afar of course. You were the best teacher I had." He reddened as he looked at his feet for a moment. "I wasn't stalking you, just interested in your success." When he looked up, his composure had returned. "You're opening your own hotel. That is so amazing. And in a few days. What the hell are you doing here?"

I wondered the same thing myself. "A long story, but I'm going to need your help."

"Let's get a table. Maybe the one in the corner over there?" He motioned to the far side of the bar next to a baby grand, just like the one Teddie used to play, except this one was black to his white.

"Sure."

"You want your Champagne?"

"No, it's gotten warm."

He raised an eyebrow, but offered a hand, which I ignored as I slipped off the stool. Taking the hint, he didn't pull out my chair at the small circular table. We settled ourselves in the enveloping club chairs. The noise of the casino, slight as it was by Vegas standards, muffled our conversation, hopefully keeping it from any would-be eavesdroppers.

Ryan didn't seem overly concerned as he leaned back, crossing one leg, resting the ankle on his knee. His expression placid, his foot bounced. "What's your pleasure?"

A quip on the end of my tongue, my defenses and self-muzzling at low ebb, I surprised myself when I stammered, "Bubbles, not the cheapest, but not enough to make me want to shed clothes."

"Hopes dashed," he countered with an emotionless grin, as only the British can do. He signaled a waitperson and gave our order. She returned with a bottle of Veuve and two glasses. Both Ryan and I watched as she went through the routine.

Exhaustion crept through my veins with the cold numbness of anesthesia. I accepted the glass Ryan handed me, holding it.

"It's better if you drink it." He sipped his, then asked, "How can I be of assistance?"

An innocent question, but to me he seemed guarded even though his manner remained casual.

My face fell and I took a long gulp.

Ryan raised his eyebrows. "That bad?"

"Worse." I drained my glass, then held it out.

Ryan took his cue.

After two glasses, the warmth moderated the cold and I felt a bit more myself. "I've got a real problem. Actually, change that. You and me, *we* have a huge problem. How long have you been here? Five years, give or take?"

He nodded.

"Long enough," I said, a slight joke...very slight.

He cocked an eyebrow. "Long enough for what?"

"To know the back alleys and the folks who navigate them."

He sobered. "Oh, that *is* bad."

Needing to shake things up, I threw caution to the wind and used a verbal stick to poke the hive. "There's something going on here, in the hotel. And when it goes down, they're planning on taking everything with them."

"Everything?"

"Vegas. The Big Boss. Me." I paused and leveled a stare. "You."

He didn't seem guilty. In fact, I couldn't find a reaction if he had one.

I made a sweeping arc with my arm. "They'll take this, too."

Still nothing. "Any idea what they're doing?" Ryan followed my lead and drained his glass, then refilled. The bottle empty, he motioned for another.

"I was hoping you could tell me." I eyed my third glass, weighing the cost versus the benefit. The immediate benefit won—I'm shallow that way.

"You knew that gal in the lounge?" Ryan asked. "I didn't get a good look at her—didn't really want one. Sometimes it's better not to know."

"It's always better to know. Didn't I teach you anything? And especially here." I sipped my Champagne, feeling somewhat virtuous that I didn't bolt it like the first two glasses, and I thought about all that could happen while the ones in charge looked the other way. "Yeah, I knew her. Kimberly Cho."

"Kim Cho?" Ryan slumped back in his chair, looking like he'd lost his best friend. "Shit."

I reached out and grabbed his arm, giving it a squeeze. "You knew her. I'm so sorry. Normally, I have a tad more tact and sensitivity."

"Only a tad, if I remember correctly." He gave me a wan smile. "It's not like that. She was a local lawyer. Made big waves. We were all worried about her."

Stokes had said she worked for him.

People are not who they seem. She'd told me that, and then she'd died. I tried to remember everything Kim had told me in Vegas. What game had she been playing? Had she been trying to take her father down or step into his shoes? Why couldn't everyone play nice and get along? Oh yeah, that filthy lucre thing. Throw a few gold coins on the ground and every snake within miles will slither your way, eating the other snakes along the way. "Do you think I could buy an island somewhere southeast of here and just disappear?"

Ryan went to work on the fresh bottle a waitress had delivered. "I'm afraid not. You'd be missed."

"The downside to pretending to be indispensable. Eventually somebody believes it."

He held up the bottle, then without encouragement, he freshened my glass.

I quit whining...for now. "Tell me about her father."

"He's hooked in with a bunch of bigwigs here." He paused, giving me an assessing look. "You do know how the game is played in Macau?"

This was one of those points where intuition told me it would be more enlightening to play dumb. "Probably not. Tell me."

"The whole town is on the take. The casino bosses and their acolytes are the government here. They pass laws to benefit themselves and enforce other laws when and how they feel like it. They dangle the foreign investors here like puppets on a string. They might enforce one gaming law strictly against us, but never enforce it against Wynn or MGM."

"And they promise a gaming concession of five hundred tables to encourage investment, then deliver permission for half as many when the construction is complete. That much I do know." I didn't add from personal experience. Ryan had been here long enough to have heard that story.

"Did you also know that the government here pays each citizen several thousand dollars U.S. every year? They get free medical care. Vouchers each year for education to spend as they see fit. Subsidized utilities, and the seniors get free or essentially free housing, if they need it." He seemed to relish his role—mansplaining clearly suited him. Another black mark on his soul.

I pursed my lips and nodded with appreciation. "Legalized graft and corruption with a payoff to anyone who might throw a big stink. I don't like it, but I appreciate it, if you know what I mean. It's exactly what would happen if Vegas was its own country."

"Precisely."

"Okay, so how does Cho figure in?"

"He's not officially part of the government, but he has his fingers in all the pies. And there's some scuttlebutt he's tied in with one of the junket dealers, which raises ugly to a whole other level."

"Which junket?"

"Not sure." Ryan glanced over his shoulder. "Best not to bite the hand that feeds you, you know."

No, I didn't know. And that's just the kind of thinking that would get our concession pulled.

Ryan plucked at his jacket, straightening it while looking decidedly uncomfortable. Lying would do that. Whitmore knew damn well Cho was a junket dealer and the head of Panda 777. If he was hoping to throw me off the scent, he was as dumb as I'd always taken him for.

I contemplated the best strategy: waterboarding, thumbscrews? I wasn't really sure. So I decided I should play dumb until I figured out the smart thing to do. Not exactly a strategy, but it was the best I had.

"The junkets do make our life possible." I tried for a bland expression, which cost me greatly. Giving that sort of attribution to the junkets, who used the Triads to enforce gambling debts, and who made book on the side, was like saying Vegas had been a much better place when the Mob ran it. I guess it depended on which side of that wall you stood. And, if the Big Boss's stories were true, once you shook the hand of the Devil, you rode that slippery slope into oblivion. The question wasn't if; it was when.

As I watched Ryan, I wondered who had him looking over his shoulder.

He relaxed back in his chair, but his hand shook as he raised his glass to his lips. "They do indeed."

"Do you know any more about Mr. Cho? "

"He likes to show off his wealth. Rides around town in a red Ferrari. Wears bespoke suits tailored in Thailand. Always has something new and flashy. Doesn't sit well with the government types back in Beijing. And their recent crackdown on gambling and high-dollar purchases has hurt our bottom line here."

I found his use of "us" to be telling. And we both knew that the crackdown would be temporary—it was the sort of saber-rattling Beijing did from time to time to keep their officials within some boundaries and to keep face with the international community. But bribery was still a way of business in China, on the mainland or in the control areas of Hong Kong and Macau.

"Did you know he tried to have the Big Boss killed?" My turn for the twenty questions.

Ryan looked impressed. "Balls." At my raised eyebrow, he recovered. "Sorry. I never knew he was your father. Not until recently anyway."

"Me either. When he and my mother told me, I thought about killing him myself, but not worth the jail time. Besides, I've grown accustomed to my creature comforts. Speaking of which, do you have a room for me?" Time to pull the curtain on this little show.

"Ah, yes!" Ryan patted his pockets then extracted a key from the one that jangled. "The owner's suite. We kept the old lock and key, since it is rarely used. The entire floor is secure." He handed me the brass key with a purple silk tassel.

"Makes me feel like a maharajah or something."

"Please, there's none of that here in the People's Republic."

I pocketed the key, then refilled Ryan's glass. "Any idea who would want Kimberly Cho dead?"

"Well, she's the second local lawyer who's been killed. The first was a young guy, Jhonny Vu." Ryan glanced over his shoulder, his gaze sweeping the area like the FBI swept a room for bugs. Apparently satisfied, he leaned forward, moving his chair closer.

I leaned in to him.

"There are rumors she helped the FBI take down Paul Zhung. Stuff like that gets you the wrong kind of attention around here."

"They still have Zhung on ice in Vegas."

"That would be only a minor impediment to Z."

So Ryan and Paul Zhung were on a first-nickname basis. Interesting. "You think he could arrange a hit from there?"

"Easily. And he'll beat that rap. You watch." Ryan looked a bit spooked along with impressed. "Rules are different here. The amount of money immense. His influence is impressive."

"He was running a wire room in Caesar's, making illegal book. Stupid, but I gotta give it to him, the man has balls. They're trying to bring him down with his tie-ins to organized crime—the Triad and the junkets dealers."

Ryan shushed me. His head on a swivel, he looked to see who might be taking an interest in our conversation. "Be careful, Lucky. Very careful or you might find yourself like Kim Cho. The walls have ears."

"Is that a threat?"

Ryan reared back, leaning away from me. "Don't be silly. It's just a warning. Macau isn't Vegas."

"I know the drill. And you're wrong. Macau is exactly like Vegas as it once was."

"Very similar in many ways, I'll grant you that. China has just started cleaning it up—or making an attempt, like the early corporate days in Vegas." He leveled a look. "Remember what happened when they cleaned up Vegas?"

I didn't feel as smug as he looked. My parents had lived through it, and I'd teethed on the stories. "Carnage. Power loves a vacuum. Take away the Mob and everyone is in the game, fighting to win."

"You have the same situation here. And the money that flows through here dwarfs Vegas a hundredfold or more. A messy business. But why don't you let the authorities worry about all this? Stay out of the way. Everyone here is a bit skittish when it comes to outsiders, and," he reached cross and patted my hand, "honey, you scream outsider."

I pulled my hand from under his as my eyes turned all slitty. Nobody calls me honey and goes unpunished. But right now I was too tired to rip him a new one. "That's where you're wrong. I scream foreigner, for sure. But when it comes to the gaming industry, I am far from an outsider."

"True." Ryan shifted uncomfortably. "This is a dangerous game. I'd hate to see you hurt...or worse."

"You and me both." I didn't throw out my normal I-can-take-care-of-myself-bullshit. When it came to Macau and the Triad, I wasn't at all sure of my skills. Breaking noses seemed almost laughable. "You said the junket dealers. Give me the inside skinny on them." As a casino exec, I knew there was what the public knew and what the hotel people saw—often different by a magnitude of ten.

"Nobody has proven it, but the scuttlebutt is the junket dealers, at least the largest of them, make private book, using our tables for the game."

"Explain." I sipped my drink, but the bubbles weren't settling my stomach. My gut was not happy, and through the years I'd learned to pay attention.

"So, part of the game is the junket dealers give credit to their Chinese National customers. A clever way to circumvent the currency export limitations. It used to be the mobile credit-card machines being used to extract cash from mainland accounts, but the government shut that down."

"Along with a general crackdown on luxury spending." I nodded. I knew most of this story.

"Right. Well, apparently, the junket dealers have found a way around, if you will. It works like this: if one of their players wagers ten million, then they've wagered ten times that with the junket dealers."

"Sort of a virtual game on the game?"

"Exactly. If they win a million from the house."

"They win ten million from the junket dealer." I knew this game—huge upside, but the downside matched and was far worse.

Ryan's voice took on a more ominous tone. "And if they lose a million at the tables..."

"They are in deep. And the Triads enforce the debts."

"We've had a few murders recently that have sent the city into a bit of a tailspin. As you might imagine, that's a bit out of the ordinary here. And then Jhonny Vu...and now Kim." Ryan leaned forward, lowering his voice. "The war has started."

And they had Romeo.

*T*OO tired to move, I slumped down in my chair, my legs stretched in front of me. I watched Ryan move through the bar, then down the steps and onto the casino floor. Unlike his earlier approach, this time he didn't greet anyone. Instead, he cast a quick look over his shoulder toward me. Hunkered in the dark corner, I knew he couldn't see me, but he knew I was there. He probably felt me watching him.

Funny what guilt could do.

I wondered what he was guilty of. Exactly how far had he gone?

That was when I saw her.

The girl with the dragon tattoo. God, I felt a book coming on. Dressed in black as she had been on the boat, she leaned casually up against a slot machine. She was watching Ryan, too. She didn't duck out of sight as he approached and passed her. If they acknowledged each other, I couldn't tell. Once he'd passed by, she waited a beat or two, her eyes scanning the casino, the bar.

I hunkered lower, even though I knew the shadows hid my presence.

Apparently satisfied, she turned to follow Ryan.

I lost sight of them both among the gamblers and the machines and tables. Bolting out of my chair, I rushed to follow. With hands on the railing, I swung myself down the three steps leading to the casino floor, then took off at a run, not caring whose attention I drew.

Dashing and darting, I found a few dead ends and startled

a few servers when I burst into a prep kitchen, but didn't pick up the trail of the mysterious young woman. Pausing on the arc of one of the bridges crossing the indoor stream that separated the lobby from the casino, I pivoted, pretending to be a corporate exec scanning my territory, whatever that looked like.

On my second pass, as that fickle bitch, Luck, would have it, I spied the girl hiding behind a clump of rushes on the opposite bank of the stream to my left. Hard to see in her in black, she'd parted the tall fronds and was peering intently at something or someone in the lobby. She had an angle on me so I couldn't see exactly what she was looking at, but, whatever it was, it was riveting. Good for me, bad for her. I'd closed half the distance before they saw me. Like a startled rabbit she bolted from her hiding place and ducked around the corner.

Skidding into the turn off the bridge, I caught myself with one hand to the floor. Regaining my footing, I charged off, racing after her. Down a back hallway. One of the side doors banged shut just as I rounded the corner. Without slowing, I slammed though.

A streetlamp silhouetted a slender figure running, hair flying. Twisting, she angled a glance back at me, then put her head down and ran. I ran after her. Not gaining, not losing, I managed to just keep sight of her as I rounded a corner or jumped a hedge, or bolted across three lanes of traffic. The streets narrowed, the traffic thinned, the hush of darkness slipped in around us. My breathing ragged, my legs growing heavy, I willed myself to keep her within just-a-glimpse sight. Somewhere deep in my gut a tiny alarm sounded. For some reason, it seemed the young woman was slowing, waiting, making sure I could follow.

A trap?

No doubt. But I was tired of always being two steps or more, as I was right now, behind. I relished a fight—at least then I'd have an adversary, someone tangible, flesh and blood in front of me, someone who perhaps I could wring some answers out of.

When I rounded the last corner into a tight, dark alley, and

I saw her waiting in a doorway, I had my answer. I didn't need to look behind me—there would be someone there blocking my exit. I was good with that—I'd brought my badass.

I slowed to a walk, ignoring the music leaking from the windows overhead, the laundry flapping loosely, the only evidence of a breeze that ruffled the stagnant humidity. The stench of garbage and fermented vegetables told me I wasn't in Vegas anymore, that I didn't know the rules. But I knew people, and, despite our outward differences, inside we are all the same.

The girl leaned against the door jamb, her arms crossed, her face open and admiring, which threw me. I was happy to see she was as sweaty and out of breath as I was. She eyed me as I stepped in front of her. Balanced on a six-inch step, she was eye-to-eye with me.

"How you get so tall?"

"Lucky, I guess," I said in an offhand, I'm-tough sort of way. Even though I hated games, apparently I could still play, although perhaps not well.

A point she made when she reached for the goose egg on my temple, which I'm sure was now turning a rainbow of colors.

"So why am I here?"

"You follow me."

"You let me."

That got a grin. Without the frown, she was a pretty young woman. She stepped aside, inviting me in. "I show you."

Without hesitating, I stepped past her.

Funny the things you'll do when you're out of options.

CHAPTER EIGHT

DARK and narrow, I followed the corridor, the young woman dogging my heels. Walking slowly, I allowed my eyes to adjust to the dim interior. Closed doors on either side. Strains of music...and sex. Astringent covering the musky sweetness.

Same setup, different country.

Miss Minnie's without Minnie.

But a whorehouse just the same. Like I said, inside we're more alike than we think.

Why was I here? What did the young woman want? Time to find out before things got any worse, if that was possible.

By my reasoning, I had two advantages in this game: surprise and being pissed-off.

I stopped, turned, and grabbed the young woman behind me, pinning her arms. Before she could react, I curled one leg behind hers and pushed. We both fell. Letting her slight body break the fall of my not-so-slight frame, I made sure I stayed on top, holding her arms above her head and her legs with mine hooked across her shins. My weight and size ensured she couldn't escape, at least not easily or quickly.

Her breath left her in a whoosh. Pulling great lungsful of air in an effort to replace what had been knocked out of her, the woman gasped and wheezed, her face turning red.

"Slow down. Easy." Her eyes burned a hole in me, but she

did as I said.

"Me your friend. The only one," she managed after a minute or more.

"You are not my friend. You helped kidnap the one friend I did have, giving me one hell of a headache and heartache in the process." She moved underneath, slight shifts, testing.

"You not know when to shut up and stay out of it."

She got that right. I could feel her coil. Pressing harder on her hands and her legs, I used my weight and for once I was glad for every ounce. "Don't."

Maybe the hint of crazy that tinged that one word made her do as I said, but she stopped, relaxing underneath me. "You seem to know all about me, so it's my turn. Who are you? What is that dragon on your arm? Why did you want me to follow you?"

The door we'd come through banged open, hitting the wall. I glanced up. A tall figure in a short skirt, with long hair flowing behind her, burst through the opening. Backlit by the light over the doorway, her face remained in shadow.

Something familiar.

She stopped, clearly a bit lost in the darkness.

The hint of gardenias floated on the wind she'd let in when she'd opened the door.

Terrific. Now I was outnumbered.

"I bring you for him," the young woman said, rolling her eyes back toward the door behind her.

"Him? Him who?"

"Lucky?"

That one word shot straight through me.

The figure reached to the right and clicked on a light, bathing us all in a weak yellow glow.

Blond, tall, trim, with legs a mile long and blue eyes I'd know anywhere. A frisson of exploding emotions bolted through me.

Teddie!

In a female server's uniform, makeup, blonde wig, and...I

narrowed my eyes...yes, a pair of shoes that looked remarkably like a pair of Manolos I used to own. Five-inch knock-me down-and-fuck-me shoes.

Oh, I'd love to knock him down. But the rest? Not anymore.

Letting loose of the woman underneath me, I sat back on my heels. "You're alive," I whispered, afraid if I said it too loudly it would shatter the dream.

Beneath me, the young woman balled her fist and swung her arm, landing a perfect strike just below my sternum, doubling me over.

My breath deserted me. She pushed. Angling her legs for leverage, she rolled me to the side and wiggled out from under me.

My hand found the wall. I collapsed to a seated position. My vision swam.

Teddie rushed over to me. I could hear him, feel him, smell his gardenias and his fear. "Lucky, stay with me." He reached for me.

I tried, but I couldn't.

My world went black.

JABBERING in an unfamiliar language. Smells. The heat of bodies pressed close. I tried to make sense of it as I swam toward the surface of consciousness.

"What is that horrible sound?" I mumbled. Grating, it hit every nerve.

"Somebody kill the music." Teddie's voice, fear tempering the hint of a chuckle, sounded so familiar, comfortable, like an old sweatshirt and PJ pants.

But it couldn't be him. He was lost. I tried to think. I wasn't sure where. Of course, that's what being lost was about. My thoughts folded over and over like plaques in my brain, trapping thoughts, making holes, leaving me adrift.

A dream, that's what this was. It must be. Nothing made sense.

A warm, solid, male hand squeezed mine. Hot breath caressed my cheek. "Honey, come back to me." Definitely Teddie's voice.

"I can't. I love him."

His lips brushed my cheek. "I know. But open your eyes," he whispered.

Struggling against the darkness, the warmth of this place, I forced my eyes open. Tiny slits, but I got them open. Assaulted by the light, they teared. Someone thumbed the tears away, leaving a cool streak of wetness. Opening them further, I gasped as the world rushed back in.

I curled up, trying to get an arm underneath me to lever myself to a seated position. So undignified lying on the floor as I was. A blinding pain. The world tilted and spun. I pressed a hand to my head, then instantly regretted it as pain radiated. "Romeo?" Fear jump-started my heart. "We have to find him."

Life focused. I looked around and gasped. "Teddie! You're really here. I thought..."

He was alive!

And, if I could still read his face, scared but happy. I let my gaze roam over each plane, each facet—I knew them all by heart. Yes, I could read him—even under all the pancake makeup.

The man I used to love.

I figured if I kept telling myself that, one day I'd believe it. Seeing him on his knees, bending over me, alive, breathing— even though I wanted to shoot him myself, I was overcome.

Despite my best efforts to stop it, I felt the warm flush that used to flood through me whenever Teddie was near. And I felt somehow less for feeling that way—as if my body cheated of its own accord. But how did one override one's heart? Was it possible to love two men, but be with only one?

Could one be a treasured friend and the other the love of

my life?

Simple questions so rife with disaster.

One thing I did know: Teddie still looked better in a dress than I did.

Although he could wear a dress and heels with aplomb, and despite the conclusion folks normally jumped to, Teddie was anything but gay. Ditch the dress and he oozed virility and enough pheromones to have half the female population swooning. I would like to say I was immune, but that would be a lie.

"Romeo?"

Teddie shook his head and waited. He knew better than to push my buttons when I was beyond tired, hardwired to the pissed-off position, and scared beyond rational thought. Guess he could read me, too.

I waited for the anger, but it didn't come. Relief flooded through me instead.

Teddie was alive.

And that alone caused a flood of mixed emotions.

Finally, I'd corralled my runaway feelings enough to trust using my words. "Do I want to hear why you are dressed as a geisha and lurking in a whorehouse off a back alley in Macau?"

"I'm not a geisha. Geisha's are Japanese—"

"I *know* that. I just like the word, okay? I'm sure you get my point, Harvard boy." Teddie had an MBA from Harvard and a music degree from Juilliard—the double whammy, smart and sexy. He also had a penchant for weaving elaborate stories, which muted his shine just a bit.

He helped me to a seated position, my back against the wall. Standing, he shooed the ladies out of the hallway and back into their rooms. I hadn't even noticed them, not really, just a sea of out-of-focus faces swirling behind Teddie. Once the hallway was clear, the music, if that's what it was, screeching again, Teddie joined me anchored to the wall. Our legs stretched out in front of us, our feet touching the wall on the other side.

Everything was smaller in China.

So many things I wanted to say, to do, not least among them was to throw my arms around his neck, pull him close, and breathe him in. So, in an effort to keep my dignity and my self-respect, I decided to take the high road. "Can we talk here?"

He stood and extended a hand. "Let's go upstairs."

Still a little wobbly, I finally felt solid over my feet about halfway up the narrow, rickety staircase.

As if he knew, Teddie, who had held tight to my hand, let go. "It's just down this way."

I followed him. Oh, to have a tight ass like his. "What's down this way?"

"My room."

"You're staying here?"

He pushed a door open, then stepped aside. "Can you think of a better place for me to hide?"

He had me there. And, from my experience, if the girls didn't want you in their house, you weren't getting in.

His room was small, large enough for a twin-sized bed covered in a faded cotton quilt, and a small dresser, the wood stained by cigarettes left to burn too long, glasses left to sweat in the humidity, and scarred by neglect or at least a lack of appreciation. Wallpaper, sloppily applied, peeled in spots. The paint, chipped and thin and dulled by time. "No bathroom?"

"Down the hall."

"Taking sharing to a new level." At Teddie's silent invitation, I sat on the edge of the bed.

Thoughtful when he wanted to be, he held up the wall across from me. He left the door ajar.

"Is there anyone up here?"

"No. These are private quarters, and all the girls are working tonight. Besides, I've yet to meet one who speaks or understands anything but the most basic English."

"Other than your friend with the tattoo."

"Ah, yes, Ming. She is resourceful."

"What's her story?"

"Not sure. I only have bits and pieces." He narrowed his eyes. "But, if I had to guess, I'd say she's been waiting for you."

"Me?" Did the whole goddamn world know I was coming? "Why do you think that?"

"A hunch, but you'll have to ask her."

"I will, if she decides to leave me conscious the next time I run into her."

Teddie smirked. "A heavy hand when a light one would do, she reminds me of someone else I know."

"I prefer to consider myself exuberant." I shifted, moving back on the bed and pulling some pillows to stuff behind me. "What did she do to you?"

Not wanting to continue as the topic of conversation, I waved his question away. "You've been here long enough to at least sniff out a trail. Give it to me quick and dirty; we haven't much time."

Playing the part, he gave me a sultry look. "In any other setting that would be quite an invitation."

At this moment, for some odd reason, I was finding men impossibly irritating. "A man, dressed as a woman, inappropriately innuendoing me in his bedroom is not attractive."

"My opportunities are few; I take them when I find them." His voice teetered on the edge of a hurt.

"Forgiveness doesn't happen just because you want it to."

"You've forgiven me." He seemed so sure.

Had I? "Forgiving and forgetting are two different things. But I don't want to talk about this. Not here. Not now."

"I knew you'd come," he whispered.

I looked into his eyes and managed a controlled voice. "I didn't come because of you."

We both knew I lied.

More in control of my faculties than before, I let my eyes roam over him, seeing under the costume while he was lost in a past and the loneliness of a world apart. Still broad in the right places, and narrow in the rest—he had a butt most women would kill for or fight over—Teddie looked like Teddie. Oh, there was a bit of haunt in his blue eyes, and stress drew the skin tighter over his cheekbones. He'd lost some weight. But he still looked like the man I had loved. But looks could be deceiving, as they say.

Teddie pushed himself off the wall. Reaching down, he shucked one shoe, then the other.

"Hurt, don't they?"

"Pain is relative." I was pretty sure he was going to keep beating that dead horse when he said, "Cho and Gittings had a twelve-hour jump on me, probably longer. I had to be a bit careful getting into the country."

The way he said that made me sure I didn't want to know how he'd accomplished that singular feat, considering half the known world, including a couple of international agencies, was looking for him.

"You know, if the female-impersonator thing doesn't work out for you, you could take this International Criminal thing and run through Interpol with it." A man of countless gifts, Teddie could be anything he wanted to be. If he wanted to use his considerable talents for the Dark Side—well, I shuddered at the possibilities. Thankfully, to date, he had yet to show any hint of a sociopathic personality. Selfish and vain, yes, but that meant he was destined to break hearts, not kneecaps.

At this moment, looking at him, the memories so close, I wasn't sure which was worse. I laughed at myself. Apparently, I was the one in four with sociopathic tendencies—I'd read that statistic somewhere. Sorta made me look at my fellow man with a jaundiced eye, which really fogged up my rose-colored glasses.

Teddie erased my smile with a serious look. "They're thirty-six hours ahead of you. Without you here, I didn't know where to start, but since you and your family are the targets, I figured your hotel was a good place to stake out."

As I watched him, my mind wandered a bit. I really envied his casual confidence as a woman. Maybe that should worry me...or both of us. "And you decided to become a cocktail waitress because?"

"There is no such thing. Did you know nobody drinks

LUCKY THE HARD WAY

while gambling here?" He looked surprised.

"Curiously enough, as one of the casino executives in charge, I do happen to have a grasp on that little factoid. Here the patrons are serious gamblers. In the U.S., they are serious partiers. Either way, the house comes out ahead."

"I didn't know."

I looked at Teddie and thought what he didn't know was legion, but I didn't say that. What would be the point?

He must've sensed we had exhausted that line of conversation. "No one is looking for a woman," he said finally answering my question.

"Not entirely true. The FBI knew you'd left the U.S. disguised as a woman."

"Well, they haven't found me yet, but good to know—I won't be quite so brazen. Besides, women here are invisible, in case you haven't noticed."

"Unless the men want their services."

"I'm not their type."

"You hope. You do sort of stand out." Tall and blonde in a sea of something else and with legs to die for? Not their type? He was fooling himself. "Did you see Kim before she was killed?"

"I'd caught a glimpse, and started to follow but got waylaid by a drunk Russian wanting bottle service in one of the junket rooms upstairs. Trust me, you do not want to piss off anybody traveling here with the junket operators, especially a Russian."

"I'm hoping 'waylaid' is one word, not two."

He rewarded me with a smile, which didn't do a thing for me—well, except for sending a warm rush through every capillary. "Did you see anyone else? Like maybe the person who killed her?"

Teddie shook his head. "No."

"I did." We both whirled at the voice.

The young woman with the tattoo. Carrying three glasses, she used her foot to nudge the door open. How long she had been standing there was anybody's guess, not that it mattered—apparently, I had no secrets here.

She handed me one of the glasses. "You drink. It hot."

"Who killed Kim Cho?" I pressed, knowing the answer, hoping I was right.

"You drink." Ming's voice held the hardness of steel.

Force wasn't always the answer; I knew that. So I retreated...for the moment. Let her have a small victory, soften her up, a good strategy. Yeah, right. "What is it?" I sniffed at the amber liquid as I held the glass by the rim. A vaguely floral scent I couldn't place.

Teddie accepted a glass. The third she kept for herself.

I motioned her over, then exchanged glasses with her, which got a wry half-smile and what I thought was a fleeting hint of respect.

Ming shut the door, then leaned against it. "My grandfather, he a healer. Has a shop in the central district in Hong Kong. This is his most strong medicine. Give much power."

Testing the heat, I took a sip. My body's response was immediate—it wanted all of it and right now, if not before. I'd experienced that once before—an ill-fated trip to Spain, a case of food poisoning that left me only able to crawl short distances, and a homegrown cure made of green apples, brandy, lemon juice, and sugar. So, trusting my gut, I blew on the brew until just below scalding, then drank it down.

Ming and Teddie followed my lead, although in a slightly more measured manner.

Curiously, I felt better. Mind over matter? Who knew? At this point, I didn't care. "That stuff is potent. Your grandfather have anything that will impart superpowers?"

"Superpowers?" A furrow of concentration buckled the skin between her eyes. "What is this?" She looked to Teddie.

Teddie waved her off. "Ignore her."

I leaned over and set the glass on the floor, then fixed Ming with my best grown-up stare, such as it was. "You want to tell me what's going on?"

"Bad men make it bad for everybody. We stop them."

"We who?"

She stood a little taller. "We women."

Struck dumb for a moment, I must've flapped my mouth like a guppy, then I regrouped. "Women." It wasn't a question. "You have no idea how much I'm loving this."

Teddie seemed to be enjoying the whole show as well.

A smile split Ming's face, and, for the first time, I realized how young she must be. Eighteen? Nineteen?

"How many women?"

"Many, many women. We all start out here or another place the same. Now many work in casinos. We see everything. We know much."

"You work here?" The thought squeezed my heart. "How long?"

"Four year, maybe five."

Teddie's eyes mirrored my own anger and profound sadness. Women, under attack the world over. No wonder humanity was going straight down the slop-chute.

Ming handed Teddie her glass, then tugged up a sleeve, exposing her tattoo. "This how you know."

The answer to one question! Hopefully there would be more to come. "What do you want with me?" I asked, unsure how I played a role in their plan.

"You big powerful woman. Kim tell us. You make men afraid."

Amusement flashed across Teddie's face, so I studiously ignored him. "I'm not sure I agree, but I will do what I can to help. What do you want me to do?"

"You smart. You know business. So you know how to fool men. We want you to tell us how to do this."

"You want me to make a plan?"

She nodded, clearly happy I understood or was at least following. "Yes, you lead us. Help us take power back. Make bad men pay."

"Okay, okay." I took a few moments to process. I'd asked for a friend and I'd gotten "many, many." This could work. "You going to tell me who killed Kim Cho?"

The question exposed the lethal under Ming's carefully

arranged exterior. "She my friend, very good friend."

"Mine, too." Okay, it was a little lie.

Something told me not to push Ming, so I waited, which used every ounce of my mythic Herculean strength.

"You help us?" Ming was on the fence; I could see that. A game of verbal poker: who was going to show their cards first and hope the other kept playing. A tough call.

"I'll help you."

She flicked a glance at Teddie.

"You can trust her."

The fight left, leaving only the pain and a need for revenge I could hear in her voice, see in her eyes. "That man, the *guai lo*. He come with Mr. Cho. Frank say he bad, bad man. He kill Sam." She swallowed hard, blinking rapidly. "He kill Kim, too."

"*Guai lo?*" Teddie asked.

"White devil in Cantonese," I answered. God knew I'd heard that enough around Mona's place when I was a kid.

Teddie looked impressed.

I didn't disabuse him of any misguided esteem he might have for me. "Irv Gittings."

Ming nodded as she crossed her arms, hugging herself. Irv Gittings had that effect on almost everyone.

Not me. Not anymore.

I'd never taken a life, but I'd looked into enough eyes of those who had to know, justified or not, taking a life exacted a huge price. When it came to Irv Gittings, I was prepared to pay.

I shot a look at Teddie. If he could read me as well as I thought he could, then he knew Irv wouldn't get out of this alive, not if I had anything to do with it.

"Frank and Sam. They were your friends, too?"

Ming nodded. "Good men."

Which explained how Sam Cho, "hired assassin," could've missed killing not only my father at short range but me also, however at a slightly longer range. But it didn't explain Sam

Cho, Teddie, and the murder of Holt Box. If Sam didn't kill him, who did? I need that to get Teddie off the hook.

A troubling thought best left for a less troubling day.

And Frank Cho—Ming's revelation explained him, too, and how easy it had been to get him remanded from the state prison into my care, and Romeo's...

Romeo.

Some pieces of the puzzle had clicked together—I loved it when that happened. But now it was time to go on the offensive.

"Together we can do this, Ming. I will come up with a plan to help you. But right now, I could use your help."

CHAPTER NINE

*N*O one would ever know the Chinese frowned on ostentation by looking at the owner's suite. The beautiful statuary—probably so old that if I blew on it, it would turn to dust. Large jade animal figurines—tigers mainly, but the largest one was of a dragon, which made me smile. Symbolic of power and good luck for those worthy of it, dragons held a special place in Chinese cultural symbolism. I'd learned a lot from the Big Boss and his dollar-bill origami. The Big Boss would get a huge kick out of the latest twist to this adventure.

He worshipped women and was appropriately scared of us. I loved that about him. For an old-school Wiseguy he was remarkably evolved.

Heavy silk draperies hanging floor to ceiling and falling to rest on the floor in pools of exquisite cloth. The furniture wasn't my style, but I knew it was expensive—I'd seen the bills. The place was probably bugged. I didn't care, but Ryan's nervousness and veiled threats had me looking over my shoulder.

No doubt about it, I felt exposed...and totally out of my comfort zone.

I wondered how Stokes had gotten on with the police.

Kim Cho was his man. And one of Ming's women.

To be honest, after meeting Ming, I was feeling a glimmer of optimism. When pushed, women as warriors had no equal.

The trick was getting them to tap into that strength.

For eons we'd been taught our physical weakness meant we had no power.

Oh, so very wrong.

In a way I felt sorry for Agent Stokes. Okay, not really, not until I figured out which team he played for. But I really felt sorry for Kim Cho. And, with nowhere to turn and no one to turn to, I had to let the FBI try to find Romeo while I waited, keeping myself available for the kidnappers to find me.

They would. They clearly wanted something. I just wished they'd hurry.

She'd been helping the good guys and we'd let her down. Of course, some of us hadn't been let in on the secret. I'd deal with Stokes later. Right now, I needed to cut Mona off at the knees, and I needed a good baseball bat.

Brandy answered on the first ring.

"Hang on, I'm patching in Jerry."

My tone took the chipper right out of her voice. "Okay."

"Lucky, it's been awhile," Jerry said, his voice deadly serious. "What's cookin'?"

"You got anything for me?"

"Not yet, but we're working on it. A lot of video to go through and I'm not that familiar with the property there. Took me a bit of time to get oriented."

"Okay, understood. Keep working on it. I want to know who in our happy little band of brigands was in the hotel when Kim Cho was murdered."

"If I find one of them on the tapes, I'll let you know."

"Good. I hate to add to the workload, but I need something else. Jerry, can you pull up some photos of the collection of antique arms we bought to showcase around Cielo? Specifically, I'm looking for an ivory-handled knife."

"What's so special about the knife?"

"It was the one buried in Kim Cho's chest."

"Fuck."

"I know, right? But somebody was either very sloppy or

sending a message. Message received, and, if I could, I'd like to appropriately thank the sender."

"You're not going to do something stupid, not without me having your back, right?" Jerry's concern vibrated through the line.

"Please, stupid is what I do." I didn't tell him about Ming fingering Irv Gittings in Kim Cho's murder. Everybody here had an agenda, and Kim Cho's warning about people not being who they appeared to be kept pealing like a Sunday church bell in my subconscious.

Jerry could often pull a rabbit out of a hat, and it'd be interesting if he could pin the murder on Gittings as well. While in China, my version of murder investigating mirrored a good reporter's—at least two objective sources for everything.

Sometimes it was best to not jade the researcher, to let them come to it clean, so I left all the juicy stuff for Jerry to find. I put him on speaker on my phone, then worked through my photos, choosing several good shots of the knife. "I'm sending the photos I have. And, given that this is Macau and I'm a foreigner, they are likely all I'll ever have."

"Gotcha." His phone pinged in the background, announcing the arrival of the pictures. "Got them. We've got something else going on that we need to talk with you about."

A problem I could solve! Oh, happy day! "Fire away."

"Got a problem with Mona."

My heart sank. Mona had no solution.

I have this theory about life and death—it's sort of silly, but it works for me. I think that when people die, they come back somewhere else where no one they knew would likely see them again. I've met long-dead friends and acquaintances before, or at least their doppelgängers, and right now was one of those times.

My mother was standing in front of me, or rather an ephemeral image was.

Of course, Mona wasn't dead, but she would be when I got home.

And the fact she wasn't really here saved me from rotting

in a Chinese jail.

"I heard about the hackers. How bad is it?"

"Bad," Jerry and Brandy said in unison. Understandably, Jerry's was the more expressive of the two—he had more experience with my mother.

"Jerry," I said after I'd let the ramifications of my mother sink in a bit, "can you bring Sergio on the line?"

Sergio Fabiano was our Front Desk Manager. Handling Mona's epic boo-boo would take all four of us and a lot of luck.

Jerry went off line for a moment. I could hear Brandy breathing, but neither of us said anything. Romeo loomed between us—of course, I knew that and she didn't, which made the whole thing darn near impossible. I fought the urge to blurt everything out, which would only make us both terrified. One of us was enough...more than enough. But I couldn't resist jumping into the silence. "How are all the preparations going for the opening? Anything I should know about?"

"Everything you and I went over before you left is in place and ready to go. We've been doing lots of run-throughs with the staff, fine-tuning. It's all really good. Don't worry."

"With you at the helm, I don't. Thank you. Let me know if you need me to step in anywhere."

"Of course."

Jerry came back online, releasing me from my agony. "We're all here."

"Good. It sounds like we have a major problem."

"You're telling me," Sergio sounded exasperated as he dove into my conversation. "Mr. Jackson, from New York?"

"The one who brings his family and his mistress?" I asked, knowing how this was going to go.

"Yes, but the wife, she does not know about the mistress."

"Yes, we put them on separate floors with a note in the file to make sure to keep them separate, even though Mr. Jackson has keys to both rooms. The instructions are explicit."

"Exactly."

I could almost hear Sergio slap his thigh as he flicked his stylishly long hair out of his eyes. By all accounts, with his chiseled physique and smoldering good looks, he was a babe magnet. I didn't get it. He was far too fussy for me. The first sign of the age apocalypse, no doubt.

"But someone, she changed the computer,"Sergio continued in his inimitable Italian sort of way, which set my teeth on edge. "The seven-year-old-son walked in on—"

"Don't tell me." I made a mental note to alert the legal department as I tried to figure out how to spin the PR nightmare.

"It is not so bad. The lady, she was alone, taking a bath."

I'd seen Mr. Jackson's mistress. I'm sure the boy would be ruined forever, but not traumatized. Of course, he'd probably have all his daddy's money someday. The thought made me sad and angry...wasted energy, I know. My Don Quixote complex. "Okay. Sergio, alert your staff. Make sure they actually think before doing. These hackers are famous for getting in the computer systems and causing all kinds of mischief: rebooking people to already occupied rooms, playing with the locks and the keycards, making reservations, changing charges, the sky's the limit. What we can think of, they've already done. Consider them to be one step ahead at all times."

"Yes, ma'am."

"But what do we look for?" Brandy asked.

"Anything out of the ordinary." Even as I said it, I knew it to be an impossibility. We were talking about Vegas, where everything is out of the ordinary. "You'll know it when you see it—if you look closely enough." With nothing more to add, I switched gears. "Jerry..."

"I'm on it. I'll work with the IT guys and try to shut these kids out, at least out of the most sensitive areas to start. What about gaming?"

"They won't hit that. Federal felonies are a deterrent. The thing about these kids is this: they don't want to totally mess things up; they just want to see if they can hack the system, and they want us to know they can. There is an upside here, although slight: we will learn our vulnerabilities, and, considering the sensitive information we have about our patrons, it might not be bad to know if all of our expensive security really works and all the high-priced consultants are worth what we pay them."

Nobody discounted my theory, but I knew we all were wondering the same thing: great info to know, but at what price?

"Brandy?"

"Yes, ma'am."

"I'll need you to handle the fallout. There are going to be some seriously ruffled feathers by the time our guests leave. Can you handle it?"

"She already has Mr. Jackson, his wife, and his mistress eating out of her hand," Jerry said. "But she still has to do something about the sign out front."

"Great." I paused. "Wait. What?"

"The sign has been reprogrammed," Brandy said, her tone not happy. "We're working on it."

Even though I knew I'd regret it, I couldn't resist asking. "What does it say?"

"Girls Direct to You followed by the number to our main reservation line."

I burst out laughing—I couldn't help it. After my day, self-control was at a low ebb. "Next thing you know, we'll be hailed in the national media as the only honest business in Clark County."

Pretty soon all of us were chuckling. "Right before an official visit by the Vice Squad," Jerry added, trying to sober us up.

It didn't work.

"That's all I got," I said. "Somebody might want to check with accounting and see if the Girls Direct to You revenue should be broken out as its own line item."

"Don't anyone do what Lucky says," Jerry's voice held a distinct lack of humor, which I found a bit party-pooperish.

"There's one in every group." I tried for a grouse, but the giggles didn't help. "Has anyone heard from Miss P?" As I'd said, my right-hand-man was off gallivanting around the world on her honeymoon, which I thought was sort of a waste. If I had someone like the Beautiful Jeremy Whitlock, Miss P's new husband, waiting to fulfill my every wish and meet my every need, no matter the sights outside the hotel, I'd never see a one.

"You're kidding, right?" Brandy said, obviously sharing my wavelength.

"Stupid question. Anybody else have something helpful to add?"

"I'm going to double up the reservations staffing so we can slow down and think things through," Sergio said.

"Good call."

"I have your approval?" Sergio always covered his corporate ass if not his real one—at least that was the scuttlebutt in the employee lounge.

"Of course."

"Anything else?" I waited a beat, but no one said anything. "Good then. Keep me updated. And do what Jerry says. Despite my inappropriate humor, we have a huge problem, or potential problem on our hands. Jerry, can you stay on the line?"

I heard the others click off. "Okay, Jer, I get the message. This will probably blow up in our faces. Tell me what I need to know." I could picture him, tall, thin, ebony skin, bald head polished to a shine, a perpetual crease between his eyebrows, yellow stains on his forefinger and middle finger from his chain smoking—stress relief. I'd quit warting him to give them up. Wild Turkey still sang my Siren song so who was I to judge? "What time is it there?"

"Lunchtime. Why?" He'd have on his ubiquitous suit, a pair of loafers, a touch of gold at the wrist.

"Where I'm sitting feels like a parallel universe."

"In some ways it is."

"And some ways not so much." I thought of the games people were playing here, lives and livelihoods hanging in the balance. "Where are you?"

"Security. I've got some extra staff watching the feeds."

He'd be standing, legs wide, like a captain guiding a ship as he stood in front of the banks of monitors, each receiving a discrete feed from the eye-in-the-sky cameras in all the public sections of the property. "We're jumping in the moment we see something going screwy, but we're playing catch-up. Somehow we need to get out in front."

"What about getting a couple of the whiz kids from UNLV?"

"Not following." Jerry's voice sharpened with interest. "Go on."

"Put them in with the hacker group. Let them infiltrate and see if they can turn a couple of the kids with the best skills, or at least give us a leg up as to what exactly they are doing before we suffer the fallout."

"Ah, defeat from within. I like it."

I could hear the tobacco sizzle as he pulled on one of his cancer sticks. "We also need to look for where they've hacked into the system." My brain was coming on line, thoughts lining up. "The stuff they're playing with is behind a gazillion levels of security. I'd be willing to bet they have an inside track. Have someone go back to when they arrived and check each video feed. Follow each one of those kids until you can map their movements through the hotel. They have to have a central meeting place. Start with the kids carrying their own suitcases, or using carts because of the weight. They'll be the ones moving the equipment in."

Jerry exhaled, a long slow, steadying breath—his way of buying time while he thought. "You've done this before," he finally said.

"Not exactly, but close enough. If you know the game, you can figure out the equipment necessary and look for that. Enough said." I had no intention of going into detail about the guests who were running a BDSM Dominatrix Palace of Pain in one of our super swank villas in the Kasbah. Being very visual, I think I was still a bit traumatized—I'd seen more than I ever wanted to even imagine.

"Your mother..." Jerry started in.

"Don't start." Sitting on the edge of the bed, I let myself

fall back. I loved my mother, I really did...just not right now.

Jerry chuckled. "She is amusing."

"Well, since I'm not there to run interference, you handle her and then see if you still think she's such a barrel of laughs."

"Point taken. But you should know one of these hackers has attached himself to your mother, follows her around like a lovesick schoolboy."

"Interesting."

"Maybe we could use that?" Jerry asked.

"You think it's wise to let Mona be a part of the solution to the problem she created? Remember the turkeys?" My mind reeled at the thought.

"Yes, but..."

I cut him off. "Remember the virginity auction? This is much the same. The plethora of potential pitfalls makes me nauseous."

"Piqued."

"What?"

"Plethora, potential, pitfalls, piqued, just correcting your alliteration."

"Do we pay you more for that?"

"No, but you should. Anyway, about the hacker kid and your mother, I'm just letting you know. How and when you use that info is up to you."

"Great, leave me holding the bag." I rubbed a hand over my eyes. My feet dangled over the end of the bed, so I kicked off first one shoe, then the other, sailing them into the corner by a beautiful black lacquered credenza inlaid with mother of pearl.

"You *are* the Vice President."

"Buoyed by my incompetence, I have risen to my high-water mark. Now, go do your job and leave me alone to figure out how to save the world as we know it."

With a laugh and an, "I'll keep you updated," he rang off.

If only I'd been joking.

I held the phone pressed to my ear like a seashell, still

hoping to hear the whispers of home.

Jean-Charles would be knee-deep in prep for his restaurant opening that would coincide with my hotel opening. Panic welled—I needed to be there. But I had to be here. The very definition of a lose-lose proposition.

I checked my watch. I had changed the time, so it was no help in telling me what time it was at home. Then I looked at my phone—the world time app. Bingo. Fifteen hours behind in Vegas. Jean-Charles would be home just preparing for the day.

I punched his speed dial, and amazingly the call went through and started ringing. A modern marvel. I remembered when it took an overseas operator and a bag full of gold to call across the ocean.

Someone answered, then fumbled with the phone. Finally, Jean-Charles's sleepy voice came on the line. "Oui?" He didn't sound happy.

Damn. He must've had a very late night, not unusual in our business. "Hi." My throat constricted. Oh, how I wanted to roll over and greet him properly. The distance stretched through the scratchy, hollow connection.

"Hi." His voice warm and sleepy, he conveyed all I needed in that one syllable.

"I miss you." I couldn't think of anything to say. I wanted to tell him everything and nothing at the same time. Life intruding into my happy place—I couldn't handle it, not now. "Please tell me you are good. Christophe is good."

"We are devastated without you."

Now he sounded awake and happy despite his "devastation." His French penchant for hyperbole as well as butchering American idioms were two of my favorite quirks. Hearing his voice warmed all my parts all the way through. But, despite the warmth, I felt like crying. I squeezed my eyes tight, fighting, resisting.

"I am so happy to hear your voice," he said. His accent, like everything else about him, was delicious. "I've missed you. It is not the same when you are not here."

All of that made me delirious and despondent at the same time. "It's not the same wherever I am if you aren't with me. How are you? How are things going at the restaurant? The hotel?"

"They are fine. I am once again having problems with the seafood purveyor, and I had to fire one of my kitchen staff—I found him walking out with five Kobe tenderloins." He paused, then cleared his throat. "But this is not why you called, and it is not important. How are you? Have you made any progress?"

"It's exactly why I called, Jean-Charles, to hear your voice and get a dose of normal."

"You are okay?" Worried undertones crept in between his simple words.

"I don't know. Physically, yes." Tears welled; I couldn't stop them. They traced hot trails out of the corners of my eyes, dripping into my hair as I lay on the bed. I didn't care. "Everything is different here. I can't tell the difference between the good guys and the bad guys. Something is going down, and I haven't but a hint of what it might be."

"You will solve this. I know you."

"But, will I be in time?" Time to save Romeo? Time to keep Teddie out of jail? Time to give Irv Gittings what he so richly deserved? Time to save my world?

Time to have my dream?

"You will do your best, and that is all you can do. You are amazing, and that you try so hard, give so much, this is everything."

"Yes, but..."

"No. It is everything."

"But is it enough?"

"It has to be."

I let the tears flow and silently cried. Weakness was not a new thing. Embracing it was. Perhaps in my weakness I would find the strength to do what I needed to do. "I want to come home."

"And you will. So, as you say, right now, you may have a

few minutes to whine, to be weak, and then go bash butt."

There it was, a tortured idiom—and I found my smile. "Kick ass?" Tugging the sleeve of my sweater over one palm, I dabbed at my eyes. The tears still flowed, but at least I'd found a hint of me.

"Yes, this."

"You're right." First things first—find Romeo. I didn't tell Jean-Charles that I'd temporarily misplaced my sidekick. My problem. I'd fix it. "Now. Give me a few more stories from normal life. How is Christophe?"

"He is a tyrant! He makes me prepare your happy-face pancakes for every meal!"

"With chocolate chips?"

"Yes. And then he scolds me for not doing it like you do. You must come home soon. He will be the death of me, and, worse, he will turn into an American with such horrible eating habits and he will die young and fat."

I chuckled through my tears. "You make that sound like a fate worse than death."

"You have traded sarcasm, puns, and clichés for irony?"

"Never! Just adding weapons to my verbal arsenal. Perhaps it's a sign of maturity."

"And that would be sad. The child must always live inside each of us."

"I got that down." Smiling a bit now, I swiped again at my tears—sun peeking through a rain shower. Time for the storm to pass and kick some ass. I felt better—better than I had since I'd left home.

"What is this? Down?"

"It means you're an expert at whatever it is you have down."

"Americans. This makes no sense."

"Slang isn't supposed to. All languages use it to identify the true natives. French is no different."

I heard a squeal from his end, then an *oof.* "Good morning, Papa! It is afternoon now—you slept late. Chantal must go to school. You must make happy-face pancakes."

Christophe had pounced—their mid-day morning was underway.

Jean-Charles groaned dramatically. "I will, but you talk to Lucky."

Christophe's excited chatter rolled through the line. Hot tears flowed again as I let his enthusiasm warm my heart and fill me with determination to hug him again very soon. He finished with a "Je t'aime," then handed the phone to his father.

My, "I love you, too," landed somewhere in the fumbled exchange on their end.

"I will tell him," Jean-Charles said when he'd retrieved the phone. "I love you, Lucky. You be safe and come home to us."

"I will. I love you more." I choked on a sob as I ended the call. He didn't need to hear me cry.

I had no idea how much time passed while I let all my worry and fear flow out of me. Probably not long, but it seemed like an eternity. I so didn't like wallowing in all that, so not like me. But sometimes you just had to deal and then get over it. There would be no place for fear or worry in the hours and days to come. Fear was always there. Courage was finding a way to persevere despite it.

Closing off thoughts of all I could lose, I summoned my courage.

I had a mile-wide revenge streak, so, once tapped, it powered me back to myself. Fatigue was another thing altogether. I couldn't move and I doubted my ability to form coherent sentences, much less cohesive plans. Finally, I tossed the phone toward the nightstand—it missed, ricocheting out of sight.

I thought about looking for it. Maybe later.

I thought about a shower. With no one to snuggle up to, I couldn't work up the energy.

My eyes closed, my thoughts drifted...

I couldn't sleep, not now.

But I did.

My dreams were jumbled, chases through the dark,

monsters...

A voice jarred me back to battle mode.

Teddie's voice. Muffled. "Lucky? You here?"

CHAPTER TEN

"LUCKY?" More insistent now. Still Teddie's hiss—I'd recognize it anywhere.

I opened my eyes, reorienting myself. Macau... it all came flooding back in a heart-racing jolt of adrenaline.

"Lucky, answer me!" Yes, definitely Teddie—I'd know that demand anywhere—and for sure not a dream.

"Why are you asking? You know damned well I'm here." I sounded a bit more irritated than I was. I guess I really hoped it was one of the bad guys.

My head throbbed. The goose egg was now more of a chicken egg, but still as sore as ever. My crying jag had left me with a headache. My stomach growled, telling me what it thought. I'd lost all concept of time.

A muttered curse, a soft knock, then the key worked in the lock.

I'd managed to push myself up on one elbow when Teddie's face appeared through the door opening, still made-up, the rest of him still sporting the now wrinkled employee uniform.

"Any word from Ming?" At the thought, hope bloomed.

"It's only been a couple of hours."

"That long?" Groggy, I swiped at the mental cobwebs. Self-conscious, I ran my fingers through my hair, not that it would do any good. When had I last had a shower? The grime of travel made me feel sticky, so much so I even offended myself. "My hour supply is dwindling."

"Time is running out for both of us. But the girls all work varying shifts, and there was someone Ming needed to talk with at Tigris. I'm sure we'll hear something soon."

Not much to say to that. If he had more specifics, he would've given them to me. "You trust her?"

"She's got more skin in this game than we do."

I cringed at his choice of words. "Good point. How'd you get a key to my place?" Before he could answer, I changed tacks. "What took you so long?"

Teddie pushed the door open then disappeared. He reappeared behind a white-cloth-covered cart with various silver domes dotting its surface and what looked like a Champagne bucket with the capped neck of a green bottle sticking out. Maneuvering the cart into the room, he kicked the door shut behind him. "You look horrible."

"Trying to ingratiate yourself, I see." Pushing myself up, I paused, sitting on the edge of the bed while my world stopped spinning. "If it's any consolation, I feel worse than I look."

He stepped in front of me. Reaching out he touched the goose egg on my temple, pain in his eyes. "Who should I kill for that?"

His touch was warm, comforting. Now a dull throb, the headache had moved way down on my radar, pushed into insignificance by the rest of my pain and worry. "Not necessary."

He pulled back, as if the connection had burned, a look of surprise on his face. "Want to tell me about it?" When we'd talked at his place, we hadn't touched on my adventures—we hadn't the time, and I hadn't the wherewithal.

"I'll get to it." Despite my assertion to the contrary, I doubted I looked worse than I felt—that would be impossible. "What time is it?"

"Three o'clock, give or take."

"In the morning?" If he was right, then my catnap was

longer than I'd hoped.

Teddie returned to his cart, both hands on the bar. "Your ability to find trouble amazes me even still."

"This time it was easy; I followed trouble here."

He didn't look the least bit chagrined, but he did stop with the personal once-over. Turning to survey my little chunk of Macanese real estate, he looked for a place to set up. "This room isn't up to your usual standards. I thought you'd have at least a suite."

I pointed through the set of large double doors at the far end of the bedroom. "It *is* a suite. You came though the private entrance. Staff is not allowed in here when the guest is present." I gestured toward the rest of the suite. "Don't let me find you in here again. I'll call the management."

"Cute."

"You think I'm joking?"

That wiped off his grin. He turned and pushed the cart into the main living area.

A bit wobbly on my feet, I padded after his cute ass. "That uniform accentuates your assets. If I ever decide to join the other team, I'll look you up."

He wobbled over on one heel, twisting his ankle, which made me smile. He'd been the one who'd taught me how to walk semi-comfortably in heels. I'd never have his sashay, but after a few lessons, I wasn't in fear of breaking a bone.

"Nervous?" I asked.

"Only if you've forsaken your chef fetish and have gone back to hot cross-dressers."

"You're not a cross-dresser."

"Today, I am." His pace slowed as his mouth dropped open. He stopped in the middle of the grand room, doing a slow pirouette, table and all. "Wow." Fourteen-foot ceilings, extravagant furnishings and finishes, a dining room table that would seat twenty, a one-hundred-inch flat screen on the far wall, and a wall of windows extending the full length of the room.

Both of us were drawn to the window. Macau in all its

incongruity unrolled at our feet. A jumbled, low-slung city of apartments that, to an American eye looked like tenements crawled over the hills, punctuated by a high-rise casino, or a lower office building, but there were few of those. This was a town built on gambling.

Neon signs flashed their come-ons. Dramatic lighting backlit the ruins of St. Paul's Cathedral sitting atop the hill in the middle of town—a testament to fleeting sanctity, but maybe I was the only one who saw it that way, perched as it was over this den of iniquity.

"Just like home," Teddie whispered.

The wistfulness in his voice tugged a heartstring. "In more ways than you can imagine."

He tore himself away from the window and returned to the table and its mounds of covered plates. He pretended to be absorbed in the various plates, setting the table, arranging everything just so.

"You didn't change?"

"The girls got off work. With one bathroom, finding time to myself is a bit problematic."

"You can use mine." Once we'd shared a soap-on-a-rope...a lifetime ago.

"I was hoping you'd say that." He reached under the skirted table and pulled out a backpack, which he tossed on the couch. "Before I forget, I brought some things."

Nothing I thought of to say would heal the hurt between us, so, for once, I kept my mouth shut. I didn't offer to help—Teddie had always insisted on doing the kitchen work. I guess this qualified. As I watched him set the table, arrange plates and fill glasses, I missed the old us. "You wouldn't happen to have any of your mother's coconut oatmeal cookies under one of those domes, would you?" I don't know why I said it, why I gave him an insight, an opening to my heart.

He paused, taking a deep breath, remembering as well, a distant look in his eyes. "If only."

Desperate to get the conversation back on solid ground, I asked the first thing that came to mind. "So, how'd you score the broom closet at the whorehouse?"

A dramatic pause—Teddie was always great at timing. "The head of customer relations at your place."

"Cindy Liu."

"Yeah, she took a shine to me right off."

"I see." I always said that even when, as now, I didn't see. I wondered what her angle was. "And Ming?"

"Through Miss Liu."

"And they know you're a wanted man?"

"Haven't a clue. They just know I'm a guy, which, curiously, isn't all that unusual here."

"The Thai boys."

Teddie shrugged but couldn't hide his frown. "The deeper you dig, the more you discover Macau really is like Vegas."

I didn't want to know about his brushes up against the male prostitution world. As a female impersonator and the assumption people made as to his sexuality, I'm sure his stories would turn this semi-pacifist into a fully automatic gal.

He continued with dinner preparations. "The worst part is the bathroom thing. But on the upside, they're really great about finding me clothes."

"Is 'that's great' an appropriate response? I'm a bit at sea."

"That'll do."

"You sure they don't know who you are?"

Teddie sighed and gave me a look; this one I could read loud and clear. "No. I'm not sure. I'm not sure of anything anymore. But I got this. Quit worrying." He gave me his patented cockeyed smile. "What's the worst that could happen?"

I knew a rhetorical question when I heard one.

Finished, he dusted his hands together then pulled back a chair, holding it for me. "Dinner is served. I won't ask if you're hungry; I can tell by that feral look in your eyes."

Three lifetimes ago, I'd picked at the food on the airplane...with Romeo. Knowing Jean-Charles had prepared it made it difficult for me. On the other hand, the kid had wolfed his as if it was his last meal. I swallowed hard—my analogies of late needed some work. But Teddie was misreading a bit. I was feeling feral, all right—hungry to rip the necks out of the men who had Romeo. And what little patience I'd had evaporated.

With heaviness hanging between us, the only thing to do was to fall back on my cocktail party inane chatter skills. "Life on the lam looks like it agrees with you. And I see you still have a pair of my shoes." I took my place. Teddie pushed in my chair, then took the chair next to mine.

"In swiping them, I saved them. Funny how things often turn out differently than you expect."

Everything else had gone up in the fire. I still hadn't dealt with the grief of a vanished existence yet. I could feel it moving, shifting inside, like that alien baby Sigourney Weaver had to fight. "You don't have to rub it in." I breathed deeply, trying to identify what might be for dinner. "You didn't answer me before. How'd you get in here?"

He smiled a tight smile. "From my time at the Babylon, I know a few back-hall tricks. I placed an order through room service, then strong-armed the waiter into letting me in. I told him you had called for me as well. We exchanged a wink or two and voila!"

"There are so many things I don't like about that, but at least you brought food." The ease between us returned as if nothing had happened—as if Teddie hadn't left, Holt Box hadn't been killed, and I hadn't fallen in love with Jean-Charles. But he had, and he had, and I had, making promises in the process, and there were rules about that. And there wasn't a moment I didn't wish Jean-Charles was here.

"Food *and* Champagne." Teddie pulled the bottle from its ice bath. Knowing me as he did, he tackled the cork first before uncovering the plates. I tried to read the label—Laurent-Perrier, famous for their rosé bubbles. He poured for both of us then lifted his glass. "To friends."

As I clinked my glass with his, I resisted the urge to fall into the camaraderie of old. Teddie had fooled me once. Fool me twice, then shame on me. And, I was tired of letting myself down, so I kept my guard up.

With a flourish befitting a fancy waiter, Teddie uncovered the dishes one by one, releasing aromas that had me snapping up morsels with my chopsticks before his performance was over.

"You know the set of brown chopsticks is for serving. The ones you're using are for eating." Teddie smiled at me over a plate of something delicious but not quite identifiable.

I popped a morsel into my mouth then dug in for more. "Your point is?"

"I get it. Who wants to waste time with transferring the stuff when we can eat it out of the dish?" He poked around at the meat I was ladling into my mouth. "What is this?"

"Some kind of shredded pork with something fermented in it," I said through a full mouth. "We probably are supposed to put it in those little sesame pockets, right?" I pointed at the pile of dainty circles of bread that looked like a very thin pita pocket, one side covered with seeds.

"Haven't a clue." He gave me the grin that used to melt my heart.

I'd be lying if I said I didn't feel mine crack.

My hunger surprised me, of course I really hadn't thought about food that much. The image of Kim Cho flashed through my synapses almost ruining my appetite...almost. I'd never been one to be thrown off my feed, not even by murder. Not a fact to be proud of, but hey, lately I'd vowed to embrace my imperfections. So I ate, my chopsticks tangling with Teddie's as we grappled for food.

When I felt a bit sated, I leaned back, set my chopsticks down, grabbed my flute of Champagne, and gave Teddie my best flat stare. To be honest, it was a bit disconcerting having dinner with a man in a dress and full make-up. Teddie and I had always kept business and pleasure separate...before.

"What's with the get-up?" I asked, even though I thought I knew the answer.

"For one, they're not looking for a female—I told you that."

"Yeah, well, I'm running on fumes and Mona..." I started to

go there and decided against it.

"No need to explain. Mona! I understand," Teddie said, and I knew that he did. "I am a man on the run," he continued. "At least, according to the mug shots I've seen salted around on various media outlets."

"Not good."

He pursed his lips and shrugged. "Maybe not, but I'm getting a lot of attention, which means I've stepped on the toes of some powerful folks."

"Bait."

"And switch," he gave me a grin that lacked his normal hint of jaunty. "I hope."

"Not a bad plan, only one minor snafu." The reality of losing Romeo and Frank Cho came crashing back, sucking the air out of my lungs. "I'm assuming you think we're going to exchange Frank Cho for you?"

"Wasn't that the plan?"

I wondered how he knew that, but not for long. He had a mole in my office...or my family. "Have you been talking with Mona?"

"No," he gave me a blank stare that didn't begin to hide the lie.

"I figured." My parents' pillow talk—Mona had to have found out from the Big Boss. Empires fell from within, if history was any lesson. "Well, then," I took a sip of my Champagne, "I guess you know the punch line, then."

"What?"

I filled him in on Frank...and Romeo.

When I was done, Teddie refilled our flutes then leaned back. "Shit. They got the kid?"

I took a slug of my Champagne. "I didn't keep him safe. To be honest, I never saw it coming. Taking Frank, sure. I figured our odds at getting him here and keeping him here were fifty-fifty at best. But Romeo?"

"Why?" Teddie seemed genuinely concerned. I'd always liked that about him. "Why'd they take the kid? He's not a part of this, is he?"

"Not until now. He wasn't even supposed to come. At the last minute, the Sheriff insisted."

"Is that odd?"

"I have no idea. This is my first inmate transfer, but I suspect other forces were at play."

"Who?"

"The Big Boss, and perhaps a friend of his here." I eyed the bottle of bubbles. Anticipating my need, Teddie beat me to the bottle, wiping the water off, then refilling my glass. "You make it impossible to have any self-control." I winced at my choice of words—fact of it was, the words were true...in all aspects. As part of my heart, Teddie was so wrong, but, oh, so right. "In taking Romeo, they effectively pulled off a two-shot swing. We not only lost our advantage, but they also gained one. Now they have something, or someone, to trade."

"But what for? They got Frank Cho."

"Exactly. And the fact they felt they needed Romeo makes me think there is much more at stake here than I realize." Or than the Big Boss had told me, but I didn't air that bit of family dirty laundry. "That's what I need to find out. I need to know what it is they really want."

"And they left you alive so you could give it to them."

"Lucky me." I trotted out my lame whine, but this time it was actually true. "Anything of interest you might be able to tell me?" I tried to give Teddie my serious face, but damn, I was so happy to see him, laughing, talking walking, living, breathing.

"It's not easy being a woman."

"Tell me something I don't know." I raised an eyebrow. "Every man ought to be required to spend a few months living as a woman—male/female relations would improve dramatically."

"That'll never fly," Teddie scoffed.

"Unfortunately, there are probably several Constitutional constraints, but with a viable female candidate running for president, you never know."

He looked like he took the unspoken threat seriously.

"Can you tell me what you've been doing since you got here? Why the getup, really?" I settled in for his story with the fresh glass of bubbly.

"Like I said, the whole dress-up thing was to get out of one country and into another. The authorities weren't looking for a woman."

"Travel documents?"

"From your friend Freddy the Finger, Easy Eddie V's partner?" He looked to me for confirmation that I understood. Apparently, I didn't give him what he was looking for. "You know, up on Rancho in front of the big market?"

"You are so hangin' with the wrong crowd." And he'd been learning the wrong lessons from me. Teddie and Romeo, both. How could I be such a bad influence?

"All depends on what you're looking for. I scored a license and a passport, the ink dry and everything, inside of two hours."

"I'm supposed to give you an attaboy? Seriously? You do realize running was probably the stupidest thing you could possibly do?"

He glanced out the window, the lights painting his face in garish hues. "It certainly limited my possibilities to only two: win or lose." His gaze shifted back to mine, his blue eyes all dark and smoldering. "But I've always been an all-in kind of guy."

Ah, the play. I was wondering how long he'd wait. I brushed it aside. "Okay, so you got out of the U.S. and into Macau and presumably Hong Kong. What did you do then?"

"Got a job here."

"How?"

"Your recommendation carries a lot of weight."

"My recommendation?" I was too tired to be mad.

"Forged on your letterhead. I always could sign your name better than you could."

The Force was strong in this one, Obi Wan. But he'd gone to the Dark Side. "I'm not even going to address the breach of trust that was." I raised my finger as he opened his mouth.

"And that letter could make me an accessory after the fact, as guilty as you are."

He shrugged. "Then you're safe."

"Proving your innocence has been a bit problematic."

"If it makes you feel any better, I *am* sorry. But desperate times and all of that."

That sounded like one of my lines. "And what position did I recommend you for?"

"Well, I put down dealer and that almost blew my cover. The HR lady knew you would know that foreign nationals can't work as dealers in Macau. Dealers have to be Macanese."

"Which causes a huge employment issue for the casinos. Steve Wynne tried to solve that problem. He went to the government and asked if for every Macanese promoted, he could hire a foreigner to fill the spot vacated, but no dice."

Teddie looked at me, wide-eyed.

"Never mind." I waved a hand excusing my trip down a side street. "Of interest only to someone like me who actually has responsibility for thousands of employees. So, exactly how did you become one of my responsibilities?"

Starting to answer, he snapped his mouth shut. Clearly switching tacks, he began again. "A bit of histrionics and she relented, probably to get rid of me and to not risk insulting you. I left her office as a newly minted roving server. Finding a uniform that fit was a bit of a struggle."

I could identify with being the largest woman in the room—just another thing we now shared. "I'm so proud. Crying to get a job—you probably set womankind back twenty years or more. And what have you learned?"

"The Japanese tip the best. Men can be pigs. High heels are excruciating. And I really want to get upstairs to the junket rooms, one in particular."

I leaned forward, crossing my arms on the table, my glass empty. "Which one?"

"Panda 777."

"Ah, Mr. Cho's room."

Teddie looked like I'd stolen a bit of his thunder as he

reached down his décolletage and extracted a folded bit of newsprint. Moving a few now-empty dishes, he cleared a place, then pressed the newspaper open between us, turning it so I could read it.

A photo, grainy. A man half-turned from the camera. The headline was in Cantonese.

Teddie gave me the gist. "This guy was seen fleeing the scene of an attack. He beat a guy senseless with a brick, right on the street in broad daylight."

"A brick?"

"An unassuming weapon that most wouldn't take notice of."

Like a baseball bat.

"He looks familiar."

"He does?" Teddie flipped the paper around to take another look. "You know, you're right. He does. Any idea where we might have crossed paths with him?"

"No. Must've been here." I flipped the photo back so I could memorize his face—evil and remorseless, his was one to remember, and steer clear of. "Who did he attack?"

"Vu. Jhonny Vu." Teddie waited a beat until sure of my attention. "Kimberly Cho's partner."

Ryan Whitmore had mentioned him—but he'd failed to mention he was Kimberly's law partner.

What had the two of them uncovered?

I blew out a breath, launching my bangs skyward. "And the man in the picture? You've seen him."

"Yeah."

"May I keep this?" Anticipating his answer, I took the paper, refolding it.

"Sure. Shortly after the attack I saw that guy riding the private escalator to the Panda 777 gaming rooms. Hell, he still had the brick."

"And?"

"He hasn't been seen since."

Grabbing my chopsticks, I shoveled some rice into my

mouth. "Tell me something good," I said between mouthfuls.

"I've been promoted."

I paused, my chopsticks halfway between the plate and my mouth. "You've been here, what, two days?" I smelled a rat.

"I have proven myself capable," he said with an air of mystery, as he gave up on grasping a bite of mystery meat, stabbing it instead.

"I don't like the way you said that." Hovering my chopsticks over the plates, I waited for an explanation and searched for my next morsel. I snagged a shrimp. "You going to tell me what you're up to?"

"Not yet. But I'm getting closer. I've been moved upstairs, to the junket rooms."

"Out of the frying pan."

Suddenly not hungry anymore, I put my chopsticks down. "It's too dangerous. I don't like it."

"There's no other way. It's not like you can roam around here unnoticed. But, curiously, dressed as a woman, I can."

We both smiled at the irony.

He had a point, but I didn't have to like it. Worse, I had nothing to counter with. "You don't know how to play with these lowlifes. You'll never know they're onto you until it's too late. Don't go being a hero, okay?" Even as I said the words, I wondered who I was trying to make feel better.

"At the first shiver down my spine, I'll cut and run and find you or Stokes."

The lie tripped off his tongue so easily, which didn't make me feel better. "I mean it, Teddie. Don't bullshit me."

"I know you do." He reached across the table, moving a few of the plates so that he could grab my hand and hold it. Staring across at his made-up face, all I saw was Teddie underneath—but that's all I'd ever seen. "You need to let me make my own choices."

"No, I want to control everything; keep everyone safe. That's my job."

"No, it isn't. And it doesn't work that way." He gave my hand a tight squeeze, his skin warm against mine. I'd been cold since I'd left Jean-Charles. "We have to get Gittings."

"And Cho," I reminded Teddie. This whole thing wasn't all about him although sometimes it felt that way.

"And Kimberly Cho's murderer." Teddie heaped more on our overflowing plate.

"And therein lays the problem."

"Stokes hasn't proven very trustworthy," I said, thinking out loud.

Teddie released my hand then picked up his chopsticks, holding them over the feast like a fisherman holding a spear. "Stokes? My take is he's above board, but ineffectual." Teddie made his stroke, stabbing a scallop. He gave me a self-satisfied grin, the old Teddie leaking through. "He's a Fed."

He acted like that explained everything. I hoped he was right.

"Besides," Teddie continued, "there isn't anybody I'd trust in this hotel."

I weighed his words, giving them the gut test. My gut told me he was right, except perhaps for one person...I was still thinking about her, wondering if I dared inch out on that limb.

With dinner cold, our bellies full enough, Teddie abandoned me to my thoughts. He took a shower and donned a hotel robe, then fell asleep on the couch in the living room.

The comfort of old friends in a land of few.

I'd retired to my part of the suite and cleaned up, too, choosing loose black slacks, a gun-metal gray silk shirt, and walking shoes. As I shrugged into a light jacket, I checked on Teddie. Standing there, looking at him, innocent in slumber, I resisted reaching out and brushing his cheek. Letting my eyes roam, I felt like I was looking back in time, at a me I used to be.

A chill raced through me.

You can never go back.

Who had said that? The Big Boss? Mona? Then I realized it had been Teddie.

But that doesn't mean you can't move forward. He'd said that, too.

I pulled my jacket close around me, grabbed a scarf and

my purse, then headed for the door. I'd made my decision. I had to find someone to give me a boost, a hint, to start me on the trail. That's all I needed—I could take it from there.

I needed to find Cindy Liu.

And nobody could know.

CHAPTER ELEVEN

CINDY LIU lived in Coloane.

Once I'd gained access to the Guest Services Office, a trip through the secure intra-hotel system and I had her address with no one the wiser. Bypassing the public areas of the hotel, I took the rabbit warren of hallways reserved for the staff, eventually working my way to the employee entrance. Before pushing into the night, I tucked my hair behind my ears, then wrapped the scarf to hide it and as much of my face as I could. When I pushed through the door, the guard didn't give me a second look, just a nod as he went back to the small book he was reading, something graphic...very graphic from the glimpse I caught.

The air held a damp crispness, the night sharp and clear. Hands in my pockets, my head down, I stayed out of the lights as I covered ground with long strides. My destination, the Grand Lisboa, was a few blocks away. Its full rainbow of neon lit the night sky, but, like a mountain in the distance, its proximity proved elusive. I needed a cab, but hailing one in front of my own hotel would show up on our video feed, and right now, I wanted to run under all the radars, especially our own.

The rhythm of the city changed as night pressed on toward morning. The wee hours where only saints or sinners were about, each trying to rescue the other from a fate worse than death. My time of night. Never sure which side I could claim as my own, saint or sinner, I felt comfortable either way. I rewrapped the scarf, pressing its warm folds into crevices to keep out the chill. My hair and my height drew attention. One, I covered; the other I couldn't do anything about. Despite Macau being a gaming destination, most of the travelers here came from this part of the universe...in other words, I could run but I couldn't hide.

As if I knew what I was doing, I cut through several side streets to make sure I wasn't followed. Circling through a park, a man in a trench coat pulling a small wagon caught my eye. He didn't look dangerous...in fact, he looked hungry. I stepped behind a tree and watched him for a moment. Staking out a spot in what would be a high foot-traffic area when folks actually rolled out of bed, he started setting up in the light of the streetlamps. The wagon unfolded into a small table. Then he began to pull out his wares, arranging them on the table.

A knockoff man.

Again an unsettling analogy, but this one made me smile. What was China without cheap knockoffs?

Content that he was after only my wallet, I left the comfort of my tree, ducked my head, and charged off.

I'd almost made it past him when he called out. "You look like a Louie girl."

The Siren call of normalcy. "I must look stupid, too," I said as I slowed, giving his table a once-over. "Although these fakes are really good."

"My fakes are the real deal." He honed in on my nanosecond of weakness like a hawk sensing movement in the grass below. "I get you anything you want and nobody will know it's not from the manufacturer. You like Louie, Prada, Jimmy Choo?" He reached for the lapel of his coat, tugging it open. "Only the best. I have Rolex, Patek Phillippe?"

I raised both my hands, a meager defense against his high-powered tactics. "No, no. I'm in a hurry. Thanks, though."

"You come back," he called after me. "I always here."

Chuckling, I shook my head. A businessman honest in his dishonesty—something about that intrigued me. Back on one of the main roads, lost in the conundrum, cocooned in the noise of the steady stream of cars and scooters, I didn't recognize the sound of a small motor at max RPM until it was almost too late.

Behind me, bumping up the curb, throttle open.

I dove to the left into a row of bushes. He screamed by, so close. My ankle connected with metal. I yelped as I rolled. Back on all fours, I craned to follow the scooter. A hooded figure, all black. A foot out, taillights blinking, he slowed, then wiggled through the traffic and turned for another pass. Riding low, his chin on the handlebars, he accelerated toward me.

A wall loomed in the darkness behind the row of bushes, blocking my escape. With no way out, I turned to fight. Frankly, I welcomed it.

Bring it on, asshole.

As I kept my eyes on the approaching scooter, I felt around me in the darkness for anything I could use as a weapon. Under a bush, my hand closed around what felt like a two by two. I pulled it out and brushed it off. A remnant of the massive building in Macau, the board was surprisingly solid. A small gift.

But a two-by-two was perfect. About three feet in length, it was more than adequate, although another foot would've been nice. The scooter guy throttled back. I hazarded a peek. A hundred feet or so, but he was idling now.

Crouching, bouncing on my toes, my weapon at the ready, I calculated the closure rate.

Standing on the pegs, he peered into the bushes. For once the Fates had given me an opening, a slight advantage, but it was all I needed.

My breathing settled and confidence returned...until the kid pulled out a pistol and started shooting randomly into the darkness. Muffled pfffts, and a ping or two off the brick. Of course, the Fates would give him a gun and me a puny bit of wood.

Better odds than I was used to.

One shot pinged over my head, one to my left. I flinched and braced against the inevitable pain to come as I forced myself to take deep breaths.

No matter how strong my flight response, I couldn't run.

Running would give him a target.

Fight not flight, a fitting epitaph.

But if the shooter got me, he was going to have to work for it.

Pressing back, I kept still, hoping my little spot wasn't one of his random ones. By the time he neared, he was barely moving as he peered into the darkness. Even though I knew he couldn't see me, I felt exposed.

I forced myself to remain still.

Closer. I could hear his engine clearly now—the timing was off slightly; the engine ticked like a drunken clock. I almost thought I could hear him breathe. But hearing anything that subtle above the pounding of my heart and the rush of blood pulsing in my ears was impossible.

Emboldened, he raised up, peering into the bushes as he eased along. Maybe he thought he'd shot me already. Maybe he knew I didn't have a gun.

Twenty feet.

Stay still, Lucky.

Breathe.

With both hands, I gripped my bat, gauging its length, testing its heft, measuring the clearance I would need. This could work; it had to work.

Wait, Lucky. Wait.

Calm flooded through me. My brain cleared. The moments slowed.

You got this.

A shot hissed to my right. I felt a sting. Focused, I didn't flinch.

Five feet.

He pulled abreast.

Now!

I stepped out of the shadows, both hands gripping the end of the two-by-two that I held down against my right leg. Bracing on my right leg, I coiled.

Surprised, he reared up and back.

Stepping into my left leg, I swung like Alex Rodriguez with the home-run record in sight and the season dwindling.

I caught him right across the bridge of his nose. He tumbled off the back of his scooter, which wobbled for ten feet or so then fell over on its side, its engine still humming. Before anyone noticed, I grabbed the guy by his hoodie and pulled him into the bushes.

Asian. Male. Tough. Like a bad movie. Should I feel bad for racial profiling? Not.

Out cold.

A broken nose that gushed blood. Tomorrow he would have two shiners and a lot of explaining to do.

But tonight he'd solved my transportation problems.

And my weaponry problem. His handgun was a new Sig .40 S&W—perfect for concealed carry. I'd counted five shots, so I had at least five more. In too much of a hurry to check, I eased the slide closed, stuck it in my Birkin, and tried not to think about all the laws I was breaking. This wasn't Vegas. I couldn't throw myself on the mercy of the court and expect the DA to save my ass.

Just having a gun here could get you into big trouble.

Unless you were law enforcement...or you had paid someone off...or you didn't care about getting caught.

But I wasn't, so the swashbuckling needed to go. If I was going to be a felon, I needed to be more careful.

Quickly, I checked the guy for any ID, not that I expected to find any. I was wrong. His angry mug stared at me from a local driver's license. I couldn't read his name nor even pretend to pronounce it—not that it mattered.

I'd seen his face before.

The guy in the photo Teddie had shown me.

The guy who'd killed Jhonny Vu, Kim Cho's partner.

A thought gripped me—the idea so strong, so powerful, so

compelling I knew what it must feel like to try to resist an addiction.

His gun. I could shoot him right now. Eliminate one horror from the gene pool. Murder wasn't that big a deal here—hadn't I been told that a thousand times?

Oh, I wanted to. So bad I could almost taste the victory, the satisfaction...the revenge.

But I couldn't.

Some lines even I was afraid to cross.

A quick pat down of the guy. He wasn't wired, so if he was working with a team, someone had to have eyes on him.

I stuck my head out of the bushes looking for more bad guys, or cops alerted to gunfire by a concerned citizen. But nothing. No movement. No one rushed in my direction. No one hurried toward the fallen scooter. No one slinked between the shadows.

A lone wolf?

Last time he'd underestimate a woman.

A lesson forcefully delivered. I could live with that.

Before I left, I checked his pulse, then dragged him further back into the bushes.

Anybody could've sent him to hassle me, and right now I actually welcomed it. *Bring it on, assholes.* At least fighting felt like doing something, no matter how unproductive defending myself might prove to be.

After stuffing the shooter's ID back in his pocket, I changed my mind. It could come in handy later, so I transferred it to my purse.

Save Romeo first. Then my hotel.

Nothing mattered until I had Romeo safe and back in Brandy's arms.

The scooter was as light as it looked. The first twenty feet or so, I wobbled a bit, but then I found my balance and opened the throttle. Bending low over the handlebars, I stayed tucked in tight to the traffic, which, to my delight, was mostly trucks at this hour. If anyone was looking for me, I wanted to be hard to find.

Macau, like its sister, Hong Kong, was a maze of bridges that connected the outer islands with each other and with the mainland. The key was finding the right bridge. As I followed the red line on my phone's GPS, I prayed Siri was fluent in the nuances of the back streets of Macau—a leap of faith, since that woman could get me lost on the major arteries in my own backyard.

The truck traffic was heavy through the Cotai Strip. The hotels, large hulking edifices, sat back from the road. Nothing about this place drew me in. Good thing I wasn't their prime demographic. Trucks peeled off and chugged up the long drives, then around to the loading docks of various properties.

So the traffic had thinned to almost none as I gunned the engine out of the Cotai Strip toward Coloane. A few miles past government housing that looked pretty posh, and which had one of the best views on the island, then winding through neighborhoods of houses along the coastline—real houses on an island where few could afford five hundred square feet in a pre-war building to call their own, and I arrived at the outskirts of the tiny village of Coloane. Amazingly, Siri actually got me within spitting distance of where I wanted to go with only two wrong turns that were somewhat my fault—reading a map upside down is not a skill I'd perfected.

Once in Coloane, the streets turned dark, the street lamps were weak and the distance between them great, so much so that I traveled from one pale pool of light through darkness to the next. The large lighted expanses in front of the garish casinos of the Cotai had given way to tight row houses. The few businesses were still shuttered at this hour.

All but one.

Where the main street bent hard to the right at the water, lights shone through the front of Lord Stow's Bakery, drawing me like a beacon in a storm. Baking was an early business, Lord Stow's, a legend. And, for once, luck swung my way.

In a two-story stucco building with turquoise shutters bracketing windows on the top floor, and tile roofing, the bakery looked, if not ready for business, then at least welcoming to the weary traveler with its steel shutters pushed back and the storefront open.

Figuring it wouldn't hurt to be extra careful, I parked the scooter across the street behind a little park area. After hiding it behind a couple of trash cans that had taken some abuse, I pocketed the keys. Ignoring the scurrying sounds in the dark corners, I paused under the lone tree's large canopy and scanned the streets and alleys. Minutes passed while I stood still, waiting, watching for movement. After several minutes, nothing looked out of the ordinary—in fact, there was no movement I could detect, so I stepped into the open, strolled across the street, and into the small shop.

The baking was done at the back of the long narrow space. Ovens lined the back wall, their maws open, belching steam, begging for the next tray of yeasty goodness. In front of the ovens, several white-clad people worked over a dough table. Long glass cases set out from the wall to my left, the space behind them defining the selling area. Taller cases lined the wall to my right, the shelves laden with pastries and breads. One machine held cold drinks, its motor laboring. A short maze of velvet ropes zigzagged in front of the counter and across the store. Apparently, this place could draw a crowd.

A lady at the back, sensing my presence, turned and welcomed me with a smile. She looked familiar. But she couldn't be. I didn't know anyone out here on the tip of the island. Everyone was starting to look like someone I should be afraid of. First the knockoff man, now the baker. She was making egg tarts for Chrissake, very famous egg tarts, but this wasn't a James Bond movie with a pistol-packing pastry chef. Which movie had they filmed in Macau... I couldn't remember.

Teddie would know.

Laughing at myself, I shelved my fear—still, there was something familiar in her smile.

"We're not quite open yet," she said in English.

Clearly, my hiding in plain sight was not an effective strategy.

The no-nonsense yet warmth of her tone rang a bell of recognition. I was losing it.

Breathing deep the pungent aroma of strong coffee and the

sweet promise of buttery, custardy tarts baking, I tried for a smile. "I know. I'm sorry. I've wandered a bit far. Would it be okay if I had some of that incredible coffee I'm smelling while I waited for a friend...and maybe a tart when they're done?"

She poured me a cup and I swore her eyes saw through all my lies. "Here you go. On the house. The tarts will be done in a few." She pointed to my shoulder. "You've got a bit of blood there."

I'd forgotten. Adrenaline, they ought to bottle the stuff and sell it as an anesthetic. Same shoulder they'd winged at Miss Minnie's, but slightly higher this time. Matching stripes that looked like the mark of a wild animal or a decoration from the military. "I'm not very good on the scooter," I said, trying for casual, hoping for convincing.

"I have a first-aid kit if you'd like," she said, as if bloody Americans appeared before dawn all the time.

"No, that's okay. Thanks."

She motioned me toward a tiny table tucked in the corner. She'd clearly pulled it inside from its normal spot on the sidewalk—there wasn't room in here to turn around twice, much less for a table, even one for two. But the corner was a perfect place to see and not be seen. Dear God, I was starting to think like a James Bond wannabe. I wondered if they still had the Bottom's Up club in town? Or was that in Hong Kong? Or that floating casino Daniel Craig laid waste to? I hadn't seen either in a long time, but I was sort of hoping for a Hollywood ending to my little adventure.

The clerk returned to baking preparations, chattering all the while to her hapless male counterpart who kept a stoic face and focused on kneading dough.

As I settled in and pulled out my phone, I wondered if the clerk wanted a job in a casino. Never turn away a paying guest—although she hadn't let me pay yet. I figured, by the end of the hour, I'd pay one way or another.

Cindy Liu answered before the first ring, her voice sharp but with the huskiness of sleep. "Cindy Liu."

The hour wasn't even sociably early. I didn't feel bad. "Cindy, Lucky O'Toole here. I apologize for the hour."

"Yes, Miss." Any hint of sleep vanished from her voice. "Not to worry."

"Just call me Lucky. Remember, we had this discussion before?"

"Okay, Lucky, what can I do for you?" The no-nonsense I'd grown to rely on returned to her voice.

"I need to find Sinjin."

Cindy was quiet for a bit, probably weighing how to react. "What you need with him?"

"Help to find my friend." I gave her a very short run-through of the salient points of my last twenty-four hours, leaving out the sensitive stuff.

"He more important than your hotel?" She measured her words.

"Of course." I answered too quickly and in doing so showed a few too many cards. "What makes you think anything is wrong with the hotel?"

"Bad things happening in Macau. Everyone afraid, but not you."

"Oh, I'm terrified."

"Smart lady, but that don't stop you."

"I'm stupid that way."

"But you want your friend?"

"I won't stop until I find him."

"I like you. You're good people." Her voice warmed...slightly.

"A gross misjudgment, I assure you. Give me time, I can change that opinion."

This time she actually laughed. "You are at Lord Stow's?"

"How did you know that?"

"My sister works there. I can hear her—she talks without stopping. Give me ten minutes. Stay out of sight." With that, she rang off.

I had nothing to do but dig into the warm tart Cindy's sister slipped in front of me with a nod and a shy smile. I knew there'd been something familiar about her—and I was glad I wasn't seeing bad guys in every innocent baker.

Even though I had taken my time, savoring every bite as I pressed into the corner out of view of the street, I was eyeing a second tart when Cindy Liu stepped into the shop. She unwound the scarf around her head and shook out her hair.

"You saved me from myself," I said as I rose to greet her.

Ten minutes and the woman was completely put together. Skirt, sensible shoes, pressed blouse, and loose shawl to cut the cool morning air. She made fashion look as easy as an afterthought. I wanted to ask her how she did that, but now was not the time, nor did I really want to trot out another of my deficiencies, struggling as I was with so many already.

I'd lost Romeo. I sent Teddie off like a Christian to fight the lions. And I was chasing a ghost.

"Americans," she shook her head. Her tone evidenced her displeasure with our culture. "More is not always better."

"You'd never make it in Vegas."

She gave me a look I couldn't read. "I'm sure you are right." She motioned for me to follow as she turned on her heel. "Come, we haven't much time."

I grabbed her arm and turned it over, exposing her forearm. No tattoo.

She didn't resist. "Not all who fight carry the mark."

"And that makes it difficult to tell which side you're on."

Cindy pulled her arm back and tucked it under her shawl, which she pulled tight, unable to fight the shiver that rippled through her. "Actions will show you."

"If I live."

Light tinged the east as we headed outside. I followed Cindy across the road to a small dock area where fishermen readied their boats...very small boats...with nets that smelled of last week's catch.

"Where are we going?"

Cindy glanced at me, a cool apprising glance. "You want Sinjin?"

"Yes, of course."

"Then you come." With a curt nod she continued down the

dock, stopping in front of a spot with a particularly tiny boat. A small, dark man stepped to meet us with a snaggle-toothed smile of black and broken teeth. His face creased by the sun, his eyes hooded dark holes, his body thin and ropey, he looked ageless, even with the thin spikes of white hair growing from his head like tufts of grass. Exuding the vibrancy of a much younger man, he extended a hand. I took it. Calloused, hard, it matched the rest of him. I winced at the vigorous squeeze as he pumped my hand twice.

Cindy smiled as she gave him a kiss, one on each cheek in the European tradition. "This is Mica. He will take you there."

I eyed the small boat—my seaworthiness was limited to large vessels, and unwillingly to those. "There, where? You do know there are sharks in these waters?" I thought of the shark net to protect the swimmers at Repulse Bay, which was actually on Hong Kong Island, but not that far as the shark swims, which didn't make me feel better. "And I don't have any water wings," I stammered.

They both ignored me. Instead, they looked at the lights twinkling across the water. A quarter-mile, no more, separated us from them. "You go there," Cindy said, confirming my fear.

"And where exactly is that?" Macau and its islands threw off my sense of direction.

"China."

My heart skipped several beats. "You mean China, like mainland China?"

"Yes." Cindy and Mica both seemed untroubled by this.

"Won't the authorities consider it bad form if I enter the country illegally?"

Cindy pursed her lips and nodded. "Quite possibly. So, you mustn't get caught."

"And if I do?"

"You have gun?"

"Yes."

"Then shoot yourself." For a moment, she didn't smile.

Everybody wanted to be a comedian.

I eyed the boat, rocking on the easy swells, then Mica,

standing there as if he hadn't a care in the world, which I guess he hadn't. If he got caught, they'd only take his boat.

"Cindy..."

She put a hand on my arm. "It okay."

With no one else to trust and a desperate need to find Romeo before there wouldn't be anything left worth saving, I nodded and stepped into the boat. Mica settled a dirty blanket across my lap as if I was the Queen of England. I clutched my Birkin like a shield, feeling the false confidence of having a gun I knew I wouldn't use. "I would like to come back alive and not in shackles looking at a firing squad," I whispered to him.

He smiled with as much understanding as if I'd spoken Swahili.

It took several pulls on a motor that probably hadn't been manufactured in this half of the century before it caught with belches of smoke.

As we motored quietly across the open expanse, I didn't even try to engage Mica in conversation. My Portuguese was nonexistent and I didn't think this was the time to trot out my intimate knowledge of Cantonese curse words. So I sat on the narrow wooden bench and clutched the sides of the boat as I tried to shake the images of being rowed across the river Styx. And here I'd hoped my demise would be a bit more dignified.

Halfway across, Mica killed the engine. Other fishing boats, dark shadows moving across the water, glided past. No one said anything as they motored into a new day. Water lapped against the sides of the boat, which rocked in the wakes of the passing boats. Lights shone in a tall building on the shore as we approached. Several smaller ones clustered along the shore. But there were no car headlights beaming through the darkness, no movement. Mica paddled the rest of the way, sliding us silently into a small dark pier. The last gasp of night crushed in around us. I huddled, trying to make myself small.

Mica motioned for me to get out.

"Here? You can't be serious."

He nodded and grinned.

I didn't like his grin. I pulled out some bills and pressed

them into his hand, unsure whether I was paying for my own execution. Without looking at the money, he pocketed it, then helped me out of the boat. With a nod, he backed the boat out, turned it, and paddled toward Macau.

Leaving me alone in the dark.

I stood there, shivering, more out of fear than cold as I tried to think of stories for the authorities when they finally caught me, an illegal in their country. I'd heard about Chinese jails—cold, damp, a piece of bread, if the rats didn't get it first. Light brightened the sky behind me but left my little bit of coast in the gloom.

Behind me, I heard Mica's engine sputter to life.

I rooted in my purse, my hand closing around the gun. I transferred it to a position at the small of my back, held snug by the waistband of my pants. A bit too snug. Maybe Mona was right—a cleanse was in my future. The thought nauseated me. Or maybe that was fear that roiled through my stomach.

Alone with no one to call and fresh out of ideas, I was as close to giving up as I've ever gotten. I wondered how the article would read in the RJ. Would they be kind? Would they vilify me? Would they even remember?

One little boy would remember.

The smell of baby soap, as strong as if I was...home. The reality hit me; why it took so long I don't know.

Everything, okay, not *everything*, but a lot rested on me.

And I could handle it. I had to.

Stokes. Maybe he would come get me. Not a perfect solution, but if he got me out of China, I could handle the rest. I pulled out my phone. As I was scrolling through for his number, a sound stopped me. I cocked my head, trying to catch it again.

I palmed the phone, hiding the light, then crouched down. Not much to hide behind, but at least I was a smaller target in the soft light of the new day, quickly brightening.

Footsteps rustled through the grasses. I dropped my phone in my bag, then grabbed the gun, holding it at the ready as I turned toward the sound. Silently, I racked the slide and strained to see into the darkness. Crouching further down, using the grasses to hide me, I held my breath, listening. And I had absolutely no idea what to do. Shoot my way out? Yeah, that'd be a good plan—talk about making a bad situation worse.

My hand shook as I tried to keep the gun aimed. What was it they said—only a fool feels no fear? Well, at least I wasn't a fool. Although, given my recent string of choices, that could be debated.

"Lucky?" a voice hissed.

How did they know my name? Thoughts tumbled on a wave of panic.

"Lucky? Are you here?"

My heart skipped a beat. Could it be? I waited.

"Lucky?"

Yes, yes, I knew that voice! Joy rushed through me. I didn't dare believe. "Romeo?" I whispered. Raising up, I called to him again, this time louder. "Romeo! Over here."

The footsteps, faster now, he rushed out of the darkness.

I had a moment to brace myself. Then he hit me, grabbing me in a bear hug.

We staggered together, holding on.

Oh, God. He was alive! We held each other tight, gathering strength, killing a fear. When my heart had steadied and I'd started to accept that he was here and okay, I disengaged and held him at arm's length. Amazingly, he looked... fine. Oh, maybe frayed around the edges, but his eyes were bright, his smile at full wattage. Even his cowlick still stood in defiance.

"How?"

A voice from the darkness answered. Male. Authoritative, with a hint of British. "Courage is rewarded."

I turned toward it. I knew this voice. "You! From the jetfoil."

He stepped into the light. I almost gasped; well, I probably did. The man in front of me embodied the best of each culture, Caucasian and Asian. Jet-black hair, worn straight and long, chiseled features, wide-set eyes, a strong jaw, broad shoulders, narrow hips, and long legs. That's all I could see in the barely-light morning. The color of his eyes remained hidden, but for some reason I knew they were green. He wore a flowing white shirt gathered in front with a string that he hadn't tied and loose black pants, tight on his hips, then tucked into black boots.

I'd just been dropped into a romance novel.

I gave him a raised eyebrow. I so did not need saving...well, given that I was in his country illegally, maybe just a little bit of saving.

"Sinjin, I take it?"

He bowed low. "At your service."

CHAPTER TWELVE

"**DON'T** you think you're taking this pirate thing a bit too seriously?" I stepped in front of him. The slight widening of his eyes hinted that he wasn't used to a woman being so bold, or one that was his physical equal. Yep, his eyes were green.

He looked a bit sheepish. "It adds to my mystique, and besides, the locals like it."

"Well, I don't like the whole heavy-handed pirate bullshit. Not one little bit." Fisting my right hand, I held it in my left. Pivoting off my right foot, I threw my elbow at his jaw.

Bone met bone in a meaty thunk. He dropped like a stone.

Not out cold, but I think he got my message.

I stood over him as he propped himself on one elbow, rubbing the spot where my shot had landed.

"Your displeasure is so noted." He shot an amused glance at Romeo. "You warned me. And you were right; she is impressive."

With a hand on my arm, Romeo stopped me from further action I might soon regret. "He's a bit of a drama queen, but he plays for our team."

"You told him I was impressive?"

"I had to tell him something." A smile lifted one corner of his mouth. "And then you had to hit him."

"I owed him. Besides, he hit me first—well, Ming, a young

woman in his employ, did on the jetfoil. *And*, he took you." I whirled on Sinjin. "Do you have any idea what my last ten hours have been like?" Had it really only been such a short time? It felt like an eternity trapped in a bad movie with no laugh track.

He gathered himself into a seated position. Then, pulling his feet in, he grabbed his knees. "Unfortunately, I do."

I let him get his equilibrium—I'd hit him pretty hard—then I extended my hand, helping him to his feet. He wobbled a bit before finding his land legs, which gave me a taste of the revenge I craved.

"Why did you take Romeo?"

Sinjin rolled his head side-to-side and blinked rapidly. "Remind me to never make you mad."

"You won't need reminding. Now, tell me, why did you take Romeo?"

"Romeo, he didn't lie. You are impressive." He worked his jaw. "I don't think it's broken."

"Do I look like I care?"

"I get it. You're steamed up." His posture relaxed, but his smile was tight. "Do I look like I care?"

Tit for tat and all of that. "Okay, we're even."

"Hardly," he said, his tone stepping on any possibility that he might be joking. "My family owes yours an incredible debt." Before I could ask what, he motored on, answering my question. "Bait. I took your friend for bait. I needed you to come to me. I needed to see what you were made of, where your priorities are. And I needed you to trust me. If I came to find you, then I would have none of those things."

Trust you?" I spluttered.

Opening his arms wide, he was all innocence. "Detective Romeo is unharmed."

Well, there was that. "What about the ten years I lost worrying about him?"

"That I cannot restore." He actually looked a little hangdog when he said it. Either he was an exceptional manipulator or he was sincere. Unfortunately, I had no idea which.

For no good reason, I went with sincere, and I prayed to the Great Goddess that I wasn't making one more bad choice when it came to a handsome man. This one could get us killed or worse. "I'm not sorry for hitting you." I tried not to pout when I said it.

"I'm not sorry for taking the young detective."

"Hey," Romeo started to object.

Sinjin and I both shot him the same look, shutting him down.

He raised his hands in a defensive gesture. "Okay, never mind. Just forget about me, a hapless pawn in a larger game."

"Well, look at you." I copied Mona's superior look. "All grown up and becoming a regular junior smart-ass."

The kid actually winked at me. I lost my bearings for a moment.

Time was short, and I didn't have the ego to carry this any further with the pirate. "Means to an end," I said, refocusing on Sinjin and trying for a bit of understanding as I tried to take his measure, sadly, without much luck. I couldn't get past the dark-haired, younger Fabio thing he had going on. The personification of a wolf in sheep's clothing. For some odd reason, clichés weren't providing the entertainment they used to. "We are more alike than makes me comfortable," I admitted, more to myself than him.

He graced me with a smile—it took my breath. I may have left my heart in Vegas, but I still could appreciate a gorgeous man oozing dangerous.

"I had it coming," he agreed. "After what Minnie told me, I should've known you wouldn't give up without a fight."

"Minnie?" It was my turn to be surprised. "When did you talk with her?"

"Before you went to see her."

"*She* set this up?"

"Set it in motion would be more accurate." Sinjin looked around—the day was brightening fast. "We are exposed. We need to move to a safe place."

"I'm here illegally, and I'm hanging with a wanted man.

I'm running low on bargaining chips so, you won't get any objection from me." I let him herd me toward the road, with Romeo bringing up the rear. "I hope we don't have to walk far. I don't have much time."

In the shadows ahead of us, an engine started. Lights flicked on, and a car emerged from its sheltered position at the side of a building then eased to a stop in front of us. A large black SUV. So much for subtle. With an unnecessary flourish, Sinjin opened the rear door for me.

His act was getting a bit old. With one foot on the floorboard, I paused in the door. "If we're the good guys, why do we have to break the law and hide in the shadows while the bad guys operate in plain sight?"

His face closed into a frown, then he shrugged. "It is China."

Romeo rode shotgun next to the driver, who appeared not to have any interest in his passengers. Sinjin took the spot next to me in the back.

I didn't give him time to relax. "Tell me about Minnie."

"Mr. Cho, he is not her husband. Even though pimping is illegal here in Macau, prostitution is not. Minnie..." his voice broke. He swallowed hard and took a moment to regain his composure. "Minnie had no choice. She did what she had to do to survive."

"And Cho?"

Sinjin shot me a sideways look—it wasn't hard to read the hate in it. "Mr. Cho took advantage."

An old story, but it still inflamed every shred of righteous indignation I had. "How'd she get out?"

"She didn't, not for a while anyway. Minnie's one smart lady, though. She convinced Cho to move her to Vegas, let her be the conduit through which his laundered money is invested in real estate. It's an old story and a gambit the bad guys have been running for a long time." He swiveled to look at me. "Did you know the U.S. is one of the few countries that allow foreign investment above 49%? Every other country worth investing in won't give a foreign person or entity majority control. It is wise to withhold this, don't you think?"

"You and I are singing the same song. But, another problem for another day."

"It is actually worse, but Minnie made it work for her. It is possible to get a U.S. visa by investing in real estate."

"Buy your way in." I sighed, somehow a bit defeated. In our desire for largess, we Americans could be so stupid.

"But, as you say, another day." He shifted back to look straight ahead, his eyes constantly flicking between the mirrors.

His posture remained relaxed, so I did, too—relaxed being a relative term.

"What about her sons?"

"Frank and Sam?" Sinjin found something about that amusing.

"What?"

"They are not her sons. They could be Mr. Cho's sons. He claims them, but nobody knows for sure. Hell, Stanley Ho has seventeen children that he claims, but many suspect he has more. Mr. Cho could be the same."

"Easy to sire, hard to parent."

"No doubt."

"Tell me about Ming." I shot him a raised eyebrow. "I know you know her."

"Yes, but I did not know you did."

"There's a lot you don't know," I bluffed, trying to raise myself in his estimation. This wasn't personal; this was professional. I was aiming for partner, not pawn.

"Apparently."

"Ming seems to hold Frank and Sam in high esteem. If they're such good guys, can you explain what they were doing in Vegas shooting at people and getting tossed in jail?"

"Frank went to save Minnie, then got crossed up with your legal system somehow. Sam went to get Frank. Nobody knew Gittings would get to Sam, and then try to take Minnie out so he could angle to be her replacement for Cho."

"That's what happened?"

"According to Frank."

It sorta made sense. Sorta. "Why did Gittings want to be Cho's guy? Ol' Irv is more of a lone wolf."

"Frank thinks Gittings killed somebody. After that big singer went tits up, Gittings got all freaked. Told Sam he needed to get out of the country. Cho was a great way out. And I'm sure Gittings figured having his protection while he figured out the local game wouldn't be bad either."

"And he promised to deliver Frank in return?"

"Yeah."

"Which I guess he did." Another thought derailed me as my heart hammered. "He admitted to killing someone."

"Well, not exactly, only that he was involved. Tried to pin it on a friend of yours, I believe."

"I was sure Sam Cho killed Holt Box."

"Possible. It depends on how hard Gittings sat on him. Sam was a little slow. He'd do anything for Frank."

"Sam's dead. So how do I prove Gittings did it?"

"Sam lived for a bit after Gittings shot him."

"I didn't know. Did he talk to anybody?"

"Minnie."

"You know what he said?"

"No. She didn't tell me; she told me to protect you. That if you live, and you bring down Cho, for the girls, she said, then she'll give you what you want."

Okay, so much for partner—I'd been a pawn from the get-go.

The more I railed against playing games it seemed, the further I got drawn into them. I wondered what would happen if we all refused to play and dealt with each other directly. Probably homicide, not that that was ruled out at this point anyway.

"I want to talk to Frank."

"In time, but he won't go over Minnie's head. He wants Cho gone more than most, especially now." Sinjin shifted from looking at me to looking out the front window—never a good sign. "Kim really was Miss Minnie's daughter, the daughter Mr. Cho kept as collateral when he sent Minnie to the U.S. Frank was in love with her. They were to be married."

"Oh." My heart fell. Minnie had pretended to not have any interest in Kim to protect her. My heart broke for all of them. Anger filtered in through the cracks—anger and revenge. "So Frank and Kim couldn't have been brother and sister."

"No, Minnie was Kim's mother. Mr. Cho was not her father. Frank and Sam, nobody really knows where they came from. Minnie isn't their mother, though, not blood mother anyway, but she feels strongly about those two boys."

"So Kim really was Minnie's daughter?"

"Yes, and she was my sister."

"What?" At a loss, I squeezed his arm, offering a connection; that was the best I had. Words failing had happened to me a lot lately. Maybe I was getting older and a bit softer. Maybe with perspective came a heightened awareness of the pain in the world. Life could be cruel, but people often more so.

Terrific. Life was giving me insight rather than solutions.

"I'd warned her. We all had. And then they got Jhonny Vu, a warning she chose to ignore. She wanted Frank, and she wanted Cho taken down." He gave me a sad half-smile. "Perhaps, with your help, she will get one wish in the afterlife."

My resolve solidified. "If I have to shoot him myself."

"Another would step into his place. We need to get them all."

"All? You want me to get *all* of them?" My voice screeched like a sour violin note. "You can't even take care of Cho."

"We can come up with a plan."

I felt my eyes grow round, and, once again, words fled.

Where was Peter Pan to fly me off to Neverland?

I watched the scenery outside the window roll by. A simple life, a simple land—so far from the glitz and ugliness on Macau and the wealth and opulence of Hong Kong—both so close, yet light years away from the small houses, the bicycles resting on their sides in the yards, the lights shining in the windows as folks started their day.

No wonder the Chinese loved the whole yin and yang thing—they personified it. Of course, I guess we all did, as it was some sort of Newtonian Law, equal and opposite reaction and all of that, but right now I felt like blaming it on the Chinese.

I couldn't talk about a plan right now; my brain was whirling from what I'd been told and what I didn't know. At this point, I wasn't sure which was more terrifying. "Tell me about Minnie. How did your mother escape Mr. Cho's...influence? Even in Vegas, I'm sure he kept her on a short leash."

"He had a rope around her neck, yes." His eyes shifted back to mine. "Your father."

Of course. My father had a hero complex of epic proportions. He'd saved my mother...sort of. He'd saved Minnie. And so many others that I would lose count if I tried to tally his scorecard. There was a special place in heaven for him, despite what he may have done that he didn't want me to know about.

"Do you know a Vito Morgenstern?"

"Of course."

"What does he do?"

"He is the Governor of Macau. Why?"

Was Sinjin playing me for a chump? "There is no more Governor of Macau. That office went out with the Portuguese."

"You want to tell that to Vito Morgenstern?"

From the look on his face, I knew the answer to be no. "Which team does he play for?"

"His own. But he is a man of honor." Sinjin seemed to understand that there was a debt to be paid somewhere, somehow.

"My father..." I started to tell him then thought better of it. Some secrets shouldn't be told.

"A friend if you need him, then." Sinjin was smarter than he looked. Of course, any man dressed in pirate garb looked about as smart as a woman wearing short shorts to a board meeting. "Your father. My family could never repay his kindness."

"That's never the deal. No repayment necessary." I shifted in my seat, a bit anxious. "So, what's your skin in this game? What do you want?"

"I want my country back. I want to finish my sister's fight." He waived my next question away. "Not political autonomy, but personal. Greed and corruption are endemic. The Triad assaults people in the daylight, flaunting their power. We are afraid."

"But everyone who wants a job has one. And crime is low."

"But at what cost?" The look in his eyes turned hard.

Clean it up or let it ride? Vegas had faced the same choice in the Fifties.

"The cash pipeline out of China has slowed to a trickle," Sinjin continued, his voice stronger now. "The mainland government is making a big show of cracking down on money laundering and the purchase of high-end goods from real estate to fashion."

"I know the bribery hasn't slowed down—the ghost cities that nobody wants built in the middle of nowhere are totems to greed and corruption."

Sinjin pursed his lips as if he was impressed. "Public money converted to private."

"It still needs to be laundered to be of any use," I said, starting to see more of how the game was played. "Cho has essentially usurped our casino as if he'd bought it. A cash business, a casino is the perfect venue for cleaning dirty money."

Sinjin looked out the window. The angry look on his face betrayed his thoughts. "He's got a sweet deal."

"Until the authorities finally grow too greedy and take all his profit to allow him to continue." I was picking up some of Sinjin's anger. "Then they shut us down and jerk our gaming commission. Any idea how we can shut Cho and his cronies down, without losing our ass...ets?"

"Maybe." His eyes had turned dark and serious as he turned to look at me.

"I'm ready for your plan." I braced myself. "I think. The goal is ambitious, so I've no doubt the price will be high."

"One hundred million U.S."

Oh, that figure sounded awful familiar. He couldn't mean...could he? Not yet willing to shoulder the enormity of what I thought he had in mind, I let him unwind the story at his own pace...as I thought about how to pull it off.

"With the added scrutiny of the mainland government, the men like Cho have been forced underground. They still have the money coming in, but where to put it has become an issue. A huge black market has burgeoned. Men who will smuggle money out of China."

"But what then if they can't use banks?" I fed him the hanging curveball, even though I already knew the answer.

"They use someone like me."

"A pirate?"

"Of course not. That is only a game. I actually work in Hong Kong; I'm a legitimate businessman."

"Really? What do you do?" I had him pegged as a thief, a jewel thief most likely.

"I run an international hedge fund."

That wiped the smug right off my face. He was not only a thief; he was a thief of epic proportions. "Really?"

"Quite." He proffered a hand. "Sinjin Smythe-Gordon at your service. Cho forced Minnie to give me up, as he made her do with Kim, although he kept her. My adoptive parents left Hong Kong before the changeover. I was educated in the U.K., then decided to return. There is more...opportunity here."

"Do you accept investments from Mr. Cho and his cronies?"

He pressed a hand to his chest in mock indignation. "That would be illegal. The Chinese are rather strict about the source of funds."

"Right. I'm sure you've figured a way around that."

He didn't confirm or deny.

"So, what's the angle? How do we get them?"

"On the side—" he plucked at his shirt as if saying it was a costume, "—I am in procurement." He actually said that with a straight face. "I acquire expensive things the bad men want."

Ah, a common thief on the side. "How?"

"I steal them."

Feeling pretty proud of myself, I resisted showing any of my hand. Like I said, he wore danger like an intoxicating cologne.

International crime folks had long speculated that famous stolen works of art disappeared into private collections in the Far East, but nobody had proven it...nor had admitted to it.

"It is a place for the men to put their money where it will at least retain its value and most likely appreciate."

"But they can't bring the pieces to market."

"You are thinking too small. You are thinking only of the public market."

"I see." I shifted again—I couldn't get comfortable. At some point, knowing his secrets would make me an accomplice. "So you place stolen goods in the mansions of the corrupt men, for lack of a better term?"

He nodded.

"Like what?"

"Famous pieces."

As I feared. "So you know where..."

"Everything is."

"Holy shit." I settled back and let out a long breath. "You're like a time bomb."

"Isn't it great?" he said without a smile.

"How does the game go down exactly?"

"A man chooses his item. I am notified. I decide when and how, or even if I will steal it for him." Sinjin gave me a look I couldn't read. Was there a warning in there? "I am very good, but I am expensive."

"How are you paid?"

"The gentleman in question must open a special account.

It is for the purpose of a specific transaction. He makes arrangements to transfer the amount into the account."

"Are you a signatory on the account?"

"I have access. Remember, this is not the United States. Banking is rarely as regulated in other countries as it is in yours."

"And we have the last economic recession to show for it. Oh, and the Savings and Loan debacle." I don't know what my point was—I was stalling for time as I thought.

Romeo watched my face. Then he grinned and said to Sinjin, "Lucky's hatching something. I can see it."

"Is this a good thing?" Sinjin asked my young accomplice.

Romeo looked like a kid anticipating Christmas. "Well, it's usually scary as hell, but it works out okay in the end."

Both men turned to look at me, waiting. Sinjin crossed his arms. Romeo practically drooled. And the three of us were going to wrest the Vegas of the Far East from the clutches of the Evil Empire all by ourselves.

A plan started to take shape. I pushed myself higher in the seat. "If we want to get rid of the vermin, we have to exterminate them all, as you said. If the prize is large enough, we can lure them all in."

"Agreed, but can we get them all?" Sinjin looked interested, or like now it was he who was three steps ahead.

Romeo's eyes got bigger and bigger. He knew me well enough to be afraid.

An all-in kind of gal.

Teddie.

"No, not all of them. Even God couldn't do that without a flood. But we can cut the heart out of the beast, then let the authorities who really do want to clean the place up take care of the rest. Not a perfect solution, but I think one we both could live with?"

I gave both men time to think, then I looked at Romeo. "I'll put you on a plane. There's no guarantee we all won't go down in flames and end up rotting in some Chinese hell-hole."

His face seemed to age ten-years, which meant he looked

all of twenty-two, but that got my attention. "No, thanks. You've been there for me every step of the way. Now it's my turn."

"You've already saved my life once, maybe twice. I think that gives you a pass on this one."

He nodded as his eyes got a faraway look. "Once. But there are no balanced scales in friendship."

I narrowed my eyes at him. "Is this place rubbing off on you? That sounds suspiciously like one of those obtuse Chinese proverbs."

We both looked at Sinjin, who shrugged. "If it is not, it should be." Then he looked at me. "What do you have in mind?"

"Oh, I think you know. You set this up."

"Set what up?" he said, his voice flat, his manner almost careless; yet, underneath I sensed a spring wound tight.

I pulled a pamphlet out of my Birkin and opened it, spreading it wide so both men could see it. I pointed at the largest photo. "Do you know this watch?"

Sinjin's eyes narrowed. "The Patek Phillipe. Worth twenty million American dollars."

"Twenty-Five. It's a beautiful thing, isn't it? One of a kind." We all stared at the full-color photo of the pocket watch. To me, the price seemed a tad steep, okay, like super ridiculous—but that whole demand-and-supply thing was obviously at work here. "But you knew that, didn't you?" I speared the pirate with a look.

His dark eyes met mine.

"You brought me here because you want me to help you steal not only it, but the whole collection. One hundred million, you said."

Romeo choked, then coughed.

"All of them are in my hotel. But you know all about that. And I'd be willing to bet my hotel that Mr. Cho wants you to steal it for him."

"Would you bet your hotel?" His voice dropped to a whisper. "What about your life?"

"Are you trying to talk me into this game or out of it?" I folded the brochure and put it back in my purse. "Stealing that watch, or trying to, would be suicide. But, with help from the inside, you might be able to pull it off. But," I angled myself toward him, "if you want my help you have to tell me the whole plan."

"Can I trust you?" he asked, which seemed a bit late to me.

"Any one of us is as trustworthy as our goals for being a part of it."

He flashed that damned smile again. "Okay. I'll tell you what I need, and, if you can pull it off, you tell me what I will have to pay to get your help. Deal?"

I swallowed hard then took the hand he extended. "Deal."

CHAPTER THIRTEEN

I'D just made a deal with the Devil. I knew it, and I couldn't do anything about it. It was the only chance I had to somehow make all of this right. I couldn't bring Kim Cho back, but I could finish her job, exact her price.

For the girls, Minnie had said. No, for the women, young and not-so-young, everywhere. A lofty goal, even one that had me a bit in awe. And with no one to trust and two days to do it.

Talk about being all in, and all crazy.

With hands on his knees, Sinjin relaxed back. "I need a schematic of the security grid."

"No."

He raised an eyebrow.

"If I give it to you, you can hack in and you don't need me anymore. You tell me when and how you need the grid to go down, and I'll arrange that."

"You could be making a cage." The muscles in his cheek bunched as he clenched his jaw, the only sign of his irritation.

"Indeed. But if it's a cage, it will catch us all."

"And what do you want in return?"

"Romeo to be your bag man." I ignored the wide eyes Romeo shot me.

"You want the boy to keep his eye on me?" Sinjin tried to hide his scoff.

"A small thing to ask, don't you think? And you taking out Mr. Cho. That's part of your plan, right? He killed your sister and enslaved your mother. Your revenge is my family's gain. Consider your debt paid in full."

"You said no repayment was necessary."

"True, but I'm just helping you walk away with your head held high."

He threw his head back and laughed. When he'd sobered, he wiped off the last vestiges of a grin. "You win, Lucky O'Toole. God help me."

"God help all of us." I couldn't believe that making a pact with the Devil actually had me feeling pretty proud of myself and hopeful for the second time since I'd left home. "What are your plans for Frank Cho?"

Romeo swiveled around and gave me a look, one I recognized and didn't like. Then he delivered the *coup de grâce*. "Sinjin here let Frank go."

For the first time in a while, I became keenly aware of the cold metal of the gun pressed against the small of my back. "Why would you do that?" I asked, turning to get a good look at Sinjin. My voice had gone all strong and cold, my eyes tightening to slits.

"Whoa," Romeo said. Smart man—he knew that look.

Sinjin seemed unaware of his imminent death. "It is best to use your enemy's hand to catch a snake."

"Oh, great. Now you're going to go all Oriental on me."

He shrugged. "Thought I'd try. But, really, the proverb is a good one. Mr. Cho is most vulnerable from within. His narcissism will never let him believe someone close to him would betray him. Not until it is too late."

"And you think Frank is your guy?"

"I know he is." Sinjin wiped a hand across his eyes.

"Tough gig being a pirate?"

"No, that part is easy. No rules." He speared me with a look. "But revenge?"

"Best served cold?" We were both playing with that hot potato. With no pithy erudition of my own, I watched the scenery roll past. "Where are we going?"

"I'm taking you home, to your hotel."

A cold sweat popped. "I don't have any explanation for the border guards."

"Let me handle it."

I had no choice, but I knew either we'd sail through or we'd all never be heard from again.

Sinjin waved at the border guards who nodded and motioned us through.

Once clear, my stomach unclenched and I relaxed back. "Man, I would kill for stroke like that."

"Sometimes it requires that," Sinjin said, rather nonchalantly to suit my tastes.

"Toto," I said to Romeo.

"We're not in Vegas anymore." The kid finished my line.

Everyone smiled at the reference, even the driver who had maintained a stoic expression up to that point. "The expansion of Western culture will be the Communist's downfall," I said, then instantly regretted going all political.

"You mean greed?" Sinjin asked. "Indubitably."

"Are you safe traveling here?"

"No one knows my face, except the two of you. There is a fairly high price on my head, in case you're interested." Sinjin didn't seem concerned.

"You needn't worry about us. But I assume Frank Cho could pick you out of a lineup?"

"If he'd wanted my head on a spit, he could've had it long ago. We were to be family. Even in death, Kim joins us. Frank will not stop until the men who killed Kim are dead themselves. If he fails, I will finish the job."

"Men?"

"In China, no one acts alone. And the person responsible is never the one with the knife in his hand." This time it was he who reached across and squeezed my arm. "We are fighting different battles, but the same war. Trust me."

My entire world rode on the decision I made. Trust him—

or not?

I thought about it for a good long while, and he left me alone with my struggles. Finally, the driver turned the big car up the drive to my hotel, stopping at the valet stand. "We have a deal. I will honor it, whatever it takes. For the girls."

Sometimes life requires a person to put everything on the line for the things she believes in. This was my time.

"Especially for the girls." He turned to face me more fully. "When you see Mr. Cho, and you will, spar with him a bit. Make him think you're desperate; that you'll give him anything to get your hotel back and get your father out of their bulls-eye."

I bristled at his instructions. "Are you telling me how to play the game?"

"The game is played a bit differently here, half a world away from Vegas. The Asian culture is..."

"Enigmatic?"

"Arrogant, especially a man when dealing with a woman."

I leaned away from him. "You want me to grovel?"

He actually laughed. "Impossible. But you're a businesswoman, and a damn good one if how you've manhandled me is any indication. So, make a deal."

"Technically, I don't think you really need me."

"Maybe not. But the watches won't be here long, and I don't have time to plan as fully as I would like. You are the key to success, for all of us. Besides, in another way, you make my position much stronger. There are so many things that could go wrong when stealing the pieces; our marks could get twitchy and pull out. Having insider help sweetens the pot. You will help lure your sheep to slaughter. That's what you want, right?"

I started to object, then gave up. Yeah, Mr. Cho's head on a platter would be perfect.

Sinjin pulled out his iPhone, and, using his thumbs, he navigated the screens. Holding the phone so I could see, he asked, "This is your number?"

It wasn't really a question if he knew the answer, which I

could see he did. I nodded anyway.

He punched in some numbers then hit send.

My phone dinged.

"Now you have my number. I know I don't need to tell you not to identify it in any way."

"Can you set up one of your dummy accounts? That's what it is, isn't it? You're not really doing business through a real bank, just a virtual one. Am I right?"

"The virtual world is a great place to hide." He tapped in some more numbers. "Here's the routing number, the account number, and the style on the account." I raised an eyebrow. "I set it up for something that hasn't come together just yet. We can use it. It is safe. I don't need to tell you not to breathe a word."

"Not my first rodeo, cowboy," I said with more confidence than I felt. "But you sell me out, I'll shoot you myself."

"Likewise." He didn't smile.

SHOULDER to shoulder as we stood in front of the Tigris, Romeo and I watched him go. Neither of us had any words, at least not for a moment. As we turned toward the entrance to the hotel, Romeo recovered first, his bottled-up words tumbling out as he bounced on his feet with the energy of a puppy at dinnertime.

"That was so friggin' cool." Worship dripped from every word and he lunged for the door, narrowly elbowing the bellman out of the way. Holding the door wide, he bowed and made a sweeping gesture. "After you."

I tossed a tight smile to the bellman as I swept through the door, then shot Romeo my best grown-up glare, which he studiously ignored. The lobby, teeming with people, offered us the anonymity of being two in a crowd. They'd changed the music. Electronica wasn't my thing, but I bowed to wiser heads than mine. The crowd seemed to pulse with the music.

Romeo caught me in two strides. "Don't you think he is so cool? A pirate!"

With a look I shushed him. "No, this is not cool; *he* is not cool. He's a desperate man who will work with us as long as he needs us. Don't be fooled."

My warning didn't dim Romeo's light. "He's a good guy. You wait." Finally, he lowered the wattage a bit. "What are we going to do?"

"*You* are going to call Brandy and tell her only that everything is fine, nothing else." I stopped, and with a hand on his arm, and pulled him around to face me. "You got that? It's very important."

People flowed around us, cocooning us from anyone with abnormal interest.

"Sure, sure. Everything's fine."

I could feel the adrenaline vibrating through him. "Then get something to eat, take a shower, and try for some shut-eye. We may not get another opportunity until this is over."

He wilted. "But..."

"No. I need to make some plans. There's nothing to do right now."

"Okay." I could see the tiredness creep over him as the adrenaline let loose its hold. "Do you trust Stokes enough to let him in on this?" he asked.

"No."

"Then how are you going to get him involved?"

"Lie."

"But that could get you jail time. Lying to a Fed is serious business." Romeo acted like he'd been absent for most of the conversation with Sinjin.

I glanced around, but people were only paying us casual attention. I pulled him close. "Minor compared to everything else." I snagged an extra key to my suite from the front desk. "Here." I took Romeo's hand and pressed the key into it. "There're two bedrooms. Take the one I'm not in." I added that unnecessarily—I wasn't dealing with Teddie, who would need the extra clarity. "If you're hungry, call room service and charge it to the room. But be very careful. People are not who they seem to be." I echoed Kim Cho's warning.

That almost snuffed the ardor of his pirate envy.

STOKES tapped his fingers on the handrail of the escalator, a distracted look on his face. He was riding down from the junket level, and I was riding up. The day was dimming—I'd taken time to clean up and find a few winks in my suite. Sleep would be at a premium from here on out.

Still below his stare into the distance, I could see him, but he hadn't noticed me. The precious seconds gave me time to think. What to do with Stokes?

I needed answers. And, if I was going to pull off a robbery of epic proportions, I'd need his help. The local authorities couldn't be trusted—I had no proof, just a healthy case of skepticism and no time to persuade myself I was being paranoid. The FBI was the only American agency within shouting distance and, more important, the only one who could round up Irv Gittings and drag him back home where he could buy off another judge.

That thought was a constant prod to my inner vigilante.

Funny how quickly I seemed to be going rogue.

As Stokes slid past, still looking over my head, I grabbed his hand then let go.

He jumped but recovered quickly. Turning, he looked up at me. "O'Toole, I've been looking for you."

In the junket rooms? I doubted it, but played along. "You found me. Meet me at the bar in the vestibule up here, but give me five."

Before Stokes could make the round trip and perhaps see where I was headed, I ducked around the corner and into the wire transfer room. A clerk sitting behind thick bulletproof glass with a slot cut in the bottom where the glass met the counter looked up when I burst through the door with a bit more energy than I'd intended.

He positioned a mic on a flexible stand. "May I help you?"

"I need the in-bound wiring instructions, all the routing numbers, and whatever else I need, if you please." I shrugged.

"Will this be local or foreign?"

Hmm, hadn't thought up that lie. "Give me both."

He narrowed his eyes, then he snaked one hand under his desk.

"Before you call Security, I'm with corporate in Vegas."

"Your name?"

I gave it to him. He pursed his lips. "O'Toole, I've heard of you. Glad you told me. I thought maybe you were the girlfriend of one of those Russians—the women are all tall and good-looking like you. The men?" He made a face. "Not so much. All that body hair." He visibly shuddered. "They send their women down here, and I have to tell them I can't do anything without the big man himself. Doesn't go over too well. I'm pretty happy for the bulletproof glass, know what I mean?"

So many questions, so little time. Which was probably a good thing—I didn't think I really wanted to know exactly how he knew about the Russians' body hair. So I nodded and said, "Totally." Which wasn't a complete lie—when it came to protection from people shooting in one's general direction, I knew exactly what he was talking about.

Tearing the top sheet of paper off a pad, he pushed it through the slot without another word. I was pretty sure he gave me a knowing wink, though, which I did my best to ignore. Some people have no appreciation for authority—I should know; I'm one of them.

I glanced at the paper. So much money coming into the hotel they had the wire instructions preprinted? I stuffed the note in my pocket, then, without a nod, I turned and left.

Stokes had scored us a table in the corner, but, considering the bar was empty, not a great feat.

"Bubbles?" he asked with a forced smile.

"No, this isn't a social visit." I took the chair across from him, but I didn't lean back—this wouldn't take long. "So, what were you doing up here?"

"Like I said, looking for you."

"Not looking for Irv Gittings? He's a fugitive from justice. I'm just a lowly corporate grunt on a toot in China."

"And I'm the President of the United States."

I shrugged. "It's your fantasy. Who am I to quibble?" Personally, anyone who fancied him or herself in the country's highest office was suspect in my book, but I didn't think it helpful to say so.

I found the motorcycle rider's ID in my purse, then slapped it on the table between us. "Well, Mr. President, want to tell me about this guy?"

As I watched him, I could see the wheels turning. A story hatching? The truth was pretty easy; only lies required a story.

"What game are you playing, Stokes?"

"It's not that simple." He leaned back in his chair and crossed his arms. "And I'm not at liberty to say."

I leaned across the table. With a finger, I poked at the photo of the scooter guy. "That man shot at me." I gave him a glance at my shoulder where the blood had dried in the dark crease of the wound. "Came pretty close, too. So, no, he wasn't trying to scare me. And, if folks around here can be trusted, he killed Jhonny Vu with a brick...on the street...in broad daylight. Then he sashayed into *my* hotel, right under your nose."

A bead of sweat trickled down Stokes' temple, catching the light.

I watched it until it disappeared into his hairline. "So, are you going to tell me what's going down, or I'm I going to have to make a stink to get the attention of your superiors?"

A tic worked in his cheek. After a quick glance around— the guy was making me even more paranoid, if that was possible, and I was in my own hotel. He met me in the middle of the table. His nose inches from mine, he lowered his voice.

"Look, I know you're frustrated with my sitting on my thumb, as you would so delicately put it."

"Frustrated?" My voice rose on a wave of anger and incredulity.

He shushed me.

I didn't take it well, but I did as he asked. "People are dying and you're doing nothing."

"The sharks have taken the hook, and I'm letting them run with the line," he said with a look that willed me to understand.

Idioms as a code. None of the folks who could overhear looked like English was their first language, so I got it. They'd never understand our convoluted vernacular.

"Until you know where all the cattle have wandered." Normally, I loved a good turn of phrase. Now they just seemed silly.

"Gotta round them all up."

"Hell of a thing."

He looked like he agreed. "Not my call."

With the knuckle of his forefinger, he pushed the guy's ID back toward me. "Keep this. Memorize his face. If you see him, shoot first."

"Everybody's been telling me the same thing. Different context, but same advice. Besides, that photo won't help much. He doesn't look like that anymore."

"How so?"

"I rearranged his nose with a two-by-two."

He seemed to take that in stride. "Are you sure the guy you assaulted and the guy in the license photo are the same guy?"

That raised my eyebrows. "Come to think of it, I just assumed. It was dark, and I'm not my best when being shot at. Although I am getting a bit more used to it."

Stokes deflated with a grudging grin. "God help me, O'Toole, I can't decide whether I love you or hate you."

"A common problem. I do tend to push either end of that spectrum, leaving not much real estate in the middle." The agent looked a little more relaxed, which made me inclined to at least give a listen to his story.

Tired of perching on the edge of my seat, as it were, I leaned back, claiming my chair. "What do you know about the guy?"

"Muscle for hire." He must've read my look—he held up his hands in a defensive position. "I'm not thinking you're stupid, just confirming what you know."

I pulled out the paper I'd kept from Teddie, smoothing it on the table. "I know this guy. And you do, too. He's killed already, and he'll kill again."

"Unless you stop him. I know where're you're headed, O'Toole, and you'd best not go there."

"I'm going there with or without your help. Your call." I had him; I could see it in the slight slump in his shoulders. Yep, I'd shouldered his burden and he was happy to shift it. Didn't really blame him. He was in a thankless and dangerous position—he wasn't calling the shots, but he and his team were taking the hits. "I can help you, but you've got to help me. Tell me what I don't know."

"Last time I got close to him he was in Vegas."

That shot my eyebrows skyward. "Where in Vegas?"

He folded up the paper as if having it would get us both shot. "Your hotel."

I hid it back in my purse. "My hotel?" Another piece to the puzzle—I could almost see the whole picture...almost. I chewed on my lip as I thought. When I'd seen his picture in the paper Teddie showed me, the guy had looked familiar, but I'd been thinking too small. I needed to widen the aperture on my lens.

"Somebody is playing with us." Now it was my turn to state the obvious. The stars were starting to align. Miss Minnie and Frank were running me, forcing me to do their dirty work, dangling the promise of exculpatory evidence for Teddie. What could it be? Something about the face in the photo—the brick man. "We better do something to shut this whole operation down."

"Not possible." Stokes looked pained.

"What do you mean, 'Not possible'?"

"Gotta let it play out. Let them show their hand."

"Well, Mr. Fed, your hands might be tied, but mine are not."

Now he looked scared. "Don't go messing in my bust."

I really did feel a bit sorry for Stokes—the FBI Ken-doll looked a bit out of his element. Maybe he really was one of the white hats. "Is there anybody who can confirm your story, this whole bust thing you keep talking about?"

"Not to you. I'm buried so deep even Jesus wouldn't vouch for me."

"I figured." I put a bit of distance between us, rolling my chair back so I could stretch my legs.

"Whoever is playing me, and you, for that matter, has his finger on the pulse around here. They were watching you, that's for sure. And they covered their ass if you got lucky." He didn't smile at the pun.

I didn't either. "I'm sorry, Stokes, but I gotta jump in the middle of this. You won't like it, so I'm not going to tell you. Besides, you'd probably arrest me."

Everybody had a story and an angle. Including me.

"Not on your life. Trust me, you don't want to know...not really."

"The last time I saw that look in your eyes, bombs started exploding. You ended up tossing one off the top of your hotel, as I recall."

"An unforgettable moment of sheer panic and stupidity."

"You have that same gleam about you."

What was it about me lately that made me an open book to the males of the species? Whatever it was, I needed to shut it down.

"I'm trying to figure out things just like you, Stokes." Technically, it wasn't a lie. "Poke the beehive, if you will."

"I'm intrigued."

"I won't compromise your position, but, if you'll hang with my friend, Jeremy Whitlock, I think we both will get what we want."

"Whitlock. The PI? He's stand-up."

"You can judge someone by the friends they keep."

"And the enemies they make."

Finally! Some common ground for me and the Fed to bond over.

"You're asking me to trust you."

"My methods might be unusual, but I've never given you reason to doubt my motive."

"No, only your sanity."

"Hell, even I doubt that."

CHAPTER FOURTEEN

I'D left Stokes at the bar pondering the black marks on his soul, or at least doing some serious navel gazing. Maybe he could say penance for a few on my soul as well—I didn't have the time.

Cindy Liu patrolled the hallway in front of a row of high-roller rooms, each one affiliated with a different junket operating under contract with the hotel.

Lately I'd developed a keen appreciation for the minefields my father had had to navigate in the Mob days of early Vegas.

Dressed exactly as she had been a few hours ago, this time Cindy Liu graced me with a smile. "You have a nice time?" Her eyes held joy at my remembered discomfort.

"Once was enough, thank you." The doors to the various rooms contained no markings, at least not that I could tell. "Which one is operated by Panda 777?"

Her carefully drawn-on eyebrows came together in a frown, pinching the alabaster skin between them. "Why you want that one?" She seemed nervous, but weren't we all?

"I'm looking for a friend."

Whatever she was expecting, that wasn't it as her eyebrows shot toward her hairline. "You no find friend in there."

I took her words as a warning. "I'm sure you're right."

Smoke engulfed me as I pushed through the door.

Expecting to find the interior dim with players huddled around tables, I was surprised to find the room well lit, the gamblers, all men, mingling and chatting while they watched others take their turns at the tables.

Teddie was sitting in the lap of a particularly hairy man, probably one of the Russians the wire agent had mentioned. And now I understood how he knew about the guy's body hair—and I knew what had happened to the Quiana shirts that had been in style for a nanosecond in the seventies. This guy had his shirt unbuttoned to his belt—a nauseating display of his hirsute paunch. He clutched Teddie, despite Teddie's efforts to get away.

They both glanced up when I walked in.

How a man treated the help spoke volumes about his character. I leveled a stare at Teddie's captor who, amazingly, reddened then released him. Teddie smoothed his uniform and fought the urge to break the guy's nose—that was easy to read in his scowl and tense posture. Wisely thinking better of it, he sashayed off to work another table.

I watched him for a moment. That man was going to have to teach me how to walk like that, swiveling like three men followed him.

Gloating over my subtle powers of intimidation, I didn't see the man sidle up behind me, but his voice sent shivers down my spine.

"Lucky, Ol' Irv is glad to see you."

Irv Gittings. My skin darn near crawled off and left me as I fought an involuntary shiver of fear and revulsion.

Gittings always referred to himself in the third person, a bit of arrogance I found grating. Even more so today.

How I'd missed his stench I didn't know. I didn't give him the pleasure of seeing the fear in my eyes. Yes, he scared me—and that gave me an advantage, I hoped. In his arrogance, Irv would make a wrong move. I just had to stay alive to catch him in it.

But I knew he wouldn't kill me in my own hotel—that would be brash even for him. No, he'd want me to die sullied in some dark alley...but he'd want me to know he'd arranged it.

I'd already dodged his efforts at least three times.

Nine lives like a cat? I was counting on it.

"Hiding in plain sight, Gittings?"

"Hiding from whom? I have nothing to fear here." He sounded so sure. "Did you like the present I left you?"

I pulled in a sharp breath. "That's a bit bold, even for you."

Holding my arm in a viselike grip just above my elbow, he leaned in close, his lips next to my ear. "She had it coming. Like you."

His breath was putrid, as if something had crawled inside him and died.

"I won't be so easy."

Although his fingers dug into my skin, jangling the nerves, I refused to give him the satisfaction of wincing. He dropped my arm as if he'd received an electrical jolt. "I've just been toying with you."

"Right." I turned to face him. A bit more bloated than I'd seen him in some time, his nose was red, his eyes watery. High stakes took a toll; I should know. Still, he wore a fake tan, a starched button-down with his initials at the cuff, and a pair of light wool slacks with flair—like a Hollywood A-lister long in the tooth and posing as a parody of himself. The hair was the same, as was the cut of the jaw, but where the A-lister understood the joke, Gittings believed the lie. "If you're so big and brave, why don't you just jab a knife in my chest right here, right now?"

He took a step back and pasted on a fake jocularity. "Now, where's the sport in that?" His Adam's apple bobbed as he swallowed hard. "The game here is way over your head."

"Beware the adversary with nothing to lose."

His smile turned mean. "You have everything to lose."

I shrugged. "At some point, you gotta go all in."

"Give it your best shot, but your father isn't here to rescue you."

I wanted to correct him—my father hadn't rescued me since I was fifteen and a drunk patron by the pool had decided I would be a perfect appetizer—but the best way to beat Irv

Gittings at his own game was not to play. But, in a way, Gittings was right. I was out on this tightrope without the net of my father's experience. One step at a time; don't look down. I kept my eyes steady, locked on his. "You came after Minnie." It wasn't a question; it was a bluff.

He recoiled from the verbal slap. A brief flash of nervous, then his mask of contrived cool fell back into place. "What are you talking about?"

"Minnie. She was shot a couple of nights ago. You ordered the hit." If he asked me how I knew, I'd be dead in the water since I was making all this up as I went.

"Don't be silly; I ordered the hit on *you.*" He ran the back of a fingernail over the red gouges on my shoulder. "The fool missed."

Me? On one hand, I was a bit unnerved, but on the other, I was happy I was a big enough stone in his shoe. Although, to be honest, in this game I was irrelevant. So, I didn't believe him for one moment. No, he'd been after Minnie and her rung on Mr. Cho's ladder. "Nice try. When are you going to get it into that empty head of yours that you don't scare me?" *Much.* Yeah, that was a bluff, too. Even I knew a psychopath when I met him...okay, not exactly when I had met him, but I was smart enough to see the wolf under the sheepskin now. And psychopaths scare everybody—like sharks, they are killing machines with no conscience, no remorse, no empathy that might be used to talk them out of it.

"I don't think he missed at all. He hit his target. Minnie's still in ICU. What do you think Mr. Cho would do if he knew you were behind that hit?"

Ol' Irv didn't have an answer to that.

Ignoring a shudder of distaste, I stepped in close so we were nose to nose. "I'll tell you what he'd do. He'd think you were trying to get rid of your competition as you try to worm your way into his organization doing what Minnie has been doing for him for years. She was his. You tried to take her out. They kill for far less here. Your death will be slow and painful."

"If you're going to threaten somebody, you better be damn sure you have the upper hand."

I thought about the knife buried in Kim Cho. I thought about Ming and her assertions. She had proven she could take care of herself, but if Irv got a whiff of her fingering him as the killer, she'd need some help staying alive. I made a mental note. Isn't this about where the Army comes riding over the hill to save the tiny band of settlers from sure slaughter at the hands of the bad guys?

I really needed an army. And it dawned on me that I had one. And I also had a gift standing right there in front of me.

I must've grinned at the thought because Irv looked a little unnerved.

I thought about Minnie and Kim.

And I thought about Frank Cho.

A man who wasn't Kim Cho's brother—he was her lover.

And he'd kill the man who'd killed her.

Even without the rest of my plan falling into place, Irv Gittings was a dead man—he just didn't know it yet.

The trick was staying alive until he was dead.

I cocked my head and gave him the head-to-toe visual undressing he loved to give all the women. "I never thought I'd say this, but I feel kinda sorry for you. You're starting to look like a dead man." I adopted a chatty tone. "Tell you what, why don't I buy you a drink?"

That threw him off. He looked at me, open-mouthed, as if not quite believing that I hadn't dropped to the floor and curled into the fetal position, begging for my life and my hotel.

"No? Well, perhaps another time." Without giving Teddie another look, I pushed past Gittings and out the door.

Back in the hallway, I started breathing again. Of all the bluffs and bullshit I'd shoveled through the years, that ranked at the top. Although it wasn't a bluff exactly, but rather more of a plan just germinating. What had Sinjin said? "It is best to use your enemy's hand to catch a snake"?

I darn near broke my arm patting myself on the back at my cleverness when I thought of Teddie. *Stupid, Lucky, really stupid.* In my need...of what, I didn't know, I'd almost blown his cover. Irv didn't know him and would never recognize him all dolled up as he was. But Irv was enough of a snake to sense my interest in someone or something. Once he did that, he'd go the far reaches of Hell to deprive me of it.

Kim Cho was the latest, and the worst...so far. Losing her hurt my heart. Losing Teddie or Romeo would rip it out and cut it to pieces.

But, I couldn't lock them in a room to keep them safe. They both were grown men...mostly. I had to stop worrying, stop trying to control everything because, if the outcome wasn't what I wanted, I would be eviscerated.

Easy to say, hard to do.

Yeah, I still cared...a lot.

Being a grown-up sucked.

Teddie was in over his head.

And he wasn't the only one.

LAUGHTER came from my room as I put my key in the lock and turned. Whoever they were, they weren't trying to hide, so I wasn't worried. But if Romeo was having a party, I'd shoot him myself. Sleep was at the top of my short list.

I pushed open the door, then just stood there.

Three faces, still red from laughter, turned my way.

Miss P jumped from the couch and rushed over to me. Throwing her arms around my neck, she gave me a bear hug as Romeo and the Beautiful Jeremy Whitlock looked on, smiles splitting their faces.

Too stunned to move, I felt tears, hot and wet, streaming down my face. "What are you doing here?" I managed to stammer. "You need to go home. It's not safe here." My heart's exposure to devastating loss had just doubled.

Miss P pulled back but didn't release me. She thumbed my tears away, keeping ahold of me with one arm. "Aw, honey, you think we'd let you have all the fun?"

She looked radiant, her short golden hair spiked, her cheeks rosy, her lush figure perfectly framed in a just-tight-enough band dress. Barefooted, happy... satisfied...she looked like I wanted to feel. And I loved her anyway.

"You're supposed to be on your honeymoon." Regaining my composure, I gently shifted out of her one-armed embrace. With the heel of my hand, I swiped at my tears.

"You're making it worse." Miss P dabbed at me with a tissue. She lowered her voice. "Have you found Teddie?"

I nodded, narrowly avoiding losing an eye with her dabbing. "He's fine."

She gave me a squeeze, and I turned to include the rest of the group, Jeremy in particular. "Seriously, why are you here? I thought you were lolling about on a beach somewhere in the South Pacific."

"We were," Jeremy said, the hint of happiness still in his voice. "We got bored. Heard you'd gone off like a bucket of prawns in the sun. Thought it'd be a bit more lively, so here we are."

Of course, they were both horrible liars, but I'd never been so happy to see two people in my life. Except having them here terrified me, too.

"Why the tears?" he asked. "We thought you'd be happy to see us." Happiness enhanced his male pulchritude, if that was possible. Golden flecks in dancing brown eyes, a light tint on the ends of his just-long-enough hair only enhanced his babe-magnet qualities. And then there were the dimples and the Australian accent...oh, and the muscled perfection on the long and lean frame. Fifteen years younger than his bride, he was totally besotted, which made him truly the handsomest man alive.

"You have no idea." I burst into tears anew.

Miss P pressed a glass of bubbles into my hand then led me over to the couch, where Jeremy and Romeo made a place between them.

Romeo looked a bit unnerved. "I didn't know you cried. I've never seen you."

"Never let them see you cry." I gave him a waterlogged grin. "Bad for that badass street cred. Apparently, I'm not as badass as I'd hoped."

"Well, you scare the shit out of me." Romeo looked serious.

There were murmurs of agreement all around. I couldn't tell whether they meant it or were just trying to make me feel good.

Miss P settled in a chair across from the three of us. I studied their faces, each of them, and fought back my tears. Such great friends, ready to ride into hell at my side, armed with nothing more than a damp cloth and a loose plan. Which was a good thing, since that's what we were doing and that's all we had.

"I had no idea how I was going to pull this off by myself."

"Neither did we," Miss P said, adding a note of home, which settled me. "Aren't you the one always preaching to us that we are only as good as the team?"

"Yes, but this is different." I sipped my Champagne and settled my thoughts. "Much more dangerous, much more at stake." I thought I'd keep the whole saving the Babylon thing out of it. After I drained my glass, I waved off a refill. Leaning forward, elbows on my knees, I tried to figure out where to begin. "I am working on a sting. One that will bring down Mr. Cho and his colleagues who have been running Macau like the Mob ran Vegas."

"A sting, you say?" A light sparked in Jeremy's eyes. "What's the bait?"

"Well, maybe a bait and switch is more accurate. The watches in the exhibit downstairs."

His reaction, and that of his bride, to my little shock-bomb were Kodak moments. "All of them?" Miss P asked.

"That's the goal."

"And how are you going to do this?" Jeremy still looked skeptical.

I told them a bit about Sinjin. "Romeo is going to be his bag man."

"Righteous." Jeremy gave the kid a welcome-to-the-club

DEBORAH COONTS

look. I hoped he wouldn't follow it with a secret handshake. He didn't. Instead, he pulled his laptop from the knapsack at his feet. "Kim Cho's brother, you say?"

"Yep, another male claiming blood relations with Kim Cho. Either Mr. Cho sowed his seed far and wide or somebody's lying."

"Let's take a look." He fired up the machine.

"Don't you need the password for the Wi-Fi?"

His eyes never left the small screen as his fingers flew over the keys. "Every hotel does the same thing: room number and last name. So easy to hack into the system it's criminal."

I'm not sure anyone but me got the irony. "Still, you need the right combination."

"Stand down near reception and listen."

"But they are trained not to speak room numbers." Even as I said the words, I knew the truth.

"Yes, and often it is the guest who verbally confirms the room number."

"You're not making me feel better."

Without looking at me, he gave me a quick flash of dimples. As Jeremy worked, I poured that last drop of Champagne into a flute then threw it back. Not a proud moment, but I was over worrying about that.

Ah," Jeremy said after what seemed an eternity. "Unless he's gone to a lot of trouble to fabricate a lineage, he's telling the truth."

"But he said he was adopted."

"True. Open adoption records."

Why couldn't everything be that easy? "We don't have time to thoroughly run him, but anything odd leap out at you?"

"Not offhand. You're going to have to go with the gut. And, if memory serves, yours is fairly reliable."

"When I don't overthink it, and this is one of those times. I need your help." I looked around the group bringing everyone into that request.

Jeremy speared me with those eyes, but he kept the dimples hidden. "So your first instinct is to trust this guy?

206

This *pirate.*" He threw off the word with a scoff. "I mean, seriously. Pirate?"

"It's worse; he's also a hedge-fund manager. I know neither of those things exactly screams trustworthy. But he's only slightly nudged my bullshit meter. He's got an agenda, but as long as we know what it is, we can figure out how much rope to let him run with." Ah, the clichés were back! Yes, I was more myself huddled in the bosom of my chosen family, such as it were. "Desperate times and all of that."

"Your fallback for making gut decisions on the fly," Miss P said.

This time it was easy to tell she was teasing.

"Just watch yourself." Jeremy looked like he thought I was a step or two down that road.

Guess he didn't understand I was dead last on my worry list.

Jeremy folded up his computer and gave me his full attention. "What plan do you have for the watches?"

Miss P bounced around on the edge of the couch like that irritating girl in my fifth-grade class who waved her hand almost before the teacher posited a question.

I ignored her. "Sinjin is going to steal them."

Miss P deflated.

Jeremy, to his credit, took my little bombshell with only a slight flinch. "And he told you that?"

Romeo, his hands crossed across his belly, his feet on the priceless antique table, gloated a bit. He hadn't taken off his shoes, which was a good thing/bad thing sort of...thing. Scratch the furniture or leave a stink so bad the place would need to be fumigated when we left? I was conflicted.

"You're no Robert Redford," I said to the young detective with no apparent effect.

He gave me a blank stare.

"The Sting?"

He shrugged. "Stuff happened before my time. I'm pretty young and you're—"

"—experienced." I gave him the slitty-eye, which shut him

up but didn't dim his grin.

So I turned back to Jeremy's question. "I had to sweeten the pot a little."

"This is going to be good." Jeremy laced his fingers together behind his head and leaned back.

"I told him we'd help him."

Nobody looked stunned. Tough crowd. Clearly, I was losing my crazy...or they were getting used to it.

"Jeremy, I need you to dog Stokes. Tell him enough to keep him on our side, but not enough that he'll stroke out."

"The FBI dude? Piece of piss." His grin and nod told me that meant yes. His wife gave him a raised eyebrow and he shrugged. "To be able to catch a criminal, it helps to have been one...or at least acted like one." Turning back to me, he wiped his smile. "But why don't we just lose him, send him off chasing ghosts or something?"

"I'd love to, but he's the only one with any authority from the good ol' U. S. of A. Once I get the goods on Gittings, I'm going to need the Fed to bag him along with the other players."

"Other players?"

"I plan on really shaking the trees around here. I bet a lot of bad apples will fall out—in fact, I'm counting on it." I didn't mention Teddie's freedom was the sword of Damocles hanging over my head. That burden was mine alone.

"Sounds like fun."

I wasn't sure I agreed, but there was a sort of satisfaction in exacting revenge in a large and painful way.

Miss P gave her hubby a bright smile, which dimmed when she turned it my direction. I seemed to be having that effect on a lot of folks these days. "And me?" she asked me.

"I need you to work with Cindy Liu, the head of customer service at this hotel. You remember her? We worked with her during the run-up to the opening."

"All business. I remember. What's going on with her?"

"Ryan Whitmore is the Head of Operations. I knew him back in the day." I didn't feel the need to explain. "He's got as much slick as anyone I know—and just a tad shy of Ol' Irv's mastery. I don't trust him. And Cindy Liu seems a bit tight with him. I don't have any proof, just a gut feeling. If Ryan turns out to fall in with the wrong team, I'm not sure what Cindy Liu will do."

"She doesn't strike me as the kind who'd compromise herself for a man."

"I've known good women with a weak spot when it came to a cad." Been there, done that, bought that T-shirt. We all probably had, but this wasn't the time to bond through the sharing of our prior stupidities. "But, for the record, I agree with you—I have a feeling she'll help us, if it comes to that. She's helped me already. But this is too important to leave the outcome resting on a hunch that she won't betray us."

If I didn't learn from my own stupidities, then that made me a fool, and I was trying very hard not to be one. Should I fail, this time undoubtedly would be my last.

"What do you want me to do?"

"Shadow her. I'll tell her it was my idea—a way for us to improve our own customer service or something like that. On second thought, I'll set it up. Would be fun to light a fire under her, see what she does." I didn't need to give Miss P any more details—she knew what I wanted.

"A corporate spy." Her voice held a reverence unbefitting of the danger.

I opened my mouth to begin that lecture. Instead, I pulled my shirt aside enough to show the top of my shoulder and two dark grooves in my skin. "They've shot at me twice, once in Vegas and once here. This is how close they came. I wouldn't count on them missing again."

My point hit home, sobering up my little band of Merry Men.

A key scratched in the door, and we all turned like felons caught in the vault. Teddie, still in disguise, strolled through, then stopped short at all of us looking at him. For a moment, life froze, then everyone but me jumped to their feet, and hugs and backslapping happened all around.

Once the merriment died down and Teddie had pulled up a chair next to Miss P's and received his own flute of bubbles, I brought him quickly up to speed.

He didn't argue with the plan. "What do you want me to do?"

"You have the most important job of all. Deliver Irv Gittings."

"In what way?"

"I need to know how I can make it look like he's the one behind all this. Where he is keeping funds, who he is manipulating, sleeping with, anything that I can use. He's new here, new to this game. Get me something I can use." Not much to go on, but Teddie was good at playing the angles. He could figure it out.

Paleness lurked under all the pancake, and I couldn't shake the feeling that I was tossing a small rodent in the case with a boa constrictor.

"I think I've already got a line on some of that. I got your message—using Ming as your messenger was a good call. She found me leaving the junket rooms, just getting off my shift. We were able to talk out of sight." At the look on my face he raised a finger, silencing me. "And out of earshot and visibility of the security system. Nobody saw us together. I jumped on it, and Ming is pulling it together. I'll know shortly what we've got."

"Ming?" Romeo asked.

I explained for the group, covering even the part where she hit me over the head.

Romeo whistled. "You met her? Like, actually were in her presence and fully functional?"

Fully functional was a stretch, but I didn't say so. "Didn't I just say that?"

"And you let her live?"

"Recruiting her to the team seemed more important." I skewered him with reality. "This battle is a gloves-off, no rules, fight to the death. Ego has no place."

For a fleeting moment, as I looked at their faces, I saw a glimmer of hope that we could actually pull this off and not end up rotting in a prison no one knew about and whose name no one could pronounce. The thought was fleeting.

"Is there anything we need to be doing right now?" Jeremy asked with false enthusiasm betrayed by his bloodshot eyes.

"It's late. Miss Liu has gone off shift. Ryan Whitmore has the night shift, so he won't be going far. I need to talk with some folks and come up with a plan. Get a few hours of shut-eye."

"And what's our part in the plan, as you see it now?" Romeo asked me, clearly worried I might do something stupid.

Too late for that.

"I will follow the money and I will follow the watches. With your help, and the help of a friend of Mona's, I will make sure Irv Gittings is left holding the bag."

Everyone raised a glass to that.

Mine was empty.

I ARRANGED for a couple more of the adjoining rooms to be opened to my suite and sent Romeo to fetch the keys. While we waited for him, the energy slowly drained from my band of Happy Homicidal Helpers. When he returned, he handed the keys out like a scoutmaster organizing his troop. Miss P accepted hers with a tired sigh. Corralling her new husband, they wandered off in search of privacy and perhaps sleep, although it was anybody's guess which time zone their bodies thought they were in.

Romeo shifted around a bit, staring out the windows. I shouldered in next to him, sharing his view. "You okay?"

"Yeah. I've always wanted to do this kind of thing. That's why I joined the force. Until I met you, I was Reynolds's grunt."

"Reynolds! I'd forgotten about him. What's he up to these days?"

"Working for me mostly." Romeo drank in the sites.

For the first time, I noticed he looked older and wiser, like he carried his world with confidence.

"How come you picked working with me over Reynolds? He had all the experience."

"And you had all the talent."

"You could see that even then?"

"As you said, I'm—"

"—experienced." He gave me a smile that could hold the world. "Couldn't have done it without you."

"Sure you could. I just accelerated your trip up the learning curve." I turned to face him. "Care to learn a new skill?"

He gave me that look—half puppy-dog-eager-to-please and half give-me-a- gun-and-tell-me-who-to-shoot—the look that had won my complicity in the first place.

"Good. This time, *you* have *my* back. You'll need to roll in Jeremy. You got your notebook?"

He pulled it out of his pocket, flipped it open, and held his pencil at the ready.

"Good. Here are the things you'll need."

TEDDIE had let Romeo and me plot and plan, remaining rooted to his chair. When I returned, settling in to my comfortable indentation in the couch, he looked like he'd been dozing. "Hungry?" he asked, one eye open.

"Let's just eat out of the mini bar." Jet lag had me guessing as to what time it was, what day it was, then I realized I didn't much want to know. We had a down moment, time to refresh.

Surprisingly, one could make a rather elegant cheese and cracker tray, with some salted nuts, but I drew the line at dried sea creatures and the jarred fermented weeds—I didn't care what sea they were from or what health benefits they promised.

LUCKY THE HARD WAY

Teddie silently chided me with a wry grin I had no trouble reading.

"I'm adventurous in every way except food," I said a bit defensively, even though he already knew that about me.

"One of your many charms." His smile lacked its normal wattage.

As a pale imitation of my vibrant self, I so got that. "Do you have to stay made-up like Mata Hari?"

We both knew the answer. I didn't know why I asked.

"I can't stay too long. Someone is bound to get wise."

"This floor should be above interest."

"You really believe that?" He gave me a look I recognized, despite the overdone eyeliner and the blue eye shadow.

"No." I wanted him to stay, and I hated myself for it. I shrugged off the need. "Have you seen Cho?"

"Briefly. He keeps a low profile. "He and Gittings had a little *tête-à-tête*. What do you think Ol' Irv's angle is?"

"I've been thinking about that." I plucked a cube of yellow cheese, hoping for cheddar. I took a bite. Close. Feeling somewhat civilized, I popped the rest in my mouth, followed by a bite of a water cracker, and then washed it all down with a sip of New Zealand Sauvignon Blanc.

Even though the river of dirty cash into Macau had evaporated down to a trickle, I bet I still knew Irv's angle. Really, it was the only one he had. "It would seem that the bit of the money funnel that might be hard for Cho to fill would be the foreign investor—the one who takes the laundered funds and buys real estate or some other blue-chip investment, through a dizzying maze of shell corporations and limited partnerships, of course. Now that Minnie is out of the picture." Another bit of bad business with Irv Gittings' M.O. all over it, but I didn't have the time nor the inclination to prove it. He'd given our judicial system the slip. Now it was time to tie the noose around his neck in a way he couldn't slip out of.

"Irv is a master of shell games," Teddie mumbled, his mouth full of fermented something. After swallowing, he gave me a grin, one of the green things wedged between his front teeth.

Feeling all passive-aggressive, I didn't tell him. "I see you've kept your flair for the obvious."

"Wouldn't want to disappoint." His smile fled as he laid his fork with concentrated precision on the plate in front of him, lining it up perfectly. When he looked at me again, I saw the Teddie I used to know in his eyes. "I'm sorry I hurt you. I never meant to. I wish I could show you what I've learned."

"I've moved on." My voice sounded steady, but my insides were jelly.

"It took losing you to realize that you meant everything."

He was saying all the right things, but I didn't believe him. And even if he was telling the truth, I didn't have the energy to teach him all the other lessons he didn't know. He still played at being a grown-up.

And, with everything and everyone riding on my shoulders, I'd stopped playing and had become one.

How I wanted to go back to the first kiss when I'd been as ignorant about life and love as Teddie still was. Such fun it was when nothing else mattered and the Big Boss was my life preserver in the tempest of life.

Teddie shook his head as if he'd been waiting for me to say something. I saw the pain on his face—I'd felt that pain when he left me for the wan little pop star. Nonetheless, I felt like a heel for causing his.

But I'd moved on. I reached across and took his hand in mine. "I'll always be here."

"Not the same." He gave me a weak smile, then pulled his hand from mine.

His touch still affected me. A warmth rather than a sizzle, but a connection solid and true. "Better than nothing, and I'm not sure you deserve it."

"True." He didn't say he hadn't slept with her; he didn't lie, and that told me he'd learned something. "So, what's next?"

As if answering his question, his phone rang—a personalized ringtone. A snippet of a song he'd written for me.

Really? Running for his life and he'd made sure that song sang when his phone rang? Even though my head didn't know what to make of that, my heart did.

Teddie let it ring. When it stopped, he started counting. Exactly when he got to ten, it started ringing again. He looked at me with a grim smile. "We need to go. The girls are ready."

CHAPTER FIFTEEN

TEDDIE didn't take me back to the center of town to the whorehouse. Surprising me, he led me to a small car parked around the corner from the hotel. He bent to unlock what I normally would think of as the driver's door for me. "One of the girls lent me this. It's a big thing to own a car here."

I folded myself into the tight space and tried not to worry about Teddie's right-hand driving skills. "With everybody gunning for me, what if I died in a car accident? How ironic would that be?"

Teddie ignored me as he settled behind the wheel and fired up the engine.

Unable to keep still, I flapped my mouth. "You do know where we're going, right? Give me the address; I can plug it into my phone." With one knee bouncing, I balanced my Birkin on the other and rooted for my phone.

"Stop worrying. When you fidget and blather like that, you make me nervous. I know where I'm going," he said with confidence, then added, "sort of," eroding mine.

"Seriously, Siri can help."

He looked over his shoulder, then pulled away from the curb. "I'm not used to this, so don't distract me."

A clever way to tell me to shut up. Getting lost sounded better than bent metal and possible bloodshed, so I let him have his way. He only scared me twice as we wound our way through the narrow streets. The traffic was light, but the trucks were starting to move with their early morning deliveries. One street we tried was completely blocked. Backing up was even more terrifying than going forward, so I stared straight ahead and braced against an abrupt stop.

It didn't come, and soon we were motoring on. "Siri?"

"Almost there."

The buildings gave way to a park, and we parked at the entrance, stopped by a closed gate. "We'll hoof it the rest of the way." Teddie didn't seem worried about heading into a dark forest, but I understood why he'd traded his stilettos for something more reasonable—Gucci sneakers.

From afar, the chain securing the gate looked locked. Teddie gave the padlock a twist and it opened easily. After letting us both through, he replaced the lock as he'd found it.

I kept pace with him as he started up the hill. Darkness closed around us, and I felt creepy things in the shadows—just like Halloween when I was a kid. Nothing was there, but my imagination loved to terrorize me. Was it only me, or did that happen to everyone? I'd never asked—apparently that little bit of truth would be too traumatizing. Something rustled in the dark. I reached for Teddie's arm, then stopped myself before I'd made contact.

"Are you scared?"

I nodded even though somewhere in my terrorized synapses, I knew he couldn't see me that well.

"Didn't you do scouting when you were a kid?" Teddie acted like he did this sort of accessory-after-the-fact-thing all the time—technically we were breaking and entering since the park was not technically open.

I tried to take it all in stride—breaking and entering was one of the lesser felonies I was contemplating. "I had a short and inglorious career as a Brownie."

He set a fast pace into the dark. "Somehow I knew that. What'd you do? Break someone's nose? Set a fire? Beat your leader at arm wrestling?"

"They took us to a place with trees, lots of trees. Like this."

I felt them closing in, looming over me, and the childhood panic returned. Once again, I reached for Teddie's arm—this time I held on. "Growing up in Pahrump, in the middle of the Mojave, I wasn't used to trees and not being able to see for a hundred miles in any direction. I got separated from the group. I didn't know where I was, and I couldn't find my way out."

Teddie patted my hand on his arm, but didn't slow down. "How old were you?"

"Seven, maybe eight."

"I bet you were scared."

"The forest was like this one." My mouth went dry with fear; my heart pounded. Something sweet perfumed the air. A soft breeze tickled the branches like wraiths whispering. "I was terrified." Unable to help myself, I clutched his arm so tightly I was sure I'd break bone.

He didn't flinch. "What'd you do?"

"I followed the trail we'd come up."

"There you go." Teddie pointed in front of our feet. "That's all I'm doing here."

My thoughts had been so rusted by fear I hadn't even noticed the small path we followed. The moonlight wasn't enough to expose us, but it let us see just far enough ahead to stay on track. I could do this. Although I wasn't comfortable enough to let go, I relaxed my grip on Teddie's arm. I'm sure he appreciated the return of blood flow.

He flexed his fingers. "We're almost there. One of the girls knows the guy with the key. She took it off him last night. No one will be here. No cameras either—it's not like an old fort is high on the list of places to break into."

"Women." And I didn't bother to point out we'd broken in.

"What?"

"Women. Calling us girls is derogatory. You'd be insulted if someone called you a boy, wouldn't you? They...we...are women. Young women. More mature women. But all of us women. Not girls."

"I didn't think about it, sorry."

"Men are used to talking down to women, underestimating us." I clamped my mouth shut. What was it with me today? I knew; I just didn't want to admit it. The whorehouses the world over, the children forced to work in them, women doing whatever they could to survive.

Men like Cho.

"Let's get these bastards," I whispered, imploring the demons that lurked in the dark.

We rounded a bend and the trees thinned. The remnants of stone walls loomed above us. The path gave way to rough cobblestone. "What is this place?"

"The old fort built by the Portuguese to defend the island. Never saw much action, although a priest, vastly outnumbered when the Danish showed up to take the island, accidentally fired one of the cannons and blew the ammunition ship and half the fleet into the next life."

"Maybe his ghost will help us. We certainly need to tap into that kind of luck or divine intervention, whatever you want to call it."

Teddie moved to our right. "Over here."

Five women gathered around one of the canons that pointed toward one of the larger casinos in old town—I loved the irony. The lights from town illuminated each face as the women turned at our approach. Various ages, all looking serious, Ming one among the five. I'd asked for the best.

I released Teddie, and he joined the women, all eyes turning to me.

With a few flicks across my phone's screen, I pulled up a picture of Irv Gittings. "Here." I handed my phone to Ming, who stood nearest to me. "Pass this around. Each of you memorize this face. And put your phone numbers in there as well with your name, or, if you aren't comfortable with me knowing that, give me something to call you." I waited until my phone had made the rounds and the last young woman handed it back to me. Afraid I might turn to stone, I closed the photo without looking at it. "I need to know where he goes, who he talks to. I want to know when he eats, when he goes to the bathroom, who he sleeps with, and where he stays. Who his friends are and who wants to see him dead, besides me."

Their expressions intent, no one backed down.

"This is very dangerous. If you are afraid, please walk away now. This man," I held up my phone, the screen dark, but they knew, "he is a killer. I know you all work the hotel in teams and you communicate via cell phone." The women who worked the Babylon did the same thing—tag-teaming their mark. Watching for a man with money to spare and either a win to celebrate or a loss to commiserate.

Once again, I powered up my phone and pulled up my own phone number. "We'll coordinate through my phone." I checked to make sure their names were in the call list. "You all have my phone number?"

Teddie shot me a look. I knew what he was thinking. At some point, I might have to hand over my phone to someone else to run this part of the operation, and I'd be flying solo. As long as I had Irv Gittings in the crosshairs, I wouldn't care.

"Wait," he said. "Let's coordinate through my phone." He didn't wait for me to argue; instead, he cut me off. "I work with these women," he said to me. "I live with them. It makes sense. Besides, you have bigger fish to fry. I'll be your backup."

The ladies nodded. No one asked for his number—it seemed they already had it. The guy knew how to work a crowd. I wasn't sure how I felt about that, especially in this context. His track record with women hadn't left me in a happy place, so my skepticism was well earned.

"Okay," I shifted to take in everyone. "But if you can't get through to Teddie or he doesn't answer, then come right to me. You got it? And I might reach out to you directly."

There were nods all around as each woman in turn programmed my number into her own phone.

"When do you want us to start reporting, Miss?" a young woman, the smallest of the group, asked. She had a fierceness about her that I responded to—a fellow warrior.

"As soon as possible. The next thirty-six hours are critical. And call me Lucky." I raised my gaze to include everyone. "All of you. We are in this together."

"I'll be in the Panda 777 junket room," Teddie said. "If any of you need help, find me. Don't worry about anything at that point other than your safety."

"And I'll be in the hotel, not sure where, but I'll have my phone. If I'm not close, I can get help to you quickly." I scanned the group, memorizing faces, and trying to step on my fear. If any one of these women got burned and we didn't succeed, they would pay the price...or their families would.

They'd been warned; yet here they were.

As I looked at them, absorbing their bravery, their spirit, I was humbled. And horrified, wishing upon all that I loved that I could do this myself and not involve anyone.

Not gonna happen. And, in a way, we were all fighting for futures that were better than our presents. I had to let go and just be grateful.

"Any questions?" I could see a few in their faces, but no one asked anything.

Then one woman in the back spoke up. "You get rid of Mr. Cho?" Her face was closed, her expression serious.

We hadn't talked about Mr. Cho. As a local, he had friends, even among the women, I'd bet. Through my life, I'd met many women who still worshiped at the altar of men who abused them. Didn't understand it, never would, but I understood it was real.

So it was anybody's guess as to the answer she wanted. I thought I knew, but only one way to find out. Any one of these women could sell us out—best to weed out the bad seeds now. I leapt into the abyss. "Yes."

A moment for that to sink in, then smiles split faces all around.

Okay. I gave myself a moment as I bowed to them. Nothing better than a plan coming together and wishes granted.

I had my army.

Ming gathered the women tighter, talking low to them in their local lingo. I started to bristle, then she turned to me. "My apologies. I know this is not nice. We said a quick prayer,

221

a warrior's prayer. I don't know the exact words in English—it is an old prayer, old words." She pulled her gang closer even still. "We are ready."

And she was their leader, the one they trusted.

So noted.

With kisses all around, which took a bit as here they did the European two-for-one thing, not that I was complaining, then the women filtered into the night, each choosing her own route out through the deepening darkness.

The darkest hours came right before dawn.

"Shall we?" I asked Teddie. Gesturing grandly toward the path, I made a show of bravery as I girded my loins to tackle the forest.

"Follow the path," he said like a New Age mystic.

My Galahad, he offered me his arm. This time I didn't hold onto him quite as tightly. By my calculations, we'd made it halfway to safety and sanity when a figure materialized in front of us shattering any hopes I had of both.

Teddie and I stopped, but the expletive was all mine. "Shit!"

Thin and lithe, the outline didn't look menacing. But somewhere in my past, someone had told me to make myself big when facing a threat in the forest. So I did...not that hard, really. To everyone on this spit of land, I was big already.

"That's for a bear," Teddie hissed.

"Not helping."

The figure stepped closer. A young woman. I recognized her. One of my vast army. Stars whirled through my vision, then I remembered to breathe. If I lived through this adventure, I'd be two decades older and Jean-Charles would throw me over for a younger model.

"Miss Lucky."

I didn't correct her. "Yes."

"I can tell you some things about that man. The other women, my friends, I didn't want to say it in front of them." She hung her head.

With a finger under her chin, I lifted her eyes to mine. "All

222

of us have done things we aren't proud of, but we have nothing to be ashamed of. You understand?"

Her features relaxed and I could see how stunningly beautiful she was. "Yes, Miss...Lucky." She glanced at Teddie.

He took the hint and moved away.

"That man?" she began.

"Mr. Gittings?"

"Yes. The night he arrived with Mr. Cho." She hesitated, licking her lips. "He bought me for the night. Big money. You understand?"

"Of course."

"He was..." She searched for the words.

I waited. She was clearly nervous, and something else. Angry? Yes, angry. That was the key to her escape.

"He was nervous, yet excited, wild almost. There was blood on him." She ducked her head for a moment. When she looked at me again, her eyes were bright with tears. "Kim's blood. I didn't know that then. He had paid. I..." She swallowed hard, but her gaze didn't leave mine, instead holding it steady, her head high.

"You are very brave to tell me these things. What was Kim to you?"

"Kim taught us we could get out. We could be lawyers, or corporate executives like you, or anything else we wanted to be."

And you could end up dead.

We both thought the same thought—I could see it in her face—but we didn't say it. In this world, this time, with all the possibilities, I still seethed that there were women who had to pay with their life to chase their dreams. Changing that was a dangerous game.

"Where did you meet Gittings? In the hotel?"

"No, there is an apartment in the hotel next door. Very fancy. He stays there. Miss Liu said it was okay to tell you, that we can trust you."

"Who owns it, do you know?"

Her brows furrowed. "You do." I must've looked shocked

as she clarified. "Your hotel does. Mr. Whitmore buys many of us for his special clients who stay there."

"I didn't know. Thank you."

She bowed her head. "There is one other thing. I don't know if it's important."

"It's all important."

"That night, a man came. Very late. He had something for your Mr. Gittings."

I wanted to correct her: he wasn't *my* Mr. Gittings. Instead, I bit my tongue, as difficult as it was.

"He brought a package." Her posture stiffened, and she wrung her hands.

I resisted the urge to tell her it would be okay, that she was safe. I couldn't guarantee that, and it infuriated me. "Did you know the man?"

She shook her head. "I only saw a little bit. And the package, it was wrapped in silk."

Intrigued, I couldn't imagine what it was that was so important she seemed afraid to breathe the words.

"It was the knife."

I lowered my voice to a whisper, I don't know why—reverence, for sure. Fear? Maybe. "The knife?"

"The one he used to kill Kim Cho."

"He told you this?"

"He bragged about it."

"Anything else he bragged about?"

She licked her lips and she looked distressed, shaking her head as if in disbelief. "I don't know what to think."

I flicked a glance at Teddie. He was getting antsy; I didn't blame him. Being caught in a closed park would not help our cause. I tried to ignore him and my growing nervousness. The girl had something to say, something important, and I didn't want to shut her down by rushing her.

"He bragged about an account he opened with Kim's brother." Her words tumbled and rushed as if she spoke blasphemy.

224

"Sinjin?"

She nodded sharply.

"I'm sure he has a good explanation. Don't rush to judge. It is a very complex game we are playing." I could see a gambit Sinjin might be setting in motion, but dang, why hadn't he told me? Secrets eroded confidence. I should know—that was my game.

I closed the distance between the girl and myself and put a hand on her arm. "What's your name?"

"Pei." Her smile wavered.

"Thank you. I won't betray you and I won't disappoint you." There I went again, promising things I wasn't sure I could deliver.

But I knew one thing; if I failed to deliver, I'd die trying.

LOST in thought, Teddie and I had ridden halfway back to the hotel when he broke the silence. "I didn't know you were afraid of the forest," Teddie said with a large dose of serious, which I appreciated.

Wound tighter than a spring, I couldn't be responsible for what I might do to the next person who gave me a hard time, even in jest. My need to hit somebody probably radiated off me in waves, like one of those machines in grade school that generated electricity and made your hair stand out when you put your hand on the thing. Yeah, I was that machine, but set higher than stun and closer to lethal. Big talker, I know—false courage, but courage nonetheless. "I'm afraid of a lot of things."

"But you always seem so confident, so sure."

"A good act. Life is about courage. And courage is being able to move forward in spite of your fear."

"You got any to spare?"

"You have enough. Maybe that's what all this is meant to

teach you."

Both hands on the wheel, he actually turned and stared at me long enough to have me twitching. "You're driving." I pointed out the window, emphasizing the obvious. "Pay attention."

"For a minute, I thought you'd disappeared and gone all Confucius on me."

I relaxed back and looked out the window. "Everyone has something to teach you. Everyone and every experience." Without the focus of driving, I usually passed the time as a passenger in sort of a fugue state, watching the scenery roll past but not really seeing. Finally, I focused. "Pull over!"

"What?" Teddie jerked the wheel, bumping a tire up the curb as he braked.

"Give me five minutes?"

Bending over the steering wheel, he stared out at the small park, dark and foreboding. "If you need to pee, the hotel is less than ten minutes. More like five. I'm sure you can hold it that long."

"I need to see a man about a watch."

"In there?" He put the car into park. "I need to come with you."

"Yes, you're very intimidating in your blonde wig and short skirt."

"It's the heavy eyeliner that gets them." He shot me his best narrow-eyed look.

I wish I didn't like him; it would make things so much easier. "Give me five. I'll be right back."

I was as good as my word. Five minutes later and I slipped back into the car.

Teddie eased away from the curb, then angled a glance at me as if he could divine where I'd been and what I'd been doing just by looking. "Want to tell me what that was about?"

"Insurance."

"You need to tell me," he insisted.

I swiveled around until I could face him—hard to do with my knees jammed against the glove box. "No. No, I don't. My game, my rules." No more letting others shoot me around the table of life in a game of emotional billiards. "I've got this. And, if I can pull it off, then everyone will get what they asked for for Christmas."

He arrowed a glance my way. Easy to read.

"Yes, even you." If Minnie lived or I got Frank alone in a room with a water board. I didn't tell him that part, of course.

Sometimes, you just have to believe.

And Christmas was the season of faith, wasn't it?

Teddie didn't say any more, which told me he had faith in me.

Frankly, I didn't know whether to be touched or irritated. How much longer would I carry Teddie before he learned to shoulder his own weight? The realization that that was really up to me smacked me right between the eyes.

If I didn't do the heavy lifting, then he'd have to choose to lift it or not. I'd been waiting for him to grow up, but I'd been toting his load. And he'd been content to let me carry it.

And therein lay the rub.

How can you love a man when he won't act like one?

After pulling to the curb around the corner from the hotel, he shifted into park, but left the engine running. "I've got to get the car back."

"Sure." I touched his cheek. "Hard to let you go. At least when you're with me, I know you're safe."

"I know the feeling. I'll run interference with the women," he said, as he stepped out of the car.

Walking around, he opened my door.

"You're in the best position to do that." I took his hand and let him pull me out of the tiny car. Wedged in, I appreciated the help

If he was surprised at my capitulation, he didn't show it.

"Give me a chink in Ol' Irv's armor. Anything. I'll work on capitalizing on it. Until then, watch him, see if you can tell who his inner circle is, where he goes, who he talks to, who he sleeps with. Anything you see, anything at all, no matter how trivial, write it down, remember it, whatever, but tell me about it. I need to get a bead on how he's plying his sleaze here."

"Okay." Teddie leaned down to push the door shut. His legs were still better than mine, which didn't bother me as much as it used to. And he wore his five-inch Lou-bous as if they were extensions. Now *that* was a pisser. Yes, he'd abandoned his kicks in the car and redonned the glam. "You're quite the girly-girl."

"Playing the part. Staying alive."

"Good point." I nodded toward his shoes. "I see you've traded up from my Manolos. Where'd you get those?"

"The girls...women." Clearly, Teddie enjoyed living in a sorority of whores.

I never liked that term much, but for lack of a better one, Mona had taught me it was okay to use it...with the right reverence, of course.

"Don't stretch them out. You know how we women hate our men to do that."

He gave me a saucy flip of his wig, then sashayed around to his side of the car, disappearing inside. The door shut, then he shifted into gear and pulled away from the curb.

"And be careful," I whispered after him.

CHAPTER SIXTEEN

"OH, Lucky, I know you're mad at me. I can't stand you being mad at me. Not right now." Mona rushed into the conversation without a hello, not that that was unusual, especially when she was in trouble.

I took her phone call in an alcove off the lobby.

"The staff has been great," she breathlessly informed me, as if I didn't already know. "And we're really close to getting the billing thing worked out. A bottle of Cristal for two dollars, a Kasbah bungalow for ninety-nine dollars a night, it's a bit of a mess, I'm afraid." She sounded contrite, and a bit frantic—so unlike her.

"Maybe someday you'll learn not to interfere." A pipe dream if there ever was one. Mona was hardwired to meddle.

Lost in worry over Teddie, I'd answered the phone without thinking, and without looking. I knew better. I didn't need enemies when I had myself as a friend. "Mother, this is not the time. Keep telling me about problems you created that I can't solve and I might reach through the phone line and strangle you myself."

"Oh, Lucky, don't be silly," she said, using her Marilyn Monroe voice. "We're talking on the cell." Her voice had that feigned I'm-too-stupid-to-live tone.

"Wrong audience for that gambit, Mother. I know your game. I also know I don't have to explain the word euphemism to you." I'd had a few hours of fitful sleep while waiting for the time difference window to open so I could call her at a respectable hour, if not a decent one, and I was running at redline. Worse, she'd beaten me to the punch, catching me flat-footed. "Mother, would you like a get-out-of-jail-free card?"

"Really?" Wariness crept into her tone.

"Do I sound like I'm joking?"

"No, you sound like you're still mad, but lately you always sound like that."

Was part of being an adult feeling like you were alone in the world? "Mother."

"You really mean it? You'll stop being mad at me? That would be wonderful. I just can't have you being mad at me..." Again, her voice trailed away, this time riding on that hint of an emotion I couldn't read. "What do I have to do?"

"Nothing, really. I heard you have one of the hacker boys eating out of your hand."

"Chip." Even in that single syllable I could hear a preen. Mother defined herself through the adulation of men. One day she'd have a rude awakening, but so far she still had her magic...whatever it was. That part of familial DNA alchemy had sailed without me.

They say daughters inherit more traits from their fathers than their mothers—one bullet missed, a whole host of others dodged.

"Chip." A computer geek with that name—either fortuitous or inevitable. I wondered which. "Does he have skills?"

Mona drew in a sharp breath. "Lucky! How dare you insinuate—"

I pinched the bridge of my nose hard to keep the amusement out of my voice. Mother could bat me around like a tennis ball, pinging between anger and amusement. "Computer skills mother."

"Oh, well, yes...of course." In my imagination, I could see her pull herself up—feigned righteous indignation, the proverbial stick up her ass.

"Good then. Have him FaceTime me in one hour."

"FaceTime?"

"He'll know."

"One hour? Oh, Lucky, I don't know. It's early for him. He stays up all night and sleeps during the day."

"I do not want to know how you know that."

"He told me." Her voice rose on a hint of indignation.

"Well, he may be an insomniac, but he is also on his way to being someone's bitch in the federal penitentiary when I get home. Convince him, Mother. If he values his life and his sexual orientation, he'll call me in an hour. And I want to see his face when I'm talking with him. But, and this is real important, Mother, he needs to be in your living room with no one else there. No one. Not you. Not Father. No one."

She dropped the ingénue act. "This sounds bad."

"It is." I didn't offer more and for once she didn't ask.

"Okay. I'll find Chip and get him here." For a moment, silence stretched between us, as if she was trying to find words for her next assault.

Frankly, I was too tired to care.

"Lucky, there's something else. Something that's not good." Her voice cracked.

As if any of this was good? But hit with the electric shock of Mona's serious tone, I didn't point that out. "Minnie? Is she okay?" Another victim of Mr. Cho and Irv Gittings would be intolerable...and just might be enough for a justifiable homicide scenario, which I'd sorta like.

"Minnie?" Mother feigned a casual tone. I knew she didn't like or trust the women in my father's inner circle. "She's going to be fine. At least that's what they told me. It's not that." Clearly, she didn't want to tell me. "You have a lot on your plate. Your father told me. Maybe this isn't the time."

"Not the time to backpedal. You opened the door. Now you have me worried. What isn't good, Mother?"

"It's your father," her voice caught.

"What has he done?" I pictured him on a plane headed this

way with a gun and a loose plan. That would be so like him, and so what I didn't need.

"He's had a bit of a setback."

I SPENT the next sixty minutes frantically tracking down doctors, nurses, anyone who would talk to me. My father was in a coma. Internal bleeding. They weren't sure why, but they knew where. They had to go back in—they were prepping him now. The doctor had been circumspect. My father was weak, he'd said. What he meant was he might not survive opening up his chest one more time.

Yeah, I recognized a euphemism when I heard one, even if my mother feigned stupidity. If the Theory of Manifestation were true, I wondered if feigning stupidity would actually bring that reality. Unsure, I thought it unwise to chance it.

With no one else to hound for information they didn't have and more than a little defeated, I moved toward the wall of windows in my suite. The Macau Tower wasn't Vegas—although people bungee-jumped off the thing like they did off the Stratosphere. One time I'd gone up the Tower and had died a thousand deaths when I realized there was a clear ring in the floor. Very terrifying to stand there, hovering in space eleven hundred feet up. My brain pegged on abject terror and refused to budge. It wasn't pretty. I never went back.

Worse, the lights of the casinos and the city brightening in the deepening darkness only reminded me of watching the same transformation back home with my father.

Desperate for news that wouldn't come, I vibrated with a need to do something, anything, yet remained paralyzed by the fact that there was nothing I could alter or change to make this better.

When my phone rang, I pounced on it. Recognizing the peculiar ring of a FaceTime call, I held the phone at eye level in front of me. "Yes?" and I tried not to be crushed by disappointment. Funny how, in an insignificant space of time, one huge problem could be dwarfed by another.

A face swam into view. A young man, clean-cut, strong jaw, wide, bright eyes shining with intelligence and mischief. "Ms. O'Toole?" He sounded nervous.

Keeping my phone in front of my face, I sagged into a chair. From the little box in the corner of the screen I could tell I looked scary enough to frighten small children. "You must be Chip." I ran a hand through my hair, which probably made it worse, but made me feel better. "Is that your real name or some sort of an inside joke?"

"Both, but my mother got the last laugh."

"Yeah, mine, too."

He leaned into the screen after glancing over his shoulder. "She's amazing. Your mother, I mean." He flushed schoolboy red.

So, we bonded over unfortunate names and differing opinions of my mother. Terrific. "Look, but don't touch."

"Oh, I know." He looked old enough to know better and still young enough to make a play anyway. Just another overachiever destined for a hard fall.

"I hear you and your pals have been having a bit of fun at my hotel." The prism of worry fractured my concentration into a thousand bits as I tried to focus.

He licked his lips, the only outward sign of nervousness, other than the tremor in his voice. "We plan on giving you a detailed report of your vulnerabilities, no charge."

"Big of you." I almost laughed at his grandstanding, but it would take too much effort. "Were you also planning on reimbursing the hotel for lost revenue, lost employee time, and lost face? By my loose accounting, the damage is in the millions." I made that part up. I was desperate. I wasn't sorry.

He ducked his head. "We didn't mean—" He cleared his throat.

I jumped into the opening. "Yes, you did. You meant every bit of malicious mischief. You cost my hotel a bundle. I should turn you over to the police. The District Attorney is a friend—he won't take kindly to you messing with my magic."

"Is that a felony?" he managed to stutter as he reared back from my coiled-rattler anger.

Why is it I always get the wiseasses? And why do I always like them? It takes some bit of asshole to make it in life today. No, scratch that, it takes balls, which is different. The kid had a set that clanked when he walked. My kind of guy—at least when I'm contemplating committing so many federal offenses that Guinness ought to take notice. "We can find out. But I guess the question is, how far do you want to push me?"

"Why do I get the impression you're going to offer me a deal?"

I rolled my eyes—I couldn't help it. Young males all seemed to have a lock on stupidity. "Maybe because I asked you to call me on the down low? I wasn't exactly hiding my hand."

He gave a self-deprecating waggle of his head, sort of a half-shrug, and half aw gee shucks. Still practically in diapers, he'd have time to work on that.

"Okay. What's the game?" he asked, as if he had a choice.

"I figure you owe me, big time. So, you want a way to make good?"

His head snapped up, his eyes sharpening to pinpoints. Yes, there was keen intelligence there. "All charges dropped?"

I shook my head in bewilderment. What he saw in Mona...

"None have been filed...yet. And you have my promise you can walk away with no liability and no criminal charges, if....and it's a huge if....*if* you help me catch a killer."

He blanched and swallowed hard. "What?"

"Oh, don't worry. My ass will be the only one in the line of fire. I just need you to work some of your computer voodoo." I could see his brain shift gears, and I knew I had him.

"What exactly do you have in mind?"

♥

*T*HE sharp stick of worry prodded me, driving a restlessness I couldn't beat into submission. Life was changing; I could feel it, like something big had shifted. Logic had accepted it; emotion railed against it.

I glared at my phone—the thing refused to ring.

Answers, solutions...good news...anything, everything...but nothing.

Teddie had gone, the others were sound asleep, and I was alone with my fear. The Big Boss. What would I do? What would Mona do? I was half a world away.

I closed my heart against the fear and focused. I had to focus.

None of it would matter if I didn't.

Cold water on my face brought me back. I half-assed the hair and makeup thing, then slipped downstairs. Nothing was going to glue the inside pieces back together, but at least I presented well.

I needed to walk.

The energy pulsed as the night got rolling, shimmering off the crowds in waves. People filled the lobby, wandering aimlessly as they strained skyward to stare at the glass sculptures covering the ceiling. Strangely, they parted to let me through, giving me a small taste of how Moses felt. Of course, I wasn't on a divine mission to lead my people to the Promised Land. Nope, I was leading my tribe down the path to Perdition. I knew the way—I'd taken the trip before.

Tigris Macau was so eerily like the Babylon but with things in the wrong place, or completely missing. Different games scattered around the casino floor. Built to hold five hundred slots and seventy tables, the gaming spaces looked empty compared to the Babylon. We'd been given a concession for half of what we'd been promised and had built for. A game. I didn't like it. We weren't the only ones. One of my Vegas compatriots had been blackmailed, the Macau power brokers refusing to grant him a gambling concession after two billion or so in construction investment—or that's how the story was presented. Shortly thereafter, he made a substantial donation to a Macanese public project. Bingo, he got his concession. Curious bit of coincidence.

Like I said, Vegas in the old days.

After my first pass through the main floor, I was convinced I'd been trapped in the *Twilight Zone*. Jerry's call caught me on my second pass, saving me from myself.

"Whatcha got?" I barked a bit too eagerly.

"Place getting to you?" he asked, a smirk in his voice.

I couldn't even summon a snort in retort. "No, life is getting to me." I tucked myself into an alcove and stuck a finger in my open ear as I listened with the other. "Before you show me yours, I want you to run a check on Sinjin Smythe-Gordon." I gave him the particulars, as I knew them, stopping short of regaling him with tales of derring-do. "Get me all the info you can."

"That important?"

"Beyond."

He gave a whistle.

"Now, please tell me you've got something, anything."

"I can place Irv Gittings in the hotel at the time of Kimberly Cho's murder."

I nodded. "Okay, good. I've got two women who have individually told me Irv Gittings killed Kim Cho. One even had him bragging to her about it."

"That trumps anything I've got," Jerry said with a hint of appreciation.

"One would think. But here in Macau, it's a galaxy far, far away. Many folks are on the take, the bad guys run everything, and the courts look the other way."

"Even when it comes to murder?" Jerry sounded like I felt—pissed off.

"I've been told so, but who knows? All I know is that asking those women to step into the line of fire would be as good as signing their death warrants. We'll have to get him another way."

"Sounds like you have some ideas."

"A few aces up my sleeve. You got anything else?"

"And I can trace the knife to one Gittings bought at auction five years ago. It belonged to Custer or somebody like that."

I wanted to tell him Custer was pretty singular, but I didn't have the time or energy to waste.

"Gittings is sure acting like he thinks he's got it knocked. I wonder why?"

"Pretty stupid, if you ask me." Jerry pulled on one of his ever-present smokes. Even this far away, the sizzle of dried tobacco burning filtered through the connection.

"And pretty dangerous. Either he's feeling like the cock of the walk, or he's got nothing to lose."

"I thought we were the ones with everything on the line."

"Maybe he thinks he's safe here, swimming with the big fish. He could be right—we have a lot to lose, and everybody who has three operating neurons knows it."

"Pretty hard to play when everyone can see your cards," Jerry agreed, but he didn't sound like he liked it.

"Unless you dazzle them with the old sleight of hand."

"Ah, cheating. I love it." His voice turned serious. "Just don't get caught."

"That's where you come in. Hang on." I left my hidey-hole and strode through the lobby, through the front door, and out to the street. I didn't want any of the hotel mics to pick up my conversation. And out here, the traffic noise would make it impossible for a microphone to distinguish the voices from the background noise and would help shelter my conversation from anyone close by. "Okay, can you hear me?" I spoke softly on purpose.

"Barely."

"Good."

"So you're really going to cheat?"

"I prefer to think of it as manipulation. But, yes, with your help."

"Oh, I love it when you talk dirty."

JERRY and I hammered out most of the details on his end, which left me feeling better but wired. With almost no sleep, I was headed for a flameout, but I couldn't do anything about it. A couple more laps around the hotel might dispel enough joy juice to let me find forty winks—heck, I'd even take twenty. Just enough to get me through. In thirty-six hours, we'd either be flying home or be fed to the sharks. That thought gave a whole new meaning to fish-or-cut-bait time.

My phone vibrated at my hip. As I stepped back into my alcove, I snatched it from its holder and squinted at the caller ID. "Hi. I was waiting to call you. I didn't want to awaken you again."

"You never need to worry about that." Jean-Charles's voice came back infused with warmth and worry. "You sound as if you are standing next to me."

"Oh, what I would do..." I trailed off. Thinking about the if-onlys...or the maybe-never-agains. As if wishing would help me find my ruby slippers and click my heels three times.

"I know this." He sighed. "It is not good there?"

"Better. Miss P and Jeremy came to help. So, our odds of success increased slightly." I hadn't told him about the Babylon. He thought I was simply trying to save Teddie's ass and bring Irv Gittings to justice. Maybe it was unfair of me, maybe not. Regardless, I couldn't talk about it, not here and not now.

"Bring Teddie back," he said, his tone insistent, almost a demand. He was getting better. A short time ago he would have flat-out demanded. "Karma will take care of Mr. Gittings."

"I'm sure you're right. I have one more thing to do, then I'll come home." I didn't tell him the downside to that one thing. He wouldn't change my mind—I had no choice. Keeping him from worry was my justification for not telling him. But really, I didn't want a lecture as to how stupid my plan was. He wouldn't have a better one—not one that would save my hotel—so what was the point?

"You know then about your father?" Pain etched his voice until it broke.

I squeezed the phone tighter, steeling against the news I hoped would never come but always feared getting. "Only a few bits and pieces." I tried to keep my voice level. "What Mona knows. I spoke with her just now."

"I have been at the hospital since they brought him here a few hours ago."

My heart swelled and tears welled. What was it with me lately? "Oh," was all I could manage.

"Your mother made sure the doctors would share information with me. She is quite formidable."

The way he said it made me smile. Mona, a skilled predator luring prey with the pretty exterior and batting-eyelid-stupid act. "Indeed. What's the latest?" I almost was afraid to ask. How would I be able to navigate the storm without the beacon of my father?

"They have stopped the bleeding. He is very weak and almost didn't come out of the anesthesia. The doctor says cautiously optimistic."

I fought my rising panic. "I don't know what I would do..." Tears traced a hot path down my cheeks. "My father...I need to come home now."

Jean-Charles's voice softened. "There is nothing you can do here."

"But I need to tell him I love him. They say that when people are in comas and stuff, if you talk to them, they hear it even though they can't respond. I need to tell him." My words tumbled over each other.

Jean-Charles let me talk. When I'd finished with the gasp of a choked-back sob, he said, "Lucky, he knows this."

"I know." And I did. Maybe I was looking for a good excuse to go home. But if we lost everything, what would we have gained? "I know. I just don't think I can do this. The stakes are too high."

"Then you really have nothing to lose."

How had my Frenchman become so wise?

"You can do this. You can save Teddie, save the hotel."

I gasped. "Who told you?"

"Your mother."

She had a bigger mouth than I'd previously thought. "I didn't want to worry you."

"I want to share your life. Trust me to handle it."

"Well, maybe you can handle it, but I'm having a damn hard time. Have you spoken with my father?"

"He is still in recovery and will be for some time. As I said, the anesthesia is taking some time to wear off."

"I'm so happy you are there. Thank you. It means everything." My voice broke. "I don't deserve you."

"You deserve the world, and I shall do my best to give it to you."

"Oh, make me earn it. I might get all entitled and difficult if you don't." My joke worked and he laughed, which gave me a smile, a weak one, but a smile nonetheless.

"You are already difficult."

"Damn straight." I felt myself come back into focus. I opened my eyes and my present reality did, too. My father was okay. "You don't have to stay. There are so many things to do at Cielo." On the theory that no news is good news, I didn't ask about the hotel—I hated problems I couldn't solve.

"I will, until your mother comes. We will, how do you say it, play tag?"

"Tag team." I would never tire of his trouble with idioms. A charming nuance.

"This is it. When your father awakens, he needs to see a family face."

"I love you." I had nothing more and nothing better to say.

"I love you, too. You can do this. You *will* do this."

"I wish I could be so sure."

"Then you will come home to me."

With that, we said goodbye, severing the thin connection

to my life.

Taking a deep breath, I stuck my phone back into its holder. Amped on worry, I charged off through the lobby, into the casino. A staircase up to the junket floors, then continuing to the mezzanine level, curved from the area next to the center bar. I took the stairs two at a time.

A text dinged. From Teddie.

Mr. Cho in watch exhibit.

Game on. I texted back.

A bit sooner than I expected.

Funny, but without knowing it, that's where I'd been headed. Turning left at the top of the stairs, then down the hallway to the end, I arrived in front of the large double doors of the timepiece exhibit. They were locked. Because of the value, the insurance company insisted we close the room early, before our revelers had time to consume copious amounts of alcohol and find all manner of mischief. I'd learned the hard way that there was no limit to stupid, especially when you had a pack of young wasted males, although I never ruled out any gender in the stupid contest. But the insurance company didn't know that public drunkenness and mischief were not part of the game in Macau. I'd given up trying to convince them.

A tough-looking guard, arms folded, stepped in front of me. A pock marked face, eyes that looked like they'd seen more trouble than I could imagine, and a nose slightly bent to one side, he gave me the slanty eye. "Closed. Come back tomorrow."

He had on a Security uniform and a nametag, so he wasn't a rent-a-cop—we owned him, and his biceps, each with a circumference larger than one of my thighs, which were prodigious. Mona told me so...often. *Now why did I feel the tug of familial bonds in her absence? I forget.*

I flashed my corporate ID. He eyed it for far longer than necessary, arousing my suspicion.

"You know the security is tight. You even reach for one of the enclosures and the place will shut down, locking you in."

"I participated in the design." I used my corporate bitch voice. And I lied. I'd hired the experts who had developed the design, but close enough.

He winced like I'd bitten him, which I had, metaphorically speaking. Finally, he relented. After fingering through a large ring of keys, he found the right one and opened the door for me.

As soon as the opening was wide enough, I breezed past him. "Lock it behind me." I didn't wait for an acknowledgement. Either he did what I asked, or he'd be replaced.

The lights in the room had been turned off—actually, we kept them that way. Each watch on its own stand and nestled delicately in silk had an enclosure of its own—a clear cube on a pedestal and lit internally. The effect was dramatic, pulling me in, making me want to see what treasure each box held. From an executive standpoint, I was pleased. From a thief standpoint, I was daunted. But, hopefully, Sinjin had as much expertise stealing things as I did running hotels.

So captured by the displays, I didn't notice a man moving in the darkness, staying out of the glow of each presentation. The guard hadn't said anything about letting anyone else in here. My heart, apparently on adrenaline overload, didn't even miss a beat.

The man didn't seem alarmed by my presence. He must've seen me walk in—the light from outside the room when the door opened would have been enough to capture his attention. If he wasn't alarmed, neither was I. Okay, maybe a little. I wound my way through the forest of expensive baubles. As I drew closer to the man, he paused, waiting. Briefly, I wondered if the guard would come running if I screamed.

A familiar profile.

Mr. Cho. As advertised.

Slicked-back hair, a mean mouth, and soulless eyes, he was dressed like he was going to a funeral: suit, starched shirt, Windsor-knotted silk tie in a pale pink—I couldn't see his feet, but I assumed his shoes would be Italian.

"This exhibit is closed," I said as I approached him,

keeping one of the displays between us, but eyeing him over the top of it. The man who had arranged to have the Big Boss shot. Of course, I couldn't prove it. There was only one other possibility, Irv Gittings, but I doubted he had the *cojones*. No, Irv usually got others to do his dirty work then left them holding the bag. Fists balled at my sides, I vibrated with anger. All things being equal, I'd really rather shoot Cho now. What can I say? I've never been a delayed gratification kind of gal.

But I wasn't running this show. Unfortunately, it was running me.

He gave me an are-you-for-real look. "When someone holds all the cards, it is foolish to call their bet."

"I returned your *son*. Perhaps you could be more appreciative." I wasn't sure where I was going with all of this; I just knew I was pissed, and with the stakes so high, the odds so long, I was feeling a bit what-the-hell.

"You think you know everything." He fixed me with an indifferent gaze, as if our game was a trifle. In his arrogance he acted as if he had nothing to lose.

We all have something to lose, I thought. I just needed to find out what Mr. Cho feared losing the most and then figure out a way of taking it from him—sort of way far afield from my normal gambit. "I don't know everything; you're right. But I do know that you've invited a snake into the hen house."

"Don't you mean fox?"

"No, the fox will eat the hens. The snake is much smarter; it will leave the hens and eat only the eggs." He looked at me as if he understood, which was a good thing, as I had no idea why I felt all Confucius all of a sudden—the place was clearly rubbing off on me.

Cho shrugged, but looked a bit unsettled. "Gittings is ... useful."

"With Minnie out of the way." Watching him closely, I said it as if I knew it.

He flinched, as his eyes that had been clapped on the bauble between us, shifted to mine. Quickly, he regained his composure.

But I'd seen it in his eyes—he was surprised about Minnie. But he didn't ask, a clever game player.

"Why are you in here?" After our little word sparring, which taught me a bit more about my opponent, I finally got to the crux of the matter.

"I couldn't arrange a private showing, so..." he shrugged, as if that was enough of an explanation.

It was. I couldn't keep him out, and he wanted me to know it. A not-so-subtle fuck you. Except, if I hadn't shown up unexpectedly, I never would've gotten the message. Right now, he might be holding one hell of a hand, but he'd just shown me a couple of his cards.

"You like these watches?" I asked, shifting his attention. A flash of gold at his wrist as he loosened his tie, then unbuttoned his collar. A Vacheron, subtle and expensive. A calling card in the circle of those who knew and appreciated, overlooked in its simplicity by those who didn't, the watch was the secret handshake of businessmen around the world.

"Calling these works of art by the same name as a Timex or Omega is like calling Chateau Lafite Rothschild just another red table wine."

Overstating, but evidence of his passion. "Although rarity drives the demand in the timepiece world. Which one do you like the best?"

He weighed my sincerity for a moment. "The centerpiece, of course. Why have anything less than the best?"

"Indeed." I followed his gaze down to the watch between us. The Patek Philippe Supercompilation. A fancy, if overlarge, pocket watch by my way of thinking. "Why is it worth so much?"

"Why is anything worth what it is worth? Supply and demand. One watch, highly complicated and exquisitely engineered." His voice warmed as he spoke, almost like a lover speaking of a beloved. Greed, love's second cousin once removed. "A chance to own a piece of history, something rare and unique that no one else can have."

"What would all of them together be worth?"

He pursed his lips for a moment. "Approaching one hundred million, I would think. With the premium you could add for cornering the market, as it were. But value is not why one would own one of these."

"Prestige."

"To have what others cannot elevates one, doesn't it?" When he looked at me, I saw the darkness inside and I almost felt sorry for him...almost. He was like a human black hole sucking everything into his ego feeding frenzy. Mixed metaphor or not, my assessment was accurate, and terrifying.

I lowered my voice. "How would you like to own them?" I could tell he didn't trust me. Why would he? "I could...facilitate that."

His gaze shifted to the watch. I thought he might drool. His inner struggle was easy to see as greed fought with self-preservation.

Greed won. He glanced around, looking at the ceiling. I knew what he was thinking. "No listening devices in here. Just cameras. I wouldn't compromise myself."

He raised his hand to cover his mouth. "Why would offer me the watches? That is a great risk for you."

I answered with a callous little gesture. "Insurance will pay, so I'm out nothing."

"It is risky."

"So is life." I met him stare for stare, even though my insides had turned to jelly. "I get you something you want. You'll have to pay for it, of course. Thievery doesn't come cheap." I tilted my head a bit and fought to keep up the appearance of courage. "But you already know that."

A flicker of surprise. "You are your father's daughter."

I took that as a compliment. "You clean some money, you get incredible treasures..." I trailed off to keep his attention.

"And you? What do you get?" He acted like he knew the answer.

"An agreement that you scale back your laundering here. Keep us out of trouble with the gaming authorities."

He let his gaze drift around the room, taking in all the

gleaming gold. "You can deliver these?" His hand still covered his mouth when he spoke.

I had him. I kept my face passive, despite the flood of emotion, the thrill of the chase. We were in the game and on the scent. "Yes."

Still, he wavered.

I waited, working on the whole nonchalant thing. Damn near impossible, given my woeful lack of restraint.

Finally, he nodded. "What are the details?"

I pulled out my phone and called up Sinjin's text message. "Here's the account number and routing instructions." I read the numbers to him, then double-checked his accuracy when he read them back. "Right, then. Eighty million certified funds by tomorrow night."

He didn't even swallow hard. Extracting a pad from his inner pocket, he jotted down the information. "The funds will come from multiple accounts."

He didn't have to explain why. Banking being what it was, I wouldn't keep large sums in any one account either.

Folding his notebook and putting it away, he gave me a tight smile. "The watches are worth one hundred million."

"The twenty percent discount is your payment for honoring your side of the deal."

Mr. Cho gave me a half-smile and a shallow bow, then, with one last look at the Patek Phillipe, he disappeared into the darkness. The light of the door opening behind me, then the returning darkness when it closed, told me he'd left.

And I was alone.

RYAN WHITMORE waited with the guard when I let myself out of the exhibit. Apparently, the guard feared for his corporate life and had called in reinforcements.

"Mr. Cho is very powerful," Ryan said as he fell into step

with me.

I'd deal with the guard later, or not. It sorta depended on the next twenty-four hours.

"I can see that."

"The government here, you do not understand."

I stopped and, with a hand on his elbow, I forced him to face me. Even though I knew full well how the game was played in Macau, I thought maybe it might be interesting to hear Ryan's take on it. "Enlighten me."

"Businessmen like Cho and the casino bosses, they *are* the government. They make rules to suit themselves and to line their own pockets. They might enforce those rules against one property but not the others. But without them, we cannot stay in business. They can shut us down, pull our concession."

"So you're worried about your job?"

He feigned indignation. The blush under the bluster told me I'd hit home.

"Of course not. Your family has been very supportive of me." He ruffled up a bit. "Although your father shot down my idea for a larger property on the Cotai. I drive through it every day on the way home, and I can't believe we made the mistake not having a presence there."

"You live out that way?" I asked, keeping the casual in my question.

"Have a nice house on the water."

Expensive. Very expensive. We paid him well, but not very-expensive well. Where was his other source of income? The big question with him was this: was he getting it on the take or just on the side as Pei had said?

"The Big Boss didn't shoot your idea down; I did. We're a small player in an increasingly oversold market here in Macau. And to build on the Cotai, we would've had to leverage everything and ruin our balance sheet. A huge price to buy into a game where the other players could change the rules on a whim.

An angry red flush colored his pasty cheeks. "You?"

I shrugged as if brushing off a fly. "My call. I made it."

Settling back, he gave me a wry little grin. "Someday that arrogance of yours will get you in trouble."

My hackles rose. I wanted to argue, even though I wasn't sure I would disagree. I wanted to tell him I knew about the apartment he kept next door—the one I'm sure the hotel paid for—where he provided young women to be used so he could gain. Come to think of it, I wanted to break his nose, for starters. But I didn't have the time to waste tilting at fictive windmills. And some secrets are best kept for future gain.

As to whether my arrogance, as he put it, would get me into trouble...

Pretty soon, we'd know if he was right.

CHAPTER SEVENTEEN

STILL on boil, I rode the escalator down and was just parking one cheek on a stool at the empty casino bar when my phone rang. An odd number I recognized: my thief masquerading as a pirate, hiding as a hedge-fund manager—he'd be a therapist's wet dream, or a cop's nightmare.

"O'Toole here."

"Where are you?" a strong male voice with cool notes of the UK and a warm undercurrent of complicity.

Sinjin Smythe-Gordon, I was right. "Lobby. Manhandling the staff."

"Do you need rescuing?" he asked with a chuckle.

"No, but the staff might." Although that sounded like a joke, my eroding self-control didn't inspire confidence.

"Meet me in twenty, north side of the hotel." The line went dead.

Fearing the phone holder clippy thing at my waist was the modern version of the pocket protector and would ruin my street cred—assuming I had any—I yanked the thing loose and tossed it in the nearest waste can. I dropped my phone in my pocket. If I sat on it, well, I'm sure they could stitch me up. To be honest, I was also chafing at the tether of constant contact. If I was going to shatter a few felony statutes, I sure didn't want to be findable.

After a moment, I pulled out my phone and activated an app called Map Me, then repocketed the thing.

Normally my happy place, tonight the casino didn't buoy my mojo. While the dedication to serious gaming improved my bottom line, it didn't make me happy. I never thought I would say it, but I missed the packs of the slightly inebriated wandering through the hotel intent on finding fun.

The Chinese were so darn serious. And the bad guys were so smug. One thing I hated was being played for a chump, as if there was nothing I could...or would...do.

With a few moments to kill I wandered into one of the pawnshops dotting the periphery. Drawn by the gleaming cases filled with watches, I stepped around a couple of men bartering with the proprietor. So many watches. All different kinds from the mundane to the magnificent.

"Is there something you want?"?" A young woman, tiny and exquisite, appeared in front of me. The requisite silk dress and unctuous attitude, she smiled in a familiar way.

Dragon tattoo on the inside of her forearm.

One of my army. Or, more rightly, I was one of hers. And they all counted on me.

"With one arm, she gestured in a sweeping motion, taking in the whole shop. "Or perhaps you have something to sell?"

"You have so many beautiful things. Are they all original?"

"All but those." She pointed to a small display in the middle of the showroom, which was piled high with knockoffs of the watches in the exhibition. "Everyone likes to own a piece of history."

"Like the little leaning towers at all the trinket stalls in Pisa."

She looked like she understood. Her eyes flicked to a man who stepped in behind me. He clutched a carpetbag, black with a red dragon motif.

He saw me standing there, and I froze. He gave me a casual bow, one a man would give any woman he didn't know, and I smiled in return.

A casual meeting. A moment of panic allayed.

"Excuse me." The girl bowed slightly, then moved to escort the man into the back.

Curious, I stepped to the display of the fake watches and hefted one. Pot metal, just as I thought. And I smiled.

With a glance at my phone, I realized Sinjin would be here in ten minutes. No more tarrying—I didn't want to be forced to walk the plank for keeping a pirate waiting.

In the lobby, the same library quiet greeted me. I felt like shouting just to shake things up. Couples strolled, not touching. The ducks paddled in the languid stream. Nothing out of place, no strident voice.

Talk about feeling useless—one problem-solver rendered irrelevant.

It's not that I was lacking problems. I was just lacking problems I could solve.

Cindy Liu chatted with a young couple at the end of the reception desk. She noticed me standing there shifting from foot to foot while she finished up. When she'd broken free, I eased her aside so we could speak privately.

"Looking for trouble?" she asked with a perfectly flat affect.

Perhaps she meant that as a joke, but I didn't hear it.

Remembering Kim Cho's warning, I eyed Cindy Liu. Was she who she said she was? Was I? "I never have to look— trouble finds me."

Her all-business manner softened to something approaching collegiality. She leaned in, which meant she was sort of talking to my boob. I leaned down to make it a little less awkward, although she didn't seem fazed.

"How can I be of help?"

"My assistant is here. Would you mind letting her shadow you? I'd love her to get up to speed on how you handle things here." I reached for sincerity.

"Your assistant?" Cindy bowed slightly, keeping upturned eyes on me. "Let me take care of a few things, then I'd be honored."

Either I lied better than I thought, or we both were playing the same game. "Thank you." I pretended to pause, as if sidetracked by a random thought. "Oh, I could use your help on one other thing."

"Anything."

"I want to know what the hell is going on with Mr. Whitmore. If he has any strange friends, I want photos, okay? Take what you can with your phone, but don't let anyone see you. These are dangerous men."

"I am am better prepared to handle them than you are," she said with an air of superiority.

"No doubt." My phone chirped. A text. *Walk around the corner. Waiting on north side of building.* My chariot, with its sexy but dangerous and now vigilant owner, was here. I got it. We didn't need to be seen as buddies any more than Teddie and I did.

"So when would be convenient for my assistant to meet you?" I asked Cindy Liu, as I dropped my phone back into my pocket. "Tomorrow morning?"

"That would be perfect."

I returned her small bow and went to meet Sinjin. Once out of the hotel, I reached for my phone.

Miss P answered on the second ring, her voice surprisingly fresh. I wondered if it was possible to exist on sex alone. If she was any proof, then the answer was yes. "How soon can you be presentable?"

"Ten minutes, maybe less."

"Make it less. I just put a burr under our Miss Liu's saddle. I want to see who she talks to, what she does, how she prepares for you shadowing her starting tomorrow morning."

"You got it."

"And Jeremy?"

"Still sleeping, but he's arranged to meet Agent Stokes tomorrow for male bonding over some Australian microbrews."

"Perfect. Keep me posted."

I terminated the call as I approached the black SUV idling where Sinjin had told me he would be. The passenger door opened on silent hinges. Wary, I stopped and stepped back until I saw his face illuminated when the interior light went on.

"Quickly," he said, his voice taut.

I settled myself in the passenger seat and pulled the door closed. I think we both felt better hiding in the night. "The dark tint. Great camouflage."

"For predator and prey." He maneuvered the car away from the curb.

"And which one are you?"

"Depends on the viewpoint."

"I would guess yours to be the one that matters." He didn't answer. "No driver tonight?" No witness, I thought, and didn't know what to make of it or what to do. Onward into battle not knowing who wore my colors and who didn't—and no one to watch my back.

"You up for a trip?" He'd changed into something a little less flashy—dark slacks, a white button-down, and a leather jacket that looked so soft I wanted to pet it.

I resisted. "No more playing pirate?"

He didn't reward me with a smile. "Not tonight."

"Are we going back to China illegally?" My phone felt warm in my pocket—the app I'd started must be working.

"I want to show you something." He darted a look my way. "We need to start making plans."

I settled back for the ride. "Sounds like fun." I said it, but I didn't feel it. Although I was ready to get this show on the road, figuratively speaking, since Sinjin was already taking me for a ride and being rather circumspect about it.

Turns out the ride wasn't far, just cross the bridge. But that wasn't the trip he'd mentioned, merely the beginning of it. He had a helicopter waiting atop one of the mega-casinos still under construction. One punch of a pre-programmed button and the gate in the perimeter fence glided open. The steel superstructure loomed like the skeleton of a dream. Lone light bulbs dotted the beams, giving enough illumination to only add to the creepy factor. As a Vegas kid, I knew all about ditching bodies in the foundations of casinos, and I shivered, despite convincing myself I was in the company of a compatriot. He wouldn't kill me—not yet. He needed me. At least that's what I told myself.

But, instead of following me down the Yellow Brick road, at any point, Sinjin could decide I was a bad witch and drop a house on me. "You could bury a body here and no one would know it." Fear was easier to handle once it was in the open. Still, I tugged my sweater tighter around myself and calculated how long it would take me to get the gun out of my purse should I need it.

Too long. Not a comforting realization.

Sinjin pulled out of sight behind a dumpster and killed the engine. "This isn't Vegas." He met me in front of the car, then escorted me to a small platform. "The sharks do a better job. Cleaner, you know. Nothing left."

I kept my nervousness to myself. "Cute."

He stepped back and motioned me onto the platform.

I looked up, way up, then back at my small little square of wood with no sides, no safety features, nothing to prevent a swan dive, or a push and a tumble. Pulling in a deep breath, I figured this was where the boys become men. I stepped onto the platform, then turned and raised an eyebrow and my escort. "Coming?"

He shook his head and smiled at a joke he didn't share, then stepped in next to me and pushed the up button. He had to keep pressing or the lift would stop—sort of like having one hand tied behind his back, evening the odds.

The familiar comfort of a false sense of security settled over me. "You do know how to show a woman a good time."

"One of my investors owns this place. He lets me use the helipad when I need to. I like the privacy."

"Understandable. Is he one of your buyers as well?"

"No, I always keep business and pleasure separate." He seemed to be making a point —I wasn't sure what it was, but I took note.

"Probably a good plan." Not one I adhered to, but I didn't admit to that. Not sure what that meant, but I didn't waste time worrying about that particular character defect—not when

I had so many more important ones.

Sinjin approached the helicopter with practiced efficiency surprising me. No driver apparently meant no pilot either.

"I'm assuming you know how to fly this thing?" He ignored me, focusing instead on opening ports and shining a penlight inside, so I answered myself. "Stupid question." Fear made me babble.

Finally, with the preflight done and both of us buckled in Sinjin fired the machine up. The rotors circled slowly, gaining speed with each revolution until they whirled with a vibration that pulsed through my chest and rattled my teeth. In the right seat, Sinjin motioned for me to don the headset. Once I had it settled, he said, "Ready?"

I tugged at my five-point harness, then nodded. *Ready as I'll ever be.*

He eased up on the collective and we levitated—a fact that always amazed me. Physics and its laws had confounded me, but, even though ignorant, I appreciated the magic. Once high enough to clear any obstructions, Sinjin lowered the nose slightly, then stepped on the left rudder, swinging us around toward Hong Kong.

Only forty-five miles or so as the helicopter flies, the ride was brief, the conversation nonexistent. I was sorry night hid the scenery—the islands in the South China Sea were beautiful. We landed on a building, one in the sea of high-rises and a forest of cranes that ringed Victoria Harbor. Thankfully, a crane wasn't part of the décor of this particular building. A key got us in, and an elevator took us down one floor to the one-hundred and twenty-third.

Hong Kong always worried me with all its buildings stretching to the sky and endless construction on reclaimed land. The city had been on a 24/365 land reclamation project since the changeover from the British to the Chinese in 1997. I wondered what they'd do when they reclaimed all of Victoria Harbor.

Of course, one good earthquake. I wasn't an engineer of course, but the combination was enough to make me queasy.

The elevator put us in a small vestibule with one desk, a

very large jade dragon, and no signage.

"Where are we?" I asked.

Sinjin stepped to a door, placing his thumb on a glass plate to the right. Another plate above it opened, exposing a retinal scanner. He waited for the machine to do its work, then stepped back and motioned me through, just as the door hissed open. "My office."

"Business or pleasure?" I stepped through and instantly felt like I had walked into Security at the Babylon. "You've tapped into our security feed at the Tigris?"

"I've been studying and timing how the feed rotates."

Finding the dark spots. "I used to do that at every property. A good thing to know."

He gave me an appreciative glance.

I felt the glow of student satisfaction when a teacher bestowed a quick compliment, which made me ashamed. *Get a grip. He's just another pretty face.* But he wasn't, not really. He was smart and manipulative, too. The triple whammy. The question was, was he a sociopath, too? "Were you going to tell me about the account you opened for Irv Gittings?"

Even though my words held the sharp point of a condemnation, he didn't even flinch. "At Mr. Cho's request. Purely business. A conduit for Gittings to invest some of Cho's money overseas."

Despite sounding legit, the whole thing stunk royally. "And you weren't going to tell me because...?"

"It's irrelevant."

I grabbed his upper arm, getting his attention. "You don't get to decide what is relevant and what isn't. My ass is on the line just like yours."

"Point taken." He shrugged my hand off. "My apologies." He spoke the words so easily, as if by rote.

"For the record, I don't believe you fund all this fancy office space, your impressive boat, and technology that would make Q quiver with lust with a bit of pirating and hedge-fund fees. You're as dirty as they are, in a way."

His eyes narrowed giving him a feral, hungry look. "How

do you figure?"

"You launder the money coming out of China, the stuff that doesn't flow through the casino. You have to. Any crook worth his salt is diversified."

My not-so-veiled insult hit home, and he puffed up a bit. "I know what you're thinking, but it seemed an easy way to fund the fight against them. Nobody in the international market wants Yuan. So, I receive them here and deposit them into accounts denominated in Hong Kong dollars. I use the proceeds for purposes you'd approve of."

"No doubt." I kept my voice flat—no sarcasm, no approval.

"Not legal by any stretch, but I figured it would be a short-term association."

"I see." I'd learned one thing by his admission—he was better than most of us at justifying bad behavior. Good to know. "How do they get the cash out of China?"

"Smuggling, the junket dealers, and sometimes they just ship it to me."

"Ship it?"

"Yeah, the shipping companies don't check packages under one kilo. So they box up a bunch of bills in high denominations. They make sure it doesn't exceed the weight— they call it an American pound."

"Slightly less than a kilo."

He picked up a mechanical pencil and started working it through his fingers as he leaned one hip against the desk. "We rotate shipping addresses so we don't trigger some unwanted attention."

"Like shipping drugs but without having to worry about the dogs." Leaning there, his arms crossed casually as if he was debating the merits of various single-malts, he looked cool and collected. Just the man I'd want on my side in a firefight.

But was he on my side? I had a feeling if push came to shove, he'd feather his own nest and leave the rest of us out in the cold. "Will you give me Irv's account number?"

He eyed me for a moment, then bent over a computer, working through the pull-down menus. He scrawled some number on a pad, tore it off, and handed it to me.

He had questions, but he didn't ask them, so I gave him a few answers. "Personal between me and Gittings. And, if I can pull this off the way I think I can, I can leave him holding the bag."

"And we walk?"

I knew what he implied. "All of us, yes."

He accepted that, or at least pretended to. He had no choice. For that matter, neither did I. Uncomfortable bedfellows for sure. "Have you come up with a timeline?"

With a hand barely touching my elbow, he moved me over to a drafting table. Sheets of schematics and construction plans covered the surface.

"These are our security schematics." I lifted a sheet. "And the architectural plans for Tigris." Feeling violated, I let my anger run loose in my words. "How dare you?"

He waited me out. "No time for that, Lucky. Tomorrow night, just after midnight. The casino will be full and Security will be busy watching that. A perfect time to steal the watches."

"So soon?" Instantly sober, I swallowed hard.

"Your people are ready?"

"Yes." One advantage to the time difference—the middle of the night here would be in the middle of day at home, and everyone would be running at full-throttle and hopefully on top of their game. Everything hinged on that.

He motioned me closer. "Then this is what I need from you."

ONCE back at Tigris, the pulse of adrenaline ebbed and fatigue flooded through me. Time for sleep, if I could. Tomorrow would be a very big day. My bedroom was empty when I let myself in. Not that I expected otherwise. I kicked off my shoes and fell on the bed, folding the heavy quilt over me.

The day was full-bore bright by the time I stirred. Someone had left a pot of coffee by the bed. Moving back so I was propped up on the pillows, I poured myself a cup full. The tiny coffee cups here in China were a travesty that made becoming fully-caffeinated a fill it, then slug it, then fill it again affair. I'd downed four of the things before I felt my blood pressure get off the peg.

After a long, hot shower, clean hair, clean clothes, and the last of the carafe of coffee, I felt more myself than I had in a long time. Stuffing my feet in the slippers that came with the room, I went to find Romeo. He was where I thought he'd be— setting up on the dining room table.

Two twenty-seven-inch screens angled together. I could hear the soft whir of the CPUs as lines of code marched down the screen, a new line added every few seconds. Romeo sat leaning back in his chair; thankfully he'd kept his feet on the floor and not on the table. But I did fear for the two thin legs of the chair he balanced on. He had a keyboard in his lap.

"That's quite a setup."

"After we talked, I got Jeremy out of bed. Good idea rolling him into this—he can procure anything. Truly amazing. I learned a thing or two."

"Not sure I want to know." The guilt of exposing my young knight to those whose values were a bit more...expedient...would weigh heavy. Of course, he hung around with me, so he didn't have much farther to fall.

"Probably not." My Defender of the Free World didn't look upset at all about most likely taking a ten-finger discount or buying hot stuff for pennies on the Pataca.

"Where's everyone?"

"Sleeping. We all had a very late night."

"Did you get any sleep?"

He ducked under the table, pulling on some cords. "A bit. Spent a good bit of time talking to Brandy." He reappeared from under the table. "I've gotten used to falling asleep next to her. Not that comfortable when she's not there."

"I understand. Is she all right? Any word on how things are going at Cielo?"

"A-okay. She's got everything under control. Don't worry."

"But if I didn't worry, I wouldn't have a job."

"But you might have a life."

"The grown-up version of you is getting irritating."

He gave me a knowing smile. "Makes you appreciate what I've had to live with dogging you this past year."

"Cute." I picked up the phone on the sideboard and ordered more coffee while I watched Romeo work. He didn't look twelve anymore, but I would never tell him that.

Room service assured me the coffee would be here in twenty minutes. I wondered if I could wait that long. The effects of the first pot were already waning, but I didn't think throwing my weight around for coffee would be a good use of my limited resources.

I pulled a chair close to Romeo and perched on the edge. "You got everything on the list."

"Yep. China, the land of reverse engineering and feigning ignorance of patents. Amazing place."

"Not if you're the patent holder."

"Sometimes the price for doing it the right way is too high." He gave me that enigmatic spiritualist expression he'd been perfecting.

"Who the heck told you that?"

"You did."

"A philosophy not to be practiced by the...inexperienced."

"I'm not as stupid as most people my age."

"Since you look all of twelve, I'm not comforted by that." I leaned forward, focusing on the screens. "Are you tapped in to Jerry?"

"Yeah. Worked seamlessly. It's amazing how these kids can hack into stuff."

I tried not to think about it, but I knew we had some work to do when I got home. "What are you watching?"

"The feed that Chip is watching. He doesn't know it, though. At least I hope not. He actually did all the heavy lifting, getting through the security into the hotel here. Amazing stuff, really."

"You worry me, Detective. So impressed with lawbreakers." I was only half-teasing. It's a fine line between criminals and those who catch them—the good guys have to think like the criminals. Just a slight dip in standards and one became the other.

"Even Jeremy said you gotta think like one to catch one. I know you feel the same—I've watched you work."

Men, reading me like a book.

"Don't do as I do, Grasshopper." Using my hands to help me up, I stood on creaky knees and tired legs. "Keep me posted. I want to know if any of the money moving into the account Sinjin gave us starts to move elsewhere. If it does, tell Jeremy to shut it down. He can do that, right?"

"That's what he said."

And it had come down to who hired the best criminal.

Oh, joy.

I settled in the deep comfort of the couch in the main room.

Time to check in with my lawbreaker. Chip and I went through the plan and timing five times, then three more after he'd hacked the security system and programmed the rolling takedown of the various cameras and security lasers. He also recorded a couple of loops, then prepared to have them run in place of the real-time feeds.

All this seemed so incredibly rushed to me. I wanted a run-through or ten, but there was no time. Make it or break it. Pass Go or go directly to jail. All in, everything on one roll of the dice. Unable to decide which analogy I liked the best, I corralled my thoughts and tried to focus. "You got it?" I asked the hacker.

"Sure."

He sounded far too casual for my nerves. "This is serious, Chip."

"Cool your jets. I got this. Done it before a bunch of times." He didn't sound like he'd seen us spying on him.

Was it a crime to hack into my own network to spy on a guy who I'd let into another network to spy on criminals? That one thought threatened to make my brain explode.

Chip. He was the key, actually. Well, he and Romeo. If they both did what they said, I might pull this off.

Romeo I trusted. Chip, not so much. Threatening prosecution to someone who broke the rules with alacrity didn't seem like much of a threat to me. Hence the back door, Jerry and Romeo.

I'm not sure what made me more uncomfortable with Chip, his weird seventies vernacular or the fact this was far from his first hotel invasion. Clearly, I needed to improve the quality of folks I consorted with. First thing I'd do when I got home...okay, the second thing. Thoughts of my Frenchman warmed parts that would only derail logical thought, so I doused them with a splash of cold reality. "You do know that if you screw this up, a bunch of folks, including yours truly will most likely never be heard from again."

"Sure."

I wish he'd quit saying that. "Easy to say sitting in the relative sanctity of Vegas."

"Irony?"

"Sarcasm. You screw this up, and I will make sure that a memory is the only thing left of you."

A text beeped. *Your father is awake and bellowing for you.* Even I could feel the curare tip of Mona's jealousy in her verbal arrow.

I'll call in a few. I texted in reply.

Texting and talking at the same time—and I thought technology was supposed to free up time, not require us to double-down. "Did you get into the wire transfer department here?" I continued peppering the kid, hoping to find the gaping hole in our plan.

"So easy you guys are either incredibly stupid or clever beyond the norm."

I felt like arguing for clever, even though I knew better. For once, I didn't open my mouth and sink my ship, letting him continue.

"Been watching the inflow and outflow, recording all origins and destinations. Anything in particular I'm looking for?"

"Yes, but I can't tell you what it will be.   Like pornography—"

"—I'll know it when I see it." He finished my tired old quote, punctuating it with a derisive snort.

Everybody's a critic. "I'll call you later.   I'll be blind, so you'll be my eyes." I tried to not let that terrify me.

CHAPTER EIGHTEEN

"WE'VE got a problem," Miss P announced as she strode into the room, brandishing my second pot of coffee on a tray with two cups. At my raised eyebrow, she said, "I relieved room service of it down the hall." She speared me with a serious look. "We have a problem."

I took the pot and poured us both a cup. "And this is a surprise because?"

"No surprise. I simply wanted to make sure I had your attention." She dropped into the chair across the coffee table from me and kicked off her shoes, then she reached for the cup of coffee I held out to her.

"Apparently, not only do owners start to look like their dogs, but assistants begin to act like their bosses." I remembered the days when she would perch on the edge of a chair, nervously plucking at imagined lint on her clothing like a sparrow pecking at empty kernels.

She seemed nonplussed—another of my coping strategies, a second cousin to fake-it-'till-you-make-it. "I'll worry about it if we are alive tomorrow."

Another pessimist, just what my guardian angel ordered. My stomach growled, demanding attention. "What meal is the next appropriate one? I haven't a clue as to the time."

"Dinner."

"Good to know. Do they have an In-N-Out close by?"

"You're not taking this seriously." Miss P seemed in a lather.

"Life is too important to be taken seriously. So what problem, among the thousands we are dealing with, has your panties in a bunch?"

"Your Miss Liu had a very emotional private chat with Ol' Irv."

Taking a moment to distill that, I realized I wasn't surprised. Disappointed for sure, but surprised? Nope. Kim had warned me—a dying gift I refused to ignore. "Any idea the subject matter?"

"One of Teddie's girls told me that Miss Liu is sweet on Mr. Whitmore, and she feels that Ol' Irv is a bad influence."

Teddie's girls threw me for a minute, but my ship righted pretty quickly. I had no more a claim on him than he did on me—his fault, my choice. "Wise, but how does Ol' Irv have any pull on Mr. Whitmore?"

"Now that's the sixty-four-thousand-dollar question, isn't it?" Miss P looked ready to erupt.

Unwilling to give her the satisfaction, I waited, feigning patience.

Finally, she caved. "Apparently, Ol' Irv is staying at Mr. Whitmore's."

"His house on the road to Coloane?" I checked my watch, calculating the time for a round trip and a bit of breaking and entering. My skills rusty, I added a fudge factor.

"No, his condo at the hotel next door."

A smile split my face. "Even better."

Her face fell. "You knew about the condo?"

I gave her an enigmatic tilt of my head, raising one shoulder as if to say, "I'm the boss, always one step ahead."

She let me have my fun. The banter was a great way to shift all the heavy we carried. "One of the young women told me Whitmore keeps it and arranges for entertainment for the whales who want to indulge in excesses but under the radar in case Big Brother takes a dim view."

"And Miss Liu goes along with that?"

"Good question, don't you think?"

Her face crumpled into a frown. "If she's in on it, that's like being betrayed by your own gender."

"Even worse than the men doing it, isn't it? We women have to stick together. Want to go on a seek-and-destroy mission? Could be dangerous." I stuffed my feet back in my shoes.

Miss P did the same, although her feet, her shoes. "I thought you'd never ask."

THAT knife. The murder weapon.

I knew what I was looking for, but I had no idea if I would find it, but I needed a chink in Ol' Irv's armor, some serious leverage, and I was tired of waiting.

Probably stupid, but, if my past had taught me anything, stupid sometimes was the way to go.

I texted Ming. *Can you give me location of Gittings and Whitmore?*

I waited, staring at my phone. Miss P said Gittings was staying in the apartment, so I knew, if he wasn't there, then we'd have a green light.

Gittings in Panda room. Will keep him there.

If he moves. Let me know.

Ok.

Miss P and I strolled out of the hotel as if we had nowhere to go and all day to get there. Nobody stopped us; nobody paid any attention, at least not that I could tell.

Soon, I was grateful for the cover of darkness. "What's the date?"

Miss P thought for a moment before answering. "The thirtieth."

"And we'll get a day back heading home?"

"Fifteen hours."

"We just might make it."

"If we don't die or get arrested."

My self-delusion running at full-throttle, I was feeling practically giddy with optimism—and amped on caffeine after having downed half the second pot. "Oh, ye of little faith. We got this."

"How are we going to play this little part of the adventure?" Miss P's voice hadn't lost its bravado.

Which left me to contemplate where bravery morphed into stupidity. Of course, I probably crossed that line the minute I got on that airplane heading here, rendering the question moot. "I'll play it. You follow. If things go south, run like hell and don't stop until you hit Vegas. Plane is in Hong Kong."

"Good to know." She hooked an arm through mine.

"When you have a chance, you might want to have it relocated to the airport here."

"Will do, but, for the record, we leave together or not at all."

"Good to know." With one hand, I covered her smaller one that rested on my forearm. "We should be okay. According to Ming, Ol' Irv is busy in the junket rooms."

Hiking up the drive of the neighboring property, I didn't even shorten my stride, fearing a slight loss in momentum would lead to total immobility. I pushed through the door, then adopted an air of authority. Miss P had loosened my arm and now let me lead the way.

The lobby was chic contemporary in hues of light purple and gray. Icicles of crystal hung from high ceilings refracting the light. Carpets of red and orange brightened and softened the grey stone tiles underneath. Cool, aloof, with barely a hint of warmth—Ol' Irv would feel right at home.

I stepped to the desk where a young man waited with his hands clasped behind his back and a look of disinterest in his eyes. "The manager, please?"

He gave me a tight-lipped grimace and a nod, which clearly pained him, then disappeared around a partition behind him.

Miss P darted me a glance as we both tried to act casual. My heart hammered and I felt on the verge of passing out—clearly a life of crime was not a good fallback if the casino thing didn't work out. Of course, riding the South China Sea with Sinjin did have its romantic appeal...

A short, stocky woman pressed into an unflattering blue-skirted suit reminiscent of the eighties, sensible shoes, tight, thin lips, and a no-nonsense attitude, stepped around the partition. "How may I be of assistance?" Her voice was a gravelly growl.

And here I'd wondered what happened to all the female adversaries in those Bond movies. My imagination revved into overdrive. I decided to keep the desk between us in case she had that curare tipped pointy thing in the toe of her shoe. I figured I had her by ten inches, too many pounds for my delicate ego, and a decade of experience. I could take her...even if she had curare on her side. "I'm Lucky O'Toole, an executive with Tigris."

"Yes."

I didn't know what that meant, but one thing for sure, she couldn't look any less impressed. This wasn't going as I'd hoped, but it was going about as I expected once I saw her. "My property next door is paying for a condo here."

"Yes?"

I'd guessed right. "I'd like a key."

"Can you prove who you are?"

Ouch. Thirty seconds later I'd given her my bona fides, obtained a key, verbally eviscerated her, and Miss P and I were now *en route* in the elevator to the top floor.

"You left her bleeding but barely alive."

I didn't hear any judge in her assessment. "Collateral damage. She knew who I was and was jerking my chain for fun."

"How do you know?"

"I fired her two years ago. I'd be willing to bet we have no more than ten minutes. She'll call Whitmore."

Miss P took that in stride. "Wouldn't be any fun if it was

easy."

"Said the bull rider at her first rodeo. Easy would be good—unexpected, but good."

"Pricy property," she said with a snarl. "Our auditors..."

"Have some answering to do." The ostentation impressed even little ol' jaded me. "At least Ryan Whitmore didn't skimp on his sinning."

"Can't trust the help," she deadpanned, without even a smidge of irony.

She needed to teach me how to do that—lately everybody seemed to read me like a book. Mesmerized, we both watched the numbers flash by. Too soon the doors slid open, delivering us to the penthouse floor. At least I had my answer— Whitmore more than likely padded his income on the side. And he curried favor with Cho to have business thrown his way—wealthy men who were looking for a woman to rough up.

The thought made me want to kill somebody. "Whitmore always was good at hiding his sins. After all these years, I'm sure he has it down to a fine art. Seeing how he pulled it off will be educational."

Apparently, there were two penthouses, an A and a B. The key was marked with a B, making the choice easy. "The B team," I whispered as I put a finger to my lips. The key actually worked a magnetic lock that opened with a barely discernible click. With Miss P guarding my back, I eased the door inward on silent hinges. No lights, no sound...apparently, we were alone.

My heart slowed just a bit as I motioned Miss P inside. Plush carpet muffled our footfalls as I shut the door behind her. "We don't have long."

"What are we looking for?"

We both surveyed the large, open great room. Couches and chairs, clustered around small tables, but in the half-light filtering through the large windows the detail was lost. "An ivory-handled knife and anything else we can use against Gittings for sure, and Whitmore for maybe. He pegs my creep meter, and I'm going to take him down whether Miss Liu likes it or not."

"Fire his ass, for starters." Familiar with my oddities, Miss P nodded, her expression serious. "Should we split up?"

"Makes the most sense, but isn't that the one decision in those slasher movies that gets the pretty blonde hacked to bits?"

Instead of buying my bullshit, she pointed behind me. "You go that way."

"And you'll go?"

"Not that way."

With our banter back, I felt better as I felt my way in the weak light. The great room was devoid of personal effects, as if carefully staged to impress. Tiptoeing, I opened doors, dove into closets, but found nothing interesting. A set of double doors at the end of the room beckoned. Pushing them open, I stepped into a large sitting room. A double-sided fireplace separated the cozy cluster of a sectional couch wrapped around an inlaid coffee table with the bedroom beyond.

A text dinged. My heart jumped out of my chest. "Shit," I whispered. Not sure why. If anyone was on this entire floor that ding just alerted them to the fact they weren't alone.

Gittings moving.

"Hurry," I raised my voice slightly so Miss P could hear. "I was right. Gittings is on the move."

Where is he?

Stairs that move to lobby.

"Five minutes." He's on the escalators at the hotel and in a hurry.

"Got it."

With a renewed sense of urgency, I fingered through the pile of magazines on the table. Nothing of great interest— mostly porn. Must be Ol' Irv's inner sanctum. I fought a shiver of revulsion.

Its burnished wood surface uncluttered, the desk in the corner hadn't been used...well not for business, at least. Ol' Irv had a desk back home...the thought made me shudder. He'd etched the names of the women he'd taken on the thing in the ancient mahogany. Thankfully, mine hadn't been one of them—even then there'd been a limit to my stupidity.

The bedroom looked a bit more lived in—the heavy damask quilt thrown back, the sheets wrinkled. The whole place had my nerves firing, my muscles twitching, my brain shouting, "Run!"

Another text. *Outside now. Running.*

Now I really did need to run. "Gotta go!"

I paused for one more look. It had to be here. Fighting the urge to run, I turned slowly, focusing, letting my gaze linger on the furniture, the credenza under the television hanging on the wall, the nightstand, the low bench at the foot of the bed, the other nightstand...

Wait.

An oblong object on the bench drew my attention. Something wrapped in a piece of cloth. I grabbed it and began peeling back the layers. Course silks with golden thread, the wrappings of a treasure.

My hands shook as I cradled the object, feeling its weight.

The thin evil shape.

Even as I turned back the last gossamer layer, I knew what I held.

The ivory handle. The lethal blade

The knife used to kill Kimberly Cho.

Quickly, I thumbed through the photos in my phone, confirming what I already knew. Jerry said he'd traced ownership as far as Irv Gittings, which was good enough for me.

It was his. He'd killed someone with it. How did he still have it?

Macau, where a life could be measured in money. I hadn't wanted to believe it, but now I held the proof. And I knew I wasn't prepared to live in a world this cruel.

"Find what you were looking for?"

The male voice held all the pain and anger I felt. My blood pressure spiked so high I thought blood would spurt out my ears. My hand sought the handle of the knife as I whirled around.

Frank Cho. Not who I'd expected.

"I'm glad to see you," I blathered.

He lifted his chin toward the knife I now held by the handle, the business end pointing toward him. "You better be ready to use that."

I dropped my hand. "I don't want to kill anybody." Self-preservation bolted through me. "Don't think I can't."

"I have no doubt." Frank seemed not to care one way or the other.

"I'm sorry about Kim."

He tried to shrug it off, but the shine in his eyes gave him away. "Then why are you holding the knife that killed her?"

"Knives don't kill, humans do." God, I sounded like one of those NRA commercials back home. True, but irritating in a condescending sort of way. I carefully refolded it in the silk. "I'm not the killer who wielded this blade, but I bet you know that."

"How do think? You're holding the murder weapon. You could've come here looking for it. Cover your trail."

"True, but then why are you here?"

"I could've followed you."

"But you didn't." I saw Miss P lurking behind him with a large bronze in her hands, preparing to swing it. "Don't!" I barked.

Frank whirled. Miss P froze. Then they both looked at me with disbelieving looks.

I extended the knife to Frank. "Here. If you really believe I killed Kim, then have at it. I deserve whatever I get from you."

He snatched the knife out of my hands, then backed up so that he had both Miss P and me in front of him. A tear leaked down his cheek. He swiped at it with the back of his hand. "He killed Kim. My father, he didn't stop him."

"That's how this business is played; you know that. Everyone is expendable, especially if they switch sides. You were going to help Kim, weren't you? I knew I wasn't wrong about you."

LUCKY THE HARD WAY

"She was right. For Macau to grow, to be like Vegas, we must be, as you say, legitimate."

One good gut-call. I relaxed just a little, fairly sure Frank wasn't going to perforate me. "My Security guy tied the ownership of that knife to Irv Gittings. He also placed Gittings in the Tigris at the time of Kim's murder through the surveillance tapes I uploaded to him. That's all I got."

"That's enough." His anger seemed to solidify into something different, something even more deadly. "How do you do it?"

"What?"

"Stay within yourself like you do."

I thought I knew what he meant, but I wasn't sure. "Draw your lines where you see fit and live on the right side of those lines."

He lifted the knife. "What would you do?"

"This isn't about me." I knew in my soul if anyone took someone I loved, I'd cut his heart out without thinking about it. "But we really do need to get out of here. Gittings is minutes away."

My phone dinged. *In the elevator.*

"Shit. We've got to run." Pushing and herding, I got both Miss P and Frank moving. "Back door? Service entrance?"

Frank turned to the left, heading through the dining room. "This way."

He'd been here before.

Behind us, the electronic lock on the front door slid open. The handle turned.

That galvanized us to a run. Trying for quiet, but in need of speed, we pushed through the back entrance.

Frank pressed the button for the service elevator. I grabbed his elbow and shepherded him through the door to the stairs. Then I corralled Miss P through in front of me.

"But it's like thirty floors," Miss P hissed.

Frank slowed. "I should go back. Kill him."

"Move. Keep going. He'll just shoot you. He knows we were there; he'll have a gun. And you have a knife. You'll never get close." I wanted to give him the whole revenge-is-best-served-cold lecture, but now was not the time.

Frank yielded to logic, surprising the hell out of me.

The three of us—Miss P in the front, Frank in the middle, me shielding from behind—raced down as fast as we could.

We didn't say anymore, just kept going round and round, descending like Orpheus into Hell.

Every few floors, I'd pause and listen for someone following, but I didn't hear anyone. I didn't like it.

At the bottom, Miss P reached to pound the bar and open the door. Reaching around Frank, I pulled her back. "Hold on. Something's not right."

Two sets of eyes turned to stare at me. "Nobody followed."

Frank nodded as the bloodlust left his eyes and cool calculation returned. "They took the elevator down."

The three of us looked at the door, imagining the evil on the other side. As if we'd summoned him, someone rattled the door.

Locked. The door could be opened only from the inside. Part of the security—hotels didn't want just anyone getting up to the upper floors. You had to have a valid room key and pass it in front of a reader in the elevator. But, legit or not, you couldn't open the stair door.

I tapped the other two to get their attention. When I had it, I pointed up.

"There's a fire escape on the other side of the building," Frank whispered.

Listening, looking, I led them up a few floors. Irv had a one-in-thirty chance of guessing which floor we chose, odds I could live with. I tried to second-guess myself—what would Irv think I would do?

I chose the seventh floor. Easing the door open just wide enough to get my head through and sneak a look, I could feel Frank and Miss P breathing down my neck, literally. The hall curved slightly to the left—I could see maybe halfway down, but the rest was around the bend.

Taking a deep breath, I pushed the door open wider and

stepped through, keeping the others shielded behind. Sticking close to the wall, I eased down the hall, heading toward the far side of the building. One step at a time, the fire escape seemed light-years away. My heart pounded in my ears. The worst part about this whole thing was we had to pass the elevators to get to the other side.

About halfway there, the elevator dinged its arrival.

Like mice in the kitchen when the light is turned on, we each scurried to safety in the doorways on either side. Miss P and Frank chose the right side; I chose the left...of course.

Pressed back as far as we could go, we blinked at each other and didn't breathe.

Voices. One male, one female. Friendly chattering in a language I didn't understand faded as the couple moved away. I sagged as stars swam in front of my eyes, then remembered to suck in a lungful of air. I sneaked a look. The hall was empty. Too afraid to speak, I motioned for my cohorts to follow as I stepped into the hallway.

The first shot winged my left arm. I didn't wait to see who was behind the trigger—I knew. Turning, I bolted after Miss P and Frank, who were one step ahead.

One floor in thirty and we had to end up on the same one.

Using the curve of the hallway, we ran just fast enough to keep Irv from getting a straight shot at us. That didn't keep him from firing. Shots thumped into the walls. A beautiful blown glass vase exploded. A light fixture was next.

I didn't bother to duck—I just ran. My breathing ragged, my legs heavy, I pushed. I couldn't slow down. One step slower, maybe two, and Irv would have a clear shot.

A shot sang next to my ear, hitting the wall.

He was closing.

"Hurry," I hissed, knowing they were going as fast as they could.

Frank hit the door first. Miss P stumbled through after him. Bending, I grabbed her under the arms and steadied her back on her feet. Bracing for the shot I knew would come, I dodged quickly to my right, putting as much of the wall between me and Ol' Irv as I could.

Next time I'd kill him when I had the chance...if I had the chance.

Some people shouldn't be allowed to live—a pretty radical thought for a staunch believer in the justice system. Ol' Irv had changed my mind.

Racing down the stairs, we'd put a floor and a half between us when I heard Irv bang through the door above us. Not much breathing room.

My throat burned as the breath tore through it, feeding lungs already starved.

Five floors.

Shit.

Bullets pinged off metal as Irv fired down the stairwell as he pounded after us. Mad and frustrated, and a bit scared, I figured. Long odds on hitting us with a random ricochet.

Only desperate men took the long odds.

As we hit the landing at the bottom, the shooting stopped. Clicks but no bullets.

Wasting ammo on emotion.

Despite sweating and breathing so hard our gasps could probably be heard in Hong Kong, Miss P and I strode sedately through the door as Frank held it open for us.

A tour group had arrived and the lobby was packed. Miss P and I filtered into the crowd as we made our way to the front door. Frank followed close behind.

A few of the tourists shot us mildly interested looks as they chattered among themselves.

Ming waited just outside the front door. She didn't have her machine gun, but the pistol in her hand was the next best thing. She took us in with one look. "Why didn't you call me? I could've helped."

"We were a bit busy." I grabbed her arm and pulled her along with us. "It's not safe out here."

"FBI over there." She lifted her chin indicating a spot across the street. "You want them to find Gittings?"

"Yes."

She spoke into her phone and men materialized out of the shadows, advancing on the hotel.

They wouldn't find him, but I didn't tell them that. I grabbed Miss P by the elbow. "Find anything?" I asked as I pulled her along, urging her to hurry.

"Enough to fire Whitmore but not enough to kill him."

"Glad to hear it. The list of folks I'd like to eradicate is pretty long, and that doesn't make me comfortable. I'm a Pollyanna—self-delusion is my happy place."

When I turned to look for Frank, he was gone.

Not that I was surprised. I hoped he wasn't doing anything foolish, then I half-hoped he was. Not really a good time, though, with the FBI scurrying like ants through the hotel. I tried not to worry about him—he'd have to do what he needed to do, then find a way to make his peace with it. "I didn't imagine him, did I?" I asked Miss P.

"Not unless we both had the same bad food for lunch."

Feeling like a fox with a pack of hounds on my scent, I didn't relax until we were both in the elevator at Tigris. Ming leaned in and punched the button for the owner's suite, flashing a card to activate it.

"You're not coming up?"

Her eyes looked deadly. "No, we need to be watchful."

I glanced at my watch. Eight p.m. "Time flies when you're having fun." I smiled at her quizzical expression as the doors slid closed.

At the last minute, I stuck my hand between them. "The man came to see you?" I asked Ming.

"Yes. Everything is in place. Do not worry."

She didn't understand—worry was my job. And Ming was the key, the only wild card I couldn't protect against. Would she come through?

One hundred million U.S. rested on her decision.

As the doors closed, I said to Miss P, "This game has the highest stakes I've ever wagered." I didn't expect sympathy from her and I didn't get it.

"You gave Frank the knife," Miss P said, as we both

watched the numbers pass all too slowly, and I had a Yogi Berra moment..

I wanted a rocket ship to Mars, and I got the slow train. Terrific. I tapped my foot as my life passed while we ascended at a glacial pace. Somehow I resisted punching the button in frustration. I didn't hear any condemnation in her voice, but I read it into the question. "He would've found it anyway."

"But you put it in his hands, knowing he had murder on his mind."

I thought about that for a moment, how I felt about it. Yeah, I'd pretty much signed Irv Gittings' death warrant. First when I delivered the *coup de grâce* to Mr. Cho. Irv had said he was shooting at me, but Irv was never known for telling the truth. The truth was his guy shot Minnie. I chose to interpret that to suit my purposes—Irv would've done the same. That fact alone should've had me filled with self-loathing, but it didn't. When I'd caught Irv the first time, I'd played by the rules. He'd used them against me, which I figured gave me a free pass this time.

Why was it always easier to justify bad behavior than good?

Knowing Ol' Irv and his Houdini skills as I did, I didn't rely solely on Mr. Cho to do my dirty work. No, I doubled up with Frank for added security.

"Justice."

"No doubt," Miss P agreed.

I heard what she left unsaid. "Maybe you're correct and I don't have the right. Maybe I'm just tired of letting bad people get away with bad things. Time to stand up. If I go to Hell, so be it."

"All our friends will be there." Miss P hooked her arm through mine. "Let's go slay that last dragon, then let's go home."

Friends—the folks who will help you bury the bodies.

"First, I have something to do. Then want to meet me for dinner? The main restaurant in half an hour?"

I left her at the penthouse floor, staring at me bug-eyed as the elevator door closed.

CHAPTER NINETEEN

RYAN WHITMORE paced in front of the reception desk.

"Take a walk with me?" I said without preamble, more of a demand than a pleasantry.

He jumped at my voice. "Lucky? What are you doing here?"

"Surprised to see me?" I grabbed his arm. "Let's go for that walk, okay?"

He fell into step although he didn't look happy about it. "What's this about?"

I moved him across the lobby toward the front door. "We can do this inside, here in front of everyone. Or you can go quietly."

He jerked his arm loose from my grip with a last-ditch effort at righteous indignation. "What are you talking about?"

"Okay, your choice." I leveled a smile. "You're fired."

"What?" He gave me a snort and smirk—hard to do together, but he pulled it off. "You can't fire me."

"You think I'm afraid of our important friends? Guess again." I glanced through the glass doors in time to see Lieutenant Uendo ease his car to the curb. "Your ride is here."

"It'll never stick."

"That's where you're wrong. You provided a service for Mr. Cho and his friends. You were the hired help, nothing more. And, as such, you are expendable. They'll find someone else."

The truth of my words hit home. I could see it in his eyes. And I was ready when he turned to run. My elbow caught him in the nose. He sagged to the floor, his hands cupped to catch the blood that gushed down his face. "You don't know anything," he growled, but he couldn't pull off the menace part.

"I know everything."

Uendo joined me, and we both stared down at Whitmore. Thankfully the lobby was fairly empty so we didn't have much of an audience. "You do make your presence known around here," Uendo said with what I thought might pass for a smile. "Good thing for Mr. Whitmore here I was next door. Given more time, I'm sure you would do more damage."

He was closer to right than I'd realized. Still itching to shed more of Whitmore's blood, it was clear my self-control had got up and went. "This is my hotel, and I take care of my own." Bowing to him, I continued, "With the help of the local constabulary."

He looked at me with new appreciation, then he reached down and grabbed Whitmore by the elbow, tugging him to his feet. "You'll get us an amount that he stole?"

"May take a few days."

"Not to worry. We have a nice cell for him, so take your time."

I watched him lead Whitmore through the doors, then stuff him in the back of his car. Whitmore hung his head as the door closed. He didn't glare at me; he didn't dare.

Cindy Liu rushed to my side as Uendo pulled away from the curb, then disappeared from sight. "Was that Ryan?"

Before answering, I turned and looked at her.

She seemed to wilt under my stare. "You don't understand."

"That's where you're wrong. I understand all too well. We've all loved the wrong man."

"I didn't know, not at first."

"I believe you. But it's what you didn't do when you found

out that worries me."

She bowed her head and wouldn't look at me. "I know I have done wrong, but I am the one who called Minnie. We needed help. She sent it."

"She did?"

Cindy looked up, holding my gaze. "She sent you."

AS I waited for Miss P in the restaurant, I contemplated what to do with Cindy Liu. What would I have done in her shoes? Women needed to learn their power—she was no exception. And she needed to develop a keener eye for good men, but she hadn't let Whitmore compromise her position. Actually, she'd reached out for help she could trust, even knowing Whitmore would get caught in the crossfire.

All qualities I could live with.

Miss P pulled out a chair and plopped into it as she graced me with an odd smile. "Normally, I can think of no better dining companion, but tonight, the two of us, this whole thing has the feel of a last supper."

I offered her a menu. "Well, then, I'd order the most expensive thing on the menu. The Big Boss owes us that much."

And so we did: Kobe steak for me, Abalone for her. No matter how much I tried to expand my palate, sea snails just didn't qualify as food. We washed it down with a lovely Laurent-Perrier rosé Champagne.

We took our time and I tried not to think of Miss P's characterization of our fine repast. She regaled me with stories of her honeymoon, leaving out the good parts.

When she'd wound down and our plates had been cleared but dessert had yet to arrive, I asked her, "What would you do about Cindy Liu?" And I told her what Cindy had told me.

"If it were my choice, I'd give her Ryan Whitmore's job."

I raised my glass. "Exactly my thinking."

WADDLING like the pigs we were, Miss P and I wandered back to the owner's suite. "Here we are," I said as I strode into my suite, using the front door this time. "In case anyone was wondering."

I expected Romeo to answer, but it was Jeremy who replied. "Sinjin and Romeo are going through things now. The cameras go down and we trigger the looped feed in ten minutes."

He sat where I'd left Romeo a short time ago, keyboard in his lap, hunched in front of the screens. One screen looked like before with lines of code marching down it. The other held the camera feeds from the exhibition room divided into ten quadrants, each showing a single feed.

I grabbed a chair and nestled in close. "You guys tested the earpiece?"

"Romeo can hear us." He showed me a small device that had been sitting on the table between us. "We can talk to him using this. He can't reply, but we should be able to see him soon."

"Sinjin won't be able to see the earpiece."

"It fits in the ear canal like a tiny hearing aid. State-of-the-art."

Miss P pulled a chair in next to mine. She set a glass of red wine in front of me and another in front of Jeremy. "To settle nerves."

Grateful, I took a couple of sips, but no more.

The feeds Sinjin wanted looped stayed on screen a few seconds, then rotated so we had several angles of each watch in its case.

"We'll see the real feed, but Security will see the loop?" I knew the answer, but I needed to hear it from Jeremy.

"Yeah. If your buddy Chip has tapped into the right wires at the right places."

I tried not to think about that. "Some of the young women helping us will be wandering near the exhibit, others on the lobby floor near the escalators up to the exhibition level. They will alert us if the feeds are looped properly and Security is heading that way."

"With this much at stake, Sinjin and Romeo will have seconds to run."

"Sinjin and I worked that through. There's really only one protected escape route. They'll have to go out that way regardless." I didn't tell Jeremy I had one hundred million U.S. riding on it. Romeo knew that, and he knew what to do.

The three of us fell silent as we focused on the screens. Dark, the lighting on the watches casting an eerie glow, the room looked empty. I scanned across the feeds. "Which one will be looped?"

"This one, the main feed from the exhibition." Jeremy pointed to the top left quadrant.

Turning the small transmitter over in my hand, I asked Jeremy, "If I punch this, Romeo can hear me?" My thumb hovered above a small button.

"Yeah. Don't shout. Whispering would be best. They'll be close together and in a very quiet place."

He didn't need to clarify. "Got it." I pressed the button. Lowering my voice, I brought Romeo up to speed. "We can't see you yet." I glanced at the timer on the screen. "Thirty more seconds. Ming said the package is in place. If, for some reason, you take a different route out of the building, we'll see that and make sure you are intercepted."

Jeremy shot me a sideways glance. "What are you up to?"

"Covering my ass. But there are so many moving parts, so many unknowns, that it's anybody's guess whether this will work."

"Tell me. I can help."

I pointed at the screen as the timer click to five. "We're almost on."

Without blinking, I stared at the monitor, relaxing, waiting. The clock hit zero. An almost imperceptible flicker, then the image continued as before. "Did you see it?"

"Yeah, it switched." Jeremy nodded, his nose inches from the screen.

I pointed to a feed at the bottom—a hallway, one I knew. I'd used it to get out of the hotel when I went to meet Sinjin for the first time. "That one did, too."

Jeremy flicked a hard glance my way, the golden flecks in his eyes turning to ice. "You sure?"

"Yep. I was watching for it. I didn't know which one, but I figured he had a plan he wasn't telling us about."

"The bastard."

"Well, at least we know how he plans on leaving the hotel." I laid a hand on his arm. "Don't worry. I've got this." Kim's voice echoed in my empty head. *No one is who they seem.*

My phone vibrated in my lap, making me jump only slightly. I'd put it on silent—my nerves were completely shot, and I didn't need the cattle prod of its siren call to flat-line my heart rate.

"Mother. And right on time, too."

"You haven't called your father. It's important."

"Not now, Mother."

Thankfully, she didn't argue. "Here's Chip."

Before I answered I texted Jerry back at the Babylon. *Everything good?*

His answer was almost immediate. *We're seeing what he's seeing. Money starting to come in. Five installments so far, each ten million. Running a back trace now.*

"Chip? What do you see?"

He told me exactly what Jerry had said. So far so good. "Are you tracing the funds back to their origin?"

"Hold." In the background, he asked Mona for some paper and a pen.

The simplest things are often overlooked. I tried for patience while I waited for Mother to deliver and I worried about what I had overlooked. Soon I heard scrambling and

Chip came back on the line. "I got five of them. More are coming in. You ready?"

I put him on speaker and pulled up the message function on my iPhone. Before I responded, I found Stokes's number and started a new message to him. "Fire away." I typed in names and addresses, double-checking them, then hit send. "And you've taken down the alarms, right? And nobody is the wiser?"

"Child's play."

"Stokes is ready, right?" I asked Jeremy.

He answered with a nod, his eyes never leaving the screen. We both were riveted, and I sensed Miss P's attention next to me—hard to miss, she'd practically crawled into my lap to get a better view.

"Chip?"

"Yo."

"Take the fifty mil and route it through Irv Gittings' account then wire it where I told you. You got it?"

"On it."

"Make sure no one can touch a cent of that money or I'll cut it out of your hide a dollar at a time."

"You might be surprised, but it's fun to use my skills for the forces of good."

"I'll make a white hat out of you yet." I didn't remind him he was helping me steal more money than either of us would see in a lifetime from some very bad men. His complicity was hidden; mine, not so much, leaving me to suffer a severely damaged chance at longevity. I could live with that. "Call me back when all the money is there." My phone fell silent. I texted Jerry. *Still good?*

You'll be the first to know if something goes sideways.

My heart pounded as I watched Sinjin and Romeo as they slithered through the exhibition hall, stopping at the display of the Patek Phillipe. Of course, they'd pick the most expensive to pinch first.

In fact, I was counting on it. Another smile. Yes, the line between good and evil was very thin indeed. How easy to erase part of it and peer through.

Romeo set the bag, one with a dragon logo on the side, on the floor. I smiled.

I had the answer to another question.

He and Sinjin both grabbed the glass enclosure, each taking two sides. I could see Sinjin counting, then they both lifted.

The glass came away from the pedestal.

"Anything?" I asked.

Jeremy rotated through the other feeds.   "No alarms. Chip is good."

I started to breathe again, although shallowly. "This sitting here with nothing to do is a killer."

Sweat beaded on Jeremy's brow. "Done this before. Never liked it."

"I'm with you."

"Me, too," Miss P whispered.

I'd even led my North Star of Virtue astray. Not good. I'd counted on her to save my sorry soul.

Sinjin lifted the watch with gloved hands, passing it off to Romeo. Romeo pulled a box out of the hatch in the pedestal, secured the watch in its silk nest, then placed the box in the bag.

All going according to plan.

They did two more watches. Only eight more to go.

My phone vibrated, and I practically leapt out of my skin, elbowing Miss P in the process. "Sorry."

Miss P shot me a sympathetic smile as one of her hands fluttered to cover her heart.

Expecting Chip, I was surprised to see an unfamiliar number.

"Miss Lucky?" A breathy, female voice.

"Yes."

"This is Pei. The bad man?" She stumbled over the words as if afraid to say them.

"Yes?" My heart hammered.

287

Irv Gittings—the one big unknown in all of this. I'd sort of counted on him running from the brick-wielding man in Mr. Cho's employ about now. Apparently, that hadn't happened.

"The bad man, he took Teddie."

"What? Where?"

"We are watching. He took him from the junket room. They are on the moving stairs to the bottom now." I looked at the screens, at Romeo and Sinjin stealing the watches, at the money moving, at Jerry watching Chip, and me watching it all. "Fuck. On my way."

I handed the transmitter to Romeo to Miss P. "If he gets in trouble..."

She looked at me with wide eyes. "Make it up. Jeremy can help you." Turning to Jeremy, I said, "When the info on the next fifty mil comes in, send it to Stokes and light a fire under his ass to go round up the previous owners of the money." I rattled off Mona's phone number. "Call Mother, tell her what's happened. She'll convince Chip to give you the goods." I sounded a bit more convincing than I felt.

"Where are you going?"

"To take care of Ol' Irv for good."

I guess they both saw murder in my eyes as Miss P paled and Jeremy half rose. "I'm going with you."

I motioned to the screen as I stood and pushed him back down. "You can't."

"Lucky." Worry weighted Miss P's one word.

"My fight."

"WHERE are they now?" I barked into the phone as I tried to suffer through the slow ride to the lobby. Someone with cloying cologne exuberantly applied had recently ridden in the thing, and the cloud that lingered added nausea to my list of woes.

"Going to the front door. He has a gun."

So did I. I'd pulled it from my purse and stuffed it back into the waistband of my pants—probably wouldn't be helpful to run through the lobby with it in my hand, terrifying the locals.

When the opening of the elevator doors was barely wide enough, I arrowed myself through sideways then took off at a run, startling many of the folks lingering in the lobby who parted like the Red Sea. I hit the front door and burst through in time to see Irv stuffing Teddie in a black sedan.

"Stop them!"

That froze everyone as they looked at me then swiveled around looking for what I was talking about—not that anyone understood English. Apparently, they understood anger and panic, as they scurried away from me.

I pushed through the few remaining who were immobilized by the sight of an angry Amazon shouting in a foreign tongue.

Too late I skidded in behind the car as it accelerated down the driveway. Irv Gittings' face mooned me through the back window. I didn't see Teddie, but I knew he was there, and I prayed he was all right.

Why was it always a black sedan? Did people unwittingly buy cars that match the color of their soul? Mine was red. Okay, it really wasn't mine, but I liked the red.

Red. The Chinese loved red—the color was everywhere. Something about fire and joy and good fortune, I couldn't remember.

As long as Irv Gittings didn't have what he wanted, Teddie would live.

And, I'd be willing to bet, what Ol' Irv wanted was me.

It wasn't an ego thing, just a reality thing. I'd messed with his magic and he wanted to punish me for it. I glanced around. I had to follow them; I couldn't let them get away. Of course, if my theory was right, they'd wait. They'd make it easy.

Setting a trap, if I'd just take the bait.

Okay. I'll bite.

An unfortunate man wheeled into the curb in front of me on a new Ducati.

A Ducati...a red Ducati.

I took it as a sign.

As he stepped off, I threw a leg over, turned the key, and was gone before he even got his helmet off. Laying low over the handlebars, I followed the red taillights blinking in the distance. Slowing for a curve, the driver accelerated when I closed half the distance between us.

Game on.

We wound through town, climbing gently, the streets deserted, the roar of the bike echoing off the dark apartments lining the streets. Content to follow, I stayed far enough back, using corners and delivery trucks to shield myself so that, if they wanted to shoot, I'd present a bit of a challenge at least.

The streets narrowed, the complexion changed. Restaurants and small commercial stalls lined the streets with apartments above. I slowed, the bike thrumming with energy under me. Around the next corner, I skidded to a stop. A delivery truck backed across the road in front of me. Yelling and waving, I finally got the driver's attention and he pulled forward just enough to let me wiggle the nimble bike behind him. But I'd lost minutes—a lifetime.

No taillights in front of me.

I'd lost them.

Fuck.

And then it hit me: this could be a great ruse to pull me off what was going down at the Tigris. I didn't know and I couldn't think about it. Romeo, Jeremy, even Chip and Mona, had to do their part.

I had to trust them. For once, I had to make a choice, to count on others. Romeo had saved my bacon before—he wouldn't let me down. Not if he could help it. Jeremy, too.

I imagined my phone vibrating with messages, but I couldn't look at it. Winding through the narrow streets, I looked for the car. A late-model luxury sedan. Not too many in this neighborhood.

My heart pounded and my palms were sweaty. I tried not to think about what would happen if I didn't find them...if I didn't find Teddie. Truly I didn't know, but I knew Irv was capable of anything.

Finally, after several lifetimes, I saw the car, doors open, at the foot of Senado Square, the center of Macau. The wavy tiled pattern alternating black and white was as iconic as the neo-Mediterranean buildings, leftovers from the colonial occupation.

Now I knew where they were going, the ruins of St. Paul's. Once the largest Catholic church in Asia, now, after several fires, all that remained was the very grand façade, lit at night as a beacon. A beacon to whom and for what, I didn't know, but it loomed above me, calling.

Just the sort of place Irv Gittings would pick for a showdown.

God, I hated the melodramatic.

Cars weren't allowed in the square, and I decided to leave the bike. Going on foot would be a little more stealthy. Once I killed the engine, the night and its smothering quiet tucked in around me.

I kept to the shadows, occasionally stepping into the moonlight to get my bearings. Once, I thought heard footsteps behind me. Stopping, I waited, but they didn't continue.

My imagination playing tricks.

Of course, the blood pounding in my ears didn't help.

When I started again, I picked up the pace.

Finally, I reached the steps leading up to the cathedral. And I'd been right.

Irv Gittings, standing in the light of the floods that illuminated the structure, stood at the top step, Teddie clutched to his side, a gun to his head. "I know you're there, Lucky. Step out where I can see you."

Teddie flinched away as Irv pressed the gun to his temple.

Irv pulled him in front, using Teddie as a human shield.

My gun in my hand and ready to fire, I stayed in the shadows as I eased around to my right.

Where was the driver? Irv and Teddie had been in the back seat, so, unless Google was making great strides with a driverless car in Asia, there had to be a third person.

Darkness shrouded the fronts of the buildings around me. The columns and the doorways sheltered me as I tried to figure a way to even the odds a bit.

"Lucky? Show yourself." He lowered his gun and pulled the trigger.

Teddie yelled and sagged.

My heart leapt into my throat.

Teddie held a hand over his thigh above his knee.

Irv had shot him! An eternity in hell roasting on a spit over an open fire was too good for him.

"Don't do it, Lucky. Go back. Irv's a dead man. I am, too." That last part he said through gritted teeth. He didn't know about Minnie and Frank and what they knew. Irv probably did, but, in case I was wrong, I didn't enlighten him.

"Another one for the other knee, Lucky."

I had nothing. Taking a deep breath, then another, I steadied my nerves.

Now or never, I was all in.

I stepped out of the shadows, my hands held high, my gun showing in my palm facing outward. "I'm here. You got me. Let Teddie go." Staying to the left, I started up the stairs toward them.

The driver stepped out of the shadows across from me, an evil smile slashing across dead features. I recognized him from the paper, and his two shiners and broken nose that I'd inflicted. The brick guy. The man who killed Kim's law partner.

And things had been going so well.

"Stop there, Lucky. Throw your gun away."

I weighed my options. Not many. Take a shot. Teddie and I could die. If I don't, we die anyway. "Okay, okay." I dipped like I was going to kneel to put my gun on the ground.

Irv didn't give an inch. He knew me well.

In one motion, I raised my gun and squeezed.

Teddie yelled.

I pivoted and fired off two more rounds. The brick guy dropped to his knees, his hands pressed on his chest. His eyes caught mine as blood oozed between his fingers. Then he toppled over face first.

All over in a second, although it seemed like a lifetime.

Turning, I bolted toward the top of the stairs. Irv had staggered back. Teddie, a heavy weight in his arms, worked against him. A red stain bloomed on Irv's right shoulder. His arm fell limp. He struggled to raise it, to point the gun. He couldn't.

I had a clear shot. Slowing, taking the stairs two at a time, I sighted on his chest.

He dropped Teddie, who crabbed away from him, dragging his leg. The bullet I'd fired had gouged his upper arm, then buried itself in Irv's chest.

Millimeters.

Irv raised his arm, slowly. I could see his hesitation, and I knew what he was thinking. Fast and quick? Or slow, waiting for the bullet?

Enjoying this, I increased pressure on the trigger. "Your choice, asshole."

Something below and behind me yanked his gaze away.

I didn't turn. I was close now, so close I could smell his fear. And I wouldn't fall for his cheap attempt at distracting me.

Something whizzed by my ear.

Irv's eyes widened. His gun clattered to the stairs. His hands found the hilt of a knife that protruded from his chest.

An ivory-handled knife.

Irv crumpled, then rolled down the few steps between us, coming to rest at my feet. On his back, for a moment he was there, looking up at me. Then his eyes went blank and he was gone. I expected angels to sing and the Devil's minions to swoop in and gather him up and cart him off to eternal damnation.

None of that happened, damn it.

I lowered my gun and took a step back, as a man stepped in next to me.

"You beat me to it, Frank. How'd you find us?"

"That was my Ducati you stole." We traded smiles, and I could tell we both were thinking the same thing: Kim was watching over us.

Teddie had pushed himself to his feet. Standing above us, favoring his right leg as blood oozed down it, he stared at us, then at Irv. "It's over."

To Teddie, Irv had been his only hope, the only one left who could exonerate him. Killing Irv had just sentenced him to a life on the run.

"It may be over, but not in the way you think. This man here," I put a hand on Frank's shoulder as I fought the urge to kiss him, which would've embarrassed us both, "he's got a story to tell. Don't you, Frank?"

"Have you done what you promised Minnie?"

"I promised her I would risk everything to do as she asked. I could not promise I would succeed."

"So, you don't know?" He seemed surprised by that.

"No. This was more important."

He glanced between Teddie and I, then gave me a small bow. "Indeed. I will tell your friend my story while I take him to the hospital."

"I'm afraid I'm going to steal your bike again."

"Be my guest. I have one of the hotel limos."

CHAPTER TWENTY

WHEN I burst through the front door of Tigris everything seemed...normal. I didn't like it. First, I tried Ming. She didn't answer. I didn't want to call Jeremy—he needed his phone to talk with Jerry and Chip.

So I did the only thing I could—I hit the elevator and headed up to my suite.

The door was unlocked. I palmed my gun and eased it open.

Laughter filtered out. Then the pop of a cork.

Jeremy, Miss P, and Ming stood in a circle. Everyone had a glass out for Jeremy to pour.

Miss P had two. "Oh, Lucky, there you are." Jeremy filled one of her glasses and she held it out to me. "Come, let's celebrate."

I set my gun on the table by the door, then accepted her glass as I joined the group. "Glad to see you guys aren't beating the bushes looking for me. Weren't you worried?"

Jeremy scoffed. "Hell, no."

Miss P rolled her eyes. "Worried sick. Bruno, here," she tilted her head toward her hubby, "was ready to scour the city. But Frank called, told Ming what happened." Her grin faded. "Teddie's okay?"

"He was standing when I left. Frank said he'd take him to

295

the hospital. We probably ought to check on him in a bit. I did leave Frank with a bit of a mess and some explaining to do."

"Should we go help?"

Normally I'd be the one to bound off looking for a windmill to tilt. "No. His fight. His city."

Miss P looked relieved as she sipped the Champagne Jeremy had poured for her.

I seconded that emotion. "Where's Romeo?"

"On his way," Jeremy said, holding up the transmitter for me to see. "I told him he was missing the party. Of course, he couldn't reply."

"But we know he's okay?" I pressed.

"Yes," Ming said. "I was hiding where you said. I saw him. He was not far behind me, and I walked in right before you."

"And Sinjin?"

"Disappeared." Disappointment tugged the corners of her mouth into a frown.

Despite local custom, I gave her a quick hug. "Don't expect people to live up to your expectations."

She looked like she understood, but I also could tell the next time the two of them met, Sinjin was in for an ass whipping. I'd like to be in on that, but I wanted to go home—and really, I had no expectations for him to not live up to. He didn't owe me a thing. Now for the big question—the answer to which would seal my fate. "The watches?"

Faces fell, followed by uncomfortable glances all around.

So not good.

I was just starting to imagine what jail would be like when a voice sounded behind me. "The watches? Got them right here." Romeo strode into the room, holding the bag aloft.

I rushed over to him, spilling my wine. "The real ones?"

Romeo had a raised bump on one temple, and his smile looked a little wobbly.

I grabbed his arm and led him over to the couch. "Sit. Did he hit you?"

"You told me he probably would. I was prepared for it, but

he still caught me by surprise. The fakes you had Ming stash in the pedestal of the last watch—I was just able to make the switch right before. I thought maybe he was onto me. But we got all the way to the hall leading outside. That's where he hit me. When I came to, the bag was gone, and so was he."

"So these are the watches you went back for?"

"Yeah."

"How do you know they're the real ones?"

"I did like you said: I took a flower in there and then put it in the bag as we were stealing the watches." He opened the bag and held it out to me. "Dig down under the boxes. You'll see the flower is still there. I didn't put it on top because I thought maybe Sinjin might be smart enough to look."

I reached in, pawing through the priceless watches, and pulled out a battered rose. And then it hit me, "It's really over."

"You haven't asked about the money," Jeremy reminded me.

"I know this sounds odd, but the money was the least important part. Stolen goods. But tell me about the money."

"We took half—well, your buddy Chip took half out of Irv's account as you asked and left half there." When I opened my mouth, he held a hand up. "Chip wired the money into that offshore account I told you about that I have for, well, cases like this. I took a screen shot and sent it to Stokes, who rather gleefully said he'd show it to Mr. Cho, who was his guest in the back of a patrol car."

"So you made it look like Irv had already taken half the funds?"

"Just as you said. Brilliant, by the way."

"With Irv dead, we don't really need Mr. Cho after him."

"On the contrary," Jeremy countered with a shit-eating grin. "We've stolen a lot of money from some very bad men. If we put them on Irv's trail, so much the better."

"They might come sniffing around, though," Romeo said, ever the detective.

I jumped in. "I've thought of that. So, if you guys don't

mind spending one more day, that will give me time to take care of a few things, and get Teddie stable enough for the long ride home. What do you say?"

"We can go out on the town," Romeo said, sounding not really that enthusiastic.

"How about you lay low. Order a feast from room service, anything you want. Then get some shut-eye and we'll head home tomorrow?"

"I've got to get this equipment back to the bloke I borrowed it from," Jeremy said.

"I need to get seriously wasted," Romeo added. Tonight had probably taken years off his life, but from the look on his face, it was worth it.

I turned to my assistant. "Miss P, what's your pleasure?"

"I think I just need to sit for a bit."

"Offer up some thanks for me, would you?"

She smiled at my soft tone.

"Would you be so kind as to get the plane moved to Macau?"

"It will be here in the morning stocked for the flight, the pilots rested and ready."

"Thank you."

"And, Romeo, if Minnie is able to talk, you might have one of your guys at home go talk to her. She's got a story and it's important."

He looked like he understood as he rose and stepped away from the group and pulled out his phone.

"Where are you going?" Ming asked.

"If you'll come with me, there's someone I'd like to introduce you to."

VITO MORGENSTERN lived in a rather unassuming

apartment halfway up one of the many hills dotting the city. He had a view, but he didn't advertise it—just that fact alone made me inclined to like him.

My father's faith in him guaranteed I would trust him.

When I pulled into the drive and up to the front door, Ming put a hand on my arm. She hadn't said one word the whole drive. "Are you sure about this man? He is very powerful."

"Yes, and when I leave, you will need powerful friends."

"You do this for me?" She seemed taken aback.

"For you, and Pei, and the other women, most of whom I'll never know. For Miss Liu. But you have to promise me something."

"Yes?"

"If Ryan Whitmore gives you any trouble, you will shoot him for me."

"Oh, I will do it myself."

"Good." I opened my door. "Come on, let's do this. I need to stop in at the police station, then go bust an old boyfriend out of the hospital. Maybe then I'll get to go home."

Ming hung back as we approached the massive wooden door. "Why no guards? No guns?"

"Real power means you don't need any of that."

The door opened before I could find the bell.

Vito was exactly as I expected, a short, wizened Jewish guy with a firm handshake, a bald head, a big smile, and intelligent eyes. He met us at the door himself, wearing a silk robe and slippers.

I was surprised to realize it was still early. Time had lost all meaning.

Except I needed to get home.

"Lucky!" Vito bellowed, his voice much larger than his body. "He pumped my hand up and down. "When your father called, I was so excited to get the chance to see you again. Of course, the first time I saw you, you were much shorter." He grinned up at me.

"You knew?" It seemed a lot of folks knew the Big Boss

was my father long before they shared the secret with me.

"We helped each other out back in the day." He herded us into a large great room with expansive views and comfortable furniture. A grand piano was tucked into the far corner. Photos graced the wall next to it—eight by tens, seven by fives, all framed in black with a white mat and hung in a mosaic of memories from waist-high to almost the ceiling.

I paused to drink in some of old Vegas. Vito lurked at my elbow. He pointed to a photo. "There's your father and myself when we were young and mean enough to think we could make something of ourselves." He pointed to another. "Here's one with your mom."

They looked so young, so ready to tackle the world, so sure the future held only greatness.

We all pass through that phase.

We sat in a comfortable sectional. When everyone was settled, I opened the conversation. "Vito, this is my friend Ming. She's a very fine young woman, but, like most of the fine young women in this city, she needs your help. Here's the deal. I've got eighty million U.S. I managed to reroute from Mr. Cho and his friends. I trust those men were no friends of yours?" I asked Vito pointedly. I was pretty sure I knew the answer—the Big Boss wouldn't steer me wrong—but I wanted to see what he'd say.

"On the contrary. They make life very difficult for an honest businessman like me." Vito managed that with a perfectly straight face.

"Really?" I must've sounded skeptical.

"Yes, didn't your father tell you? After he pulled my ass out of the fire back in Vegas, I decided to make it as a legit businessman. Oh, he was chapped when he found out I'd crawled into bed with the Wiseguys."

"He was?"

"Yeah, we used to call him Prince Valiant. So incorruptible your father was. He made it his way, though. Never compromised."

So that was the secret my father didn't want me to know?

Or Vito was shining me on for my father's benefit. I didn't really care which was true. The truth was what I believed—at least when it came to my father.

"And you?"

"An honest businessman selling gaming equipment to the casinos."

Honest meant different things to different people, but I wasn't in a position to quibble. One thing I knew about him for sure—he didn't run girls for other men's pleasure, and that was what mattered.

"Okay," I continued, anxious to make sure the doctors on the small spit of land didn't kill Teddie. "Actually, I misspoke before. I don't have the eighty mil; my friend Ming does."

She looked at me with large eyes, blinking rapidly. "She will use this money to better the lives of all the young women here who need to get out of their present circumstances, if you follow?"

Vito smiled and shook his head. "You are your father's daughter."

So many people had said that I was starting to believe it...and like it. "Ming will need your wise counsel and your protection. I don't need to tell you there could be Triad trouble."

"No. I have my own ways of dealing with the Triad. They do not scare me."

"Well, you are old, but Ming is not. Nor am I, although I feel old at the moment. And, the Triad scares both of us."

Vito threw back his head and laughed. "You have nothing to fear. I will offer you both my protection."

I leaned over and patted Ming on the knee—she still sat ramrod straight like a statue. "You can't do anything better than that. Are you up to this?" I should've asked her first, but I didn't want her to say no before she met Vito. "You can get out, but now is the time. After this, I don't think it will be possible."

She gave me a steady stare. "For the girls."

"For the women."

Then she smiled, reminding me how young she was. "Yes, this."

"May I leave you two to work out the details?"

Vito and Ming looked at each other. "Tea?" he asked her.

Her courage kicked in. "Please."

Still too early for the house staff to be awake, Vito excused himself to go find the kitchen.

I eyed my young pupil. "You make a hard bargain with him."

She nodded.

"He is a man of honor. He will do as he says."

Vito returned. "I rousted the butler. He will bring tea shortly."

I rose. "I've a plane to catch." I turned to go. "Oh, Vito, one more thing. Watch Ming, she has a pirate friend who is a bit shifty."

I CAUGHT up with Detective Uendo at the steps leading up to St. Paul's. With daylight breaking, the place looked totally different than it had a few hours ago. Much less sinister. The bodies had been carted off. Probably not good for tourism to leave them around.

"When are you leaving?" he asked as I approached. He was standing in almost the exact spot I had been standing when I'd pulled the trigger.

"We can't leave without your clearance."

"I heard the FBI rounded up a bunch of our upstanding citizens early this morning. Waves are being felt all the way to Beijing."

"Really? How clever of them."

"I also heard the watches at your exhibit had been stolen."

I pursed my lips. "If you check them, you'll find that is not true."

"Not now." He gave me a sideways look.

He turned to look out over the stairs leading up to the cathedral ruins. "So, if someone stood right here, do you think it would be possible to shoot someone up there," he pointed to the top of the steps, "narrowly missing an innocent man. Then turn and drop an armed man over there." He pointed where the brick guy had fallen.

"They'd have to be really lucky." I managed that without even the hint of a smile. Yes, my luck had turned. And, curiously enough, I liked Uendo.

"That's what I'm thinking," he said, patting the pockets of his coat like Columbo before him.

"So the guy up there was shot?" I pointed to the top of the steps.

"Before someone planted a knife in his chest. The same knife used to kill Kim Cho."

"Wonder how that knife came to find its way here?"

"Bad police work. I will find who was responsible."

Yes, I liked Uendo a lot.

"Will you let us go home?"

"Yes, with a proviso."

That raised my eyebrows. From his tone, I thought perhaps a prison sentence might still be in my future. "What?"

"Frank and I will clean this up." He swept his arm to include all of Macau. "But, if we call..."

"I'll come running."

He grabbed me in a hug, surprising us both.

ROMEO'S text caught me on the way to the hospital, rerouting me to the airport.

I found my gang huddled in a small building at the Macau

airport, watching through the window as the G-650 taxied up. The adrenaline in all of us was waning. Miss P leaned on Jeremy, safe in his hug. Romeo held up a pillar in the corner, and Teddie lounged on a sofa that had seen better days, his leg, bound in white gauze and tape, rested on a chair he'd pulled around in front of him.

I sat down next to him. "How's the leg?"

"Flesh wound. Amazingly it just tore through muscle but missed everything that would hurt worse."

"Or kill you."

He looked wrung out without even the hint of sparkle he usually had. "Are we really going home?"

"No. Somewhere over the Pacific I've asked the pilots to pull over so I can throw you out."

He sighed and let his head fall back against a pillow someone had stuffed behind it. "Wow. Home."

I patted his hand resting on the couch between us. His skin was cold. "It really is over."

"You believe Frank?"

"I don't have any idea what he said or what his story is. The police should be talking with Minnie, I hope. We'll piece it together."

"You put everything on the line to get me off."

"It's what friends do."

I left him sitting there, not sure what he was feeling or how I felt about any of it. Well, happy that everything had turned out okay, but totally clueless as to how I felt about Teddie.

We'd always been best as friends. I'd like to get back there...if we could find the new normal and start over. Who knew? But there'd always be a place in my heart for Teddie.

I wandered over to Romeo. "I assume you gave the watches to..."

"Miss Liu and the police. They were headed to reinstall them in the exhibition hall. Dear God, I thought she'd never let me go."

"Why?"

"She thought she'd be fired, and then you gave her the

grand poobah job. She was beside herself."

"Yeah, I'll talk to her when the dust settles. I just didn't have any more corporate in me, you know? Been coloring outside the lines for a few days. Need to remember what it's like to live in the real world."

He got a glazed sort of faraway look. "I know what you mean,"

I leaned into him and whispered, "So, how did it feel to steal them?"

He glanced around to make sure no one was listening then leaned in closer. "Hell of a rush."

"Awesome, right?"

"You and me," he said as he looped an arm around my shoulders, "we push the boundaries. Always will."

MISS P and Jeremy took one bedroom. We put Teddie in the other and gave him a pain pill. Romeo and I were stuck with the chairs in the main cabin—they unfolded to lie flat, so it wasn't a horrible hardship. Besides, at this point I felt I could sleep standing up if someone just propped me in the corner.

We'd reached cruising altitude, the pilots had dimmed the lights, and Romeo had poured us some of the Twenty-Five— we'd put a dent in the Big Boss's stash.

It was déjà vu all over again when Romeo plopped down across from me in the club seating area. "You talk to JC?"

He always called Jean-Charles that, which chafed my formal chef a bit. "Yeah, he said he'd be waiting."

"I'm a bit whacked, but, by my calculations and with the pilots' complicity, we just might make it in time for the fireworks."

"Fireworks?"

"It's New Year's Eve—well, it will be when we cross the date line again. Right now, it's New Year's Day. Happy birthday, by the way."

I leaned back. I'd forgotten. "Been a birthday to remember."

"Even though you didn't remember it was your birthday."

"Grasshopper, you should show a bit more respect for your elders."

We clinked our glasses and I thought it had been a damn great birthday. "Were your guys able to talk to Minnie?"

"Yeah, she's still singing, but the gist is that your father was the target. Sam Cho wasn't even there, it was the guy you shot, the brick-wielding dude."

So that's why he looked familiar. "Wow."

"I know, right? Anyway, Teddie wasn't supposed to be there. He interfered, and Holt Box took the blow meant for your father."

"So how did Ol' Irv figure into that?"

"He was stepping on Sam. Sam reached out to his Mr. Cho, who sent the assassin guy. Then Irv shot Sam because he could link him to the murder. And killing a country-and-western icon garnered a bit more heat than Irv could handle."

"Wow. Holt Box was collateral damage?"

"Yeah. Minnie has Sam's story on tape. He gave it to her in case anything happened to him."

I took a slug of whiskey. "Poor Sam, he just wanted his brother back."

"Irv promised Sam he'd spring Frank if Sam killed your father."

"In the end, Sam couldn't do it."

"No. And, according to Minnie, he was beside himself that Holt got in the way and then up and died."

"I'm not quite sure I believe Sam was as innocent as Minnie would like us to believe. But, if she's got his tape and it exonerates Teddie, that's all I care about. Why do you think he confessed like that?"

Romeo sipped his whiskey. "He probably knew Irv would try to take him out, and would probably succeed, it being Irv's home turf and all. And he wanted Irv to fry if that happened."

Sounded good to me. At this point I didn't know which way was up.

"Did you ever hear from Sinjin?" Romeo asked.

I pulled out my phone and showed him the text I'd gotten as we were boarding. It said simply, "Well played."

"You think that's the end of it?"

I stared out at the inky black sky and the Milky Way slashing across the sky. A lightness on the horizon illuminated the curvature of the earth. We were indeed flying high. "Oh, I have a feeling this isn't the last we've heard from Sinjin Smythe-Gordon. Bad pennies always have a habit of turning up."

"For the record," Romeo said as he got up to root through the candy basket, tossing me a pack of peanut M&Ms, "I liked him."

When he again took his seat, he poured the candy onto his tray table and sorted it by color.

"Grasshopper, you have learned a thing or two."

"Sometime you feel like a nut... Regardless, Sinjin was a cool guy."

"Yeah, I liked him, too. The lure of the dark side. But I didn't trust him, and that saved me a prison sentence and my company one hundred million U.S." I pulled up the map function of my phone, the one that had tracked my helicopter ride with the pirate. "And, I know where he lives."

EVERYONE slept most of the way home, me included. My dreams had been vivid and full of adventure, pirates, and the color red. The sun had set, and the brightness of the day stayed behind us as I felt the pilots pull the engines back, drifting down in a final approach to Vegas.

What would home feel like?

The last few days had been spent in another world and I'd

almost forgotten my reality—not the heart of it, but the pace, the smells, the normalcy of it. And I felt energized, but more at peace than I'd ever been.

I waited until everyone disembarked before I made a final check of everything. Perhaps I was looking for the me I'd left behind. But she wasn't here anymore.

Travel, it changes a person.

And it dawned on me that I'd never called my father.

Jean-Charles waited for me at the bottom of the stairs, as he'd promised. In fact, he'd never made a promise he hadn't kept. Just the sight of him took my breath. Christophe waited next to him. When he saw me at the top of the stairs, he launched himself up toward me. Jean-Charles smiled over the boy clambering toward me. I crouched and caught him as he reached the top. Drawing him tight, I breathed him in. Baby soap and mischief. And I was right back to being me. "I have missed you so much!" I whispered in his hair, afraid to let him go.

He clung to me like a tiny human monkey, his hand fisted in my sweater. "You came back. You promised. And you did."

I leaned back as I tickled him just a bit.

He rewarded me with a giggle.

"Of course, I came back. You doubted me?"

A serious look darkened his eyes, and I knew he thought of his mother. I couldn't take that hurt away, but I could show him people didn't always leave, especially not when they made promises.

"I will never leave you."

We both fell into Jean-Charles's embrace.

"You are home," he said simply, but his voice reverberated with emotion.

"Home." I thought I understood the full breadth of the word for the first time.

Jean-Charles stepped back. He tried to take Christophe, but the boy would have none of it.

"He's good."

"You okay?" my Frenchman asked me.

"Way more than okay."

"Good," he clapped his hands, and Christophe started giggling. "It is someone's birthday, and there is a very big party, with fireworks, and fancy food, and handsome men."

"The hotel?"

"It is more perfect than you dreamed. That Brandy, she has saved the day with your father and all."

"My father?"

"He has driven us all mad wanting the most perfect birthday for his daughter. Have you spoken with him?"

"Not yet."

Jean-Charles looked like he understood.

"Papa!" Christophe wiggled so much I thought I'd drop him. "You forgot to say the presents." Then he clapped a hand over his mouth. Clearly, he'd been instructed not to say anything.

Jean-Charles tried to look stern and failed miserably. "Yes, there are also presents."

"Well, good. You know how much I love presents."

The first whistle of a firework launching drew our attention. Fired from the top of Cielo, it burst in an explosion of colors and light.

Jean-Charles took my elbow. "Come, my love, the party is starting."

"What did you wish for for your birthday, Lucky?" Christophe asked.

"To be home. Right here. Right now. With my two most important men."

"So your wish came true." Christophe seemed to accept that, as if this kind of magic happened all the time.

As I looked at them, their faces alive with excitement and love, I thought perhaps he was right.

Magic happened all the time. And *that* was the best present of all.

NEVER THE END, ONLY THE BEGINNING....

Thank you for coming along on Lucky's wild ride through Vegas. For more fun reads, please visit www.deborahcoonts.com or drop me a line at debcoonts@aol.com and let me know what you think. And, please leave a review at the outlet of your choice.

Novels in the Lucky Series

WANNA GET LUCKY?
(Book 1)

LUCKY STIFF
(Book 2)

SO DAMN LUCKY
(Book 3)

LUCKY BASTARD
(Book 4)

LUCKY CATCH
(Book 5)

LUCKY BREAK
(Book 6)

LUCKY THE HARD WAY
(Book 7)

Lucky Novellas

LUCKY IN LOVE

LUCKY BANG

LUCKY NOW AND THEN
(PARTS 1 AND 2)

LUCKY FLASH

CPSIA information can be obtained
at www.ICGtesting.com
Printed in the USA
LVOW10s1536200717

542033LV00011B/600/P